A DEVIL NAMED
HERNANDEZ

Also by Mima

Fire
A Spark before the Fire
The Rock Star of Vampires
Her Name is Mariah
Different Shades of the Same Color
We're All Animals
Always be a Wolf
The Devil is Smooth like Honey

www.mimaonfire.com

—MIMA
A DEVIL NAMED HERNANDEZ

iUniverse®

A DEVIL NAMED HERNANDEZ

iUniverse books may be ordered through booksellers or by contacting:

iUniverse
1663 Liberty Drive
Bloomington, IN 47403
www.iuniverse.com
1-800-Authors (1-800-288-4677)

Because of the dynamic nature of the Internet, any web addresses or links contained in this book may have changed since publication and may no longer be valid. The views expressed in this work are solely those of the author and do not necessarily reflect the views of the publisher, and the publisher hereby disclaims any responsibility for them.

Any people depicted in stock imagery provided by Getty Images are models, and such images are being used for illustrative purposes only.
Certain stock imagery © Getty Images.

ISBN: 978-1-5320-4391-8 (sc)
ISBN: 978-1-5320-4392-5 (e)

Library of Congress Control Number: 2018902126

Print information available on the last page.

iUniverse rev. date: 02/21/2018

Acknowledgements

I would like to thank Mitchell Whitlock and Jim Brown for helping me write the back cover synopsis for A Devil Name Hernandez. Being able to perfectly sum up a book in a few short lines takes a great deal of talent and skill. Thanks to Jean Arsenault for her many hours of poring over a laptop, helping me with the editing process. I would also like to thank everyone who has supported me over the years and took the time to read my books, write reviews, share posts on Facebook and Twitter, distribute bookmarks, interview me or even say a kind word. Thank you all so much!

CHAPTER 1

We never know when a memory will forever be captured in our hearts. The mind collects the facts; time, place, the colors, while our souls absorb the emotions captured in those mere seconds, the smallest parts of our days on earth. Some are beautiful in nature while others simply bring us to our knees and yet they're all a vital part of who we are, proving that our journey is relevant. Though we may live many seconds, many moments, many days, the memories that shape us will someday be reduced to a flash. It is up to us to make them matter.

No one knew this better than Jorge Hernandez. He managed to escape death on many occasions and having done so, knew the value of living. You had to grab what you wanted, with no apology or reluctance because life won't deliver great love, fortune or wealth to your door. You had to go out and capture it with that passion the demonstrated your commitment. Life is not for the faint of heart.

His mind often slipped back to his youth, a time when it never occurred to him that he would someday be a man in his 40s. Having entered the dark world of the Mexican drug cartel Jorge assumed that, like most rock stars, he would die young. But his early demise wasn't meant to be and for that reason, Jorge eventually recognized that this was a sign his life had purpose. This took place during his 30s and specifically on the day his daughter Maria was born.

No one and nothing had brought him back to earth like holding that tiny infant in his arms for the first time. She was him. There was no doubt that the child was a Hernandez. Regardless of his tormentous relationship with the mother Verónic, a woman who showed up for his money and drugs then refused to leave, that child would become his world. She was barely minutes old when Jorge knew that his life was about making hers better. Over the years that would mean eliminating Maria's drug-addicted mother, then later the grandparents who threatened to take his daughter away and finally, moving to Canada to put her in a private school to shape her into a better human being than he could ever be. His daughter would one day rule the world, he was sure of it.

Although during his 20s, when Jorge was a young man full of piss and vinegar, he arrogantly assumed that *he* would one day rule the world. A Mexican who frequently worked in California, he catered to the many rich assholes who were happy to spend money on some of the best cocaine in the world. He didn't care if they got addicted. He didn't care if they got sick. He was determined to do one thing; Jorge Hernandez wanted to rule the underground world. He would be a legend.

In those days, he spent most of his downtime partying at the home of an associate, a man well into his 40s who was deeply rooted in both business and politics. Ralph Borowiak made people believe that he was a family man who cared about the good of the community when, in reality, he was a man who profited from the illegal drug trade. He had a way of smoothing things over to get Jorge's product into the US with no problems, no questions and certainly no consequences. That was the beauty of being a powerful person. Jorge quickly realized that it was power that made him a rich man with the ability to create his own rules, while everyone else simply got out of his way.

Of course, Ralph had another secret that he hid carefully, and that was of his homosexuality. While young women often partied at his mansion, giving him chaste kisses on the lips, it was a 20-year-old Colombian man named Diego Silva that was the object of his lust. A sugar daddy to the young immigrant with the huge, brooding eyes, he didn't care that his Latino plaything wasn't faithful, as long as he was accessible. In return, Diego lived in a beautiful apartment, took courses, and dressed in the finest clothing. A man of style himself, Ralph insisted that his young boyfriend be dapper in appearance and worldly in his presentation.

A particular evening often came to mind when Jorge thought back to those days. It was one of the many nights he sat at a small coffee table, cocaine lined up before him while he pondered which one of Ralph's *putas* he would fuck later, except that this night was different. Unlike the others, Diego sat on a nearby couch and not joined the others while they danced. Appearing bored, his scrawny legs pulled up beneath him, he silently watched Jorge snort his first line of coke of the night. Through watered eyes, he noted Diego's morose face and after he felt the burn of the drug as it reached the back of his throat, Jorge gestured toward the white powder and nodded for him to take a turn. Diego merely shrugged.

"No, really, is this true?" Jorge abruptly asked, his English still not where he would've liked it. But he felt comfortable when speaking to the Colombian. "What? You sick or something, Diego?"

"I'm still not feel good after last night."

"Ah, last night, it was a rough one for you, was it?" Jorge teased as he sniffed and rubbed his nose, suddenly realizing that the music had switched from Nirvana to some older Mötley Crüe. 'Ten Seconds to Love' poured through the speakers, the heavy base causing the room to vibrate, or was that just him? Ralph Borowiak was energetically dancing with a small group of young women as if he was having the time of his life, making them giggle at his stupid moves. "Does he not know it is 1995, not 1985? What's with this music?"

"I dunno," Diego shrugged apathetically, his large eyes looked down. A strand of long, black hair fell across his face and he quickly brushed it aside. Diego appeared unusually nervous and awkward.

"So last night, what happened, you look sad my friend," Jorge commented casually as he leaned forward and inhaled his second line of cocaine, this time feeling more at ease, his reaction much more subtle. Sitting back in the chair, he bit his bottom lip. "Does your ass hurt or something?"

To this, Diego grinned, his dark eyes grew warm and he puckered his lips in a seductive way. "Maybe it is someone else's ass that does hurt today, *amigo*."

To this, Jorge laughed and shook his head. "Oh, my friend, your English, it is so broken, as is mine. I am hiring someone to help me with that though, you should also look into this. Cause these Americans, they do not like our English to be bad. They want us to fall into the *melting pot*, as they call it. They do not want to be reminded that we are not from here."

"I find English, it is a struggle for me," Diego admitted self-consciously with a shrug. "I do not want to sound bad but it is hard."

"Your *señor*, ask him to get help as I am doing," Jorge grabbed his pack of cigarettes as his eyes landing on a scrawny white ass that walked by him. "He will pay. You, what, suck his dick another day of the week? I am sure you will anyway, am I right?"

Diego seemed to enjoy being teased and glanced over at his sugar daddy, who continued to dance with the small group of women. Ralph looked after the women as well as his young boyfriend but of course, it was in a very different way. He supplied the girls with drugs and in exchange, they partied with him in the mansion, while his family lived in a modest residence in another part of California. Apparently learning that your husband is gay is grounds for divorce. Jorge wondered how his ex-wife could've *not* known.

"I will look at it," Diego appeared noncommittal with the subject but Jorge knew he would listen. After all, hadn't he taken his advice about looking into some college classes? There was a part of Diego that silently sought guidance, to learn how to survive in this world. Ralph showed him one way but Jorge wanted to teach him independence. As much as he had little in the way of relationships with people, there was something about the Colombian that made him want to help even though he owed him nothing.

"So, Diego, what is going on?" Jorge asked, making another attempt to learn what was troubling his friend. Feeling relaxed and wired at the same time, he inhaled his cigarette. Pointing at the small line of coke left on the table. "You had a little too much last night?"

"Ah," Diego attempted to hide his emotions with his usual, jerky body language; his quick, abrupt shrug, wrinkling his nose, puckering his lips in an obnoxious way, his eyes avoiding Jorge's, he didn't speak at first but finally found his voice. "You know, I was hung over and then I had to do this thing…"

"What?" Jorge asked and leaned on his hand while the other guided the cigarette back to his mouth. "With Ralph, you mean?"

"Nah, just, I call Colombia," Diego continued to look everywhere but at Jorge, his eyes drifted across the room. "I thought maybe *Mama,* she would talk to me now. You know, now that time passed but no."

Jorge nodded glanced down at his naked legs, wearing a t-shirt and shorts, his clothing much more casual than when he was working. His minded drifted back to a previous conversation when Diego confessed being disowned by his father for being gay. It didn't surprise Jorge that his mother would not speak up against her husband. Some of these old people were rigid in their beliefs and if the man said no, their wife would obey.

"So, no?" Jorge gently asked.

Diego didn't reply but merely shook his head, his eyes downcast and for a long moment, neither spoke.

"Diego, I wish I could tell you that this will change," Jorge said with all the kindness he could muster, carefully choosing his words but knowing that nothing would give his friend comfort. He missed his family. "But it is not likely, my friend. These people, they are not about to change their minds on such things. I wish for you that she would but if your *Papa* tells her no then, she will not accept you. Their world, it is old-fashioned."

"She will not change," Diego solemnly replied, his sad eyes hesitantly meeting with Jorge's. "My *Papa,* he owns her."

"I *am* sorry Diego," Jorge spoke sincerely. "But I cannot lie to you, *amigo.* This will not change. I know my *Mama,* she listens to my *Papa* and he does not like me. He hasn't since Miguel died. He blames me. He *hates* me. Neither look me in the eye. It is not easy for me but it would be more difficult if I did not accept it."

"Why does he blame you for your brother's death?" Diego asked, almost seeming relieved about the change in topic. "He fell off a dirt bike, did he not? As a child?"

"Yes, a dirt bike *I* was driving," Jorge replied as he put out his cigarette. "And not supposed to. He fell and died immediately and then my *Papa*, he beat me bad, I thought I would die too. My mother, she was in the next room. She did nothing for me. So me, I know where you are coming from Diego. Family, it is not the people we are born to, it is the people who are there for us, who are loyal."

These words seemed to perk up Diego and for the first time that night he sat up a little taller, his eyes grew wider.

"If someone comes in this room now Diego and hurt you, do you think I would sit here and do nothing?" Jorge asked, raising his eyebrows and finally shook his head. "My family are those loyal to me and in turn, me, I am loyal to them. I would kill for my family. My *real* family."

"I do the same for you," Diego appeared emotional and nodded.

"I know you would," Jorge replied with a nod. "You, my friend, you are my brother now. You are my family."

It was a conversation that was close to Jorge's heart. Over twenty years later he could still remember every little detail as if no time had passed. Those words had defined his relationship with Diego. Perhaps it was a conversation that made him a little more human in a time when he showed no humanity.

The two young men would eventually go their separate ways only to meet up again years later at Ralph Borowiak's funeral. It was at that time that they would reconnect for a business venture that would bring them together again and forever change their lives.

CHAPTER 2

Jorge Hernandez rarely asked his wife about her past. Although he was well aware that Paige Noël-Hernandez was as much a ruthless criminal as he was, for some reason he didn't feel the need to learn the details. She was an assassin while he a *narco* and while both of them were aware how the other made money, there was an unspoken rule to never share too much information. This wasn't due to a lack of trust but simply because it was better that way.

Jorge had met his wife in what would seem like an unsavory way the previous year. She was hired to kill the man originally booked for his hotel suite but due to a mix-up and his aggressive nature, it was Jorge that ended up in the room and not the pedophile that was her target. Once she made this realization, Paige was planning to cut her losses and walk out the door but he persuaded her to stay for a drink. Within a few short weeks, they were living together with his 10-year-old daughter in a Toronto apartment. It was hardly material for a chick flick or romance novel but it was a story that gave Jorge great pleasure telling to select friends.

"Who knew?" Jorge shared a look with his wife as he pushed a strand of her blonde hair aside and gave her a kiss on the cheek while across the table, Diego Silva looked slightly perturbed by this story. The three sat together in a small, elegant restaurant in the richer area of Toronto, a place that demonstrated wealth with no apology. People boldly expressed their value and had no hesitation or shame in doing so; not that Jorge Hernandez did either. He simply preferred power over the money. You could sell your soul to the devil for money but not everyone could get power. Only a perfect mix of arrogance, confidence, and charm created true dominance. Without the correct proportions, you were only fooling yourself, as fools often did.

Paige was more thoughtful, gentle in her mannerisms. She absorbed her surroundings with quiet reflection and to those who didn't know her, appeared non-confrontation and sweet. Jorge had seen her be both soft as a kitten and fierce as a lion and although he loved both sides, there was only one side of Paige Noël-Hernandez that anyone wanted to be on. Few women had the right mixture of softness and ferociousness, it was a delicate balance that only she had managed to perfect and it was why Jorge fell in love with her.

"I'm sorry, Diego," She finally spoke and reached over and gently touched his hand. "I know it's not exactly the kind of story you wish to share at a wedding. We certainly didn't meet in the most…" She turned her head slightly and exchanged looks with her husband, their faces only inches apart before returning her attention to their mutual friend. "Conventional way? Romeo and Juliet, we are not."

"It's fucking twisted, that's what it is," Diego spoke abruptly as he pulled away from them while his dark, brooding eyes studied their faces with a look of perplexity and frustration. "How the hell am I going to tell that story at the wedding? You guys aren't making this easy for me."

Both Jorge and Paige grinned, briefly exchanging looks with one another, neither responding. They had asked Diego to plan a small ceremony for them to share with friends, family and most importantly, Jorge's ten-year-old daughter, in an effort to make up for their secret, impromptu elopement a couple of months earlier. Neither had any interest in a traditional wedding but knew that Maria was heartbroken she hadn't been included in the first one.

"It's bad enough you two hid the fact that you were already married from me, your *best* friend, for weeks!" Diego continued to complain as his eyes grew in size, while his anxiety kicked in causing him to twitch and jerk while he moved toward them like a brooding storm cloud. "Now I gotta make up something to cover this up in my speech."

"Calm down," Jorge raised his hand in the air, indicating for Diego to back off. "Relax. It is all good. You know, this wedding, it will be a nice celebration for us to gather as a family. This is more for my daughter than anyone, so just make a nice little speech and that is all."

"I can't believe you won't allow me to have it on Valentine's Day," Diego continued to complain as if he hadn't heard a thing Jorge had said, now ignoring the fact that both the bride and groom were grimacing at the suggestion. "It would be so romantic and you know….it would be a cool day…"

"Ah! I feel ill even thinking about it," Jorge commented as he reached for a glass of lemon water. "This idea that Valentine's Day has any meaning, it is ridiculous to me. Love should be celebrated every day not once a year, that's just lazy. I hate it. A terrible holiday."

"I have to agree," Paige spoke smoothly, her eyes fixated on Diego, her quiet disposition managed to calm Diego as his shoulders deflated slightly, his face relaxed. It was moments like this he reminded Jorge of a little boy who sought acceptance from his mother, and not a 40-something-year-old homosexual man who desired a friendship with a woman.

"Yes, yes," Diego hesitantly admitted. "You are right, Paige, it would be overkill but you know, we do have to decide on a date soon. We have so many other decisions to make but the date, it is the most important one."

"How about tomorrow?" Jorge spoke flippantly and was automatically the recipient of a glare.

"Like I can throw a wedding together in a day!" Diego snapped, his original fire regaining its strength as he leaned forward on the table. "What do you think I am? A fucking magician?"

"Hey, you said pick a date," Jorge shrugged while Paige grinned beside him. "I gotta date for you."

"You know what, Jorge?" Diego clearly didn't enjoy being teased as he tilted his head, while his eyes squinted. "Don't be an asshole."

"Ah, Diego!" Jorge continued to torture, finding pleasure in Diego's discomfort. "This meditation that Paige is teaching you, it is clearly not working. You're anxious and angry."

"Cause you're an asshole," Diego repeated, his face relaxed slightly as he glanced toward Paige. "Meditation, it teaches me to live in the moment and at this moment, I'm feeling *frustrated*."

Jorge laughed and placed his hand on Paige's thigh. "We should get going. Maria will soon be finished…whatever activity they have at that school of hers. We must pick her up."

Paige didn't reply but nodded then smiled at Diego, who appeared to calm down.

"We do appreciate your help," She spoke gently. "He's just teasing you. But if you have thoughts on the date, anything else, do keep us informed. We've made a lot of progress."

"But really, Paige," Diego leaned in as if to confide like Jorge wasn't there. "We should've picked the date first. We kind of are doing this backward."

"You're probably right," She gently agreed. "Things have been so busy with Christmas, the dispensaries opening, all these changes…." Her voice drifted off and she glanced toward Jorge, who raised his eyebrows and made a face.

"Jolene," He added, referring to Diego's younger sister and their business partner. She had given Jorge many reasons to distrust her. If Jolene Silva hadn't been Diego's sister, Jorge would've killed her by now. His hatred and distrust for the youngest of the two Colombians was beyond the point of repair.

"I know," Diego appeared apologetic and shrugged. "But she's been better lately, maybe we can trust her again. We're all she has and she has to be loyal to someone."

"She has no reason to be loyal to me," Jorge referred to the woman who had helped start their sex party planning business a couple of years earlier. The immediate success caused the crew to open a Toronto office. The elitist parties were difficult to get into and an ideal place to launder money and sell drugs. Although Jorge had since made connections throughout the country to push his product, Toronto continued to be the main cash cow. Although, these days, most of his focus was on the dispensaries and the real drug of choice: marijuana.

"She should," Diego began to rant. "After all, she is in Canada because of you. She has work, a career because of you. Her life, it is much sweeter than if she was still in Colombia."

"Ah, from your lips to her heart," Jorge commented and leaned back in his chair. "I somehow doubt she sees it in the same way."

Diego frowned and looked away. Jolene had also caused her brother a great deal pain after having an affair with his friend, Chase Jacobs, a man whom Diego had fallen in love with years earlier. The two had been close friends and Diego did a great deal for the young man, a half-indigenous boxer, taking him under his eager wing much in the same way Ralph had once done for him. Except, of course, Chase was straight. Everyone knew that Diego wanted more than a friendship with him but this affection had never been returned.

"Anyway, I'm monitoring the situation," Diego stated and although Jorge merely nodded and said nothing, he was quietly having Jolene watched for months. It was a perilous situation. He would sleep better at night if she were dead. "I promise you that."

"Monitor carefully," Jorge reminded him. "We, the three of us, we are in this together, remember that."

"I do," Diego said with sincerity flowing through his eyes when he looked back at Jorge and then Paige. "I swear."

Jorge didn't reply. He believed him but he also felt that Diego's emotions might complicate things and the last thing he wanted was another complication. He didn't want to see Diego's judgment clouded and although he had expressed this opinion in the past, he wasn't quite sure that it was reaching his friend's heart.

"Now tomorrow," Jorge continued. "We have a meeting to discuss business and the new dispensaries that are in the process of being opened. I want to own this city soon and this is just the first step in taking over the entire industry in Canada. But I have a doctor's appointment first, so we can only meet around noon."

He noticed that his wife looked away and he gently touched her arm. "Paige, it is fine," He insisted. "The doctor, he is keeping an eye on things and I am doing better."

She didn't appear convinced.

"You are doing great," Diego confirmed, his eyes lit up as he looked at Paige, almost as if reassuring her. "You quit smoking, you almost never drink….you don't eat everything put in front of you anymore."

"Hey, I was never that bad," Jorge complained. "I must be careful. Canadian food, so fattening and your healthy foods so expensive and yet, your government makes no connection between this and your drained health care system. Me, I was healthy till I move here and although my heart is full of love and happiness," He gestured toward Paige lovingly. "My body, not so much, you know?"

He unsuccessfully attempted to make light of the situation but he knew his health was not great. Although Jorge assumed the doctors only wanted to get him on a bunch of pills to help their friends in Big Pharma, he refused to listen and instead changed his diet, quit smoking and continued to exercise daily. Paige, of course, she worried so he tried to give her the softer version of the truth.

"But I'm better now," Jorge continued. "So do not worry about me. Worry about your sister and keep an eye on her."

"I will," Diego assured him. "I got both eyes on her."

And so did Jorge.

CHAPTER 3

"Diego and I, we go back many years," Jorge quietly commented as his SUV eased toward Maria's school on the chilly, January evening. Traffic was moving slowly, causing him to feel somewhat claustrophobic as anxiety filled his body. He ignored it. "I trust him with my life but Jolene, I will never trust again. Regardless of what she has attempted to tell us, I know she wanted me dead but she is Diego's sister. What can I do?"

"I've actually given this a great deal of thought," Paige's voice was smooth, warm and soft, instantly causing Jorge to relax, he briefly glanced in her direction. Her face was radiant and full of love. "I didn't say anything throughout the holidays but I had an opportunity to speak with Hector recently and I told him about Jolene…about what happened."

"Ah, should we really tell Hector about this?" Jorge asked with skepticism in his voice, thinking about the man who was known as a 'problem-solver' within their community. "You know I do not like to get him involved unless necessary."

"Jorge, that's why you have health problems," Paige spoke with unexpected defiance, contrary to her usual, gentle nature. Her words jolted him since it was rare for her to take such a strong stand. "You take everything on yourself. You don't ask for help. Sometimes we need someone else to weigh in. Sometimes we need to admit that we aren't sure what to do."

"But Hector," Jorge shook his head while he continued to keep his focus on the traffic. Taking a deep breath, he continued, "Yes, he has helped me in the past but we are talking dicey situations. He is not who you go to if you are having a fight in the schoolyard, you know?"

"The idea that someone might've been setting up your murder is hardly the same as a schoolyard fight," Paige was insistent, her stance strong, while she watched him from the passenger side. "Plus, I didn't exactly ask him to take care of the situation. He was in town on business before the holidays and we met to discuss Jolene."

"He has a business relationship with Jolene as well," Jorge reminded her with some irritation in his voice. "How do we not know that he will go back and talk to her about your concerns or worse, what if he is helping her out?"

"Jorge, I've known Hector longer than Jolene," Paige returned to her usual, calm self. "She worked for him. I worked *with* him. There's a big difference. They no longer have a working relationship unless she's in a jam. I thought I would sound him out and if I felt it was safe to do so, I would go ahead and explain your…predicament with Jolene."

Jorge didn't reply but thought back to a few months earlier when he first discovered that Diego's sister had communicated with a religious fanatic who wanted him dead. At the time, she gave some wishy-washy excuse why she had talked to the right-wing protester but regardless of Jolene's insistence of innocence, her explanation fell flat. As Jorge often said, if you weren't sure, it was better to put someone else's head on the chopping block rather than to find your own there later. This was the first time he hadn't followed this instinct and it wasn't sitting well.

"Ok, so, what did you learn?" Jorge remained unsure of his wife's decision to speak with Hector. Although the man had been good to him over the years, he feared that if contacted too often with issues, it would be a lot like poking the bear. The man was a powerful force in Latin America and someone you wanted on your side and definitely not against you.

"I learned a few things," Paige gently replied as they pulled into the school parking lot, his daughter Maria waiting by the exit, having a lively conversation with a woman Jorge recognized as one of her teachers. "But let's just say that Jolene made a lot of enemies before she came to Canada."

Jorge shifted into park and shared an intense look with his wife, his body relaxed and a feeling of peace filled him as he silently listened.

"There's a reason Diego got her into Canada so fast," Paige continued as Jorge's gaze fell on his daughter, as she slowly started to move away from the teacher, as if attempting to wind up their conversation. He briefly wondered what they were talking about since Maria had a bad habit of sharing too much information with strangers. "I'm wondering how her enemies in Colombia felt about her sudden disappearance and if they know that she's now in Canada."

Jorge continued to listen, his eyes staring off in a daze, he bit his bottom lip and allowed her words to drift through the SUV. Maria rushed toward the vehicle, a huge backpack swung over her shoulders, she gave them both a quick wave. On the passenger side, Paige continued to quietly speak.

"My guess is that they don't," Her words were barely above a whisper as the backseat door swung open and the little girl quickly hopped inside. Paige's tone suddenly took an upbeat turn. "Maria! How was your day?"

"It was good, thank you for asking," Jorge's daughter was unusually official in her answer as she closed the door and reached for her seatbelt. "I had a good day in class and our play practice went well too."

"So, you were talking to that teacher over there," Jorge ignored everything she said as he put the SUV back into drive and moved ahead, a fake smile on his face, he waved at the woman his daughter was speaking to moments earlier. "What were you talking about?"

"Just the play," Maria replied. "I told you, *Papa*, I will not discuss private manners with people anymore. I know how mad that makes you."

"*Cariño*," Jorge immediately felt his anxiety intensify as he looked in the rearview mirror. "It is not that it makes me mad so much as that it is not appropriate. As I keep explaining to you, we are new to this country and we want to fit in. We cannot talk about your mother's drug addiction issue or about her death. We cannot talk about your grandparents and their deaths and how things were when we were in Mexico. These are things that we do not share with others."

"What about me getting kicked out of school for bringing a knife?"

Maria giggled, clearly provoking him on purpose. Jorge felt his anger melt away as he watched her in the rearview mirror. His beautiful daughter's large brown eyes glowed with warmth as her little body leaned forward in the seat. A long strand of black hair fell on her face and she quickly pushed it away. On the passenger side, he could tell Paige was attempting to hide her grin.

"Maria, come on," Jorge heard his own tone relax even though he didn't want her to think this was a joking matter. "We must not talk about these things. It may give people the wrong impression about you. I know you have spent a couple of months at this school but you are still quite new."

"I know, *Papa*, I know," Maria smiled sweetly and shuffled uncomfortably in her seat. "I was teasing you."

"Ok, very good," Jorge attempted to sound stern but somehow felt it was lost on his daughter.

"But *Papa*, had I told others about the knife incident, I think I would be justified since those other kids were bullying me," Maria continued as she pulled out her phone and started to tap the screen. "Can a woman not defend herself?"

Jorge bit his lip, unsure of how to answer that question. He didn't want his daughter to show compliance or be a powerless victim but on the other hand, he didn't want to send the message that bringing a weapon to school was acceptable either. Realistically, schools were stringent on their rules and yet, he found they often didn't help with the problematic situations or offer any real tools for children, especially young female children on how to protect themselves. As much as he hated to think about it, the rules for little girls and boys seemed very different and didn't realistically reflect the world that they were living in.

"Yes, a woman should always defend herself," Jorge insisted and glanced at Paige who also appeared to await his response. "Unfortunately, these schools don't give you children realistic ways to do so. Young girls should be taught self-defense in schools."

"They feel it is teaching aggression," Paige spoke evenly but her eyes said otherwise as she glanced in his direction. "Perhaps it would be a good idea to look into self-defense classes for Maria."

"Teaching aggression?" Jorge got stuck on the first comment as they sat in traffic, a suddenly drift of snow fell on the windshield and in the back seat, Maria was clapping her hands together.

"It's snowing!" She spoke excitedly. "I'm so excited! There's hardly been any snow since I moved to Canada."

Jorge ignored her remarks as his forehead tightened in frustration. "You know, I do love this country but yet, do Canadians not realize that there is a dangerous world out there? I do not think that teaching my little girl how to defend herself is exactly encouraging violence. I just, I don't understand."

"I agree," Paige spoke in her usual relaxed manner as she glanced out the passenger side window. "Maybe you should take it up with the school. I think it's a reasonable request. You certainly pay enough and they talk about preparing the children for the future. That seems like a good way to do so because regardless of how sheltered some of these kids lives are, there's a good chance at least some of them will run into some.....dicey situations."

Her choice of wording was not lost on Jorge who raised an eyebrow and nodded. "No one is ever that sheltered," His voice was little more than a murmur as he glanced at a pack of gum beside his phone, briefly craving a cigarette but realizing that this was merely a sign he was feeling tense.

"*Papa*, I would love to learn self-defense," Maria spoke excitedly from the back seat. "Uncle Jesús, he tells me that I should learn it and he has shown me a few things to do if I am ever attacked."

"Jesús has?" Jorge found it amusing that his longtime work associate had made this suggestion. He had also mentioned it shortly after Maria was caught with a switchblade in her Mexican school. It was good to know that the man who had often protected Jorge's daughter was also teaching Maria to protect herself. His loyalty was one of the many reasons why Jesús was now living and working in Canada, helping to open dispensaries throughout Toronto and soon, across the country. Cocaine may have been what opened the door for Jorge but times were changing and weed was the future.

"Jesús said that he wanted me to be ready if someone ever attacked me," Maria continued and Jorge noted that Paige was giving a nod of approval from the passenger side. "He taught me what to do if someone tries to come up behind me or attempts to grab me, everything."

"So you know what to do?" Jorge asked, his voice growing excited. "If someone grabs you, you know how to look after yourself?"

"Yes," Maria insisted. "He showed me how to hit with my elbow if someone is coming from behind and how to twist their arm if they grab me. He also said if it was a man to 'kick him where it hurts and ask questions later' and of course, run away."

Paige tilted her head, unsuccessfully attempting to hide the fact that she was laughing but on the driver's side, Jorge was unsure of how to take in this information.

"Ok, Maria, don't be casually kicking a man there unless you really think he's going to hurt you," He cringed slightly as he thought about his daughter attacking every man or boy who offended her in the smallest way. "I am serious."

"*Papa*," Maria spoke with wide-eyed innocence as they got closer to their apartment. "I won't. You know me, I am not normally a violent person."

"Good, let's try to keep it that way," Jorge reminded her, suddenly feeling exhausted. "However, I want you to learn proper self-defense, not just the moves Jesús taught you. Although, I do appreciate that he did so."

Maria nodded enthusiastically and looked down at her phone.

Jorge's eyes met Paige's and she gave a knowing smile. "After all," He began in a low voice, sensing that his daughter wasn't really listening, "One never knows when they will be in a vulnerable situation."

Paige nodded but didn't reply. It wasn't necessary.

CHAPTER 4

"The most frustrating thing is that no one believes that I feel better," Jorge pointed out as they sat in the waiting room. Paige watched him with skeptical eyes. Did his wife fear that he would die? Sure, he had a few incidents where he passed out or felt light-headed but since he quit smoking and made a genuine effort to change his eating habits, Jorge felt he made a vast improvement. Not that he could capture this in words. "I don't know, I feel good in the morning and I'm not tired as often. I'm not as cranky as I used to be and my body, it feels good. I'm a teenager again, maybe even better."

Paige broke out into a grin, her eyes lit up as she reached forward to touch his arm. They shared a quiet moment before a young, white woman called his name and Jorge immediately stood up to follow her. Paige stood up too.

"What? Where are you going?" He asked stupidly as if it wasn't clear. "You can't come in the office with me."

"Sure I can," She gently replied. "I want to hear what he says."

"I will tell you what he says."

"All of it?" She pressed and appeared hesitant, her large, blue eyes studied his face and for a moment, he feared she didn't trust him. Noticing the young woman impatiently waiting for him, Jorge quickly nodded.

"*Mi amor*, of course, I tell you everything," Jorge insisted as his fingers brushed her hand as he started to walk away. "Everything is fine, do not worry."

Appearing somewhat satisfied with his answer, Paige returned to her seat and Jorge gave her one last smile before following the young woman to the doctor's office. Surprised to find the older man already there glancing over some papers in a file, Jorge attempted to read his expression. Fear crossed his heart when he considered what terrible prognosis this man might be preparing to give him. Hadn't he followed most of his instructions since his original visit the previous fall? In a rare moment of vulnerability, Jorge felt anxious. He had a gun pointed at him many times and yet, this was much more frightening to him.

The doctor looked up and his face brightened, something that wasn't lost on Jorge as he said 'good morning' and cautiously sat down. The young woman slipped out of the room and closed the door behind her and it was only then that the doctor spoke.

"Good morning to you as well, Mr. Hernandez," He closed the folder, possibly because he saw Jorge attempting to read the notes. Shouldn't patients be allowed to read the information doctors had about them? Wasn't it a right to know about your own health?

"So, doctor, what is the good news?" Jorge attempted to keep things light despite his fears. "Am I going to live another day or what?"

"I would definitely say another day," The doctor replied with a reluctant grin, his eyes appeared tired as if he had worked many hours, even though it was only 10:28 AM according to the clock across the room. "In fact, I must admit, I see a vast improvement in your most recent tests."

Of course, he was referring to the many, *many* tests that Jorge had to endure over the past weeks. Blood tests, heart tracing and others that were slightly more invasive but at the end of the day, he had done almost everything asked of him despite his argument that they were actually *looking* to find something to make him a sick man and keep in the hospital. Of course, he did this accusation in a charming way, manipulating his infectious smile to appear flirtatious to the women, while almost as pleading for understanding from the men.

"My wife, you know, she could probably use the break if you put me in the hospital," Jorge had awkwardly joked at the time, although his worst fear was to be admitted to that terrible place. People often went into that sterile, unpleasant building and never came out. If he was going to die, he wanted to do so like fireworks in the sky not fading away in a backless gown, surrounded by death.

The doctor that he dealt with throughout this ordeal was starting to feel more like a friend than the man who could potentially give him terrible news. He sat back in his chair and shook his head. "I don't know what you've done Mr. Hernandez but I do see a lot better results from these tests than I expected. Now, having said that," He leaned forward and opened his chart again despite Jorge's prying eyes. "Jorge…" He said his name in the Spanish pronunciation that sounded like *Horhey*, causing him to cringe in response.

"Oh, I'm sorry," The doctor continued after noting his reaction. "I keep forgetting that you prefer the English pronunciation. At any rate, I can go over these tests with you but for the most part, I feel there's been a significant improvement, considering your original assessment. Your blood pressure is the most notable improvement of all, which was originally one of my biggest concerns. I'm not saying you're completely out of the woods and I'm definitely not suggesting you go back to your old ways, but I will give credit where it is due."

"I thank you," Jorge spoke solemnly, his mind gratefully accepting these words and for a moment, he wasn't sure how to respond. "I tried to do better but I was afraid it was too late, you know?"

"Well, you know, Mr. Hernandez," The doctor once again closed his file. "The body is a complex machine but at the end of the day, when you treat it well, it often does the same for you. Many people sit in that chair and are told that they need to change their lifestyle and although they agree wholeheartedly, they often don't stick with it and unfortunately, there is only so much I can do if they aren't willing to listen to my advice."

"Yes, I do understand," Jorge nodded. "So what happens now?"

"I will monitor you and we will do more tests in a few months to see if you are continuing to improve but right now, what I'm seeing here on paper, does reassure me."

Perfecto. Jorge felt relieved when he left the office, stopping briefly in the washroom, he threw out the prescription the doctor had passed him on the way out the door.

Paige appeared skeptical when he relayed the news to her a few minutes later. Jorge repeated everything the doctor said, adding a bit more flair, to emphasize the vast improvement in his health.

"He said you had the body of an 18-year-old?" Paige raised an eyebrow as they walked toward the SUV.

"Yes, I believe it was something like that," Jorge insisted and reached for her hand and gave it a gentle squeeze. "He said I must have an amazing wife that keeps me young, that is what he said."

"I don't think that is what he said," She gave him an upwards gaze that made him grin as they reached the SUV. He gave her a quick kiss and opened the door for her.

"I may be paraphrasing a bit," Jorge winked at her and headed toward the driver's side and once they were both seated, he continued. "It was good though."

"You would tell me if it wasn't, right?" There was a sadness in her voice that caught him off guard.

"*Mi amor*, of course!" Jorge's eyes expanded and he leaned in to give her another kiss. "Of course. I agree, I'm perhaps exaggerating a bit, however, he did say that I am doing incredibly well and he is just monitoring me in the future but to keep up the good work. I promise."

Feeling his heart unleashed from fear, Jorge continued to brag about his terrific health as they drove to the meeting with Diego and Jolene, who took care of the sex party business, one of his primary investments. It was a meeting that he would be happy to have out of the way.

Despite Jorge's light attitude on the way there, his more serious, *bastardo* side immediately took over as soon as they stepped into the building. In the professional office in downtown Toronto, Jorge's eyes darkened to a brilliant charcoal as he arrogantly strutted in the door not even saying hello to the receptionist, he walked down the hallway. Paige quietly followed behind, she smiled at the receptionist who merely looked alarmed by the investor's rude arrival but at the same time, unconcerned.

In the boardroom, the first person he saw was his longtime business associate, Jesús Garcia López. He was having a slow, thoughtful conversation with Diego, who was standing beside him in an apron, holding a coffee pot. Jorge raised an eyebrow as he entered the room while

Jesús explained in Spanish that he had recently watched a documentary about a little-known brand of coffee that had vast health benefits. Although this kind of intrigued Jorge, he refused to show any interest.

While Jesús continued to talk, he gave a quick nod to Paige and Jorge while awkwardly rubbed a hand over his bald head. In the chair beside him, Jolene Silva didn't even look up from her phone. The beautiful, curvaceous Colombian showed no interest in the conversation taking place nor did she acknowledge that Jorge and Paige had entered the room. Her interest in the company had dropped since Jorge's confrontation with her a few months earlier, on the night she should've died. And yet, here she sat, almost obnoxiously, as if it was an inconvenience for her to take part in this meeting. Her attitude change was disturbing to Jorge and was just another red flag indicating that she needed to be taken care of in the future.

Loudly tossing his laptop bag on the table, his dark gaze on Jolene, he heard Paige pull the chair out beside him and she sat down. Glancing in her direction, Jorge noted his wife's warm smile and he quickly followed her lead, sitting beside her. Jolene merely glanced up and quickly returned her attention to the phone.

Continuing his conversation with Jesús, Diego didn't miss a beat, turning over the empty cups in front of both Paige and Jorge and filling them with coffee. They both thanked him and the conversation faded as Jorge reached for the milk, first putting some in his wife's coffee then his own, while she reached for the sugar. Her eyes briefly glancing toward Jolene, then met with his for a silent message that went unnoticed by the others.

"Chase, is he coming?" Jorge directed his question at Diego and noted that Jesús nodded while Diego answered.

"Yes, he's on the way."

Jorge nodded and took a drink of his coffee. Noting that Diego was waiting for his reaction, he nodded.

"The coffee, it is good, Diego. It's always good."

Noting that Diego turned and winked at Paige, he then reached for the last empty cup and filled it before slipping out the door. Moments later, Chase Jacobs walked in. Tall, the half indigenous man was large, resembling a club bouncer rather than the management but his intimidating size had been helpful on more than one occasion even though, at heart, he was more of a pussycat than a lion. Of course, he was loyal and at the end of the day, this was what mattered to Jorge.

"Sorry, I got tied up with a truck at the club," He headed toward the seat beside Jolene, who didn't even look up. Jorge sensed some reluctance from him before he sat down. "They were trying to short us some supplies and I had to deal with the guy."

"And it is now taken care of?" Jorge asked as Diego slipped back into the room and closed the door.

"Yes, it is," Chase spoke confidently as Diego moved to the head of the table.

"I see you have removed your apron," Jorge decided to take a moment to tease his friend, ignoring the tension in the room. He quickly glanced around the table; Jesús looked alert and eager, while Jolene the complete opposite and Chase appeared uncomfortable. With humor in his eyes, Diego curled his lips into a snarl.

"Hey, I have very expensive clothes and I feel the need to protect them," He sat upright with a forcefulness that suggested his strength. "Coffee stains, they are not easy to get out."

"My 10-year-old can get out a coffee stain," Jorge countered and noted that Diego merely shrugged, his body jerking awkwardly as it always did when he wasn't sure what to say.

"Whatever, can we get on with it?" Diego's voice boomed, perhaps a little louder than usual and Jolene suddenly looking up, as if waking from a nap. "We don't got all day."

"Now you sound like me, Diego," Jorge said with a grin and turned his attention to the others. "And Clara has been in?"

Diego nodded vigorously, recognizing the name of the lady who swept the office for any kind of listening devices or anything suspicious, particularly the boardroom. "She has."

"Well, we have a lot of things to talk about this morning. Some big changes are coming and some of you," Jorge continued and glanced toward Jolene and then Chase. "Some of you might not like what I have to say."

CHAPTER 5

"We are now in a new year," Jorge began to speak as he opened his laptop and glanced at the notes for the meeting and closed it again. "Our focus this year will be the pot dispensaries. We've come a long way from the first one we opened in November? I do not recall the exact date but immediately after, I began to buy other locations and my goal is to have 7 opened within the city before the spring. Considering 4 are already up and running, this shouldn't be a problem. The sex parties will no longer be our focus."

Everyone except Jesús and Paige looked stunned. Although it was common knowledge that this was an area that Jorge had intended to expand on, few knew how serious he was about the dispensaries until that moment. Most assumed they were merely a side business and wouldn't become the focus. Not that Jorge had let them in on his plans.

"I want Marco to put aside whatever he is doing now and update the Our House of Pot website," He referred to the new company associated with the dispensaries and noticed that Jolene was already appearing defiant. "We will soon start mail orders on our site for those who can't get to us, although I plan to eventually go nationwide. From now on, as I said, this is our focus, not the party planning. Let's face it, the sex parties, they are going downhill."

"But Marco has been busy updating the site for location parties," Jolene protested. "He does not have time for both."

"No need for that," Jorge insisted as he glared at Jolene. "No more parties outside the club. Pot is our priority now and these out of town parties, they cost more than they are worth. I only had them in the first place to set up locations to sell coke through various bars. Cleo and Raymond's real job was to sniff out the owners that would be open to it and that has been completed. From this point on, the man who took over my former responsibilities will worry about that. We no longer have time and honestly, this is pretty established. We have to break away and my boss in Mexico, he agrees my focus will be pot. Which means *your* main focus will be pot too."

"That makes sense," Diego agreed as he reached for his coffee. "Cleo is resigning anyway but I'm not sure about Raymond?"

"We will figure out something," Jorge referred to the Chinese man who rarely stepped foot in the office, usually working remotely. "Our concern is staffing the dispensaries and starting a mail order site in BC since that is where our pot comes from, it only makes sense we ship from there. Jesús will be taking care of this duty and dealing with our partners since he has already established a relationship with them. However, he will be a busy man and will need someone here in the city to set up new stores and work directly with all the shop managers. If Beverly is interested in this job, then I wish to have her be this person."

Jolene's eyes grew in size. "But she is the assistant to me and Diego," Her protests were abrupt. "What do we do without her?"

Jorge cringed at her terrible English, something that didn't seem to improve regardless of how long she was living in Canada but unlike Diego, he didn't feel the need to point it out to her.

"You don't need an assistant, Jolene," Jorge spoke in a condescending tone and leaned back in his chair. "No more location parties. The only parties we will be having at this point is at the club," He reminded her and directed his attention toward Chase, who managed JD Exclusive Club. "Even that, I'm not sure if we will continue these parties in the future. Right now, it is only there to launder our money. You don't need an office full of people to run a few parties. From now on, everyone's jobs will be changing."

Silence. The only thing that could be heard was the clock ticking on the other side of the room. He definitely had their full attention.

"The receptionist, she will stay but her duties will eventually be connected to Our House of Pot. I would prefer the stores take care of inquiries about pricing and the warehouse for shipping concerns, however, she will take care of directing questions that come into our website and overseeing everything. Her job will grow but I feel she is up for it."

"And her pay cheque?" Diego asked skeptically.

"Of course," Jorge spoke evenly and nodded along with Diego, who appeared content.

"Now you, Diego, I think you should oversee the pot stores. Make sure they are running smoothly since Jesús will be on the road most of the time but you will be in regular contact with him," He shook his head. "I will need you to oversee everything from issues in stores, the website, communicate with Beverly daily, everything. You must also be on top of regulations and laws that are changing. If you need help with anything, you can contact Jesús or if it has anything to do with the shipping aspect. You contact Chase if you need research or a helping hand from time to time and Jolene, you can look after the sex parties but you will have to do it without much in the way of help."

Her face turned red and he wasn't sure if she was about to cry or scream. Jorge ignored her reaction.

"As I said, this is a smaller focus for us now," He continued and leaned ahead on the table. "From now on, Chase, your main job is looking after the club with day to day operations. If anyone needs a hand otherwise, you must help them if you can. I'm not sure what will become of the club in the future but for now, keep bands coming in and have a few parties."

Everyone sat in stunned silence.

"Benjamin, he will take care of the accounting and payroll for both places, if he or anyone else needs help then talk to me." He referred to the Filipino man who was their crafty bookkeeper. In fact, this man was responsible for helping them launder money through the club and sex parties and did so efficiently. They recently passed an audit with flying colors.

"Juliana," Chase spoke up, appearing confused, he referred to the Mexican woman who had come to Canada to look after Maria and to help out with party planning. In the end, the young woman also assisted in setting up the first couple of pot shops and essentially jumped in where needed. "Is she still helping get the new stores ready?"

"She will be returning to Mexico," Jorge spoke regretfully. "I could have arranged to keep her here but she decided to return home to her family."

No one replied. Jolene, he noted looked the most distressed but didn't speak but merely glanced around the table.

"Wow, that's some big changes," Diego was the first one to speak. "I have to admit, my knowledge is limited when it comes to the pot industry. I guess I have a lot of research ahead of me. Chase, you might be getting a text before the end of the day. When will these changes be taking place?"

"Immediately," Jorge spoke candidly. "Up until now, Jesús has taken on most of the workload. All job descriptions may end up changing again, depending on how the future unfolds. If anyone in the office has an issue, then maybe it is the time they part ways with us."

"What about Sylvana?" Diego asked, almost as if the Italian was an afterthought. He had only recently learned that the young, abrasive woman was Jorge's cousin; something he had kept a secret so she could spy within the office. "What are you going to get her to do?"

"Marketing, of course," Jorge replied in a relaxed manner. "Except, of course, she will be doing so more for Our House of Pot and only a small fraction of her time for the sex parties. I want her focusing on how we are going to stand up against the other online pot shops and how we can compete with the local shops here in Toronto. This will be her focus at this time and yes, Diego, before you ask, if she requests an assistant again, then perhaps we might now consider it. But don't suggest it unless she asks."

"She will ask," Diego said with a laugh. "You can be assured, she will ask."

Jorge didn't reply but simply shared a grin with Diego.

"If there are no questions, I must run," Jorge pushed his chair out. "It's a busy day."

"I have a question," Jolene finally broke her silence. "So what happens now, as in today."

"Today you all sit here and map out a plan, talk to your staff one on one and sort things out," He replied with a shrug, as if it were the most obvious thing in the world. "You are paid to think of the minor details. Starting tomorrow, the sex parties are still available but very limited, perhaps we cut back on the dates, that is up to you guys. I don't give a fuck as long as we have enough going that we can filter money through and make it clean but slow it down, so it looks legit when we eventually close it down and use the dispensaries to launder money."

No one spoke as Jorge stood up and Paige followed his lead. She had remained silent throughout the meeting. "We will be in touch. Diego, Jolene, you can set up a meeting later this week to let me know how things go and meanwhile, I got stuff to do."

He grabbed his laptop and slid it into the leather case before they both headed for the door. "*Adiós*, my friends." He sang out behind him and didn't look back. It wasn't until they were alone in the elevator that his wife finally commented.

"I think this is too much," She spoke evenly. "Your health is…"

"My health is fine," Jorge insisted as he reached for her hand. "Remember, the body of an 18-year-old. I'm great."

"But you're doing a lot," Paige calmly attempted to explain. "You never slow down. You can't run at this pace forever and not expect it to catch up with you."

"*Mi amor*, I thrive on this kind of thing," He moved in and gave her a quick kiss. "There would be no Jorge Hernandez if I wasn't running in circles. This is what I love. This is how I've always been except now, I'm moving toward the legal side so I may be in less danger."

This didn't seem to bring her comfort.

"You, my love, you worry too much," Jorge commented as the elevator door opened and they stepped into the underground parking. "Plus, once all these stores have opened, I will be taking a break. Maybe a vacation this summer when Maria has finished school for the year. We will go away to somewhere tropical and warm." He automatically shivered, his body not used to the cold, Canadian winter.

"I understand," She spoke calmly as they reached the SUV and he opened her door. "I'm not saying you should stop living your life, I just wish you would…slow down a bit. Seven pot shops in only a few months?"

"We must strike while the iron is hot, as they say," Jorge replied as she got in the vehicle and he made his way around to the driver's side and did the same. "We opened the first store and things immediately took off so we must follow the yellow brick road to where it takes us. Now we are on our way to opening 7 stores. It will be great. It's not like people will get tired of buying pot and Sylvana will find a way to win against our competition. Plus, I have some friends who will raid the other stores in the future, therefore giving us the upper hand business wise. As soon as customers come to us, we will win them too."

Of course, the idea to hire attractive staff helped too. Not that they could stipulate it in the application but Jorge was insistent on a 'professional image' but wasn't discouraging sexy attire either. Low cut tops, short skirts, handsome, stylish men, this was what Our House of Pot was getting known for as much as its superior product. As he had clearly stated during the hiring process, he didn't want 'no dirty hippies' to deal with customers.

"It will be ok, my love," He insisted while starting the SUV. "You will see, soon, we will own this city."

CHAPTER 6

It didn't take long for the dust to settle. Jorge and Paige were barely back at their apartment when he received the first in a series of text messages from those who had attended the meeting; each demonstrating who they really were when thrown off guard. It intrigued Jorge but he chose to ignore them all at first. His silence would prove that he held all the power in this situation. It was his money invested in the business, his connections that controlled the drugs and therefore, he could make the rules.

"Your phone hasn't stopped" Paige let out a gentle laugh as she walked from the kitchen carrying two red mugs. She sat their coffee on the table in front of the couch while Jorge shivered and glanced toward the thermostat.

"Do you think, my love, you could turn up the heat?" He spoke with a gentle tone reserved for his wife. Jorge felt that it was better to hold all affections and warmth for those that are close to him, his *familia*. "I seem to have gotten a chill when I was out earlier."

Without replying, she crossed the room and turned up the thermostat as Jorge took a drink of coffee. The two exchanged looks as she returned to the couch and sat beside him. They didn't speak as she reached for her coffee and hesitated slightly before taking a drink.

"This chill," Jorge spoke jovially, as he leaned back on the couch, his arm propped up on the back, "It is almost like someone walked over my grave."

To this, Paige grinned and glanced at his iPhone sitting on the table.

Raising her eyebrows slightly, she gave a quick nod. "I suspect someone has thought of it a few times."

"I suspect, my love, that someone thinks about me dying at least once a day," Jorge laughed and leaned forward to give her a quick kiss. She looked away, a grin on her face. "People, they are interesting. I find it fascinating to watch how they will react in any given situation. It is kind of like one of those snow globes that Maria was looking at last week when we were shopping. The only way you can truly enjoy it is if you shake it up a bit and watch what happens. Of course, if that does not work, you shake it a little harder next time."

"I think you've already shaken it pretty hard," Paige pulled her legs up on the couch. Wearing a basic pair of jeans and a heavy, red turtleneck, he wanted nothing more than to devour her right there on the couch but unfortunately, he felt that this would only be interrupted as his phone continued to beep with both text and voice messages.

"Oh my love," Jorge shook his head and glanced toward the coffee table. "There is no rest for the wicked, is there? I guess I should probably see what is going on."

Reaching for the phone, he scrolled through the messages and finally listened to a voicemail that awaited him. There were no surprises.

"So," Jorge sat his phone back on the table and reached for his coffee, he finished it in a few gulps. "It appears that this has brought the best and worst out in people. On one hand, Chase has ideas and on the other, Diego is anxious," He shrugged. "But isn't he always anxious, *mi amor*?"

Jorge watched her grin, her affection for Diego Silva was clear, their friendship quite strong. "He says everyone is coming at him with questions and concerns but not surprisingly, the one person doing the most complaining is Jolene. In fact, I have a message from her on the phone as well."

Paige shared a long, intense look with her husband while taking a drink of her coffee. He looked away and placed his empty cup on the table.

"This coffee," Jorge casually changed the topic. "It was very good. You're really catching on to Diego's secret formula, such as it is."

"It is such a treat."

That was when the buzzer rang. Someone was at the door.

"Shall we take bets, my love?" Jorge teased while neither of them moved from the couch.

"Is it necessary?" Paige finished her coffee and set the cup on the table. "Do you want me to leave so you can have a private conversation?"

"Oh no, of course not," Jorge rose from his seat and checked the camera to see who was at the door before pressing the button. "Some find you intimidating. You are, after all, the most successful assassin in the world. Your eyes, although a beautiful shade of blue, somehow make people edgy, is that word, my love? Nervous, you know? My English, it is good but sometimes, your words have so many meanings."

"Edgy sounds right," Paige replied as a small knock could be heard at the door and she got up from the couch, reaching for both their empty cups. "But you can only scare a willing participant." She quietly added.

"Ah, yes!" Jorge walked across the room. "Terrific point."

Jolene Silva was standing on the other side of the door, her face dark with anger. In the kitchen, Paige was rinsing out their coffee cups and putting them in the dishwasher while Jorge didn't bother to hide his irritation with their visitor.

"Oh Jolene, perhaps no one has told you that in Canada, it is rude to just show up at the door, uninvited," His words were condescending and hypocritical but he stood aside and let her in. "Even I know this."

Storming in, her distinct scent flowed past him as the beautiful Colombian ignored his comment and went right into her complaint. "What was with this meeting? Today, what was that?"

"I thought I was pretty clear," Jorge shut the door and followed her across the room while from the kitchen, Paige watched Jolene carefully; her face expressionless but her stare, intense. "We need to make changes, that is the nature of the business. Just as we moved the office from Calgary to Toronto a year or two ago, now we must focus on other things. We have to look at what makes money and pot is where the money is now, especially here in Canada."

"So you leave me to do everything for the party arrangement?" Jolene loudly protested, unbuttoning her long, green coat.

"Oh Jolene, don't bother taking off your coat, you won't be staying for long," Jorge gave her a dark glare, a hint of anger slipped into his voice. "My decision, it is final, if you do not like, we can happily change the name on the door. In fact, I *have* thought of changing the entire operation to Hernandez Enterprises since all of it, is mine anyway."

"I tell you, again and again, that I was not trying to have you killed and yet, you continue to punish me," Jolene spoke with emotion in her voice, her eyes jumping toward Paige as if she would find compassion but instead, she received a cold glare. "I do not know how I can prove this to you!"

"Jolene, I do not believe you," Jorge spoke honestly, his eyes narrowing in on her. Despite the sincerity in her voice, her story didn't add up and his instincts were rarely wrong about these things. "You, I think should be delighted to be here still breathing because most in your shoes, would not be. Now, if you excuse us, my wife and I, we have plans."

"House hunting!" Paige spoke joyfully even though her eyes continued to stare through Jolene. Her head tilted slightly, an intimidating glare shot in Jolene's direction.

"Ah yes!" Jorge agreed. "And that address, you will not know because my wife and I, we do not like unexpected visitors. What if we were walking around half-naked? How awkward would this be?"

Jolene's eyes grew in size as anger continued to fill her face and suddenly she lurched toward him as if to attack but Jorge quickly grabbed her by the throat with one hand. He watched tears form in her eyes and although he felt tempted to strangle the last breath out of her, he instead pushed her back and watched Jolene protectively reach for her neck.

"Not smart Jolene," Jorge spoke with fierceness this time. "My wife, the pretty blonde lady across the room, you do remember she is an assassin or have you forgot?"

Jolene glanced toward the kitchen where Paige now had a gun sitting on the island that separated them, her expression calm.

"Now, she's a superb assassin because she can make a death look like a suicide or an accident," He explained in a soothing voice. "She's very talented, you know? So, if I were you, I would not come in here and attack her husband."

Jolene stepped back, her eyes jumping between Jorge and Paige, she appeared uncertain of what to do as she briefly glanced at the door.

"And you," Jorge pointed at her and continued to speak as if she were a child. "You do not, *ever* question my decisions. You shut your fucking mouth and you do what I say and you thank God that you are still able to do either of those things because if it were not for your brother, I don't think you would be so lucky right now. I am loyal to him but you, not so much."

"Now, if you would kindly leave," Jorge continued as he gestured toward the door. "My wife and I plan to go check out some houses this afternoon and with any luck, we will find our home sweet home so we can get out of this cage we live in. However, be assured that when we do, you are not required to buy us a housewarming gift."

Jolene took a deep breath and glanced at Paige before making her way toward the door.

After she left, Jorge crossed the room and locked the door. He then watched the camera that indicated that she was leaving the building. Paige quietly joined him. Putting his arm around her, he let out a loud sigh.

"This one, she is going to be trouble," Jorge shook his head. "I was hoping she would learn her place but clearly, Jolene is not able to see the big picture."

"She's getting desperate," Paige commented as she leaned in closer to her husband as his arm tightened around her. "And today, she personalized the meeting, taking it as if it were an attack on her. That means she's paranoid and if she's paranoid, my concern is that she will react."

"Which means we must be vigilant," Jorge spoke thoughtfully. "Perhaps we must act before she has the chance."

"As I told you before," Paige spoke gently as they both turned their attention away from the camera. "She has some old friends in Colombia that would be anxious to see her again. Apparently, she left without saying goodbye."

"Too bad she wouldn't give us the same courtesy," Jorge muttered as he loosened his arm from her waist and he glanced toward the nearby clock. "My love, we must go soon to look at those houses. We will talk more about this later."

"So far, there isn't anything else to talk about," Paige commented with a grin. "You just have to say the word."

"I will give it some thought," Jorge nodded and grabbed his leather jacket and phone then turned to Paige. "But it seems that we will soon have no choice but to take action."

"Just say the word," Paige repeated as she headed for the closet and pulled out her coat. "Our hands would be clean."

Jorge didn't reply but calmly slipped into his jacket, his body shivered again. "There is that person walking on my grave again."

A ting sound came from Paige's pocket and she pulled out her phone to check the message. Her eyes full of surprise, she quickly attempted to hide it but Jorge already sensed her uneasiness.

"Paige, is there something wrong?"

"Nothing I can't handle," She replied and shook her head. "Let's go find our new home."

CHAPTER 7

"Today, *mi amor,* will be a beautiful day," Jorge spoke up from the warmth of the bed while across the room, Paige selected her clothing from their cramped, little closet. He couldn't wait for the day when they finally found a real home, an escape from this dingy apartment with limited space, tiny bathrooms, and tacky decor. This temporary home felt like a depressing starter apartment for a poor college student; completely uninspiring and dismal. "I have so many plans for this week but today, I think I will spend some time with Chase."

Paige's head popped out of the closet and she studied his face with her huge, thoughtful eyes, a gentle smile crept on her face as she held two sweaters in her hand, as if unsure of which one to choose. She pushed a single strand of freshly washed hair from her face and Jorge was left mesmerized by his wife, immediately sitting his phone on the nightstand to give her his full attention. Still wearing her red robe, his thoughts quickly jumped to possibly enticing her to remove it for a quick encounter while his daughter was still in the shower. However, there was simply no time. Reality could sometimes be disappointing.

"I have avoided him for so long but it *is* time now," Jorge dryly commented with a shrug. "I suspect that he will talk if asked the right questions."

"You've hardly spent any time with him since learning about his affair with Jolene," Paige replied as she selected a black sweater, returning the other to the closet, she closed the door. For a moment, Paige stood in silence but he could tell she had something on her mind. "Maybe you should ease into the conversation. Did you get the sense that there was tension between the two of them yesterday at the meeting?"

"Most definitely," Jorge replied as he sat up straighter in a slow attempt to get out of bed. "That is why I choose this as the day to meet with him, although, perhaps it is a tad too early. I suspect he might be more talkative in a relaxed environment. Maybe I should take him to a strip club."

Paige shot him a cool stare and he began to laugh.

"I am joking, of course, that would be too distracting."

"For him or you?"

"For him, of course," Jorge replied. "He is a young man in his 20s. He hasn't yet learned to control his libido."

Even before finishing his sentence, his wife was already laughing.

"Does this ever extend to men in their 40s?" She calmly asked as the bathroom door could be heard opening and the echo of Maria's feet dancing into the kitchen, as she hummed the music from a production her school recently started to work on.

"Me?" Jorge acted shocked as he rose from the bed, completely nude. "I am obviously the exception. Remember the doctor said that I had the body of an 18-year-old?"

"I bet he did," Paige teased as he walked into their bathroom.

Jorge merely laughed before closing the door. Looking in the mirror, his smile quickly faded. Truth be told, he wasn't feeling like an 18-year-old that morning. This was something he merely said to his wife who loved him very much and didn't want him to fall ill. After the doctor's dismal report a couple of months earlier, she had spent enough time worrying about his health. Now it was his job to reassure her that he was fine.

He wasn't fine.

The lines around his dark eyes were growing deeper, the white hairs popping up among the black ones and he woke most morning with a sense of dread. Although he had quit smoking the previous year, there were many days he craved a cigarette but Jorge credited himself with avoiding the 30-year habit for about three months. The truth was that a part of him deeply mourned his former life in Mexico. Although he loved Canada and it was better for his wife and child, there was a part of him that was left in his birth country and Jorge wasn't sure if it would ever return.

These were the thoughts he didn't care to spend much time entertaining. Once you allowed your mind to travel to dark places, it was sometimes difficult to get it back again. He was lucky. Despite how terribly Jorge had treated his body over the years, he was still alive. He had a beautiful wife and daughter and all the wealth any man could wish for and yet, something felt wrong. It was simply his fears rising to the surface.

Hearing Paige singing out to Maria to hurry since traffic would be heavy, he took it as a cue to get in the shower. It was time to push this nonsense aside and start his day.

It was during breakfast while he checked his emails and the latest news that Jorge felt his depression return. Every story was so dismal. The world was falling apart and powerful people were doing everything to destroy the environment, the poor, the weak; money ruled the world and although he was a wealthy man himself, he preferred to view his work with the cartel as a way of providing the poor with jobs. It was a way to give those with ambition an opportunity, just as others had once done for him. In truth, people died but it was never quite how television presented it, which is what most choose to naïvely believe. Hollywood exaggerated everything, conveniently making people believe that it never happened right under their noses even though it did.

When Jorge Hernandez walked down the street wearing a designer suit or entered a pricey hotel, when he got into his expensive SUV or spoke to people in a pleasant way with a charming smile on his face, no one ever believed he was a part of one of the largest drug cartels in the world. The media taught society that his people were dangerous with no class or education, a 'bad hombre' that you could identify immediately because of his shifty eyes and crooked smile but in reality, it was some of the most polished men in the world that were doing the most questionable things. In fact, it was at a fundraiser that a well-known politician once pointed out to him that it was often the man dressed in the best suit and whom referenced God the most that should raise suspicion.

"I'm sure there are people burning in hell for all the times they hid behind God," The distinguished gentleman commented as he and Jorge lit a cigar in a quiet room, away from the crowd. "And there will be many joining them one day."

It was just as he was about to stop reading the news and contact Chase that his phone rang. It was Jesús.

"Good morning sir," He spoke officially and judging by the noise in the background, Jorge assumed he was at the airport. To someone who didn't know him well, they would probably assume he spoke slowly to pick out the correct English words, however, in Spanish, his words shared the same gentle ease. "I am sorry to call at this early hour but I have a concern that I hope you can help me with."

Looking at a nearby clock, Jorge glanced down at his robe. "It's fine, what's up Jesús?"

"I'm having a minor problem with the last property that we were about to buy, the one on the North end of the city?" He referred to the place the two had visited before the holidays. At the time, the owner was receptive to selling but Jorge suspected he was eager for them to leave.

"He doesn't want to sell," Jorge guessed as he got up from the chair and headed toward the bedroom. "I got that feeling."

"No, he does want to sell but he just almost doubled the price," Jesús continued to explain slowly as a loudspeaker could be heard in the background almost drowning out his voice. "Maybe not almost double but it went up substantially sir."

"Ok, don't worry about it," Jorge calmly insisted when he sensed the anxiety in Jesús' voice. "I will look after this today. I will be in touch."

"Ok boss," Jesús spoke with some reluctance. "Maybe you should take Paige with you?"

"I can handle this myself," Jorge insisted, somewhat displeased with the suggestion that he needed any help but quickly realized he was right. "On second thought, I may bring Diego."

"Well, ok then," Jesús responded. "I will talk to you soon, boss."

Throwing his iPhone on the bed, Jorge ran a hand over his face and briefly considered crawling back into bed. Instead, he grabbed his phone and sent Diego a brief text with a vague explanation of the situation and requested his help. A response was immediate.

By the time he put on his white shirt, a pair of jeans and a leather jacket, Diego was waiting outside in his prissy little Lexus. Wearing sunglasses and an expensive suit, he gave Jorge a once over when he got in the passenger side.

"Are you sick or something?" He automatically asked causing Jorge to grow paranoid. Did he really look that bad?

"No, why?"

"You never ask to get picked up," Diego insisted suspiciously and then it was as if he remembered his earlier text message. "Oh, is it because I have…"

"Yes, Diego, let's get going," Jorge spoke abruptly, pointing toward the road. "I don't got all day."

Diego gave a sardonic grin and pulled out on the street. The two fell silent as the GPS spoke in the background. A few minutes went by before Jorge realized that it was giving them the wrong directions while Diego didn't appear to even be listening, as he wasn't following the computerized woman's voice.

"What? You don't take instructions from a woman?" Jorge asked after the voice once again announced it was recalculating. "Why do you have this on at all?"

"I've been experimenting lately to see how accurate it is," Diego replied and reached over to shut it off. "You know what they need? Real humans giving instructions and not a machine."

"Hey, maybe you could do that as a second job," Jorge teased him as they drew closer to the site of his seventh dispensary; one way or another. "You could scream at people that they are going the wrong way, terrorize them with your voice."

"Not *me*, I meant someone else with a nice voice and you know…"

"Manners?"

"I have manners," Diego insisted. "I'm just not really what you call, a people person."

"That's perfect," Jorge commented as they turned on the street where they were about to conduct some business. "Because that works with what I need you for this morning. I don't tell you this often my friend but this morning, do your worst."

"My worst?" Diego grinned as they pulled into the small lot hidden behind the building. "You got it."

After parking the Lexus, the two got out of the car and headed toward the entrance. The small café had been closed for over a month due to poor business management and now the owner was desperately attempting to sell. Of course, as soon as he learned of Jorge's interest and most likely, his earlier success with dispensaries, the owner clearly increased the price, seeing this as an opportunity to swindle the new buyers. Jorge had some respect for him asking more but not to such a level that it was clearly extortion, especially when considering that the building definitely needed some work.

"He agreed to meet with us?" Jorge confirmed just as they arrived at the door.

"Like he had a fucking choice."

CHAPTER 8

"He said the door would be open," Diego gruffly commented and removed his sunglasses before boldly walking in with Jorge behind him. There they found a young, white man leaning up against a booth playing on his phone, a moronic grin on his face as if he were merely hanging out at the mall and not about to take part in a business meeting. When suddenly realizing that he wasn't alone, the imbecile quickly looked up and shoved the phone into his pocket. Jorge remembered him however, Diego wasn't at the last meeting and had no idea that he was the person they had come to see.

"Get the owner," Diego demanded in his usual, gruff voice that appeared to startle, then anger the young man. Although, in fairness, this scrawny kid wearing a pair of dirty jeans and cheap Wal-Mart jacket didn't exactly present the professional image of a businessman. These young people had so much to learn and the lessons would not be gentle.

"I *am* the owner," The pale-faced man approached them and as he did, the results of living a rough lifestyle could be seen on his face. He looked high and perhaps this instilled the questionable courage in him as he stared Diego squarely in the eyes although, his wimpy voice indicated otherwise. "My dad left me this place in his will, it's been in my family for years…."

"And you managed to sink it into the ground," Jorge abruptly cut him off, as he glanced around the room, evaluating the wasted space that could be better filled when he took over. So many businesses didn't use all their room to its potential capacity, not realizing that every inch of your business costs money and should, in turn, help to make its value back. "You gave me a price, the money was about to go through, you just had to sign off and instead you change your mind at the last minute. What the fuck is with that?"

"You guys can afford it," The kid spoke with a nonchalant shrug, his milky eyes appeared almost colorless in appearance as if his life was already fading away. Homely, he struck Jorge as a loser in life, someone spoiled by his parents with no idea how to survive on his own; a typical fucking millennial. "And I got a lot of debt."

"That's not our fucking problem," Jorge replied evenly despite the fact that his heart was beginning to race and he felt a little shaky. He would never show his weakness. "You *are* going to sign off on this deal today. No more fucking around."

"No," The young man was defiant like a child and turned, walking awkwardly toward the counter. "I know I have the upper hand here. I don't *need* to sell to you unless you're willing to give me the new price."

"Well technically, *I* don't need to *buy,*" Jorge shrugged casually and shoved his hands in the pockets of his leather jacket and cleared his throat. "The thing is though, I don't got time to look for property right now or I could just as well walk away so we *are* going to make a deal today."

"Look, I get it, you two have money and you think you can pull the wool over my eyes cause I look young or cause I need to sell," The white man leaned against the counter with a glimmer of arrogance in his face. "But maybe I have other offers on the table. Toronto is a booming real estate market if you two *spics* weren't aware of that."

There was a little sound that came out of the back of Diego's throat that only Jorge could hear and although his blood was boiling, he continued to look calm. Glancing at Diego brooding eyes, he gave him a quick nod before turning his attention back toward the white boy who was about to learn a valuable lesson in life.

"My associate," Jorge glanced at Diego as he walked toward the door. "He has a little something that might make this deal a little more…acceptable."

"I somehow doubt it," The kid remarked, pulling the phone back out of his pocket, he began to tap on it with such a sense of defiance and rebellion that it almost made Jorge laugh at his stupidity. Ah! But some lessons, they are much more difficult than others.

Diego's return didn't appear to capture his attention but the first strike of a baseball bat against a vase full of fake flowers in the corner seemed to do the trick. Suddenly very alert, the kid appeared stunned as the Colombian wearing an expensive suit began to violently smash everything in sight; shattered glass was flying everywhere as a stack of dishes quickly became debris, the loud clang apparently putting the café owner in a state of shock. His mouth fell open and his eyes widened as Diego approached him. It was as if he suddenly realized that he also might be in danger that his attention quickly returned to the phone as if to reach out for help but before he could, a vigilant Diego lifted the baseball bat and without missing a beat, knocked the phone out of his hand, causing the kid to fall forward, screaming in pain.

"Oh Diego, do not break *both* of his hands, we do need him to sign the contract that he *verbally* agreed to just before the holidays," Jorge casually strode toward the young man, gently kicking the phone aside in case he had any ideas about reaching for it with the hand that wasn't red, already swelling. As if on cue, Diego rose the baseball bat and with intense fury in his face, brought it down, smashing the small device repeatedly as the white boy cried like a child on the floor. "These tears, are they for the phone? Your hands? Maybe it will be harder for you to jerk off now? I dunno but I will say, that us *spics,* we have really good business sense but we don't always play by the same rules as you *gringos*."

"Our cultures," Jorge spoke in a calm, relaxed voice. His attention was on Diego as if in deep thought, his eyes shifted back toward the sobbing man on the floor, as he grasped his injured hand, evaluating the damage. "We can learn so much about negotiating from one another, wouldn't you say?"

Diego shrugged with an evil grin on his face, his dark eyes lit up as he glanced back towards the kid and suddenly rushed ahead with the baseball bat raised over his head. The white boy started to cry, begging for mercy and it humored Jorge who put his hand up to indicate that Diego stop.

"We will wait," Jorge commented and he noted that Diego reluctantly backed off. "See, I suspect he had a little too much holiday optimism and thought he would get more money out of us but he now realizes that we are not exactly negotiating kind of folks. Plus, we cannot have all our fun at once, maybe next time, *amigo*."

"I don't know," Diego spoke gruffly, as he hesitantly lowered the bat. "I'm kind of on a roll, why stop now?"

"I will sign!!" The kid shrieked through his tears, bent forward with both snot and saliva running down his face that made Jorge look away. He was pathetic. This generation, they had no passion, no balls, just a bunch of fucking children wanting it all without doing a fucking thing. In a way, it was tempting to let Diego beat the piss out of him but then again, he knew it was important to keep the end goal in mind. Their shops were taking off and it was important to strike while the iron was hot. He needed this place.

"Very well then," Jorge commented. "We shall leave you for now. I suspect that after you stop by the hospital, you will have to also purchase a new phone, however, may I suggest that while you still have the ability to sign with your other hand that you do so. If I don't get a call from my lawyer later today stating we have taken ownership of this property, we will find you and take care of your other hand and who knows? Maybe something else?"

His eyes shot toward Diego who twisted his lips together, his eyes squinted as he nodded while Jorge continued to stay calm.

"And my associate," Jorge continued. "He can get a bit *loco* especially if he hasn't had his fill of coffee for the day. Now, if it were me, I would be careful not to press his buttons."

"I told you I will sign!" The kid shrieked as he pushed himself away from them both with tears continuing to stream down his face. "Please, leave me alone!"

"For your sake, I certainly hope so," Jorge spoke with what appeared as sincerity, as he glanced back at Diego, their eyes communicating briefly before he returned his attention to the whimpering child on the floor. "Oh and another thing, I wouldn't recommend you tell anyone about our…business meeting. Us *spics,* we don't exactly like the police.

If anyone asks, you accidentally shut the door on your hand. You're clumsy and a stupid fuck who wasn't paying attention."

The young man's face was flushed as he used his jacket sleeve to wipe away both tears and snot, while his injured hand sat like a dead animal on the floor. Swelling more and more by the moment, it was almost as if the idiot had merely begun to accept the pain and was in shock.

"No *Policia!*" Diego repeated and suddenly lurched ahead, stepping on the injured hand causing the white boy to let out a scream that resembled that of a wounded animal and not a human being in pain; it was primal, full of vulnerability and if Jorge had to guess, a sign that this child was finally becoming a man. A *real* man.

"That's *spic* for *no police,* you stupid little motherfucker," Diego showed no mercy, stepping on his hand once again, a cracking sound was unmistakable and had Jorge never heard it before, it would've made him cringe. However, this wasn't his first rodeo.

"Well, my friend," Jorge calmly commented as he turned toward Diego, his black eyes showing no mercy as he finally backed away from their victim, his dark stare continued to hold the boy hostage. "I'm glad we were able to come to a mutual understanding."

Glancing at the kid again, he returned his attention to Diego. "See, I told you he would be open to our suggestions. These Canadians, always *so* accommodating. I really do enjoy doing business here."

His lips shifting to an evil grin, Diego's eyes continued to look angry as he lifted his eyebrows slightly and nodded. "Indeed, they are."

"But my friend," Jorge turned his attention back to the victim shaking on the floor. "Like all fun things, this conversation must end. But I do look forward to that call from my lawyer later today. Oh, and can you clean this place up too? Diego, he left quite a mess and I don't got time to clean it up."

With that, he shoved both hands in his pockets, one of which had a gun but he felt it wasn't necessary today. Giving Diego a brief nod, the two of them casually headed for the door.

CHAPTER 9

Even though his family wasn't conventional in many ways, Jorge believed that they should have dinner together as often as possible. Due to everyone's erratic schedules, this was often a fantasy more than it was a reality but at least a couple of times a week, the three of them managed to get together and have a quiet meal. He wanted this for his daughter. These things mattered.

"So school, Maria, you are still doing well?" Jorge asked as he reluctantly dug into his salad, glancing at the bland chicken on his plate. His wife was a lot of things; beautiful, his sexual Goddess, a symbol of strength, power and intelligent but she did not enjoy cooking. Not that this bothered him but sometimes his rumbling stomach craved something more than store-bought, ready-made food.

"Yes, *Papa*, my grades, they are good," Maria replied as she practically danced in her seat to the soft music playing in the background. She was so full of energy and excitement that it made him smile. Luckily, his daughter had not turned out like her mother; a depressing woman who lived only for the next party, the next line of coke and little else. Fortunately, the *puta* was gone and his little girl, she was a Hernandez through and through. "I'm quite busy lately with the play that we started after the holidays."

"Yes, I noticed, you are never home," Jorge teased while reaching for more chicken; perhaps it wasn't so bad. Across the table, Paige quietly ate as she listened to their conversation. "One day you will walk in and I won't even recognize you because you'll be a teenager."

"I like to think I am already," Maria commented and casually nibbled on her food as if it were merely a snack that she barely took seriously. He sometimes worried about her lack of appetite. "*Papa*, it's not like the olden days when you were growing up, kids, we grow up faster now. We're more mature."

Glancing at his daughter, her huge brown eyes stared back with such innocence that it tortured him to think of her growing up. He had to look away and decided to make light of the comment.

"Olden days?" Jorge replied with a grin. "How old do you think I am, Maria?"

"You're in your 40s," Maria replied and sat down her fork, her head twisting back and forth as if in thought. "I think 44 but I'm not sure?" She gave him a quick glance and continued to speak. "That is old, *Papa,* you were a child of the 70s, look at how much has changed since that time. We were learning in class how people lived back then. It was so *weird.*"

Shooting a look at Paige, he noticed she was avoiding the conversation altogether.

"What, Maria, do you think was so 'weird' about those times?" Jorge was starting to second guess this idea of a nice, family dinner. It wasn't exactly turning out as he had hoped.

"You know, like the phones with the big circles you had to turn? Rotary? That must've taken forever to call anyone," Maria spoke matter-of-factly as she avoided her food and turned toward him. "We were learning about such things in class today. No computers? What did you do, I mean, to learn anything or communicate or have fun? I do not understand."

"We listened to our teachers in class and played with our friends after school," Jorge answered abruptly, wondering when his daughter became such a little elitist. Perhaps some of the rich little girls from school were having a bad effect on her. This was something he would have to monitor. "We didn't need a machine to entertain us. We went outside, got fresh air."

"Maria," Paige took over the conversation, perhaps picking up on Jorge's frustration with his daughter. "How is your play going? Are you still working behind the scenes?"

"No, I am *in* the play now," She spoke excitedly, continuing to dance around in her seat, she lifted a small piece of chicken to her lips and nibbled at it before continuing. "I told the director that I'm meant to be on stage, not hiding in the background."

Hearing these words made Jorge proud and he nodded in understanding. "That is right, Maria, never settle to be in the background when you can be front and center. I do agree."

"That's what I said, *Papa*," She spoke excitedly, her eyes doubling in size as she continued. "It's the *best* thing ever. I think I want to be an actress when I grow up."

"An actress?" Jorge spoke with disgust. "Maria, please, you are so smart and can do anything. Why be an actress? It is not easy, many actors are out of work. It is a struggle."

"But I'm going to be *better*," Maria insisted. "*Papa*, they will not be able to deny my talent."

Jorge hesitated and shared a look with Paige before replying.

"Maria, I do appreciate the fact that you are a strong-willed little girl who goes after what you want, however, I also think you need to take your time," He tilted his head and stared at her for a moment. "You're only 10. You do not need to make such decisions now."

"Ten is much older than it was in *your* day," Maria reminded him, her voice somewhat condescending as if he were the child. "Teachers tell us that we must not dilly dally when it comes to our careers. We must start working hard even now to get where we want to be in life."

Jorge turned his head and looked away.

"So, Jorge, how was *your* day?" Paige gently changed the subject.

"It was good," He commented as flashes of Diego smashing everything in sight with a baseball bat filled his head. "Diego and I went to see an associate who was having some...second thoughts about selling his property to me and well, we managed to reason with him."

Paige stopped eating and nodded.

"How did you get him to change his mind?" Maria innocently asked.

"Diego," Jorge said with a shrug before shoving more food in his mouth. "He can be very persuasive."

Paige raised an eyebrow and nodded.

"So he will sell this place to you?" Maria asked.

"Yes, he signed shortly after our meeting," Jorge cleared his throat. "And Paige, your day?"

"I was busy with my website," His wife referred to her online business as a life coach; a concept he would never understand. Why would people pay someone else so much to help them see what they wanted in their *own* life? The idea was prosperous to him but on the plus side, it was a great way to launder money from her real work and it looked good on paper if the government started to poke around into her finances.

"Do you have a lot of clients now?" Maria asked as she continued to nibble on her food. "See, *Papa*, if people don't figure out what they want to do when they're young, they become mixed up adults that have to go to a business like Paige's to get advice."

"Well, it's not really like that," Paige's voice was soft in reply. "Sometimes people are in a profession and decide that it no longer interest them. People change and grow. Their priorities change or maybe they are between careers."

"Like *Papa* when my *Abuelo* sold his coffee company?" Maria asked as she set her fork down again. She was referring to the company that Jorge was officially listed as being an international sales rep for during the many years he was actually in charge of international sales for drugs, mainly cocaine, spending most of his time in California. "Is that how you met? Were you his life coach?"

"I told you, Maria, we met at a networking event at a hotel," Jorge replied as his stomach rumbled in fury. This conversation wasn't encouraging a pleasant digestion period. Perhaps this is why his own childhood meals were often in silence. "Your *Papa* was already investing in Canadian businesses and was looking at some other options."

Paige nodded and went along with the story. "I was there…looking for investors."

"Did you end up investing in her business?" Maria asked.

"No Maria," Jorge grinned and winked at Paige. "I decided to marry her instead and here we are."

Paige smirked and confirmed his story. Of course, he couldn't tell his daughter the truth; that she was an assassin who mistakenly came to his room to kill him. Few people knew this fact. His daughter wasn't going to be one of them.

"You could've still invested in her business," Maria commented as she watched Jorge push his chair away from the table. He didn't reply to her remark.

"Ok, Maria, I notice you are finished eating," His comment was abrupt as he stood up. "Can you please put your dishes in the dishwasher?"

It was after she was in her own room with the door closed that Jorge turned toward Paige and muttered. "There is no *fucking* way my daughter will become an actress. I know these Hollywood types, I spent time selling many of them drugs when I was in California and there is *no* way."

"It doesn't mean your daughter will take drugs."

"I do not care, I also know about the scumbag Hollywood producers and directors," Jorge leaned in and whispered as his heart began to race, his fury becoming clear. "They are sexist predators who treat women with no respect. No daughter of mine is going down that road."

"OK, you have to calm down," Paige placed her hand on his face. Her voice was as soothing as was her touch and he blinked rapidly, quickly looking away, forcing himself to relax. "This is what the doctor was talking about when he said you needed to get less excited about things. This is not something you have to worry about now. She's ten. Today she wants to be an actress, tomorrow she will want to be a doctor or a lawyer."

"I like those options better," Jorge took a deep breath and closed his eyes. "I might need both one day."

Paige let out a quiet laugh and pulled him into a hug. "You can't let these things get to you. She's always going to push your buttons because you two are very much alike."

"I do not think," Jorge succumbed to her hug. "I do not think I'm like that."

"Impulsive? Determined? Strong-willed?" Paige calmly reminded him while her hand gently caressed his back and he found himself falling into a peaceful place. Jorge closed his eyes and felt his entire body press tightly against hers, as his desires began to churn.

"Oh, sweetheart, we need a new place that is bigger, where we can escape for private time when the mood strikes, you know? Here I feel like this place is so small, cramped."

"I know, I'm still looking at houses, everything is just so crazy in real estate right now," Paige complained as he reluctantly moved away from her, as she studied his face. "So what *really* happened today?"

"Oh the property owner on the North end was trying to almost double the price on us, after a verbal agreement," Jorge recalled the morning, he eased closer and gave her a quick kiss. "Diego managed to…encourage the man to sign. You know, with his hand that was still working after the meeting."

She merely nodded with a grin. "Diego wants to meet me about the wedding this week. Do you have a date you would prefer?"

"Whatever you wish, *mi amor*," Jorge replied. "Honestly, I do not care. We are married."

"Well, it is for Maria," Paige commented as she pulled him close once again. "So maybe we should ask her for a date?"

"No, this is not for her to decide," Jorge was insistent. "Allowing her to choose a date is giving her too much say in our lives. I believe this spring, perhaps?"

"Ok, well, I will make a lunch date with Diego to discuss it tomorrow," She commented as her fingers massaged his shoulders and he fell in a trance.

"And I will talk to Chase and see what I can find out about Jolene," He replied without breaking eye contact. "This world, it will soon be ours."

Chapter *10*

"Chase, we must go to lunch," Jorge spoke with a friendly tone but with an unmistakable insistence, assuring that there was only one answer to this invitation. Fortunately, there was no hesitation on the other end of the line.

"Sure," Chase Jacobs replied automatically, giving Jorge a sense of reassurance that had escaped him in the last couple of months. Not to suggest that Chase had necessarily given him a reason to question his loyalty; that is, other than fucking Jolene, whom he no longer trusted. "What time?"

"I will meet you shortly before noon," Jorge calmly instructed, giving him the name of a popular restaurant close to the club, a place where the entire group had eaten before, back in the days when they were all on the same page.

After ending the call, Jorge glanced down at his bathrobe and glumly decided it was time to get up and change. These Canadian winters depressed him greatly and although he attempted to hide it from Paige, his wife knew him on such an intuitive level that she'd recently suggested that they return to Mexico for a holiday. Jorge wasn't sure if he was quite ready for that yet. So many memories; so many *bad* memories in his home country. In fact, he hadn't been there since having Maria's grandparents on her mother's side murdered after learning that they wanted to take his daughter away. It was necessary. They knew too much.

The weight of the world seemed to sit on his chest as he rose from the chair and closed the laptop. Jorge went into the bedroom where he grabbed the first shirt and tie he could find. Even though it wasn't a business day, it was important to stay professional in appearance. Also, Paige was looking at a potential house viewing for that afternoon. It was a private sale so it was important to look like an established businessman, encouraging a sense of respect. One's appearance did matter.

He had a few errands to run, something Jorge did with little enthusiasm, feeling drained and tired. He simply wasn't himself anymore and yet, why not? He had everything a man could want; love, ambition, money, success and yet, his heart continued to scream that something was missing. There was an emptiness that he couldn't deny.

Lately, his thoughts often drifted back to childhood; the good and the bad. He saw Miguel's face every day, the kid brother that followed him around as if he were God and what had Jorge done in return? He took him out on a dirt bike that he was unable to properly drive and killed him. It was an accident and in truth, he was only a child of 12, not much older than his own daughter and yet, he couldn't forgive himself. He would've done anything to bring Miguel back, to erase that day from history but it would never happen. His brother died at 10 years of age and in some ways, Jorge died that day too.

Arriving at the restaurant early, Jorge asked for a table away from others so he could conduct a business meeting. The waitress showed him a place at the back, a quiet corner in comparison to the rest of the establishment and for this, he thanked her and ordered a Corona.

Checking his phone, he saw that Paige scheduled an appointment for late afternoon to check out the house they discussed earlier that day. She seemed optimistic and although he wanted to share her enthusiasm, Jorge wasn't so certain. The homes they had recently viewed were often a disappointment either in price, location or the structure. It was amazing the shit people would try to sell at such inflated prices.

But it was important to push back his emotions and show strength before Chase's arrival. The last thing he wanted his associates to see was any weakness. In fact, he wasn't even content to show this side to Paige but yet, it was necessary for a beautiful marriage. It was one of the lessons he had learned in the last couple of months and a valuable one.

Chase arrived early, a good sign in Jorge's eyes. He approached the table showing no signs of hesitation or anxiety but with an overall sense of positivity, something Jorge welcomed on that particular day.

"Chase," He respectfully rose from his seat and gestured toward the chair across from him. "I do thank you for meeting with me."

"Of course," Chase replied as he sat down. "It's been a long time. I know how hectic things have been."

The waitress approached before Jorge could respond, two menus in hand, she asked Chase if he wanted anything to drink and he ordered a coffee. After she left, he continued to speak.

"I've been doing a lot of thinking about the changes you want to make and I have a few ideas."

"Very good," Jorge commented while giving the menu a quick once over, already settling on his usual boring choice of chicken and rice. "I love ideas, please share yours with me."

Setting his menu aside, he watched Chase carefully, observing his every move. People, he believed, said much more in their body language than they ever did with words. In fact, words were often meaningless but yet, so powerful at the same time.

"I understand why the focus is more on the pot side of things," Chase started, hesitating for a moment to read something on the menu before putting it aside and making eye contact with Jorge. "What if we just make the sex parties less exclusive? Plan a night, throw it together and set a price. No location parties, no private parties, no themes."

Jorge thought about his words in silence. In truth, he was actually thinking about scrapping the sex parties but this was an interesting point too.

"My concern with the entire sex club," Jorge said as the waitress approached again to ask if they were ready to order. After both did so and when she walked away, he continued. "My concern is that if the wrong thing happens at one of these parties, we get sued. For example, someone gets assaulted and suddenly we get pulled through the mud. Between you and I, this is why I am thinking of shutting it down completely and make us only about pot."

"Even if they're making money?" Chase asked and tilted his head.

"Yes, it was Diego's idea to create this kind of party after he noticed how popular they were in other places but for me," Jorge shrugged and glanced around before returning his attention to Chase. "I just saw it as a way to sell my drugs. I knew it was an ideal environment and that someone who had sex with complete strangers in a public place was not likely to have qualms about drugs. As it turns out, I was right."

Chase nodded in understanding.

"And now, we're established in many clubs across the country and my interest lie more with the pot industry, so I feel everything has come full circle."

"So what does that mean for the club?"

"It means that regardless what I do with the club, you will always have a job," Jorge assured him, suspecting this was the underlying concern. Chase had two children in Alberta that he was supporting on top of his everyday living expenses. Although he stayed with Diego as a roommate, Jorge knew that this relationship would be coming to an end. Although the two were still close, it was not as close as Diego wanted and chances were Chase was feeling the tension in their friendship.

"Thank you," Chase replied with a smile. "I wasn't even thinking of that but that's definitely good to know."

"I have more than enough work for you," Jorge thought for a moment and took advantage of the silence to bring up another awkward topic. "Jolene, I'm not so sure."

"Really?" Chase appeared sincerely surprised.

"I do not feel she is with us anymore," Jorge admitted and casually leaned back, his eyes carefully observing Chase. "Maybe her heart is elsewhere, I don't know."

An awkward silence followed and like a hawk observing his prey, Jorge quickly moved in. "Perhaps, you feel differently?"

"No," Chase shook his head and looked somewhat frustrated. "I'm not so sure that Jolene has a heart."

Jorge grinned and took a drink of his beer. It certainly was going down smoother than he expected.

"I see and tell me, Chase, what makes you say such a thing?"

"I see a different side of her now," Chase confessed and Jorge showed the right amount of compassion and nodded. "She's not who I once thought or maybe she changed, I dunno."

"Interesting," Jorge nodded. "Of course, you know I must ask what makes you say such things?"

"Please don't mention this to Diego," Chase quietly requested before starting the story, his eyes full of remorse and shame. "I would rather he didn't know."

"I will not say a word," Jorge spoke with sincerity in his voice. "Whatever you say, it does not leave this table."

"Jolene and I had a..fling," Chase reluctantly admitted as the restaurant began to fill up around them. "She was insistent that we keep things quiet, which made sense because we all work together. But then it became clear that it was casual to her, that she wanted *me* to be a secret."

"And you, you wished for more?" Jorge calmly asked, making sure to show compassion. "But she did not?"

"I thought she had a sincere interest in me," Chase commented and shook his head. "I don't understand. I guess I'm a little naïve."

He was more than a *little* naïve but still, Jorge felt for him. He knew that Jolene's honeypot was probably pretty enticing to this kid in his 20s. Clearly, it was a power play. She wanted to make sure Chase was in her corner against the others. Jorge had known this from day one but made sure to let things play out and as he suspected, his patience outlasted Jolene's desires for Chase. She had thrown him to the curb.

"Chase, are we not all naïve when it comes to what our heart wants?" Jorge spoke honestly but having spent most of his life in Jolene's shoes, he did understand her perspective. That's how he knew what to expect when things got a bit serious. A player wasn't sticking around when things were no longer fun.

"I suppose," He answered with reluctance and behind him, the waitress approached with their food. After she left, Chase continued to speak while Jorge dug into his rice. "I feel pretty stupid when it comes to women."

"Ah, well, women, they are often a mystery," Jorge replied while chewing his food. "You know, Chase, you need to ask yourself what these women have in common and what attracts you. Women, good women, they appreciate a strong, confident man and my friend, I think these are areas you need to work on."

"You're probably right," Chase replied and started to eat his food. "It just seemed weird, you know, we worked together for so long and she never showed any interest in me before. It was very sudden."

"Chase," Jorge stopped eating and thought carefully about the words he was about to use. "You must be careful of women like Jolene. Believe me, there is often a reason for everything they do and as you have expressed earlier, it isn't necessarily because they have a heart. I think it is important for you to see Jolene through new eyes and listen to your reluctance about her. I think maybe you see what others have noticed all along."

"Your loyalty," Jorge continued. "It makes you believe in people who sometimes don't deserve it but as someone once told me, if someone shows you who they truly are, it is important that you accept it. I believe Jolene has shown you who she really is, my friend."

Chase didn't reply but appeared troubled by these words. It was necessary to introduce the right amount of doubt, allowing it to trickle in and slowly absorb, causing Chase to discover his own conclusion. The brain, it had a beautiful way of finding the evidence it needed when determined to prove a fact. No one ever wanted to believe they had a part in a breakup and therefore, the natural reaction was to see the other person as inferior. *Perfecto.*

CHAPTER 11

Feeling pleased with his lunch meeting, Jorge decided to swing by the office of Diego and Jolene Inc for an impromptu visit. The element of surprise was always both entertaining and informative although, rarely appreciated. Catching people off guard was often the best way to see the truth.

He wandered into the office, passing an abandoned reception area followed by a couple of empty offices before discovering Diego at his desk with Jolene standing beside him. She was showing him something on his laptop. Neither heard him walk in the room.

"Well well well," Jorge spoke abruptly, causing Jolene to jump while Diego only looked slightly surprised, unconcerned with the unexpected visitor. "Now I see why someone was able to successfully walk in and put a listening device in Jolene's office last year. I could've easily done that or worse with no receptionist and empty offices. Did you give everyone the day off Diego?"

"Hey the receptionist, she quit this morning," Diego replied with the same abruptness as Jorge carried in his voice, while Jolene stood up straight with a dark expression on her face. "Everyone else is gone to lunch."

"Clara, she was in this morning," Jolene referred to the Latina who they often called the 'cleaning lady'. Although she was known to occasionally break out a mop or broom, most of her cleaning involved locating listening devices, cameras or anything that demonstrated that their crew was being monitored. Interestingly enough, most of these devices were found in Jolene's office.

"Would it matter?" Jorge shrugged and made himself comfortable in a chair across from Diego. "I could've done a lot of damage with no one minding the store. So your receptionist quit?"

"This morning, some family thing," Diego replied with a shrug. "I asked Sylvana to watch over things but she's gone to lunch."

"I see," Jorge nodded with one raised eyebrow and glanced toward Jolene before returning his attention to Diego. "Don't bother replacing her. We don't need her. We will reroute the calls to either the pot stores or the club. There is no need for anyone to call here unless it is for one of you and in which case, you have a private line."

"But the door?" Jolene's voice was loud and Jorge merely shrugged, enjoying her frustration.

"What about it? Why would the public even come here? We change the door that anyone wanting in has to buzz and whoever is close can answer it and get the staff a security passcard each. Other than an occasional delivery or meeting, I see no reason for anyone other than staff be in here. Jolene, you can look into that today and meanwhile, maybe *you* should look after the door."

His comment was casual but he immediately saw the anger on her face. His phone vibrated before she could respond. Standing up, Jorge glanced at the number and started toward the door.

"I have an important call but make sure you get one of those security cards for me too, Jolene." He said without waiting for a reply and ignoring the look of contempt on her face, he walked out of the office. He knew a fight was about to break out between the siblings as he made his way toward the main entrance but didn't care. "Jesús, how are things in BC?"

"Sir, they are doing well," He replied from the other end of the line, his reception sounding less than stellar but chances were good he was in a remote area where the marijuana was grown. The location was secret and highly secured. So far, they only had one incident a month earlier and those involved had a brutal message to not return. It was simply the only way to do business when so much was at stake. Fortunately, Jorge and his partners were in agreement about how to handle any kind of security issue.

"Did you find a location for the distribution centre?" Jorge asked as he stepped into the hallway and headed toward the elevator.

"I did sir, I will discuss the details further when I return later in the week but it is good," He replied with a slight uplift in his voice. "Currently, we are looking at the best options for delivery of such sensitive materials. Clearly, the customer will sign to assure they receive the package. We want to negotiate with the various courier services. I do not think hiring staff will be an issue. We have some immigrants in this area who are in great need of a job and are trustworthy."

"Ok, we must keep an eye on them regardless," Jorge noted the time on a nearby clock as he stepped into the elevator. He had to meet Paige to look at a house. "Have you talked to Marco about the ordering site?"

"Yes, yes, he is on top of it," Jesús replied with a laugh. "It was actually him who made some possible employee suggestions. He knows people in need of work and who can keep quiet."

"Very good but we will keep this legal," Jorge replied as he hit the proper button on the elevator.

"Of course," Jesús spoke with a certain amount of sarcasm. "As always, sir."

Jorge grinned to himself as the elevator door opened and he walked out. People were suddenly all around him but he ignored them all until he noticed one lagging back. It was Marco Rodel Cruz, the very man he was speaking of moments earlier.

"Speak of the devil," Jorge said with a smooth laugh. "I just ran into Marco on the way out of the office."

"Oh yes! I shall leave you to talk to him then," Jesús commented as his reception started to break up again. "I wanted you to know that we are good here."

"No problems?"

"Nothing I cannot handle, boss."

Jorge knew what that meant.

"Very well then."

Ending the call, he turned his attention to the Filipino man and ushered him away from the people wandering in the hallway. "Marco, I was just speaking to Jesús."

"Ah yes, we have had many conversations, Mr. Hernandez," Marco commented with a bright, appreciative smile. "He is a good man. I'm working on the site today and we should be able to go live easily by the time the distribution centre is ready to fill orders. Until then, I have it on the websites that we will soon be offering online options in confidential packaging, which I've already discussed with Jesús as well."

"Ah yes, that is a good point," Jorge commented with a nod. "Confidentiality is important in our business."

"And the party website?"

"Give it as little of your attention as possible."

"That is what Diego has said," Marco appeared concerned and glanced over his shoulder. "And Miss Jolene, I noticed she is not happy with this arrangement."

A smile lit up Jorge's face and he nodded, "Well she must learn that things change quickly in business."

"Diego, he says we are taking a different direction?" Marco said as he continued to look eager.

"Indeed we are," Jorge insisted and glanced toward the main exit. "But you gotta excuse me, Marco. Paige and I are going to see a house shortly and if I'm not there on time, she's gonna kill me."

Marco gave an enthused smile. "Oh sir, I do wish you good luck. You were so generous when helping my family move into a nice apartment."

"Of course, my friend, of course," Jorge replied as he started to walk away. "We will speak soon, Marco."

Outside, he located his SUV and got in before sending Paige a quick text.

I know I'm running late. Meet you there?

He had just enough time to fasten his seatbelt before getting a reply.

Sure thing.

As he drove to the address his wife had given him earlier that day, Jorge called Jesús back.

"I didn't get a chance to ask if you spoke with your friends in Colombia?" Jorge asked a simple question without getting into detail. It wasn't necessary.

"I did, boss, I did," Jesús reassured him from the other end of the line with some enthusiasm. "Ohhh....I think you will like what I have to say but that will have to be for our meeting later this week when I return."

A smile lit up Jorge's face as he glanced to his right and back to the road.

"*Perfecto.*"

Arriving at the house, he noticed Paige's car already there and she was staring down at her phone. It took a minute for her to look up and see him watching her. A smile lit up her face as she got out of the car and he met her at the end of the driveway, giving her a quick kiss.

"The house, it's ok," Jorge commented as they walked toward the door. "Who know's till we get inside."

"Yes, we've had some surprises in the past," She muttered, referring to a few dumps they had visited in recent weeks.

"It is draining, this house hunting, we may need to hire a real estate person," Jorge replied as he reached for her hand. "Oh, I spoke to Jesús about Colombia. I think he's got something for us."

Paige nodded.

Knocking on the door, Jorge hadn't expected to see a Latina answered but not as surprised as she appeared, when she looked at Paige.

"Yes?" She spoke curtly while giving Jorge a dirty look.

"We're here about the house," Paige spoke evenly. "We spoke on the phone earlier? I'm Paige, this is my husband, Jorge."

Without replying, she turned and let them in while the couple exchanged looks.

"Not bad," Jorge ignored the tension and made the generous comment; to be fair, they barely got in the door so it was a bit early to offer criticisms. "Kinda small but not bad." He reached into his pocket for a piece of gum and nervously shoved it in his mouth.

"I will give you the tour," The woman's reply was abrupt and although it automatically turned Jorge off, he went along with it. Paige squeezed his hand as they followed the Latina through the various rooms, most of which were small, dank and depressing. Of course, this was quickly becoming the theme of their house hunting; either terrible or outlandishly expensive.

"It's…quaint," Paige spoke softly, politely, even though Jorge could tell by her expression that she fucking hated it. The Canadian politeness wasn't something he necessarily shared.

"I dunno, it looks like it needs work," Jorge shot out unapologetically, growing frustrated with the overpriced dumps he was finding while house hunting. "We're not really interested in fixer-uppers."

"Fine," The woman appeared uninterested in this conversation, her reply accompanied an apathetic shrug as she led them back down the stairs. "Do what you want."

"Alright then, thanks anyway," Jorge commented dismissively and turned to his wife just as they reached the first floor again. "Come on Paige, let's go."

"Thank you," Paige said and smiled at the lady, who appeared angry.

"You know, this should not have surprised me," The homeowner commented abruptly, causing Jorge to turn and give her a frustrated look.

"Look, lady, your house needs work, we don't got the time or interest," He replied defensively. "You'll probably end up selling to someone who will tear it down and rebuild anyway."

"I meant you two," She gestured toward them with a grimace on her face. "A Latino with a white woman. This, this is why my family is breaking up and I need to sell my home." She gestured toward Paige accusingly. "It's only cause you spoke Spanish on the phone that I even thought differently."

"I…I just thought you were more comfortable speaking in Spanish," Paige spoke with hesitation as if uncertain how to address the main point of the woman's comment.

"Look, lady," Jorge's voice grew angry, noting the growing frustration on her face. "I don't know about you and your….man, but that's got nothing to do with us. We just want to buy a fucking house and we don't like this one. That's it." With that, he took Paige's hand and rushed toward the door. This woman was pissing him off.

"They only like you white women cause you're submissive and you don't fight back," The Latina sharply commented. It was at this point that both he and Paige abruptly stopped and turned around, his wife appearing stunned by this comment. "They know they can control you. I can tell that you're passive and quiet. And he's a Mexican man too, they're the *worst*."

Despite the shocked expression on Paige's face, Jorge wanted to laugh. His wife, the assassin, was passive and submissive? It was hilarious to even consider. The fact that anyone associated her quiet, gentle nature as being obedient and compliant was ignorant. Of course, he also had the benefit of seeing her kill with ease, so perhaps that made this comment even more ridiculous. He decided to tease his wife by playing along.

"Oh yeah, that's totally her," Jorge spoke mockingly before returning his attention to Paige, who continued to look unsure of how to react.

Without missing a beat, Jorge let go of his wife's hand and walked ahead. Swinging around, he threw on an extra layer to his accent and pointed toward the door.

"Come on, Paige, we don't *got* all day!" His comment was harsh and abrupt and he was enjoying the questioning look on her face. "You gotta get home and make my dinner, woman. Come *on*! Let's *go!*"

Giving him a questioning look, she couldn't hold back from grinning as she walked toward the door.

CHAPTER *12*

"Maybe she's not totally wrong," Paige spoke evenly as they walked away from the house and toward their vehicles. Reaching into her coat pocket, she pulled out a set of keys and shivered as a gust of wind swept over them. Their eyes met and she shrugged. "I'm always there for you for whatever you need, maybe I am compliant."

"Oh *mi amor*, come on," Jorge quickly shook his head dismissively. Facing her, he looked into her blue eyes and placed his hand on her arm. "You're listening to that woman back there? She's obviously bitter about whatever happened with her and her man. It's got nothing to do with us and to tell you the truth, I'm kind of pissed she's projecting her shit on you. You're hardly compliant."

"But I'm always doing things for you," Paige quietly answered. "Whatever you need, I centre everything around you. You know that my biggest fear is becoming like my mother and sisters, their entire lives are about their husbands and children's schedules. They have no lives of their own."

Jorge made a face and with a quick shrug, shook his head. "Paige, it's a partnership, is it not? I mean, I'm hardly the expert but that is how I see it. You help me out and I do the same for you but *mi amor,* you must first ask. You never ask me to help you out with anything other than maybe, pick up something at the store on the way home. If you don't tell me what you need then how can I give it to you?"

Her face softened as she listened, glancing down, Paige looked back up and into his eyes. "You're right, I don't ask. I'm just used to doing things for myself."

"Well, I guess maybe that is something you're going to have to work on," He leaned forward and kissed her forehead. "Meditate on it on your fancy pillow tomorrow."

She smiled as he began to walk away. "I'm going to go pick up Maria. I will see you at home soon."

"I'm going to cook dinner," She replied and he glanced back with a smile.

"I will pick up dinner," Jorge insisted. "You go home and relax. Don't worry about that *perra* in there." He gestured toward the house. "And really, I should be the one insulted. Did you hear how she talk about Mexican men? Come on! We are the perfect gentlemen."

Paige started to laugh as she got in her little car. After she drove off, Jorge got in his SUV and left. It wasn't until he was almost at the school that he got the call.

Glancing at the unfamiliar number, he hit the button and casually answered.

"Jorge? Is this you?"

"Yes, who is this?" Jorge practically barked back as he was about to turn the corner to Maria's school.

"Esta es tu tía Rosa."

It was his aunt Rosa whom he hadn't spoken to in years. In fact, Jorge couldn't remember the last time he saw her. His only memories of her were when she used to visit his mother, especially after Miguel passed away. The two often had hushed conversations in the kitchen, halting suddenly when he entered the room. Their bond was strong but it was clear that she had little use for her nephew. If she was calling now, something was seriously wrong.

"Rosa," Jorge said as he drove into the school parking lot and wished that Maria was running late today. He wanted to get this conversation over before she got in the SUV. "What can I do for you today?"

"Your mother, she ask me to call," Rosa spoke slowly, her voice full of uncertainty. "I have terrible news. I am afraid that your father, he had a bad heart attack this morning and he..he has passed."

The news hit him just as he saw Maria sauntering toward the vehicle, a huge backpack resting on her tiny shoulders.

"What? I don't understand," Jorge spoke with hesitation. "He died?"

"Yes, I am so sorry Jorge," Rosa carried sincere regret in her voice. "Your mother, she is too upset to call. She asked if I would. I am so sorry. She said she will call you later or tomorrow."

The call ended as Maria got in the vehicle while Jorge's heart raced erratically, for a moment he felt weak because despite the terrible relationship he had with his father, this was still a huge shock. The man who had lived his life as if death was at the next corner had finally got his morbid wish. It depressed him.

Glancing at his daughter, he attempted to act normal as she threw the backpack on the floor and climbed into the passenger side. Closing the door, she looked at Jorge and fear suddenly appeared in her eyes, his stomach dropped in guilt. He didn't want her to find out this way, not as they were driving home.

"What is it, *Papa?*" She spoke reluctantly. "Did I do something wrong?"

"No, *cariño*, you are fine," Jorge hesitated and decided this was a conversation that they would have at home. "I..just...I got some news but we will talk about it at the apartment."

"No, you must tell me now," Maria insisted as tears welled in her eyes. "Is it Paige? Are you sick again? What is wrong?"

"No, we are fine," Jorge spoke honestly as he pulled the SUV into a better parking spot, one away from the school and turned toward her. "I just had a phone call from *tia* Rosa in Mexico. She shared with me some bad news."

Maria nodded and sat a little straighter as if putting her body in a strong position before learning what he had to say. How could he break this news to his little girl? Another family death; in less than a year, she had lost both her other grandparents and her mother. Could she handle this as well?

"*Cariño*, it is about your grandfather," Jorge took a deep breath, speaking in the most gentle voice he could muster while still absorbing the reality himself. "He had a heart attack earlier today and he has passed away."

Maria looked stunned by the news as tears quickly followed. Not that the old man ever had much to do with Jorge's daughter - in fact, neither of his parents did - but it was still another loss. Her family was disappearing as death took them one by one. He immediately unfastened his seat belt and reached across the SUV to hug his sobbing child, unsure of what to say, he decided to say nothing.

Once her tears subsided, the two drove home in silence. Back at the apartment, his daughter weakly got out of the SUV, attempting to pull her backpack out, Jorge quickly insisted that she leave it.

"I will take it," He said as he reached the other side of the SUV, pulling the heavy bag out, he closed the door and hit the button to lock the vehicle. He reached for her hand and they headed for the elevator.

Once in the apartment, Jorge felt his entire body grow heavy as Maria quickly repeated the news to Paige. His wife looked stunned as she pulled Maria into a hug, offering the child words of comfort while watching her husband walk by. Jorge went into the bedroom, closing the door behind him, he then went into the bathroom. It was there that he finally cried.

A chill ran through his body and he began to shake uncontrollably. Reaching out, Jorge braced himself against the sink as waves of emotions rose inside of him from a place he didn't even know existed. Through his tears, he mourned not the father who beat him mercilessly on the worst day of his life nor the cold, heartless man who hated his oldest son; he mourned the father he never had and never would.

Turning on the shower, he started to remove his clothes, hesitating after his shirt hit the floor. His eyes automatically glanced in the mirror and toward the scar that his father had left on his back. It was almost as if to spite the doctor's comment that Jorge had gotten away with 'not even a scar' after the accident that he decided to leave one himself, something to carry every day so he would never forget how Miguel died; as if he ever could.

Oh, he had beat him so bad! In a way, it made him fearless of any fight in the future and yet, it had scarred him in so many ways. Interestingly, of the many people who had seen the scar over the years, only a few had asked him about how he got it. Jorge had simply told his daughter it was a result of a childhood injury but he would someday have to tell her the truth. Why was he protecting an old man who hated him? A man who was now dead?

The warm water of the shower washed over him, giving him little comfort other than to stop the shaking. He felt numb as he stood and once again replayed that terrible accident over in his mind. After a few minutes, he turned off the water and got out. Grabbing his robe from the back of the door, he walked into the bedroom to find Paige sitting on the bed. Her eyes full of worry, she quickly rose and moved toward him.

"I'm so sorry," She pulled him into a tight hug which felt like heaven at that moment. "This must've been such a shock to you, it was so sudden."

"It was," He replied as he weakly hugged her back and gave her a quick kiss on the top of her head. "Thank you for looking after Maria, I did not know what to say or do."

"She's fine," Paige reassured him as she let him go and looked into his face. "She's looking at an online menu, we're going to order some food."

"Sorry, I guess I didn't get the food," Jorge remembered his promise and laughed.

"As if I expected it after learning your father died," Paige quietly responded as her hand gently caressed his face. "I'm worried about you though."

"Paige, you know I had no relationship with my father," Jorge commented as he moved away from her and opened his dresser, pulling out some comfortable clothing. "It's…it brings up a lot of stuff from my childhood, that is all."

She didn't reply at first but finally spoke. "Maria was asking me why you didn't talk to your father much, why the two of you didn't get along."

"What did you say?" Jorge asked as he removed his robe and started to dress.

"I said she should talk to you," Paige replied.

"She doesn't know much about the accident," Jorge commented as she watched him pull on his pants.

"Are you going to tell her?"

"I had considered telling her but I don't know," Jorge finally admitted as he pulled on his sweater. "What purpose would that serve?"

"There is so much you can't tell her," Paige spoke gently, her eyes full of compassion. "This is something, maybe she should know about him. She doesn't understand why your relationship was so bad."

"But now?" Jorge shook his head. "On the day of his death, tell her what a horrible man he actually was? Even I am not that cruel."

"But maybe you present it to her in a different way," Paige suggested as she sat on the edge of the bed. "As him being a grieving man who reacted out of his own pain."

"I'm not sure *I* even believe that," Jorge sat beside her. "You never met this man, Paige. He was as cold as ice."

"I've never met your mother either," She quietly commented and glanced away.

"*Mi amor*, you aren't missing much," Jorge said as he moved closer to her. "She is the same."

"Maybe not now that your father has died," Paige whispered.

"I have little hope she will change," Jorge commented. "But you can come to the funeral if you wish."

"Of course," Paige agreed. "Of course, I will be there for you and Maria."

"You always are," He replied and took a deep breath as she smiled at him. "Now, we must make sure Maria hasn't ordered enough to feed the entire building."

It was only later that evening, as they shared a pizza that he looked over at his daughter's tranquil face and realized that Paige was right. This was a truth he had to share with her. She must know what her grandfather was like; he would tell her after the funeral and it would be a conversation that would define his relationship with Maria.

CHAPTER *13*

"I bring my daughter and wife to Mexico, I dress up in a nice suit and am respectful at the service," Jorge gruffly commented as he watched his daughter swim in the pool outside of his home in Mexico, while he sat inside on the couch. Beside him, Paige poured herself a second glass of wine and leaned miserably against the couch. "All this for a man who hated me and yet, do I receive any respect? Nah, I am treated like an outcast."

"They weren't exactly friendly to me either," Paige commented with a long sigh and exchanged looks with Jorge and shrugged. "At first, I thought it was because I wasn't Mexican but when I spoke Spanish, they still seemed…"

"Like assholes?" Jorge finished her sentence and took another drink, reaching out to touch her thigh. "*Mi amor*, please do not pay attention to such things. They're ignorant. Most of the people you saw today, they haven't spoken to me in years and I suspect most know the work I do. Many look down at me but if I waved money in their faces, they would have no problem, you know?"

"I do," Paige seemed to shake off her mood and shared a gentle smile with him. "I'm sorry that your family is like that, I'm actually kind of surprised. I thought they would at least try to be kinder especially in front of Maria."

"Some were," Jorge reminded her as he finished his drink and set the glass on a nearby table before moving closer to his wife as he continued to watch Maria outside. "I was slightly annoyed when my *madre* decided to lavish her with affection and attention in a way she never had before and in fact, probably never will again."

"You mean when there was an audience?" Paige asked as she put down her wine glass and leaned in closer to her husband. Breathing in the gentle scent of her perfume, he closed his eyes briefly and let out a short laugh.

"Yes, that is right, it's all about appearances. That is why having her criminal son show up at the funeral was such a terrible embarrassment and yet, had I not shown up, I would've never heard the end of it."

"It must give you such mixed feelings about Mexico," Paige commented as the bitter drink hit his system and suddenly relaxed him.

Yawning, Jorge was just about to respond when he heard the patio door. Opening his eyes, he saw Maria walking into the house with a towel wrapped around her shoulders. She observed the two of them on the couch in silence, something that disturbed Jorge since his daughter was rarely quiet. Sitting upright, he stretched and nodded toward the nearby chair.

"Sit down, *bonita*, we must have a talk," His voice was gentle causing an order to sound more like a suggestion while on the other side of him, Paige stood up. "Wait, you do not have to go, you can stay."

"You two should talk," She glanced toward her stepdaughter and back at Jorge. "I have some work to do for the website."

While his wife made her way upstairs, Maria appeared hesitant to sit beside him, something he noticed right away.

"What? You don't want to talk to your *Papa* anymore?" He attempted to joke even though he could easily see the toll the day had taken on his daughter. Before she could reply, he quickly jumped in. "Look, Maria, I know there has been so much death in the last year. I wish that you didn't have to go through this but unfortunately, sometimes it's in God's hands. We cannot do a thing."

"I know," Maria commented with a sad shrug and pulled the towel closer. "I don't understand why my relatives act so strangely around me."

Jorge bit his bottom lip and thought about her comment. It was *him* that they had issues with, not his daughter. In part, they perhaps feared him, having heard notorious stories of his evil and destructive ways. He was the black sheep of his family, if not the entire country.

"Maria, that is just their way," Jorge replied with an answer that didn't appear to bring her comfort. Turning to face her, he considered the best words to explain the situation. "You see, I have not been close to the family for many years, in part because I've traveled so much for my work. I have missed weddings, baptisms, funerals, so many things and these people, I assume they probably hold a bit of a grudge."

"But you were busy working, *Papa*."

"Some people, they do not understand such things," He offered her a smile and reached out to touch her hair but she continued to appear unhappy. "I am sorry, *cariña*, that your *abuelo* wasn't very kind to you but to tell you the truth, he was often the same with me."

This appeared to get Maria's attention. She suddenly turned to face him, her eyes inspecting his as if to finally lure the secrets from her father's heart. Oh, he had so many but most, he would never be able to share with his daughter.

"Maria, your *abuelo*, he simply wasn't a kind man."

"But why not?"

"Well, I believe he was that way because your uncle Miguel died at such a young age," Jorge attempted to explain. "My brother, he was only 10, your age. I know we have discussed this before but I'm unsure if you know how he died."

"He was on a dirt bike."

"Yes, he was on a dirt bike," Jorge replied and hesitated for a moment. "And it was me who was driving it. I wasn't supposed to use it and I lost control."

Unexpected emotion crept into his voice and his daughter's eyes grew sad. He rested his hand on her shoulder and looked into her eyes. "I shouldn't have been on the bike but I was a child who never listened and because of this, I had an accident and my brother died."

"Oh, *Papa!*" Maria's eyes filled with tears and she leaned in close to him. "How terrible!"

"It was, *cariña,* the worst day of my life," Jorge spoke honestly, sincerity filled his voice. "It was a terrible mistake. I was impulsive and that is why I'm so strict with you. Sometimes when we are young, we don't see the possible consequences of your actions."

She nodded slowly. "*Papa*, tell me about Miguel."

"Miguel, he was very different from me," Jorge chose his words carefully. "He was quiet, a good child, always with our *madre*, helping out in the kitchen."

Maria's eyebrow rose as she listened.

"When he died," Jorge started and hesitated for a moment. "Your *abuelo*, he was furious with me."

"But *P*apa, it was an accident," Maria said as she leaned up against the back of the couch and looked up at him with her big, brown eyes, full of such warmth and love that it almost made him tearful again. "You didn't mean to hurt Miguel."

"I know," He spoke in a soft voice and reached out and pulled her next to him. "But your *abuelo*, he was in shock. He was grieving and I guess that he displaced his feeling of sadness and turned them into anger. He was furious with me."

Maria didn't comment but continued to listen, her face falling into a frown and for a moment, Jorge considered concealing the rest of the story. However, it was necessary to always be honest with his daughter.

"Maria, I don't know how to tell you this but on the day that Miguel died," Jorge said and paused briefly to take a deep breath. "Your *abuelo*, he wanted to punish me for what I had done. He did so by beating me, *very* badly beating me."

Maria looked stunned and sat up, her eyes widened and her mouth fell open but no words came out.

"I'm sorry to have to tell you such a terrible thing," Jorge spoke softly. "But I want you to understand why our relationship, it was not good. It was never the same. He held me responsible and I never was able to get over how badly he beat me that day. It was quite…brutal."

"Oh, *Papa*!! That is so wrong!" Maria said as she continued to react, her face full of fury. "Is that why those marks are on your back? You said they were from your childhood?"

"Yes," Jorge spoke with regret in his voice, stunned when his daughter sprang from the couch and he quickly did the same. "Maria,

I am sorry, I did not mean to upset you like this…maybe you are too young for this but I wanted you to know the truth."

Sometimes her maturity tricked him into believing that his daughter was older than 10 but yet, she was still very much a little girl.

"*Papa*, had I known, I never would've gone to the funeral today," Maria spoke with anger in her voice. "How could he be so mean to you? How could he *hurt* you?"

"Grief, Maria, it…"

"Do not make excuses for him!" Maria's eyes began to fill with tears again. "What a cruel, horrible man!"

Jorge slowly nodded, feeling helpless.

"Yes, you are right. I should not make excuses for him."

"I hate him!" Maria screamed and flew up the stairs, leaving her father in stunned disbelief.

For the rest of the day, he wondered if this conversation had been a mistake. After a quiet dinner, followed by Maria going to bed early, Paige suggested they do the same. It was only after an intense encounter that left him at his most vulnerable as he lay naked beneath the sheets that his emotions began to overflow. Paige attempted to comfort him but the day had been too intense. He felt conflicted by memories of Miguel's death combined with his thoughts of the funeral earlier that morning; the loathing of his relatives, followed by the shock and outrage of his daughter when learning the truth. It was only the tip of the iceberg. There were so many things Maria didn't know.

"Everything will be ok," Paige reminded him as he let out a heavy sigh. "Its over and tomorrow is another day. Maria will be fine. You had to tell her the truth. She's so mature and instinctual, you know she sensed something was wrong."

"I know, but the look in her eyes," Jorge moved away slightly, turning on his back he stared at the ceiling as the fan overhead propelled. "I will never forget it."

"She's resilient."

"I hope this is true."

The next morning, Maria appeared fine over breakfast, if not back to her usual self. Dancing in her chair to popular Latin music that she had found in his CD collection, they almost didn't hear the knock at the door. Paige exchanged looks with Jorge, who didn't react but instead got up and walked across the room. His mother was at the door.

"*Mama*," His voice was full of surprise as he stood aside, allowing her in the house. Paige appeared expressionless while Maria stopped dancing in her chair.

"*Buenos días,*" Paige said, to which her mother-in-law returned the greeting but then turned her attention to Maria.

"*Buenos días,* Maria," She spoke calmly, with a little more affection in her voice than usual, something that surprised Jorge but appeared to have no effect on his daughter, who gave a strained smile.

"May I speak to you in private?" His mother asked him and to which Jorge merely gestured down the hallway, toward his office.

"Do you need something, *Mama*?" Jorge asked even before closing the door, hoping this meeting would be short and to the point.

"I was wondering if maybe, I could have Maria for a while," His mother spoke nervously, as if unsure of how to act now that she was a widow. He noted that she showed no signs of the grieving wife of the previous day. "Maybe after you leave, then you can return to get her in a few weeks."

"Weeks?" Jorge laughed. "*Mama,* you do realize that my daughter, she goes to school? She cannot miss weeks of school to visit with you."

"But I feel, I feel I've missed so much time," She spoke with emotion in her voice. "When your *Papa* was still here, God rest his soul, it was difficult to see her."

"Why?" Jorge bluntly asked. "If anything, it would've been easier to see her because up until a few months ago, I still lived in Mexico."

"But your *Papa*, you know he…"

"Hated me?" Jorge said without hiding the bitterness from his voice. "Yes, I think that was pretty clear."

"Jorge, you do not understand, your *Papa*…he was.."

"An asshole," Jorge replied with coldness in his voice.

"No, you do not understand," His mother shook her head.

"I do," Jorge replied. "If Paige were to have an accident that took my little girl away, I would not hate her. I would not punish her. If Maria were to do something that accidentally led to my wife's death, I would not beat her within inches of her life. I would not whip her. That is the act of a madman."

Tears formed in his mother's eyes, one escaping to slide down her cheek.

"And perhaps, those people at the funeral yesterday, who think that *I'm* the devil," Jorge spoke abruptly and pointed toward the window. "Maybe if they knew how he used to beat his son, they might see both of us a little differently."

"What your *Papa* did, it was not right," His mother shook her head. "It was wrong."

"But you didn't stop him, did you?" Jorge spoke accusingly, not breaking eye contact for a moment. "You allowed this to happen."

"He was my husband, I could not say…"

"When someone was hurting *your* child, you could not say anything?" Jorge countered. "I thought he was going to kill me that night, *Mama*. Did you not hear me screaming in pain? Did you not hear me calling for help? Do you forget the cuts, the bruises on my back? Do you know I still have scars? Oh, so many scars and not just on my body."

His mother's body shook as her tears poured from her eyes, her sobs growing louder as his voice grew in hostility and fury. So much he had held in for far too long! But no more, Jorge refused to hold back a single word.

"You and I," Jorge pointed at her before reaching for the door. "We are done here."

She rushed out of the office, continuing to cry loudly as he followed behind, watching her run past a stunned Paige and Maria, out the door, slamming it behind her. Without saying a word, he turned around and went back into his office, where he closed the door and sat behind the desk. His spirit was weak but yet, in other ways, stronger than it had ever been before that day.

Chapter 14

"Oh, *mi amor*, you worry too much," Jorge said as he leaned forward to give his wife a quick kiss before heading for the door. "Kiss Maria for me too." His instructions were gentle as he hesitated only briefly to give her a warm smile.

"We just got back from Mexico last night," Paige reminded him in her usual, gentle voice as she followed him and reached out to touch his arm. "It was an exhausting few days especially dealing with your mother. *I'm* exhausted so I can't imagine how you must feel. You don't have to jump right back into everything."

"Oh, but sweetheart, I *must,*" Jorge insisted, reaching for the doorknob as he observed his wife's concerned expression. Still wearing her red bathrobe while Maria could be heard singing in the shower, Jorge couldn't help but feel some comfort in the worried look in her eyes. It was beautiful when someone cared about you that much; he had spent most of his life neglected of such feelings. Now that he was fortunate enough to experience them, it often took him off guard and almost made him giddy in response. Who knew anyone would ever worry about him?

Paige stepped back with a slightly defiant expression on her face and slowly nodded. "Ok, but can you try to make it a short day, at least?"

"Yes, my love, I can certainly try," He leaned forward and gave her another quick kiss. "I gotta go see Jesús now that he's back in town and Marco, he will be waiting for me at the café shortly, we must meet before he goes to work." He stopped briefly and thought for a moment. "I might also go speak with Chase. It's been a few days since our last conversation. I am curious what more I can learn now and oh yes, Diego has my new security passcard for the door at the office…who knows, I might swing by and make a few *more* changes there as well."

"That doesn't sound like a short day," Paige observed and took a deep breath. "Well, I guess I'll look into that real estate agent that Diego recommended."

"You must because us," Jorge gestured between the two of them. "We cannot waste any more time sifting through terrible houses. To me, real estate agents are vultures but then again, I'm perhaps not one to talk?" He joked before winking at her and slipping out the door.

Marco was already at the café when Jorge arrived. Seated at the back of the room, the Filipino's face lit up when he saw Jorge and gave him a quick wave. After ordering a breakfast sandwich and coffee, he made his way to the table, taking note of those sitting nearby. The place was unusually crowded compared to most mornings when the two held their private meetings; perhaps it was time to find a new place.

"Mr. Hernandez, good morning sir," Marco warmly greeted him, pushing his chair forward, he set his phone aside. "Cold, isn't it?"

"You're fucking telling me, Marco," Jorge replied as he sat across from him. Glancing toward the window, he noticed everyone walking by wearing scarfs and hats, many rushing as if to escape the bitterly cold temperature. Opening his coffee, he took a quick drink. "I got back from Mexico last night and I just heard on the radio that we have record low temperatures today. How does one get used to this?"

"I do not know," Marco shook his head and with compassion in his eyes, continued. "I am so sorry for your loss."

"We weren't close," Jorge said with a shrug. "So, Marco, what's new at the office?"

"A lot of tension, sir," Marco revealed and Jorge grinned before biting into his sandwich. "Miss Jolene, she is not happy."

"Is she ever?"

"Not so much, no," Marco replied and let out a little laugh. "Her and Diego, they argue often. I have watched her emails but there is nothing."

"She knows she's being watched," Jorge insisted as he took a drink of his coffee. He was fortunate to find an IT expert who had no scruples about hacking emails and pretty much anything else that was hackable; Jorge wasn't much of a techie so this was a positive skill in his eyes.

"You won't find anything else. You can continue to check emails but don't allow it to consume much of your time. As I've said before, our focus will be the pot stores. The website, I was looking at it this morning, it looks good."

"Thank you, sir," Marco spoke graciously. "Jesús and I have worked together on it, so I cannot take all the credit."

"I have a meeting with him after this one," Jorge glanced at his phone briefly. "I want to go over a few details with you before I go. I'm thinking about sending you to BC with him sometime soon."

"Oh!" Marco's eyes lit up. "Very good, sir."

Jorge smiled in between bites.

Twenty minutes later, he was out the door and on the way to see Jesús at his apartment. Unlike himself, his business associate was able to find a nice place in the downtown area but parking was terrible. Once Jorge managed to find a spot, he still had to walk longer than he would've preferred in the bitter weather. When he finally arrived at the door, he was blunt.

"We will never ever meet here again," He said as he rushed inside the apartment rubbing his gloved hands together and Jesús let out a good-natured laugh. "The last time I was here, I don't remember having such a difficult time finding parking."

"Last time was in the evening, I believe," Jesús reminded him while gesturing toward the kitchen table, where he already had his laptop sitting, open. "Parking was probably more reasonable at that time. Unfortunately, this building doesn't have visitor parking."

Jesús spoke so slowly that Jorge was already across the room, his coat off and was sitting down just as he finished his sentence. Gingerly, Jesús sat down.

"Hey, what's with you?" Jorge asked as he pulled out his phone and glanced at it briefly before returning his attention to his longtime associate. The two had worked together closely over the years, Jesús had many roles including as Jorge's bodyguard. "You're moving like an old man."

"Today, I feel like an old man," He commented as he reached for his back. "I must've pulled something when I was in British Columbia, I am not sure."

"Was it one of those Asian whores again?" Jorge asked with laughter in his voice.

"That, that was only once," Jesús quickly reminded him, although a grin crept on his face. "I may have pulled something when I reached for my shoes yesterday morning. I think perhaps, I must lose weight."

Jorge didn't comment but merely nodded. Jesús had always been a little heavy but his weight had increased rapidly in the last few years. He seemed exhausted most the time. Fortunately, it hadn't affected his work.

"So business-wise, we are doing well, boss," Jesús turned his laptop around to show Jorge some images. "This is the place for our new distribution center." He commented while showing some photos. "The last business that was here, they did not do so well, poor management and had to sell quickly so we got it at a good rate."

Jorge merely nodded as he observed the images.

"I have someone in place to hire and organize at this location," Jesús continued and showed Jorge a document displaying the specifics of the building and price. "I must go back later this week to see how they are doing but I don't anticipate it will take long. I also found a courier that is reasonable."

"Good," Jorge commented as he slid the laptop back toward Jesús. "I want you to send me everything so I can take a better look later. I would like you to take Marco next time since you're hiring some people he knows. Maybe he can be helpful and also, you can continue to work out details for the site."

"Yes, of course," Jesús agreed. "And the office, boss, how are things?"

"I keep making changes" Jorge replied with a grin as he glanced at his phone again. "Some of which aren't going over well but that is fine. Sometimes you must shake things up."

Jesús laughed and nodded. "You do like shaking things up, boss."

"Jolene isn't happy with me," Jorge spoke solemnly before quickly following it with a hearty laugh. "Speaking of which, you said you have news?"

"Yes, I almost forgot," Jesús continued to speak slowly and closed his laptop. "My sources tell me that she left abruptly from Colombia, as we already knew but I was surprised to learn that there are people in certain circles that believe she is dead."

"With the internet and their resources?" Jorge asked with uncertainty. "That seems unlikely."

"Do a search online for Jolene Silva, see if you find anything," Jesús offered as he pointed toward Jorge's phone. "You will not find anything. She is not on social media. She is not listed anywhere."

"These people would want proof," Jorge insisted. "They are not going to make assumptions."

"There are two groups of people who she managed to piss off," Jesús continued. "One was connected to a boyfriend and the other, connected to someone she was working with and both were very dangerous. I believe, from what I understood, both perhaps thought the other was involved in her sudden disappearance."

"Now, I do not have all the facts," Jesús continued, "I merely did some inquiries about whether someone might be looking for her."

"What about her connection to Diego? Wouldn't they find her that way?"

"Diego, you must remember, he is older," Jesús commented. "He left Colombia at a young age, many probably forgot him, if they even knew he existed."

"So if we wanted to, we could easily let some of her former connections know that she's here, in Canada."

"That is the problem, boss," Jesús slowly commented. "Do we want to open that can of worms? Do we want to bring them here, on our territory?"

Jorge considered his words for a moment and finally shook his head. "I do not know, Jesús, I'm going to have to think about this one. Either way, my patience with Jolene, it is getting short."

Jesús didn't reply but merely nodded.

"We must find a way to push her out," Jorge continued. "I'm cutting back on the party planning business, squeezing it out, which is something she does not like. But I feel that unless she is dead, Jolene will always be a threat."

"Then we must kill her," Jesús replied gently. "But Diego? This is his sister."

"And that, my friend, is the only thing that has kept her alive this long," Jorge replied and bit his bottom lip. "If not, she would've been dead months ago, as soon as I learned she was working with that religious fanatic who wanted me dead."

"Perhaps the key is to build more loyalty with Diego so that it surpasses what he has to his sister."

"I believe, we already have," Jorge commented airily. "She had an affair with Chase, whom we both know Diego lusts after and now, the two are fighting over my changes at the office. Diego is fiercely loyal to me, which only manages to irritate Jolene further and they fight; the more they fight, the more he is in my corner."

Jesús grinned and nodded. "Yes, sir, I see your point. That is very good, boss."

"Diego also helped me out with the situation at the 7th shop," Jorge continued and reached for his leather jacket and stood up. "Let's just say that we got the fucker to sign. Diego, he's an animal when his buttons are pushed."

"This is always helpful," Jesús commented as Jorge put on his jacket.

"It can and will be," Jorge agreed as he grabbed his phone and gloves. "Because at the end of the day, both me and Diego feel the same when it comes to loyalty. There is no stronger bond in this world. Him and I, we've always been family."

"So now," Jorge continued as he glanced at the time. "I must go see Diego and Jolene but first, I think I will pay a surprise visit to Chase. I believe now that more time has passed since the abrupt ending to his affair with Jolene, he might now be harboring some bitterness and this, this could be helpful."

Jesús nodded. "Yes, you do know how people tick."

Jorge replied with a grin.

Fortunately the cold air didn't seem so vicious when he left the building to find his SUV and the walk felt slightly shorter. After replying to a text from Paige, he then drove to the club to see Chase.

However when he entered the building using his own key, Jorge was met by a loud, booming voice coming from the back office. It was Jolene's and clearly, there was a little disruption between her and Chase. This made Jorge smile. A gracious, thoughtful human would've turned and walked away. But that wasn't Jorge Hernandez. He was never one to walk away from a conflict, especially if it wasn't his own.

CHAPTER 15

So, of course, Jorge barged into the office. He felt no need to knock or announce himself, choosing instead to see the drama first hand.

What he found was hardly a surprise. Leaning back, Chase appeared defenseless while Jolene, unaware that they weren't alone in the room, continued to speak so rapidly that she was difficult to understand. Although Jorge caught a few words, nothing she said made sense and he noted that she was flipping back and forth between Spanish and English; which definitely would've put a unilingual such as Chase at a huge disadvantage.

"Hey, my friends, you know what they say," Jorge hollered out over Jolene's sharp voice, immediately cutting her off, her eyes suddenly glaring in his direction. She appeared disheveled and confused by this sudden interruption as she began to blink rapidly while turning her attention toward the unexpected guest. "Make *love* not *war*. Isn't that the expression? No?"

He was immediately met with a death stare from Jolene while Chase simply appeared both embarrassed and uncomfortable. In fairness, he was still young and Jolene, she had many years of intimidating men under her belt. In fact, Jorge guessed that this was the Colombian's specialty and had been for most of her life.

"This is a private conversation," Jolene sharply commented as Jorge made himself at home, sitting on the first chair he could find, leaning back in a relaxed manner.

"Oh yeah?" Jorge shrugged and glanced again at Chase, who looked as if he wanted to crawl under the desk and hide. Although his physical appearance was one of strength and power, he was anything but when dealing with confrontation. "Funny thing is that it's my money that financed this club, not to mention that office you work in. That pay cheque you bring home, it exists because I invest in the business."

"We are on a break, having a *private* conversation," She quickly countered, showing no signs of backing off.

"Private? Really?" Jorge asked and let out a laugh. "Cause I could hear you from the door when I walked in. I'm sure half the fucking neighborhood could hear you, Jolene. Your voice, it carries."

Her eyes continued to blaze and glancing toward Chase, who was avoiding eye contact with them both and back at Jorge, she shook her head. Grabbing her handbag, which was sitting on the desk, she turned and stormed out of the office. The main door could be heard slamming about the same time as Chase began to come out of his frightened mode, slowly easing on his chair behind the desk.

"So what the fuck was that about?" Jorge didn't feel the need to hold back and in fact, was slightly entertained with this short performance. He noted that Chase was starting to relax once Jolene was gone, the only remnants was her perfume that continued to linger; some expensive shit that you buy at department stores along with the false hope demonstrated in their overpriced ads. "Jolene seems to have her panties in a knot. Perhaps you should've helped her fix them?"

Chase looked slightly horrified by this suggestion while Jorge laughed at his own joke and finished with a shrug.

"So, what is it, my friend?"

"I can honestly say that I don't know," Chase confirmed and shook his head. "I…I was here, on the phone about a band I wanted to book when Jolene flew in here, screaming at me."

"Oh really?"

"Yeah, I had to excuse myself and end the call," Chase said as his lips hinted at a grin that quickly disappeared. "Something about us all working together against her? Are we working against her?"

Jorge managed to keep a straight face and shrugged.

"Anyway, she seems to think," Chase paused for a moment as if in thought than looked back into Jorge's face. "I don't fully understand but it sounded like she was accusing me of being her enemy now because she ended the affair. She's very paranoid."

It was then that something struck him but Jorge didn't say anything, choosing to remain stoic.

"Yes, she hasn't been herself for a while," Jorge commented casually as if concerned. "Maybe there is something wrong with her brain? You know, like a mental illness."

That's when Chase's expression changed and he looked hesitant to say anything.

"Look, Jorge," Chase spoke slowly. "I have a theory but I could be wrong."

"Always," Jorge spoke calmly, knowing that this was what Chase needed to hear. "Always listen to your instincts, that is what Paige says. We, inside, we know the truth."

"I can't help but shake the feeling that Jolene," Chase cleared his throat and glanced down at the desk briefly, showing some hesitation before continuing. "I feel like Jolene might have a drinking problem."

"Is that right?"

"I thought I could smell alcohol on her breath when she got close to me earlier," Chase confessed and sucked in his lips before continuing, "my mother used to drink a lot when I was a kid and she was kind of acting the same way. I don't like to make that kind of accusation but this is not the first time and she's acting very erratic lately."

Jorge didn't reply. He simply nodded with a touch of compassion on his face while his brain had already connected the dots. However, it was on his way out after this short meeting that Jorge sent Jesús the text.

I figured it out.

The beautiful thing about longtime friendships and business associates is that few words were necessary. They often knew what you were referring to when others would be lost in the same conversation.

Deciding that it was time to touch base with Diego, Jorge sent him a quick text suggesting they have lunch.

I'm having lunch with your wife.

Jorge grinned when he saw this reply. Diego's infatuation with Paige was almost the same as that of a lovesick teenager to a pop star and although he originally found it strange, if not irritating, Jorge had learned to accept it. To think it was anything but harmless was simply the result of his many years of being cynical. Seeing the two together, it was clear that Diego felt Paige was a confidant, someone he could share who he really was with and in turn, Jorge's wife was able to do the same with Diego. They had a friendship created as much by their secret lives than anything else. However, they also had long lunch 'dates' and therefore, Jorge knew that inviting himself wasn't completely out of the question.

I can join you?

Of course! We're just talking over coffee.

He found them in a bright, beautiful restaurant that only Diego would find, in the west end of Toronto. Of course, where everyone else was clearing out after the lunch rush, Diego and Paige were sitting side by side, having an energetic conversation at the back of the room. Diego could be seen speaking with both his hands swinging in the air as if to emphasize a point. When a young woman approached him to ask if he wanted a table for one, Jorge pointed toward Diego and Paige.

"I'm meeting those two."

"Oh, they're so cute together," The young woman commented and Jorge merely grinned as she led him to the back of the room.

"Ah, Jorge, you made it!" Diego commented as he gestured toward the empty chair across from him and Paige as the waitress rushed off. "We decided to have an impromptu lunch date to talk real estate and wedding."

"Oh yeah, how is that going?" Jorge said as he winked at his wife. "The waitress over there was just telling me how you're a cute couple."

"Did she?" Paige said with a smile on her face and glanced toward Diego.

"We do look cute together," Diego insisted while his big eyes bugged out. "I'm just saying, people, they see that."

"Yes, Diego," Jorge assured him. "You look cute with my wife."

This comment came out as the waitress approached them again. Her mouth hanging open, she looked unsure whether to speak. Without missing a beat, Jorge turned his attention to her.

"My dear, would you be so kind as to get me a Corona?"

She quickly nodded. "Anything else?"

"No, that is fine for now," Jorge commented then raised his hand in the air. "On second thought, maybe I will get something to eat."

After receiving his menu, Jorge quietly scanned it but was unable to concentrate. Although his stomach rumbled, he was almost too excited to eat. A plan was quickly coming together in his brain and yet, he couldn't discuss it yet. His original reason to talk with Diego was overshadowed by the ideas pouring into his thoughts.

"Hey, what are you smiling at?" Diego suddenly asked as the waitress returned with his beer. After she left, Jorge shrugged and commented.

"What? Does a man not have a right to be happy for no reason?"

Diego looked skeptical.

"Does Paige's meditation, does it not teach you to be happy for the little things?"

"Yes, but I don't think that evil smile would fall into that category," Diego commented and returned his attention to Paige. "Is he helping *at all* to pick a date?"

"I told you before Diego, I don't care what the date is, we are already married and this is just for Maria," Jorge answered for his wife. "Now, I must ask you, did you change the office door? Do you have a security card for me yet?"

"It's back at the office," Diego replied. "You were right, we don't need a receptionist anymore. Having people buzz in seems like the best idea. Jolene isn't crazy about it but I don't know what her problem is lately."

"I just saw Jolene," Jorge casually commented. "I stopped by the club and she was there."

Although the comment was innocent in nature, he could already see Diego's face darken like a storm cloud.

"I believe her and Chase, they were arguing but I'm not completely clear on what that was about," Jorge continued as he put down the menu as the waitress approach again.

"Yes, I will have the soup and sandwich special and put this on one bill," He gestured toward Diego and Paige. "I will pay for it all. Thank you."

After the waitress scurried off, Jorge turned his attention back to them. He noted that Paige appeared intrigued with what he had to say while Diego's face had a mixture of sadness and fury. Not that this was unusual especially when the topic of Chase and Jolene came up.

"An argument?" He asked as his nostrils flared out.

"Yes, Jolene was screaming," Jorge replied and nodded his head. "Ah, I believe Chase didn't even fully understand why she was so angry. She stormed out when I arrived. I was simply dropping in to check in on the club but I guess I interrupted something."

Diego let out a disgusted grunt and looked away. Paige appeared concerned and immediately touched his hand, causing him to turn toward her, the anger falling from his face. He now resembled a sad, little boy. Women, they were so powerful and yet, so few ever recognized this fact. Paige could calm people with a mere look while Jolene's every move seemed to create more friction that negatively affected everyone. However, her power was disappearing.

And Jolene, her edges were already starting to fray.

CHAPTER *16*

There was a reason Jorge Hernandez was moving quickly to open marijuana shops all over Toronto; it was only the first step in a plan to dominate the industry. His dream was to eventually take over across the country, even if that meant doing so through various unscrupulous means. Eventually, he would propel to the CEO position of Our House of Pot, therefore moving him away from the underground world to become a regular businessman and investor. Of course, he would always have ties to the Mexican cartel since they helped to invest in his dreams but on paper, everything was legit.

The tradeoff was that he still worked for a powerful man who needed to launder money. This originally took place through sex parties because numbers could easily be inflated to make sense on the books, but more recently it was through the club and dispensaries. Meanwhile, drugs were sold at bars across the country for a reasonable cut. It was an agreement that worked for everyone.

For the most part, these clubs were trustworthy. They paid what and when expected, well aware of the potential consequences of messing with the Mexican drug cartel. However, on occasion, problems did arise. It was surprisingly rare but when it did, these issues were dealt with head-on. Jorge received a call about one of these cases a few days later while he and Paige were viewing a house in Toronto's north end. He excused himself and went into the front yard and out of earshot to take the call.

"We got a problem," Diego spoke excitedly on the phone, his voice both loud and obnoxious, indicating he was upset and unsure of what to do.

"Meet you at the usual place?"

"I'll be there."

That's all he had to say. Everyone in their inner circle knew what the 'usual place' was and when brought up, it generally meant it was something serious. The last time they met there was when someone from Chase's past was investigating their operation, a lone wolf who thought she could slither in and take them all down in one swoop. It was *her* taken down in one swoop by Hernandez. He just hoped this wasn't another one of those situations.

Half an hour later, Jorge, Paige, and Diego sat together in a small, family restaurant that often quiet, making it an ideal place to carry out business conversations with relative ease.

"One of the clubs," Diego started almost as soon as they sat down in the opposing booth. "In Montreal, he's not giving us our money. Your replacement is tied up in Mexico and asked if we could help."

"How long has this been going on?" Jorge asked, already reaching for his phone. "Does this got something to do with the biker gangs? That's why I'm not so crazy about Montreal, the bikers own that city."

"Not this place," Diego assured him. "Cleo knows the area and assured me it was good. We never had an issue till now but the guy's having financial troubles. We've had a few unsuccessful conversations with him. A lot of empty promises."

"Well, you know what's a great way to take care of financial troubles?" Jorge taped on his phone, sending Jesús a quick message before looking back up at Diego. "Fire insurance."

"If he has insurance," Diego spoke thoughtfully, his eyes narrowing.

"Let's hope he does because my next idea," Jorge remarked with a slight hesitation while he looked at his wife, "He may not like so much."

"My beautiful wife," He continued and leaned in to kiss her. "I know I keep asking you for favors but I swear, this is one of the last ones."

"The owner?" She muttered in a seductive tone as if they were simply newlyweds enjoying a flirtatious moment.

"Yes, *mi amor*, if he does not pay." Jorge gave her a sexy smile followed by a quick kiss on her cheek, where he lingered. "Devastated by his financial concerns along with his business burning to the ground, he may have to take his own life."

She merely nodded, the instructions weren't necessary. Paige Noël-Hernandez was an expert assassin whose specialty was making a murder appear as a suicide. Her record was flawless and even if the police were suspicious, there were certain guidelines that indicated a suicide and most were quick to sign off on the easiest route.

"I do enjoy Montreal," Paige replied as she placed her hand on his thigh almost distracting him from the topic of discussion. Her voice was soft and smooth, something that drove him wild. "Maybe, you could come with me?"

"It's been a long time since I've been to Montreal," Jorge replied. "Is there not a large winter carnival in Montreal this time of year? Maybe we are going to be tourists?"

"That's Quebec City," Paige replied. "But it doesn't matter, we can still go as tourists."

"Or maybe," Jorge shifted his attention toward Diego. "It will be for our honeymoon?"

"No fucking way," Diego snapped, perhaps a little louder than he intended. "I can't plan a wedding that last-minute."

"You know I am teasing," Jorge said with a laugh. "You know this whole wedding thing is stressing you out, Diego. It's not a good look for you."

"It wouldn't be stressing me out if you picked a date," Diego countered. "Just cause you two are already married doesn't mean that this day isn't important. Your daughter is looking forward to it."

"We will deal with this later," Jorge shrugged and moved away from his wife who now had both hands on the table. "Meanwhile, me and Paige might take a little trip to Montreal. Jesús enjoys setting fires, so we can send him there first."

"He likes setting fires?" Paige appeared surprised.

"Yes, he is what you might call a firebug," Jorge commented with a grin. "Jesús knows how to make it look like a wiring issue or some shit like that. He could use a bit of an adventure to take him away from the stress of figuring out the details for the dispensaries."

"Most will be opened by the end of the February," Diego excitedly switched topics. "I think the rest in March but we're putting a push on to have them all up and running as soon as possible."

"Wow, Diego, I'm impressed," Jorge spoke with admiration. "I can honestly say I have the right man for the job."

Nodding proudly, Diego smirked and sat back in his seat with a smug expression on his face.

"Ah, so Paige, for the wedding," Diego seemed to jump back into overdrive and leaned forward, his dark eyes staring through her. "How many people from your family?"

"Preferably, none," Paige spoke with defiance, despite her soft voice.

"Ah, *mi amor*, are you ashamed of me?" Jorge said and leaned in.

"No," Paige said with a gentle laugh. "I'm ashamed of them. I don't speak to my family unless necessary."

"Do they know you are married?" Diego asked.

"I told them," Paige commented and shared a smile with Jorge. "They were surprised. I was once told that they thought my 'days were over' being an old maid and such."

Jorge made a face while Diego looked stunned.

"Wow," Diego shook his head, twisting his lips in an arrogant pose. "No wonder you like murdering so much."

Jorge let out a laugh, looking down at the table. Glancing back at his wife, he knew of the temperamental situation with her family and didn't take offense to not having met them. Where his relatives were cold and uncaring, hers were nosey, perhaps a little too involved in each other's lives. This was something he preferred to avoid.

"Well, it certainly doesn't make me like murdering *less,*" Paige joked and they all laughed, Diego the most heartily.

"Yes, well, we all have relatives that are difficult to understand," Diego commented.

"Oh, and how is Jolene today?" Jorge asked as he took a sip of his coffee.

"Don't ask."

"You know, the other day," Jorge started cautiously and wondered about the best way to approach the subject. "When I dropped by the club, the day Chase and Jolene were arguing, she pushed past me and I thought I smelled alcohol on her. Is it possible she sometimes has a few drinks early in the day?"

The color drained from Diego's face, his arrogant expression disappearing and he sank back in his chair. At first, he didn't reply and Jorge wondered if perhaps he hit a nerve until he finally answered.

"I was hoping that was just me that noticed that," Diego spoke reluctantly. "I was hoping I was wrong."

"Perhaps it is me that is wrong," Jorge spoke compassionately as he leaned toward his friend. "And hey, who hasn't had a drink before noon once in a while, you know?"

"That's the thing," Diego spoke abruptly. "I don't think it's once in a while."

No one commented at first as the waitress drifted by, stopping briefly to offer more coffee. Everyone said no.

"And maybe, this is a problem?" Jorge asked after she walked away.

"It might be," Diego confirmed. "Look, I don't want to say too much cause I'm not sure myself but it might explain a lot. Her behavior has been quite erratic for months."

Jorge knew why she was drinking. She feared for her life. The irony was that her own paranoia could become her reality. It isn't what you see is what you get, it was that you get what you see. She was already predicted her future and as a result, was pulling it closer and not working to keep it away. It was a mistake many people made.

"Maybe she needs help," Paige spoke softly, her long eyelashes fluttered in a compassionate way, as if she cared about Jolene Silva. In truth, she only cared about Diego, and his sister was merely an unfortunate side effect.

"Like Jolene would ever admit to needing help," Diego commented and glanced at Jorge, who mustered up a concerned expression.

"Well, unfortunately, we cannot help those who don't want to help themselves," He made the thoughtful suggestion while in his heart, Jorge was laughing.

"Sadly," Paige began, tilting her head to the side. "He's right."

"I know, I just don't need this shit now," Diego confessed. "Chase is moving out, everything is kind of weird with him, now Jolene is crazy. She's too stubborn to listen anyway."

"Oh yes, I do know stubborn," Jorge confirmed. "Welcome to my world. *My* Jolene is ten years old and is as strong-willed as they come."

"She's been very good lately," Paige commented with a grin.

"Let's hope that keeps up," Jorge replied. "Now she wants to be an actress and I can't convince her to even consider anything else."

"Hey, did you guys find a house yet?" Diego seemed to purposely switch topics. "You were looking at a place today."

"It was just…ok," Jorge made a face.

Paige shook her head and mimicked her husband's expression. "It didn't feel right."

"Unfortunately, none of them do," Jorge insisted. "We may have to get a condo like you did, Diego."

"There's one available in my building," Diego's eyes lit up. "We could be neighbors, I mean, kind of."

"I'm not, you know, crazy on condos," Jorge admitted. "I'm more of a house man."

"Do you like the real estate lady?"

"Ah, she's ok," Jorge spoke with reluctance. "To me, real estate people are vultures in this current market. If I'm not mistaken, I think that real estate agents are part of the list of careers that psychopaths are most attracted to."

"Really?" Paige asked with a raised eyebrow. "As opposed to what we do?"

Attempting to hide his grin, Jorge scratched his chin and looked away.

"I got no comment," He finally replied.

"I got a feeling we're on that list," Diego smirked, his mood seemed to suddenly lighten.

"I got a feeling we own that list," Jorge replied and leaned in to kiss his wife. "And what better group of people than us?"

They all laughed.

CHAPTER *17*

As it turns out, they didn't have to kill the club owner. Shortly after an electrical fire burned the business to the ground, they got their money; with interest. Although slightly disappointed that he had no excuse to sweep his wife away for a weekend of murder and romance, Jorge accepted that he probably had enough on his plate and perhaps, it simply wasn't in the cards. Fate, it had a way of leading him in the right direction.

However, there are times when fate has a way of introducing circumstances that are hardly ideal. One never knew what is waiting around the corner.

It was rare Paige introduced Jorge to anyone from her past. After living a lie for so long, her friends consisted of a few casual acquaintances, people she kept at arm's length to hide her many secrets. To the outside world, Paige was a busy life coach, a woman who moved back to Toronto after spending years in various countries as a translator. Since she spoke three languages, it made perfect sense.

What most didn't know was that being multilingual was also a valuable skill for an assassin. That along with knowing about other cultures, traditions, and political environments. It wasn't just about pointing a gun but also knowing the exact place to shoot for an immediate death. It was about leaving no evidence and making a murder look like a suicide so that the police had little recourse but to follow procedure, if not their instincts. It was being unnoticeable; a ghost who could move through a room with ease, never leaving a trace. A highly skilled person becomes an assassin; their uneducated and trigger-happy counterpart became a hitman. There was a big difference.

Few people knew Paige's true identity. Those who did worked with Jorge and none of which would throw rocks from their own glass houses. However, there was apparently one other person who knew her secret and when Jorge learned this person's identity, he was not happy.

"You told an ex-boyfriend?" Jorge felt jealousy creep in with his words, tension immediately squeezed his chest so tightly that he momentarily wonder if his heart would explode in anger. "You shared this secret with him? This is unbelievable to me."

"If you would give me a minute to explain," Paige calmly replied, her face appearing unaffected by his frustration as her hand gently touched his arm. "This was a long time ago. It wasn't like we ran into each other at the mall yesterday and I dropped it in the middle of our conversation."

"Yes yes, ok, I understand," Jorge reluctantly replied and took a deep breath, something he now did when he felt his body tighten in anger. He focused on the floor beside the couch where they sat. He hated to think that anyone knew Paige's secret let alone a former lover, a man who clearly was significant if she shared this with him. "So why are we talking about this now?"

"He contacted me recently," She quietly replied. "I think he needs our help?"

"*Our* help?" Jorge shot back and immediately regretted this comment as he saw Paige's eyes widen.

"You're always telling me to ask for help when I need it," She gently reminded him.

"Ok, yes, of course," Jorge replied and ran a hand over his face. "But it didn't occur to me it would be an old boyfriend of yours that I would be helping."

"Alec and I haven't dated since…" She seemed to hesitate as if trying to recall. "Since shortly after high school. We're talking 20 years.

"Well, you know," Jorge gruffly commented with a shrug. "Some flames, they still spark.

He immediately regretted this comment.

"Seriously?" Paige raised an eyebrow, a grin formed on her lips. "You're jealous?"

"I'm not jealous," Jorge shuffled uncomfortably in his seat. "I am just not comfortable with someone from outside our circle knowing this information about you."

"He's fine," Paige replied and moved closer to him and looked into his eyes. He immediately felt himself calm down. "He's known my secret for a long time and hasn't said a word."

"He might."

"He won't," Paige assured him and glanced toward the kitchen briefly before looking back into his eyes. "He knows my secret because I once helped him with a problem."

"So he will not talk," Jorge began as he reached for her hand and started to think about this last piece of information. "What does he want now?"

"I'm not sure," Paige replied with a casual shrug. "He said he'd explain when he comes over later."

"He is coming *here*?" Jorge asked with some anger returning to his voice. "You are bringing an ex-boyfriend to our home? I cannot believe this, Paige, why would you do this?"

"Because I'm not having an affair with him," Paige gently reminded him. "I'm meeting him to discuss something of importance and I want him to meet my husband. If you prefer, we can meet him elsewhere?"

Jorge ran a hand over his face and although he felt the flame of jealousy only burn hotter, he instead pushed it down and looked in his wife's eyes. He had to stay calm and see this through.

"Ok, well, if you must," Jorge reluctantly agreed, his body growing weaker with each word. "And you are sure, he is ok? He didn't suddenly start working for the police or something of that nature?"

"Far from it," Paige let out a laugh. "Actually, I think he wants to get into politics."

"Politics," Jorge automatically felt himself perk up. "You don't say?"

Paige didn't reply but merely grinned as she rose from the couch and walked into the kitchen. While she roamed around the apartment, attempting to tidy up the cramped space, Jorge stared at his laptop, lost in thought. Sometimes what originally seemed as if it were a problem was in fact, an opportunity.

By the time Alec Athas arrived at the door, Jorge was ready for him. He felt some comfort after having done a quick background check and realized that rather than being an irritant, the man could be an asset. It was interesting how a slight shift in thoughts can change an entire situation. Who knew that an ex-lover of his wife might be a blessing and not a pain in the ass?

His presence was anything but threatening. After giving Paige a quick, chaste hug at the door, he entered their apartment with some reluctance, his eyes immediately focused on Jorge. Paige's husband didn't offer a smile but instead sized up the stranger and quickly decided that he was no concern.

Alec Athas was probably no taller than him but definitely appeared healthier. His eyes were a dark brown, his black hair meticulously cut and he wore no wedding ring on his finger. He reminded Jorge of the boy next door type that women loved when they were younger; safe, sweet, honest in nature, someone who always did the right thing. He appeared nervous as he crossed the floor with Paige, almost as if he was about to face a firing squad and not meeting a new friend.

"Alec, I would like you to meet my husband," Paige spoke evenly as they reached the couch where Jorge sat with an opened laptop, "Jorge Hernandez."

"Nice to meet you," Alec leaned over the coffee table and the two shook hands.

"As it is nice to meet you," Jorge replied courteously with a smile. "So Paige tells me that you have an interest in politics."

Alec appeared uncertain, his dark eyes growing larger and Jorge considered that the innocent look would work in his favor when attempting to win over voters. He was also attractive with olive skin, a neat, overall presentation; the classic white shirt, a nice tie and clean-shaven. Polite, friendly, approachable; this was a man who could win an election.

"Well, yes, I'm interested in running in my district," Alec spoke with ease as he sat on the chair opposite of Jorge, while he quickly glanced at Paige. "But I haven't made a firm decision yet."

"Tell me," Jorge decided it wasn't necessary to waste time. "What is it that makes you interested in getting into politics?"

"Jorge, he barely sat down" Paige insisted as she stood nearby. "Alec, can I get you a cup of coffee? Something to drink?"

"No, thank you, I just had a lunch meeting," He politely shook his head. "I'm fine."

"So politics," Jorge attempted to pick up the conversation again as Paige joined him on the couch. "I have yet to meet a person who got involved in politics for anything but power or to make changes. Which of these would you say is important to you?"

"I definitely want to make a change," Alec began to speak with more confidence, his original reluctance seemed to fade away. "I want to make Toronto a more affordable city. The price to live here, especially real estate, is getting out of control. People are leaving because they don't want to pay a small fortune just to have a home. Only the rich can comfortably live here and immigrants are often left living in cockroach-filled apartments. It's despicable. I want to make this a livable city."

"Let me ask," Jorge said while glancing at his wife briefly before returning his attention to Alec. "Has Toronto ever been a livable city?"

Letting out a sharp laugh, Alec looked down at his feet with a grin but quickly looked back at Jorge.

"It depends on how you define livable. When my family immigrated here, Toronto was a place where new residents came together, to learn about Canada, to get a job, to raise a family and add culture to a city that strived on diversity. Now, it is becoming a rich man's playground. The rich come here from all over the world to buy our property, inflating the prices and the people here aren't able to find affordable housing. In fact, my fear is that we become like Vancouver, where this problem steadily increased over the years. It's only recently that the government even started to look at the issue. I think there should some federal policies in place across the country."

"But is it the same here as Vancouver?" Jorge wondered out loud.

"Yes and no," Alec shook his head. "The government gives the impression that they are making real efforts but yet, homes are still outrageously priced, as are apartments and condos. Landlords are neglectful and vultures. My fear is that if left, Toronto will be a city for elitists, only for the rich and everyone else might be pushed out."

Jorge nodded. "Your ideas, they are provocative and I believe this is something you can easily run with but my question to you is, what would you like from us? Money?"

"If my party chooses me, I would like Paige to work on my campaign," Alec commented and immediately looked in her direction and Jorge noted this his wife appeared surprised. "Paige you are a well-known life coach. People trust you, they look up to you. If they feel you support me, this would greatly help my chances."

Jorge immediately wanted to object but bit his tongue.

"How about this," Jorge finally responded, noting that Paige was not. "I back your campaign. Anything you need. Money, resources, problems, you come to me."

Alec looked as if he was about to speak but Jorge quickly cut him off.

"In return, *you* work for *me.*" Jorge took a deep breath. "Right now, I own 7 dispensaries either opened or about to open. I may need a favor from time to time."

"I don't know if…"

"I'm not sure what you know about me," Jorge cut him off. "But I'm not a man who messes around. I'm a businessman, yes, but I make my own rules. I've been making my own rules for a long time and I'm not about to stop. I can help you out with *any* problem, any issue but you gotta help me too."

"Look I…" Alec started to speak slowly, his eyes shifting between Jorge and Paige. "I want to do everything legally….the pot thing is still iffy."

"Alec," Paige spoke sweetly, yet with some assertion in her voice. "The thing about politics is eventually, you're going to end up working with people with questionable morality and criminals. You may as well start now."

"He didn't come here today," Jorge turned toward his wife. "Because he thought we were good Christians that would say a prayer for him. He knew what the deal was, am I right, Mr. Athas?"

Paige smiled, her disposition relaxed, peaceful as she turned to look at Alec.

"I know about the sex parties and the dispensaries," Alec replied sheepishly. "I'm not sure what my district would think of that and I don't want anything negative connected with my campaign."

"Nothing will as long as we work together," Jorge spoke passionately. "You and me, Alec, we can own this city and with my help, you *will* fucking win. I can assure you of that, my friend."

There was something different in his eyes now. A strength replaced any reluctance that had lingered; perhaps he now understood.

"I believe that." His voice was quiet, yet determined.

"But as I said," Jorge slid his arm around Paige's shoulders. "You just gotta remember that once you win, and you *will*, I'm the person you're loyal to, not anyone else. As they say, you gotta dance with the one who brought you."

It would be these words that would haunt Alec Athas but his desire to win would override almost anything else. Ironically, Jorge didn't ask which political party he was running for; and he didn't care.

CHAPTER *18*

Alec Athas. Oh, how she had been in love with that boy! It was that pure, innocent love that you only experience before the cynicism of real-life moves in but until that time, it's simply the most wonderful feeling. Nothing ever feels the same again. Even Paige's relationship with Jorge was very different. Their love was deep, strong, intense but it simply didn't have that same simplicity of a young romance.

Paige had been hesitant to introduce Jorge to her former boyfriend. She knew how jealous he could be but to not introduce him would be deceitful. Alec had always been a part of her life even if they had brief periods of lost contact, in the end, they eventually reconnected. Of course, their relationship was now much different from their younger days. The simple truth is that you can never go back and really, does anyone want to? As much as she loved Alec Athas, it would never be like those days again. Circumstances, timing, everything had changed. However, she would always care for him.

They had met when she worked at the mall during her early twenties. It was one of those jobs that you thought you *really* wanted until you actually had it. Paige was in awe of the beautiful clothing, the hip feeling of walking into the popular store and thought she had hit the jackpot when the company hired her. It turned out to not be much of a jackpot. She spent most of her time watching for shoplifters and cleaning up messes left by customers; spilled coffee, snot on the dressing room mirrors, ripped clothing that customers tried on and damaged before even leaving the store. That was another thing about working at this particular shop; the prices were expensive but the clothes were cheaply constructed. So on top of everything else, Paige spent a vast amount of her time dealing with customers who wished to return the low-quality merchandise.

As it turns out, Alec was one of the customers that came in to complain about a shitty product. It was a shirt that he had bought for a family wedding and immediately noticed that the terrible stitching was letting go; unfortunately, he dropped by the store on a day when everyone else was pulling Paige's attention in different directions. It was a soft tap on her arm when she was hurriedly attempting to return some clothing to its proper rack that caused her to swing around, defensively, exhausted and frustrated, to see the cutest boy she had ever seen in her life.

"Excuse me," Alec had quietly asked, nervously stepping back. "Do you work here?"

Paige was under the heat of embarrassment and shame a few minutes later as she attempted to key in his return. Nervously hitting all the wrong buttons, it was as if her fingers suddenly doubted in size. Although she asked all the necessary questions and he was more than courteous, she couldn't help but feel overwhelmed under his gaze while behind him stood a long lineup of impatient customers. She wanted to crawl into a hole and die.

The bright side was that it was through this process that Paige learned his name was Alec Athas. She racked her brain wondering if they went to school together but if they had, wouldn't she remember? By the time he was out the door, she already assumed that he had a girlfriend and chances were, she would never see him again.

Paige was wrong. Alec started to show up at the store a few times a week. Fortunately, their conversations grew more comfortable over time and eventually, Paige figured out that he was single. A college student, Alec balanced his days between studies and his part-time job at a popular fast food restaurant in the mall. In fact, he often brought Paige free food as a way to encourage her to take breaks with him and that's how it began.

They started to spend time together outside the mall. Their shyness eventually disappeared but yet, there was still such an innocent nature to their relationship. It was real, honest and sweet but when it ended, it completely broke her heart. It wouldn't be until years later that she finally realized how deep that cut had been, ripping out a piece of her soul that would never return.

It was a few years later that she would train to become an assassin but she often wondered how differently her life would've been had they stayed together. What kind of person would she be? Would they be happy?

Not that she blamed him for her life taking a drastic turn; many things had contributed including an armed robbery and an attack at a nightclub. It was these events that pushed her to buy a gun and learn to shoot. She hadn't expected to be a natural. Paige also hadn't expected to feel more powerful when she held that gun; as if nothing and no one could hurt her again. She was no one's victim and although it was clearly her own upbringing that put her in the position to become submissive and weak, it was a place she had no intentions of visiting again.

With that, Paige developed a bitterness toward life. People were only out to hurt others. She could trust no one and if she did, they would disappoint her. Paige decided that she was a complicated person and difficult to understand which caused most to not bother with her. It would be a long time before she would see the world any differently. It wasn't until she met Jorge and by that time, hadn't she started to mellow? All the yoga, the meditation, it was necessary for keeping her balanced but at the same time, it opened her up in ways she hadn't thought possible.

Despite their breakup, Alec and Paige had stayed in touch. They had a magical way of finding one another over the years; while he seemed in awe of her worldwide travels, she envied his simple life. He got married and after a few short years, divorced. No kids. That surprised her but then again, had it really? In fact, that was a turning point in his marriage. Alec always said that when he discovered he wouldn't have children with his former wife, it was a clear sign of bigger problems. Paige wasn't so sure but his view on love had always been more romantic than her own; he felt that love changed you at the core, even the beliefs you held on to tightly could collapse under its weight.

Fortunately, children wasn't a topic that ever came up with Jorge. Not that she worried about it. He had a child so chances were good, he didn't want another one. Especially considering everything else on his plate.

"So what did you think of him?" Paige asked Jorge after their guest left and they were alone on the couch. The apartment was quiet, something that she enjoyed especially when Maria was in school and they were home alone.

"What do I think? I think he's too handsome to spend time with my wife," Jorge spoke gruffly but with a smile, he turned and winked at her. "Why can't your ex-boyfriend be fat and ugly and not a Greek God? Can you tell me that?"

"I don't date ugly men," She teased and leaned forward to kiss him. "Besides, we dated like a hundred years ago, I told you that. We aren't even the same people anymore."

"So, tell me this," Jorge said as he turned toward her, giving Paige his full attention. "How did it come about that you told him about being an assassin? You said you took care of something for him?"

"He needed help," Paige answered his question as simply as possible. "And I wanted to help him."

"But still, could you not have helped without him knowing?" Jorge asked while showing no judgment and yet, wasn't there some fear in his eyes. "Did he have to know?"

"In retrospect, I wish that I had found a way to avoid it," Paige replied and pulled both her legs up on the couch and sat in a comfortable position, sensing this might be a long conversation. "But I guess I also felt the need to tell someone. I had just returned from spending a few years in Latin America after working with Hector."

"I viewed life through different eyes," Paige admitted. "I guess I was feeling a bit full of myself over the work I had done. I had money. I felt stronger. I wasn't the same woman I was before and Alec saw this right away and called me on it."

"You mean to tell me that he was the same?" Jorge asked skeptically. "Did he not change too?"

"He did but in essence, he was the same man," Paige said with a shrug. "He has his morals and he stands by them."

"So this man with morals, he had you kill someone?" Jorge quipped and she merely grinned.

"His younger sister, Eleni was raped," Paige slowly began and she was automatically pulled back into the year 2006, listening to Alec telling her about his youngest sister's attack on a university campus. The pain in his eyes was something she'd never forget. "The rape was brutal and she ended up suffering a lot after the attack. Eleni and Alec were very close and he noticed she was acting very erratically and suggested she talk to a professional. Unfortunately, that psychiatrist she found only gave her pills and was of little use otherwise. She ended up committing suicide by overdosing."

'Oh wow," Jorge said and turned away and shook his head. "Yes, well, I do understand why he would want her attacker dead."

"It wasn't the rapist that he had me kill," Paige quietly corrected him. "He got away and the police were useless. In fact, that was one of the reasons Eleni lived in such a state of anxiety, she feared he would come back to find her. It was actually the doctor he had me kill."

"The doctor?" Jorge appeared confused. "For giving her the pills? I don't understand."

"Her psychiatrist," Paige continued. "He knew she was suicidal and he loaded her up with anxiety and sleeping pills. Lots of them and on the night Eleni did it, she called him for help and he apparently told her she had become too reliant on him and would need to figure out what to do on her own."

"But *mi amor*, are you sure this is true?" Jorge asked skeptically. "Perhaps this was just a man grieving who misunderstood some information?"

"No, there was a message on her answering machine and when questioned, he apparently didn't deny it," Paige explained. "He essentially referred back to some study where tough love was the answer, said he felt she wasn't trying to help herself. He wasn't charged."

"Well, I don't like to say it," Jorge said and shook his head. "But human life, it does not always matter to those in the position to help."

"He was a pretty despicable man," Paige replied and thought in silence for a moment. "After Alec told me the story, I started to follow him. He would go to clubs regularly and I saw him give pills to women. I was never sure what those pills were but it was clear he was abusing his power and when I reported this back to Alec, he was so furious and so full of grief that he talked about killing the doctor himself. That's when I told him the truth. I wanted him to know that I could do it and get away with it. I wasn't about to let him mess up his future. So if he really wanted him dead, I would do it for him."

Jorge nodded. "That was a beautiful thing to do for a former love, I must admit, I'm not sure I would do the same."

"One of the reasons why I've had Alec in my life for all these years is because I respect who he is," Paige quietly added. "In a way, he's a compass to what is actually normal. I sometimes need that when things get too crazy."

"So, what did you do to the doctor?"

"I followed him out of a club one night," She started to tell her story. Paige could still remember every detail. She wore a short dress and a pair of long boots and a long, blonde wig that resembled a famous pop star's hair; the disguise was uncomfortable but made her fit in perfectly with the other clubbers and fitting in was one of the top traits of a good assassin.

She watched him from afar, as vulnerable women flocked around him, many layered in makeup, wearing skimpy clothes, the telling signs of women who begged for attention. It was the same thing each time he was out; except for that night, he only handed out the pills, had a few drinks and left the bar alone. He always did on Wednesday nights possibly due to his early morning schedule. He had a very specific pattern that made it easy to plan his murder.

Paige followed him out of the club, then down the street and at the perfect time, Alec appeared, wearing a fedora with his usual leather jacket and jeans. Neither said a word as they walked a safe distance behind. Paige grabbed a hair clip attached to her purse, pulling her hair back in a bun before reaching for Alec's fedora, putting it on her own head, he silently pointed toward a dark alleyway.

"Are you sure?" Paige had quietly asked and with the eyes of a broken man, he slowly nodded before looking away. He was too upset to talk.

"All right," She softly replied and followed the doctor down the same alleyway. The psychiatrist was walking as if he were king, like nothing could take him down; how wrong he had been. It was when she said his name in a super sweet voice, as he turned around causally with a smile on his face, that Paige pulled a gun out of her purse and shot him in the head. Luckily, the music from the nearby nightclubs drowned out the noise. He fell to the ground. She knew the look of death. She knew it all too well.

Paige didn't normally have any emotions connected to a murder but that time was different. He represented any man who had ever taken advantage of a woman in a vulnerable situation, as much as he represented the pained looked in Alec's eyes. It had been the first time Paige felt any emotion when killing someone. It was also the last.

CHAPTER *19*

"Like I said in our meeting, I would like to get him elected," Jorge slowly started to explain after Alec's second visit to the apartment a few days later. He noted a faint smell of cologne lingering in the room as if he were an animal who had left his scent trickling behind. "But I do not like the idea of you helping him with his campaign. It puts you too much out there, you know?"

Paige quietly considered his remark, her eyes downcast as if her thoughts were well beyond the topic at hand and for a moment, this worried Jorge. It was a touchy situation; on one hand, he wanted to keep his wife away from her ex-boyfriend, however, he didn't want to appear jealous, like a ranting lunatic, demanding her to avoid him.

"Yes, I do see what you mean," Paige finally commented, her eyes briefly meeting with his and she looked away dismissively before rising from the couch and walking to the kitchen, where she poured a glass of water.

"I think you might be right," Paige said before drinking her water, leaning against the counter, her eyes on Jorge. "I don't think this is a good fit for Alec either. Politics isn't something I ever imagined him doing."

"What kind of work does he normally do? He did not say." Jorge casually inquired, noting that Paige's ex-boyfriend couldn't be more different from him in every way. It was interesting that her taste had changed so dramatically over the years. At least, he hoped it had.

"Alec's a counselor," Paige replied as she slowly made her way back to the couch. "He works with teenagers in the poorer sections of the city, people at a disadvantage. So he looks great on paper but I'm a little concerned this incident from years ago will somehow pop up because at the time, he made a complaint to the College of Physicians but despite all that, nothing was done. Then suddenly, the doctor shows up dead."

"That seems extreme," Jorge said with a shrug. "They got no reason to think this pillar of the community would be connected. If he was the person who got the ball rolling after his sister died, it would make sense that someone else probably reacted and not him."

"That's true," Paige admitted with a shrug. "Also, I don't know if Alec has the stomach for politics. I don't like to see his values corrupted like the rest of us. In a way, I need to know that there are still some people out there who aren't morally bankrupt."

"It is possible," Jorge corrected her. "But those people eventually get pushed out of politics. At the end of the day, the rich and powerful want their own puppets to run the show and they will make sure they're in office, even if that means undermining the good guy. And I should know. I'm one of those people."

Paige quietly nodded, her face expressionless.

"Alec, he will not necessarily leave politics being the good man he is now," Jorge continued. "Unfortunately, I may have something to do with his soul's demise. You must keep this in mind."

He was speaking the truth and it wasn't the first time he had corrupted someone for his own personal need but the way Jorge saw it, it was never a one way street. Alec Athas was no fool and knew what he was asking for as did the others before him. Just as Jorge often needed something from someone else, they often graciously took what he gave in return. Chase Jacobs had been one of those people.

Jorge decided to drop by the club later that afternoon and much to his surprise, he found a tired, frustrated man behind the desk.

"My friend, what is wrong?" Jorge asked with the compassion in his voice while his mind raced a mile a minute. "You look like you haven't slept in a week. Has Jolene returned to keep your bed warm at night?" He attempted to tease as he sat on the other side of the desk.

"The person keeping my bed warm is a whole other story," Chase said with a grin, shaking his head as he pushed his laptop aside.

"Unfortunately, I think that's contributing to my problem. Jolene found out I was seeing someone else and is punishing me. She's basically dropped her duties lately, leaving them for me and is home, sick in bed."

"Oh, is she really?" Jorge asked, intrigued to learn this news. "I had no idea. Diego hasn't mentioned this to me."

"Diego probably hasn't been in the office much lately," Chase commented with a shrug. "He's been busy with the pot stores opening so quickly. I think he's actually on the road most of the time or helping Beverly, that kind of thing."

"And you two, you don't talk much at the home?" Jorge spoke in a conversational tone, feeling it was usually the best method when it came to Chase. "You do still live in his condo, no?"

"Well, for now," Chase replied hesitantly. "I'm not home much so I hardly ever see Diego."

"So it is true," Jorge asked. "You are moving out?"

"I think its time," Chase quietly commented, his shoulders drooped slightly and his eyes shifted away from Jorge. "I'm not sure it's a good idea that I'm there. I consider Diego one of my best friends but deep down I know he wants something more and it's not healthy for us to live together. I can't give him what he wants."

Jorge didn't reply but nodded. After all, it was him and Paige that comforted Diego when he finally accepted that his love for Chase would never be returned. As much as Diego wanted to believe that this straight man would have a change of preference, it was unlikely. Although he understood both sides, Jorge couldn't help but feel compassion for Diego, a man who was like a brother to him.

"Yes, I do see what you mean," Jorge commented with a nod. "Maybe it is time for you to move. How does Diego feel about this?"

"We haven't really discussed it," Chase spoke with some hesitation, "I feel awkward since everything with Jolene."

His conscience kicked in. Chase clearly felt a sense of shame for his secret affair with Diego's sister and Jorge guessed, this was the real reason he suddenly felt the need to move out of the condo. He remained silent and nodded in understanding. Jolene had managed to poison a friendship just as she poisoned everything else in her life; her dark soul luring others in and bringing them down into the dirt of humanity.

"Tell me something, Chase," Jorge jumped back into the conversation as he glanced around the office. "Do you mean that Jolene is no longer helping you? Are you taking care of all the details for the parties by yourself?"

"Pretty much," Chase replied and waved his hands around. "We only have a few parties but Jolene dropped everything on my lap at the last minute and then started calling in sick. It was clearly on purpose."

"I am thinking," Jorge spoke slowly. "I am thinking we do not schedule anything new until we see what Jolene is doing and we may have to cancel some of these events."

"What about the rest of the time," Chase asked awkwardly, as he shifted in his chair. "It might seem strange if the club is only opened a few times a month. Do you still want me to book bands?"

"We will do something else. Perhaps," Jorge thought for a moment. "We should rent the space to other people; companies and individuals between our own events. That way, you only must worry about keeping the place presentable, collecting the money and it minimizes your workload. Also, we can have timeframes filled in even if the club is empty. It's a great way to…wait, has Clara been in today?"

"She actually was a little earlier," Chase referred to the company 'cleaning lady'. "I haven't left this desk since."

"I was going to say, if we have spaces booked off for various events that aren't real, it provides a great opportunity to move some money through the business. It will solve some problems for us both. What do you say, Chase?" Jorge moved to the edge of his chair as if he were preparing to leave. "Does this sound like it could work?"

"Definitely, that sounds great," Chase automatically showed signs of relief, his eyes brightened up. "I can do that. I will call Sylvana to make sure no parties are posted."

"Very good," Jorge nodded as he stood up and Chase awkwardly did the same. "Figure out the details, the pricing and so on and let me know. We can then contact Marco to make changes to the website and

Chase…..why are you moving like someone kicked the shit out of you? Did you fall asleep at your desk?"

"Ah, it's just, this girl I'm dating," Chase awkwardly replied as he moved around the desk slowly, almost as if he couldn't walk properly. "She's into kinky stuff."

"Like what?" Jorge asked as Chase stiffly moved toward him. "Shoving a dildo up your ass? You can barely walk, my friend."

"S&M," Chase replied with as much discomfort in his voice as his body. "I dunno, it's a little out there for me but she's into it."

"Let me get this straight," Jorge hesitated and pointed at Chase. "You, who is the boxer, has a woman beating him with a whip or some shit?"

Even the words made Jorge feel a little ill and he flinched.

"Yeah, I mean, it's kinda weird, I know," Chase replied and finally managed to stand up straight, towering over Jorge in height not to mention size; the man was massive, resembling a football player and not a submissive. "It's her thing, I guess and….

"My friend, that is fucked up," Jorge insisted as he backed away slightly. "How do you find pleasure out of such things?"

Chase looked as if he was attempting to find an answer but didn't reply.

"Chase, let me give you some advice," Jorge said with some reluctance, not one to usually get into someone's personal life. "As much as I'm into some kinky things, as much as I love to devour my wife, you will not find me whipping her….or vice versa for that matter. That's a lot of fucked up, do you see what I mean?"

"I do," Chase spoke as he moved awkwardly. "I didn't want to seem….like I wasn't open minded and she was really hot and…."

"Where did you meet this demented woman anyway?" Jorge sputtered out and shook his head. "Like a dating website or something like that?"

"I met her at Maria's school when I was picking her up one day," Chase spoke reluctantly.

"What? A bored housewife that gets off on whipping men?"

"She's actually a teacher," Chase quietly replied.

"A teacher? At my child's school?" Jorge shot back. "Are you fucking kidding me?"

"No, I mean, we used to talk all the time when I picked up Maria for you and…she asked me out and I thought she was cute…"

"She teaches at *my* daughter's school?" Jorge repeated and took a deep breath. "This is all I need, some S&M freak teaching my daughter. This is just wonderful!"

"Trust me," Chase replied with a grin on his face. "I don't think she's anything like this at school. In fact, she seemed like the regular girl next door until she got me back to her apartment. That's when things got a little crazy."

"No, my friend, a little crazy is leaving bite marks on someone's ass," Jorge spoke defiantly. "Not whipping them so hard that they cannot walk the next day."

With that, he turned and headed for the door.

"It was actually two days ago," Chase replied as Jorge reached the door and he turned around.

"That, my friend, should tell you something."

CHAPTER *20*

Needless to say, Jorge was much more observant when he picked up Maria at school that day. He usually preferred to wait in the SUV but after hearing Chase's disturbing comments about one of the teachers, Jorge decided to show up a tad early and go inside. What he found was a bunch of parents, mostly moms staring at him; but of course, he was a good-looking man, wearing a shirt and tie under his expensive leather jacket. He noticed years ago that women seemed to smell money a mile away but in an interesting twist, liked to pretend that money didn't matter. One of the many ways women lied.

But that didn't matter. Ignoring the intrigued glances around him, Jorge was somewhat relieved when his phone rang. It was Paige.

"Hey *mi amor*," Jorge turned away from the crowd.

"So, you're picking up Maria?"

"Yes."

"Really?"

"Why is this a surprise to you?" Jorge asked as he started to walk away from the others.

"It's just that you're usually busy around this time of day," Paige replied and he could hear chopping in the background. "Is everything ok?"

Jorge laughed. "Well, I'm better than Chase is today."

"What do you mean?" Paige asked with some uncertainty in her voice. "I don't understand, was he supposed to pick up Maria?"

"Nah, I will tell you later," Jorge said as he glanced around the corner to see the children streaming into the lobby. "That man, I think he needs help. That is all I'm saying for now."

"Ok," She replied with reluctance and a laugh. "Well, you'll be happy to know I'm cooking dinner. I'm following a video online. It looks pretty simple."

"Ah! Beautiful!" Jorge replied just as he spotted Maria rushing toward him. "I cannot wait, *mi amor*, it will be wonderful. See you soon"

He ended the call and turned toward his daughter.

"*Papa*, you're inside, you never come inside," Maria spoke with hesitation in her voice. "Did the principal call you?"

Jorge halted, ignoring the stream of people making their way out of the building. "Why do you say that, Maria? Are you in trouble again?" His brain quickly returned to their days in Mexico and the specific incident when she took a switchblade to school to protect herself from bullies. "What did you do?"

"Nothing, *Papa*, I swear," She insisted in a way that automatically made him suspicious as he watched his daughter squirm.

"What did you do *princesa*?"

"Nothing, I swear!" Maria replied, her eyes growing in size. "I've been good. My marks, they are also good."

"And the other kids?" Jorge pushed. "Are you getting along with the other children?"

"Yes, of course, *Papa*."

Although he was slightly suspicious, Jorge didn't reply but gestured toward the door. He gave a quick glance around for the wacko Chase was dating but only noticed other parents walking their children outside. As it turned out, it was a good idea for him to show up at the school that day. Perhaps his daughter needed the fear of God instilled in her. The last thing he wanted was for her to start getting in trouble in Canada too.

As soon as they got outside, Maria started to talk excitedly. Noticing that her backpack was heavy, Jorge stopped to reach for it.

"Let me carry this for you," Jorge insisted and Maria appeared doubtful when he reached for it. "A gentleman always carries a heavy bag for a lady."

"You never carry bags for Paige," Maria insisted as she passed it to him.

"What the hell is in here?" Jorge ignored her remark. "Rocks?"

"Books."

"Books?" Jorge shook his head. "Isn't everything on a laptop these days?"

"Some but we also have books," Maria replied. "*Papa,* you said a gentleman always carries a lady's bag but you never carry Paige's."

"I do not think I have to carry Paige's purse," Jorge grinned as they made their way to the SUV. "Not to mention that it's not as heavy as this here."

"*Papa,*" Maria quickly shifted gears as if she forgot what they were talking about. "I want a cat."

"What? No, *niñita,* we cannot in an apartment building," Jorge insisted even though he honestly had no idea. The last thing he wanted to deal with was a cat.

"*Papa,* when we finally move, can we get a cat?" She asked just as they reached the SUV.

"We'll see," Jorge reluctantly answered. "I think Paige might be allergic."

"I want a black cat and call it Visa."

Jorge opened the door for her and placed her backpack on the floor. Walking around to the other side, he assumed Maria would be on to another topic before he got in the SUV but he was wrong.

"I always wanted a cat and I think Visa is a cool name," Maria continued to rattle on as Jorge left the parking lot, his mind on the series of texts that he was suddenly receiving on his phone. Of course, he couldn't look at them with his daughter in the vehicle or she would scold him for texting and driving. Not that he would be texting, just reading, but she would still react.

"Well, we will see…" Jorge attempted to change the topic but that was when Maria reached over and turned up the radio, which had only been a quiet hum until that point. 'Dr. Feelgood' poured through the SUV as his daughter attempted to dance in her seat, her mind finally off the cat topic. Jorge reached forward to turn it down a bit, feeling that the song possibly hit a nerve due to the subject. He was slightly alarmed when his daughter reached forward and turned it up again and louder.

She ignored his warning glances.

"Maria! The radio, please!" Jorge reached over again and turned it down.

"But *Papa*, it's a song about us."

"Maria, it is not a complimentary song about Mexicans," Jorge said in the calmest voice he could muster. "It is a song about….anyway, it does not matter, it is not a flattering song about Mexicans."

"Oh no, *Papa*," She replied as they stopped at the light and he turned toward her. It was at that moment it happened. His daughter's huge eyes stared at him with such innocence and in a split second, a flash of her mother crossed over like a dark cloud that would forever haunt him, her eyes narrowed and he swore it was Verónic's voice that said the words that would break his heart. "I mean, drug dealers, like you."

Jorge froze on the spot. Breaking out in a cold sweat, it took him a second to realize that traffic was once again moving and he quietly followed along. His tongue was frozen, while everything else was an echo; the music, his daughter's words, he could barely focus for the rest of the way home. For the first time in his life, he was unable to speak. He didn't have an answer or a sharp reply but fell completely silent. It was to the point that when they finally drove into the underground parking for their apartment building, Maria started to cry.

He turned off the ignition. The garage had never been so silent, so dark and dreary as it was at that moment. He remained silent. He couldn't even look at his daughter, even as she cried hysterically from the passenger side.

"*Papá, ¿por qué no estás hablando?*"

Rubbing his forehead, Jorge didn't know if he wanted to scream or cry, his body was weak while his heart raced erratically. This was a nightmare come to life. This was the day he dreaded forever. No longer could he fantasize about gently breaking the truth to his daughter after her 18th birthday; she was 10 years old and knew everything.

"*Papa*!" She continued to cry hysterically, her arms now thrown around him and much to his surprise, Jorge felt tears falling from his own eyes as he took a deep breath and turned toward her. He felt as if his body were floating back down to earth, finally out of his trance, he managed to find his voice.

"*Niñita*," He began to speak, stopping to clear his throat and wipe a stray tear away from his cheek as his daughter's watering eyes stared back at him. "I cannot ever lie to you. It breaks my heart to confess this, but it is true."

His phone beeped again but he felt too weak to look at it.

"I know," Maria sniffed. "I'm sorry, *Papa*, I should've not said anything."

"How long have you known?" He finally managed.

"*Mamá* told me," Maria replied and Jorge turned away as anger swept over him.

Puta.

"Your *Mamá*, she did not always tell you the truth," Jorge made a half-hearted attempted to explain although it seemed redundant at this point. "But unfortunately, this time, she was being honest."

Turning toward his daughter, he felt shame when he saw the love in her eyes. In a way, it frightened him. Had he normalized such a savage lifestyle? He didn't want any of this for Maria. She would be better than him.

"*Papa*, everyone in Mexico, they knew," Maria whispered. "At school, the other students, they all knew."

"Not here, right?" Jorge's thoughts raced. His daughter shouldn't be judged based on his decisions.

"No, *Papa*," Maria insisted as she wiped the tears from her face. "I promise, I do not tell."

"Don't ever tell anyone."

"I won't, *Papa*, I promise."

Although he wanted so badly to believe her, Jorge wasn't sure. His daughter didn't have a great track record when it came to keeping secrets.

Together, they got out of the SUV, Jorge walked around and grabbed her backpack and they silently got in the elevator while Maria reached for his hand.

Arriving at the apartment, the bold spices could be smelled before they even opened the door as Paige attempted to cook some new dish in the kitchen. She was so busy turning off burners and removing pots, it took her a moment to realize that something was wrong. Her eyes quickly summed it up.

"What…what happened?" She rushed out of the kitchen wearing a sweater and yoga pants, her hair in a messy ponytail as her eyes drifted between Maria and Jorge. "Is everything ok? Did something happen at school?"

She directed her last question at Maria who shook her head and started to cry again, causing Paige to rush toward the little girl while exchanging looks with Jorge.

"What's going on here?"

"I told *Papa*… that….that I knew he was a drug…." Her sobs cut off the words as Paige pulled her into a hug. Sitting on the couch, Jorge took a deep breath and shook his head.

"She knows," His words were barely a whisper. "Her mother told her everything."

"Everything?" Paige's eyes grew in size.

"She knows…that I'm part of the cartel," He spoke clearly and Paige simply nodded. "I hadn't realized she knew."

"I upset *Papa*," Maria suddenly pulled away from Paige. "I didn't mean to hurt his feelings or I never would've said."

"It's fine, Maria," Jorge spoke gently as the little girl sniffed and nodded. "I'm not mad at you, I just wish…I wish you did not know. I feel…ashamed that you know."

"Oh, *Papa*!" Maria rushed to him and the two embraced again. "I would never be ashamed of you. *Te Amo, Papa*,"

Paige appeared as stunned as Jorge had felt in the SUV. She glanced toward the kitchen and back again, as if unsure of what to do.

"You know, Maria," She finally spoke up and the little girl moved away from her father to look at her stepmom. "Your father is more of a business manager now. He manages a lot of people and actually, it's more….it's more marijuana dispensaries than anything and they will soon be legal in Canada."

"Yes!" Jorge quickly agreed. "I am trying to get away from my old ways...I mean, I am working more toward a more legal kind of business."

"It's very important you never talk to anyone about this," Paige continued, her eyes full of soothing compassion, which was something Jorge needed as much as his daughter at that point. "It's our secret. If anyone ever tells you they know this about your father, you must say you don't know anything. He worked as a salesperson for his family's coffee company and now, he invests in businesses in the Toronto area. That's it."

"I know," Maria sniffed and nodded. "I never tell anyone these things."

"The only people who you can talk about this to are," Jorge spoke up, his normal voice returning as his heart began to slow down, no longer pounding erratically in his chest. "Diego, Jolene, Chase, and Jesús. Do not discuss this with anyone else and do not discuss it in public places. We cannot trust that people won't be listening."

Maria nodded in understanding and stood up. "*Papa*, I will go wash my face before dinner."

After she was out of the room, Jorge reached for his phone, once again beeping, as Paige sat beside him on the couch.

Glancing at his missed text messages, he wanted to scream. Could this day possibly get any worse?

CHAPTER 21

"Boss, I'm sorry to interrupt your day," Jesús spoke with some hesitation, a clear sign that something was wrong. "We must talk soon. Where are you?"

"Home," Jorge replied as he saw Paige turning off the burners in the kitchen while his daughter watched him attentively.

"Ok, we cannot meet there," Jesús automatically insisted. "The club?"

"Ok, I'm heading there now."

Ending the call, he saw Paige and Maria looking at him. Both expressed disappointment and concern in their eyes.

"I won't be long, I promise," Jorge spoke gently as he stood up and glanced at Paige then his daughter. "I got to meet Jesús at the club."

"Can I come?" Maria asked, already started to walk toward him.

"No, Maria," Jorge shook his head. "You must stay here with Paige and eat your dinner. I won't be long." He turned his attention back to his wife, although he knew she understood. "I will eat when I return."

Jorge's legs felt heavy when he started to walk toward the door while his head was swimming, telling him that he should stay with his family; but what could he do? Clearly, something serious was going on for Jesús to request a sudden meeting.

When he arrived at the club, Jesús met him at the door and gave him a concise overview of the situation as they headed for the bar. "Someone was found snooping around the warehouse," Jesús referred to the location where the pot was grown.

"Was it the police?"

"No, I do not think it was the police, I have made certain they do not come near," Jesús spoke with a calm strength that assured Jorge that whatever took place in BC, it would soon be taken care of with swift and careful actions. "However, we had to shoot him. He was threatening one of our workers."

"Threatening?" Jorge asked just as the door opened and Chase walked in with a paper bag in his hand. The aroma of food filled the club which caused Jorge's stomach to rumble as his associate stiffly walked in their direction, not appearing surprised to find either of them standing there in the midst of a conversation.

"He had a gun pointed at one of the Filipino women that works for us," Jesús spoke calmly, his hand up in the air as if to assure Jorge. "But it is ok. She is fine and will not say anything, however, we had to shoot him and ask questions later, given the circumstances. So now, we must get rid of the body. Hector is on his way and I'm about to take a plane out after this meeting. The men looking after things at the warehouse are following our instructions but they need help disposing of the body and, I must have a conversation with the lady who was in danger."

"I thought you said she wouldn't talk?"

"She won't," Jesús assured him. "She's a family member of Marco's and we know he's quite loyal. In fact, he has already left for BC to speak with her, as an extra insurance policy. And I must leave soon or I will miss my plane."

"You need me?"

"No, boss, we will be fine," Jesús reassured him while giving Chase a strange look as he slowly got closer. "Why is he walking like that?"

"Trust me," Jorge assured him. "You don't wanna know."

"I will trust you on that," Jesús commented as he started to walk away, giving Chase a quick nod as he headed toward the exit. "I will text you as soon as I know anything. If I send messages asking about Maria, you will know it was resolved and I'm on my way back. Otherwise, I will call."

"As soon as you know anything."

Jesús gave a quick nod before exiting the club.

Chase looked back and forth between the exit and Jorge. "What's going on?"

"We had a little situation in BC," Jorge replied. "It's being taken care of as we speak. Jesús is heading out to make sure everything is ok."

"Oh," Chase replied as the smell of food continued to make Jorge hungry. "So, everything's fine?"

"More or less," Jorge said and pointed toward the office and the two started walking. "Maybe not so much for the man who just had a gun on one of our employees but from our end of things, I guess you could say, everything is fine."

Chase didn't reply as they entered the office and he stiffly moved behind the desk while Jorge sat on the other side. Grabbing his phone, he sent a quick text to Paige stating that he would be home soon.

"So Chase, I must tell you something quite alarming that happened earlier today," Jorge said as he put his phone away. He noted Chase paused when taking his food out of the bag. "It has to do with Maria."

"Is she ok?" Chase automatically responded, his eyes full of concern.

"She is but me, not so much," Jorge admitted as his mind slipped back to the conversation that took place a little earlier that day. "Maria, she knows what I do. She knows about the cartel."

"But who told her?" Chase asked as he placed both hands on the desk as if forgetting his food. He leaned back in his chair. "Or did she overhear something?"

"Her fucking mother, that is who told her," Jorge answered while shaking his head. "Apparently, she has known for some time. That woman, she was a poison in my life, my daughter's life. Even after her death, she haunts us. She did everything to destroy my daughter. Her words, her actions, everything and yet, they call me the devil? She, Chase, *she* was the devil."

"Fuck!" Chase shook his head. "Why would she tell her? Who the fuck does that to their kid?"

"A snake, that is who," Jorge replied as the anger rose in him. Taking a deep breath, he finally shook his head. "but, what can I do? I cannot lie to my daughter or she will never believe me again. I told her that yes, this is true. Of course, I didn't tell her about anything else or about Paige but I did confess that I worked for the cartel."

"Does she even understand?" Chase wondered.

"In Mexico, this is in the news often," Jorge replied. "Fortunately, my name didn't make the news. I made certain of that because once your name is in the news, the police, they must do something to make the public happy. The media, Chase, they are the most powerful force out there. They can destroy a person in a second."

"Did you pay them?" Chase asked hesitantly as he reached for his food. "I mean, to not speak."

"Pay?" Jorge replied with a grin while raising his eyebrows. "It was a simple matter of how much they valued their lives. Those who valued their lives kept quiet. That was a message I sent out early on when one reporter, he thought he would investigate me. I found out and his family's home burned to the ground. No one dared since."

Jorge noticed that Chase didn't ask if anyone was in the house when it burned down and perhaps, it was better he didn't. He merely nodded in understanding as he dug into a pile of rice.

"At any rate, it didn't matter in the end," Jorge commented and took a deep breath. "My daughter learned the truth much too young and I guess, that is my punishment for the lives I've destroyed over the years because having her know this truth about me, is killing me but there is nothing I can do now."

"I'm sorry, Jorge," Chase shook his head between mouthfuls of food. "I know there are things I would never want my children to know about me either, so I definitely relate. And for what it's worth, I get what you mean about the mother. Audrey and I had a terrible relationship and she often held my kids over my head. As much as you love your children, sometimes the person you have them with is another story."

"It is a complicated situation," Jorge agreed. "But that is life, you know?"

Chase silently nodded.

"So tell me, my friend, why are you still here if you are in pain?"

"I gotta catch up on my work," Chase shook his head, depressed. "Jolene is still out and I'm stuck trying to get this party ready for the weekend. You would think that after all the times I've helped with them over the years, it would be a piece of cake but it's a lot of work to do on my own. Getting supplies, making sure everything is taken care of, that you have enough staff available, it's been hectic."

"How about….I must have someone to send here to help you, no?"

"I don't think so," Chase gloomily shook his head. "Everyone is so busy at the office with the pot shops."

Jorge thought for a moment. "I have an idea."

Grabbing his phone, he immediately made a call.

"*Mi amor*, I must ask yet, another favor from you," Jorge spoke lovingly into the phone.

"Does this have to do with that call you got earlier?" Paige asked, her voice in an even tone. He could hear dishes rattling in the background.

"No, actually," Jorge replied. "It is to help our friend Chase with party planning. Jolene, it seems is *ill* this week and she left him in a bit of a mess. The poor man is working day and night. I would like to tell him to go home and rest since he's also in a great deal of pain."

"Pain?" Paige asked. "Weren't you supposed to tell me something about that earlier?"

"Oh, my love, I will let *him* explain that to you," Jorge said with humor in his voice, teasing Chase, who grinned and looked away. "Would you be available to pop in tomorrow and help him out for a bit? I know you are good at planning things."

"Sure," She replied with no hesitation. "Are you coming home soon? We have a plate of food ready."

"That would be beautiful," Jorge replied. "I am heading there shortly. How is Maria?"

"Fine," Paige replied with no further explanation.

"Were you able to discuss things with her?" Jorge asked.

"Yes, of course," Paige replied as the dishes continued to clatter in the background.

"We shall talk about it tonight," Jorge commented while his eyes grazed over the food Chase was eating. "I will be home shortly."

After finishing the call, he noted the look of relief on Chase's face.

"Paige, she will meet you in the morning," Jorge informed him. "She will help you with whatever you need."

"Thank you so much," Chase said as he swallowed a mouthful of food. "She doesn't mind?"

"Of course not," Jorge replied. "Paige is superwoman, she can do anything."

"I'm seeing that," Chase commented as he stopped eating for a moment. "Please, thank her for me."

"Thank her yourself in the morning," Jorge insisted as he stood up. "Now I must go home and heat up my dinner that I missed. You, go home and ah....take it easy, Chase. Paige will help in the morning and tomorrow, I shall pay a visit to Jolene to see how she is doing. I may have to borrow Paige when I make this visit."

Chase didn't reply but nodded in understanding.

Too many things had diverted his attention lately but he wasn't about to let that snake slither away.

Chapter 22

"She said it was *cool*, can you believe this?" Jorge asked as he slowly got into bed later that night. His movements were slow as if he were an old man after a very intense day. At one time, he could've taken anything thrown his way then sleep like a baby but lately, the events of the day often haunted him long after he went to bed. Dreams, nightmares and overwhelming thoughts that had a way of racing through his mind all night long.

Paige offered him a sympathetic smile but didn't reply at first, instead, she slid her hand over his naked back as he quickly checked his phone, mentally counting how many hours it would take Jesús to arrive in BC and get rid of the body. Chances were that he wouldn't hear any news until the middle of the night. Although Jorge knew that there was little to worry about with Hector on the job, he would be more comfortable once the situation was resolved.

"My daughter," Jorge finally sat his phone on the nearby nightstand and turned his attention to Paige. "She watches all these American TV shows that have criminals so now, Maria thinks that my lifestyle is cool. Can you believe such a thing?"

"I'm wondering," Paige slowly began to speak as if choosing her words carefully while moving closer to him, her voice barely a whisper. "If maybe Maria started to watch these shows in the first place because she knew about your…lifestyle. Perhaps she wanted a better understanding and knew she couldn't ask."

Jorge considered her words and sadness crept through his heart as he nodded.

"Today when she told me, it almost killed me to hear those words, Paige." He confided as he looked into her eyes. "How could Verónic tell these things to a little girl? To hurt me? To make my daughter hate me? I do not understand."

"Verónic was clearly a *deeply* disturbed person," Paige observed as she gently pulled him closer. "But she's gone now, so she can't do any more damage."

"And yet, since her death, her ghost haunts me," Jorge commented and took a deep breath, closing his eyes for a moment. Whether it be Verónic's parents threatening to take Maria away or the discovery that the *puta* thought nothing of snorting coke in front of his daughter, Jorge felt as though she hadn't died. She was still causing misery from the other side of the grave.

"All we can do is deal with each thing as it comes up," She continued to whisper, her soft lips touched his cheek for a quick kiss. "Over dinner, her biggest concern was upsetting you. I suspect she has a pretty vague idea of what you actually do."

"Let's keep it that way," Jorge commented as he turned more toward his wife just as her hand reached under the covers, immediately taking his mind off his worries as he sunk down into the bed.

It wasn't until the middle of the night that he awoke to the sound of his phone vibrating. Grabbing it from the nightstand, the text told him everything he had to know.

Hope Maria is doing better. I will see you sometime tomorrow.

The next morning, Jorge woke early and quickly showered and dressed. He had a busy morning ahead, all his vulnerabilities of the previous day had slipped away into the night. In fact, it was almost as if a weight were lifted from his shoulders. Perhaps it was having another truth on the table that somehow brought him relief because it was one less secret he had to hide. At least, for the most part. Although his daughter knew about the drugs, she didn't have to know the full extent of his crimes; murder, torture, threats and, collusion These were things Maria could be blissfully ignorant about that for now. After all, despite her mature attitude, she was still a child.

"Good morning *princesa*," Jorge sang out as his daughter later wandered out of her room. Yawning, she made her way toward the kitchen, where Jorge sat with his coffee in hand and laptop opened. Without saying a word, she leaned in and gave him a kiss before heading toward the fridge. "Did you sleep well?"

"Yes, *Papa*," She replied while opening the fridge door and pulling out a container of yogurt. "But I'm still tired."

"Maria, come sit with me for a moment," Jorge insisted and pointed toward the nearby chair. "Let us have a quick conversation."

Sitting the yogurt on the counter, Maria hesitantly followed instructions.

"Now, as we discussed yesterday, I am not angry with you about our conversation. I was just very sad that you learned these things about me," Jorge clarified.

"But *Papa*, I made you cry."

"I was upset because, *niñita*, I'm not proud of the kind of work I have done," Jorge spoke honestly. "I'm not a doctor or a lawyer, I do not have a degree and I have helped contribute to a terrible problem in our world. It is not as you see on television. You must understand that, Maria. This is something I never want for you."

"I know, *Papa*," She spoke with such innocence devotion in her voice that he felt his heart soften. "I will continue my studies and when I'm a bit older, I will become a famous actress."

Jorge opened his mouth to say something but decided it was perhaps better to pick his battles for the day. He merely nodded as she stood up and went back to preparing her breakfast.

"*Papa*, you never did tell me if I could get a cat, did you discuss it with Paige?" Maria asked as she reached for a bowl in the cupboard. "I will look after it myself."

Jorge didn't reply. Feeling slightly defeated, he realized that it wasn't even 7:00 yet. Fortunately, Paige walked out of the bedroom as he was closing his laptop. She was already showered and dressed, a smile on her face.

"Oh, my love, good morning. Unfortunately, I must leave now," He pointed toward the door while his eyes glanced toward an oblivious Maria in the kitchen. "Diego and I, we are having breakfast."

"Ok." Paige nodded in understanding as he leaned forward and gave her a quick kiss. "I will text you later."

Turning toward the kitchen, his eyes met with Maria's and her smile was a gentle breeze through his soul. "*Te amo*, have a good day at school."

In response, she dramatically blew him a kiss as if she was already a movie star.

With a smile on his lips, he headed out the door.

Diego was already at the coffee shop when he arrived. Sitting at the back of the room, his eyes squinted as he held the menu away from his face, Jorge started to grin.

"You need fucking reading glasses," He gruffly insisted upon arriving at the table, causing Diego to shoot him a dirty look. "Why don't you admit it, my friend, you're getting old and blind?"

"I'm not *old* or *blind*," Diego snapped as he closed the menu. "Did you come here this early only to insult me?"

"Not *only* to insult you but I'm not gonna lie, it has been, so far, the highlight of my day," Jorge grinned as he stole Diego's menu and glanced at it. "Don't you find it interesting that I'm older than you and yet, I'm more handsome and still have my eyesight?"

Diego didn't reply and Jorge glanced up to see a scowl on his face as he reached for his coffee.

"Smile, Diego, you would look much more attractive if you smile more," Jorge continued to tease as the waitress approached.

"Could I get you a coffee?" She directed her question at Jorge and then turned her attention to Diego. "Or are you ready to order, sir?"

"Yes, thank you," Jorge answered for them both. "I will have a coffee and do you happen to have a menu with large print for seniors like Diego? You know, like those library books with bigger print for those with vision issues?"

The waitress looked unsure of what to say and Jorge merely waved his hand in the air.

"I will take your breakfast special, scrambled eggs, brown toast and bacon. Diego, do you wish to have the same?"

After the waitress took their orders and walked away, Diego immediately jumped in.

"*Hijueputa*!" He leaned forward, his dark eyes grew in size, only causing Jorge to laugh. "I can see perfectly fine, in fact, I can see the grey around your ears and you call me old?"

"Don't get all *loco* Colombian on me," Jorge insisted as the waitress returned with his coffee. After thanking her, he returned his attention to Diego. "And please, you're as grey as me without a little hair dye. I just let mine go a little longer."

Diego squinted and then pointed accusingly at Jorge "And, I will have you know, I do have glasses. I just choose to not wear them. Your eyes, they become dependent if you wear them too often."

"Oh Diego, you need a boyfriend, you are wound up tighter than a 40-year-old virgin on his wedding day."

"Hey, don't worry about me," Diego insisted. "So what's going on, why are we here the morning?"

"Well," Jorge began but hesitated again, this time as the waitress approached with their breakfast. After she left, he promptly continued. "Your sister, what is wrong with her? She's been home sick all week."

"Jolene?" Diego asked as he shoved a piece of bacon in his mouth. "She never takes a day off."

"According to Chase, she's taken the week off, apparently sick?" Jorge replied and raised his eyebrows. "Does that sound familiar?"

"Not to me, it doesn't. Chase didn't tell me this," Diego replied. "Do you think she's really sick?"

"I was about to ask you the same question," Jorge said and bit into his toast. "My thoughts are, no, she is not."

Diego didn't reply but some of his original feistiness seemed to instantly fade, causing Jorge to have some regret. He quickly changed the topic.

"Oh yeah, Jesús had a situation in BC."

"I heard," Diego spoke through a mouthful of food as he reached for his coffee. "Yesterday."

"I got a message in the middle of the night, I believe it's resolved,"

Jorge continued as he picked at his eggs. "I will learn more later when he gets back."

"Who was this guy? Should we be worried?" Diego asked as he picked up another slice of bacon. "Hopefully there's no more coming looking for him, if you know what I mean?"

"Let us hope not," Jorge said and reached for his coffee. "I'm not fucking around with anyone who comes near our operation. We shoot and ask questions later, as far as I'm concerned."

An hour slid by as the two discussed the further details of the new pot shops including opening dates and Diego showed him pictures of the recent work done in the various locations. Impressed, Jorge nodded and grinned.

"You do good work, Diego," He spoke and noted the look of pride on his friend's face. "We need more people like you working with us."

"You should clone me," Diego joked as his eyes squinted in a rare smile.

"Ah, let's not go that far," Jorge joined in with a grin. "The world can only handle one Diego."

It was as they were about to leave the coffee shop that Jorge noticed a text from Paige on his phone.

A cat? We're getting a cat?

"Oh, I must attend to my wife," Jorge spoke as the waitress dropped by with the bill and he immediately grabbed it before Diego, as the waitress walked away. "We had a stressful day yesterday with Maria. She surprised me by saying she wanted a cat and then she surprised me again by telling me she knows *what* I am."

"What you are?" Diego appeared puzzled at first and in sudden realization, his eyes bugged out. "As in."

"Yes," Jorge answered his question and shook his head. "Verónic, if she wasn't dead already, she might've been after that conversation."

"She told her?" Diego leaned in close, his eyes expanding in response to Jorge's nod. "Oh fuck! Wow, that must've been a surprise."

"To put it mildly," Jorge replied. "It was not a good day but now, we move on. I must meet Paige and together, we are going to see Jolene. Check out what illness is taking her from work."

Diego made a face and looked away.

"I know she is your sister," Jorge spoke respectfully toward his friend. "But lately, she is a lot of trouble."

Diego didn't reply.

CHAPTER 23

They met in the parking lot of Jolene's apartment building after Chase dropped her off. Immediately, Jorge could sense that Paige had something on her mind rather than the task at hand. She approached slowly, with an apprehensive expression on her face which only grew more wary with each step. However, it wasn't until she was close that Paige spoke.

"A cat? We're getting a cat?" She asked with no judgment in her voice, although her eyes were telling a different story. Immediately beginning to shake her head, there was clear reluctance on her face. "The apartment is already so small. Jorge, as much as Maria insists that she will look after it…"

"Ok, so first," Jorge felt his heart soften upon seeing his wife's clear reluctance over the issue of getting a family pet. It was rare that Paige protested something so when she did, he would listen. "To begin with, I did not say we would get a cat *now,* in fact, I did not say we would get a cat at all. This is Maria attempting to push the issue. I said we would think about it after getting a house. I figure by that time, it will be forgotten. For now, we can say pets aren't allowed in the building."

"She saw someone walking out with a dog this morning, so that's not going to work," Paige said and shook her head. "You must be careful Jorge because Maria sees that you're in a vulnerable situation now, and I think she is trying to use that to her advantage to get what she wants."

"I know, *mi amor,* I know," Jorge admitted with some reluctance as he reached for her hand. "But I feel such guilt over everything."

"She'll be fine," Paige assured him and squeezed his fingers. "I think maybe you might be projecting some of your own uncertain feelings on her. Not to say she doesn't feel that way too but I think maybe a part of you sometimes wishes you had a different..lifestyle."

"That I became something like a doctor or lawyer and not a *narco?*" Jorge grinned and pulled his wife closer. Giving her a quick kiss, he squeezed her hand back and started to move away from the SUV. "Yes, of course, but we are our decisions. Sometimes they aren't the best when we are young, you know?"

"Oh, believe me, I know," Paige grinned as she followed his lead as they started to walk. "Always looking over your shoulder, wondering what is around the corner? I can't imagine a life where you can just live with ease but then again, would we want that?"

Jorge didn't answer but merely smiled in response.

It wasn't until they were in the elevator going toward Jolene's floor that either of them spoke again. This was after sliding in the door behind an occupant who was leaving to avoid buzzing the apartment.

"And Chase, how is he doing today?"

A smile eased across Paige's lips. "I suspect better than when you saw him last. I recommended he take a bath with Epsom salts tonight."

"Epsom salts, is that not used in making meth?"

"He can make all the meth he wants but first, he needs to take a bath in it so he feels better," Paige teased as the elevator door opened and they stepped out.

Jorge laughed. "So did he tell you what happened?"

"Yes, he told me about it," Paige nodded with a smirk as they approached Jolene's apartment. "The fact that he's so uncomfortable somehow doesn't seem to make it worth it."

"No kidding," Jorge commented as they arrived at Jolene's door and he casually knocked. "How are the party plans?"

"Great, we got a lot accomplished this morning."

The door swung open and a rather disheveled Jolene answered. Stunned, Jorge almost didn't recognize the woman who was normally immaculately dressed, with a full face of makeup and perfectly groomed hair. She looked as if death had taken over. Pale, her face was so dry that it looked as if it were about to crack into a million little pieces while her eyes were glassy, hopeless and full of fear upon seeing them on the other side of the door. Not saying a word, she invited them in.

Wearing a frumpy sweater and a pair of yoga pants, she shuffled ahead of them in a pair of pink, fuzzy slippers, the smell of body odor lingered as she walked across the room. Closing the door behind them, neither Jorge or Paige commented, both completely stunned by what they saw, exchanging looks before their eyes took in the state of the apartment. Dishes, clothing, and garbage were everywhere. Although Jorge had seen much worse in his day, this was an upheaval for someone like Jolene.

Thankfully, it was Paige who made the first comment with a gentle voice, showing no judgment. Her words were simple, to the point and yet, showed a sense of compassion.

"What's going on Jolene?"

"My life, it is over, that is what is going on," She spoke in a slurred, delayed manner as she sat on a couch full of more clutter.

They both approached Jolene as she raised her hand in the air.

"You are here to shoot me, no? That is it, right? You want me dead for a long time, Jorge, this must be...like a record for you, to have waited so many months." She halted and started to laugh in an exaggerated manner as she leaned back on the couch. "Except, you bring her, so you will have her do the dirty work. That is the plan. Make it look like I suicide? Maybe had a slip fall of some kind?"

Paige didn't respond nor did she react. Instead, she shared a look with her husband and he took a deep breath and thought for a moment.

"Jolene, how long has this been going on?" He finally asked the question that would start the conversation. "The drugs, when did it start?"

Appearing surprised by both their reactions, Jolene's eyes filled with tears and she began to shake. Taking a sharp breath, an unexpected painful cry filled the room as she looked away in shame. Shaking her head as tears began to stream down her face and she wiped them away with her sleeve. "It has been a long time."

"How long, Jolene?" Paige's voice seemed to bring her back as she turned toward them with a look of pleading in her eyes.

"I don't know, since Colombia, on and off," She confessed in a hoarse voice. "I would sometimes do a little cocaine when I needed the energy and when I worked all night parties in Calgary but it was nothing serious, you know? I controlled it, it did not control me. I would drink when I was anxious to relax and then it became more and more since moving to Toronto. I felt a lot of pressure to do things right, you know? I was overwhelmed. I do not know. I guess none of this is an excuse but somewhere it became…my every day."

"Things, they kept getting worse and worse," Jolene continued as she sat up straighter. "My decisions were not good and I felt like everything, it got out of control. I couldn't even think right from wrong. *Ahora soy un desastre.*"

"Why didn't you tell anyone?" Paige gently asked. "Why wouldn't you tell Diego?"

"Diego, he would've criticized me. He would have told me to get my act together and be angry with me. I could not do." Jolene continued to slur her words, her broken English was much worse, in this state.

Jorge grew impatient but didn't know how he should proceed. Weighing his options, it was a tumultuous situation especially considering it was Diego's sister in question. Loyalty was important to him and even though Jolene had proven to not have such a trait, Diego had always been by his side which complicated the situation.

"Jolene, I gotta tell you," Jorge slowly started even though he had no idea what he was going to say until the words left his mouth. "It's the fact that you once helped out a man who wanted me dead that makes me not so compassionate."

Beside him, Paige folded her hands together tightly but her face remained tranquil. He knew his wife and Jorge was certain of what she was thinking.

"I tell you," Jolene spoke in barely a whisper as she hesitated to clear her throat. "I tell you before that I made a mistake. I thought that when these men publicly protested the sex parties that it increased our business. I did not know he wanted to kill you."

"See that's the thing," Jorge spoke thoughtfully. "I never believed that and the more time that goes by, the less I believe it. In fact, right here and now, I do not believe you *at all*. I think you wanted me dead. I think you wanted me out of the picture, maybe so you and Diego could take over. Maybe you wanted me dead because I put too much pressure on you. Maybe you're working for someone else.

"Why I want you dead?" Jolene asked as tears formed in her eyes again. "You give me so much. You give me a job, I am a Canadian citizen, because of you. Why would I want you dead?"

"How much of the coke have you been keeping for yourself?" Paige carefully inserted the question. "Maybe you thought he would find out? Were you selling some and keeping the money for yourself?"

"I pay!" Jolene quickly protested. "I pay my way. I do not steal!"

"You know what never added up to me," Jorge directed his comment toward Paige this time. "That whole thing with that Luke Prince guy, back in Chase's hometown. You know the one who accidentally shot his son, so we *purposely* shot him?"

Paige raised an eyebrow. Of course, at the last minute, she was contacted to murder Luke Prince since Jolene claimed she was too overwhelmed with emotion to do the task. At the time, Jorge had let it go, more stunned to learn Paige was even involved.

"What I tell you, it was true," Jolene said and turned her attention to Paige, perhaps because she knew trying to raise compassion from Jorge was impossible. "But I did, I did also have some drinks and took a pill for anxiety, it made me feel funny and I knew that Jorge would be angry if he knew. So I call Hector. That is why they send you, Paige."

Jorge nodded in understanding. That did make a little more sense.

"She *did* seem a little off," Paige confirmed with some reluctance. "I just assumed she was upset though."

Jorge wondered how often her decisions were clouded by drugs and alcohol. Why hadn't any of them noticed sooner?

"Going back to the religious nuts, your story just doesn't add up," Jorge said as he shoved both hands into his pockets; one of which held his gun. "There's no way protesting my hotel would bring attention to the sex parties. No one knew the connection. That's why I don't believe your story."

"See that is the thing with lies," Jorge continued as he took a big breath, his nose flared out in anger, his fingers caressing the gun in his pocket. "If you are going to tell them you should at least be good at it first. Unfortunately, with your clouded judgment, I guess that was not possible and then you made the even bigger mistake of thinking that I wouldn't learn the truth. A very, *big* mistake."

Fear encompassed her face and tears rapidly slid from her eyes when he pulled a gun out and pointed it at her.

"The problem is we keep going in circles here and yet, nothing makes more sense now," Jorge continued in a hushed tone.

His last words caused Jolene to suddenly collapse on the floor, at his feet, her body shaking uncontrollably as she sobbed for her life. She started to beg, to plead for him to not kill her but it was only under that pressure that the truth would come out.

"It was not my idea," She said in almost inaudible words as she lay on the floor. "I was told to do."

Jorge and Paige exchanged looks.

"Text Diego, tell him to come here." He spoke in a gentle voice toward his wife who nodded and he quickly changed his tone for Jolene. "Tell me a name now, Jolene, or your brother will get to see you bleeding to death on the floor."

"No, please, no!" Jolene begged as she sat up. "I tell you now, I tell you who."

"I got my listening ears on Jolene," Jorge replied in a mocking tone. "I had them on for the last few months and yet, why am I just hearing of this now?"

"It was *policia*," Jolene said as she continued to sob uncontrollably. "Jorge they want you dead because they say, you are untouchable. They cannot do so they tried to get these crazy, religious persons to do it."

"Then why didn't you tell me this before, Jolene?" Jorge felt himself growing more frustrated. "Why did you hide this from me?"

"Because they say that if I do not cooperate," Jolene replied, her body shaking rapidly now. "They will have me deported to Colombia and I cannot go. I made some bad decisions when I was there before, this is why I had to leave quickly."

"Bad decisions seem to be your thing, Jolene," Jorge snapped. "So now you are telling me it's the police that wants me dead. Finally! Something that makes senses. So, who wants you dead in Colombia? Who did you get involved with?"

He asked the question but it wasn't necessary she even answer. Jorge knew.

"Jorge," Paige said as she approached, cutting into their conversation. "Diego is already on his way. He was a little worried. I guess you must've told him you were coming here?"

Deciding to put away his gun, Jorge noted the look of relief on Jolene's face.

"Yes, I mentioned it at our meeting this morning."

"Oh, he is going to be so angry," Jolene nervously rose from the floor. "He's going to be so mad at me."

Paige reluctantly pointed toward the door. "I'm going to meet him downstairs," She said in a quiet voice as Jolene rushed around attempting to clean before her brother's arrival. "And tell him what's going on."

Jorge merely nodded and watched her walk out the door. Everything finally made sense. If the police took him out, heads would roll because his lawyer had proof of their collusion; many would fall from their pedestals. So finding someone else to do the dirty work was the answer. Oh! How it all made sense! As Jolene rushed around like a lunatic, attempting to tidy her place, Jorge was finally seeing the big picture as it pieced together.

His thoughts were abruptly interrupted when Diego suddenly threw open the door and walked in with Paige behind him. Fury filled the Colombian man's eyes as he glared across the room at his sister, who looked as defenseless as she had been when Jorge had a gun to her head earlier. Rushing over, she began to explain.

"Diego, I am sorry, it was the drugs, the drugs that…"

He didn't respond at first but listened as his sister began to speak rapidly in both Spanish and English. Her eyes pleading, her face full of hope, Jolene attempted to explain herself but it was when she started to relax, as the sun suddenly peaked through the window that Diego lifted his arm and with one, harsh movement, he backhanded his sister.

Chapter 24

"*Qué coño, Jolene?*" Diego roared at his sister while Jorge and Paige stood back in disbelief. His eyes burned with such rage that it lit a flame through his body, as he shook and continued to scream. "I am DONE! We've been down this road before and I am fucking done. I told you last time that you had one chance to get your life back on track and that was it. But you fucked up Jolene!"

Glancing at Paige, Jorge noted that she was easing closer, a hand in the air. Although she carried her usual calm demeanor, there was an unmistakable troubled look in her eyes. "Ok, we all need to step back for a second and calm down."

Diego turned and gave Paige a desperate look causing her to continue to speak softly. "Everyone is upset. I understand that but we've got to think about this for a moment. We need to work together. There is someone out there who wants Jorge dead or maybe all of us. This isn't the time to fight."

"But Paige," Diego began as he turned in her direction. "You don't understand."

"I don't have to understand," She replied and shook her head. "Whatever is going on between you and Jolene, is between the two of you. I think we all have an issue with her now but it doesn't matter because we have to work together to figure this out. Plus she clearly is an addict and even though that's not an excuse, it is something we must consider."

"Yes, I am sorry, Diego, I truly am," Jolene spoke to him, her eyes pleading as she touched her face where he hit her moments earlier. He simply turned away.

"Now," Paige continued and took a deep breath. "Jolene, I need you to tell us who you spoke with, did he give you a name?"

"He just say he is the police," Jolene said as she nervously played with a ring on her hand. "But I know it was true, he had a badge."

Paige and Jorge exchanged looks.

"Did you get any other information? When did this happen?" Paige calmly asked. "What did he look like?"

"It was probably 5, 6 months ago," Jolene said as she glanced at her hands while soft lines formed on her forehead. "I…I don't know, it was around same time religious groups start to protest us, shortly after because he talk about that when he made me get in the car."

"Why would you get in the fucking car, Jolene?" Diego shot the question at her. "If he wasn't arresting you, you could've said no."

"He did not give me choice," Jolene insisted as her eyes jumped to Diego's face. "He said either I get in the car to have a conversation or he would arrest me."

"For what?" Diego continued to interrogate his sister.

"Possession.

"Possession?"

"I had cocaine in my purse."

"So?" Jorge finally found his voice after watching everything play out. "Lots of people have drugs on them, guns, you name it, you didn't have to open your purse. You just deny it and keep going."

"A woman who was with him, she saw me with it in the bathroom," Jolene attempted to explain, her voice started to shake. "I was at a coffee shop for lunch and they must have followed me. The woman, she was not wearing a uniform, she dressed more like a teenager so I did not think anything when she talk to me in the lady's room. She saw the cocaine in my purse."

"How could she see it in your purse? Don't you women have little pockets to hide shit like tampons and stuff?" Jorge spoke sharply.

"No, she walk into the ladies room and my purse, it was open,"

Jolene spoke with some hesitation and stepped back. "I did not know it was so visible."

Jorge opened his mouth to say something but immediately closed it. His eyes briefly met with Diego's and suspected he was thinking the same thing.

"Ok, so, let's get past the bathroom thing," Jorge decided it was time to switch gears. "They saw you, used that as a way to get you in the car to talk and so tell me, Jolene, what did you say? What do these guys know about me? About all of us?"

"They only talk to me about you," Jolene replied as she looked at Jorge. "They seem to believe that without you, it does not matter. That everything would fall apart and so, their main focus was you."

"And it never occurred to you to warn me," Jorge asked with a shrug. "Haven't I done enough for you Jolene? Does loyalty not factor in? Didn't it occur to you that we might also protect you from their threats?"

"I did not think you could," Jolene replied and glanced down at her hands again. "They know things about me that no one knows. They tell me that they deport me to Colombia and that I will be killed, that they will make sure that those who wish to see me dead will find me right away. They show me pictures of the last woman who made enemies with these people and what they did to her body. I was so scared. I did not know what to do."

"Manipulation," Paige spoke evenly. "It was their way of terrifying her to do what they want."

"Ok, so they show you a picture of someone who was mutilated?" Jorge asked as he stepped forward and shrugged. "I'm guessing and what?"

"They tell me that they want you dead because you're untouchable," Jolene continued and her eyes met with Jorge's, even if with some hesitation. "If they try to arrest you or kill you themselves, he said at the very least, they will lose their jobs."

"Lose more than their fucking jobs if they try to kill me," Jorge shot back. "What else you got Jolene?"

"They talk about these religious fanatics and how they wanted you dead," Jolene insisted. "That they wanted me to help get them closer to doing so. That I was to work with them. I was to say that I wanted out of this business but could not do because you controlled me, so I would help them."

"And so you jumped in with both feet," Jorge spoke sharply as he stepped forward again, spotting the fear in her eyes. "And don't bother to tell me."

"I could not."

"You could've Jolene," Diego yelled. "You made a choice. You chose to help the *policia*. You made a decision. Jolene, *no policia!*"

"Do you not see?" Jolene snapped back. "I did not choose. If I tell you, they would send me back."

"How would they know?" Diego snapped at her. "Fuck! Jolene! Come on!"

"They would know!" She shot back, her voice full of emotion. "You do not understand. This man, he would not leave me alone. Every time I turn around, he was at my door, on my phone, calling me, showing up places I am. I was scared to tell anyone because they would know."

"So when the listening device was in your office last year?" Diego asked.

"It was them," Jolene's eyes grew in size. "They went to Gracie. They were working on her too. They say they would go to everyone I know and have them work against me."

"Yet another reason to tell us, Jolene," Diego insisted. "What the hell were you going to do, let them kill Jorge? You think they weren't going to come after the rest of us including you? How naïve are you?"

"No no! I was not going to let that happen," Jolene insisted. "I decide to take care of it myself."

"Wait, you were going to kill this guy?" Jorge asked and shrugged. "Again, you should've told me."

"I waited too long," Jolene said in a calm voice despite the fear in her eyes. "Do you not see? I was terrified and couldn't tell at first and by the time that I consider it, it was too late. It would look suspicious so I kill him myself. Hector, he helped me."

"You do realize, we have an assassin right here," Jorge spoke in a condescending manner and pointed toward his wife. "She could've done this without blinking an eye and made it look like an accident. Why wouldn't you just do that?"

"Again, I left it too long," Jolene replied, her eyes widened as she spoke. "It would look suspicious to you."

"So, you killed the guy and *still* didn't tell us?" Diego snapped and shook his head. "Why not then?"

"You would never trust me again," Jolene spoke with both her hands moving through the air as if to give emphasis to her point. "Why did I not come forward sooner? That is what you would've asked, all of you. So I hid it. I figure, the problem, it was taken care of and we would move on. I did not expect Jorge to find that email."

"So why not tell me *then*?" Jorge asked and shook his head. "I don't get it."

"You would've been angry I hadn't told you sooner," Jolene replied and shrugged. "So I say that I was talking to the religious people so they would protest and bring attention to the business. At worse, you would think I am stupid to do this stuff behind your back, you know?"

"Ok," Paige spoke up. "So, if I'm understanding this correctly, the man who wanted to kill my husband is dead? Was there anyone else working with him? Who was the woman?"

"I do not know the woman, she is maybe a police officer too? She was only with him that one time." Jolene said with a pleading voice. "I figure if I make this man go 'missing' that if there were others, they'd get the message. That is what you do, am I right, Jorge?"

He reluctantly nodded in agreement.

"I'm not so sure there aren't others," Diego said as his eyes jumped from Jorge to Paige. "Who was *he* working for?"

"It could be anyone," Jorge said and took a deep breath, his mind going in a million different directions. "Jolene, when did you kill this man?"

"Just before you approach me about the emails," Jolene spoke in a small voice.

"Has anyone approached you since?" Paige took over at this point.

"No," Jolene replied and shook her head. "But I am nervous, you know? What if there is more and what if they are watching me?"

"Another reason why you should've told us sooner," Diego insisted, shooting her a dirty look. "We're supposed to be a team here, Jolene. We could've helped you take care of this problem."

"The last time I admit anything," Jolene seemed to regain some of her original confidence. "You both get angry with me. Diego, you wouldn't even look at me and Jorge, you walked out pissed off. Why would I do again?"

"You mean the time you told us that you lied about killing Luke Prince?" Jorge asked and shoved both hands in his pockets. "Then you admitted it was Paige, whom I had just met? You thought we wouldn't react to that?"

"Trust, Jolene, it's a two-way street," Diego snapped. "You can't expect us to trust you when you're hiding secrets from us and tell us lies. That's not how trust works."

"I know!" Jolene replied and put her hands up as if to surrender. "I swear, that is all. I have no more secrets to tell. You know everything."

"We *better* know everything," Jorge snapped at her and turned his attention toward Diego. "Get your sister to rehab. Make it a long stay if you can because I don't wanna look at her again until she's sober."

Giving a reluctant nod, Diego ran a hand over his face. "I'll take care of it."

"Good," Jorge replied and turned his attention to Paige. "I gotta get out of here."

Without replying, she merely nodded and the two headed for the door.

CHAPTER 25

There was a fire in his eyes that was like no other. Paige Noël-Hernandez had met many people in her life but never anyone like her husband. It was how he appeared to take everything into consideration even when he wasn't; that daring, bold look he got in his eyes as he stared through people. It was the way he shot her a quick glance from across the room, telling her everything she had to know. Jorge Hernandez always had a plan, if not a conscience.

Jolene had survived another round of inquisition. Barely, by the skin of her teeth but she had managed to get out alive; which was nothing short of a miracle. Jorge's sudden shot of compassion was more about keeping his enemy close than it was about caring. After all, they might still need information from her but the damage had already been done. She could've come forward long ago but only did so when there was literally a gun to her head.

However, Paige held back. This was more her husband's battle than her own. It wasn't until they were back in the SUV and driving home, that she expressed herself with the same brutal honesty that was usually reserved for him.

"I want to kill her," Paige said in a quiet voice.

Jorge turned his head, his eyes expanding in size. "Seriously?" They were stopped at the red light and he almost didn't notice that traffic start again. "I'm surprised."

"You're surprised?" Paige challenged him. "Really? Because of her stupidity, you could be dead now. She's selfish. This entire thing, it's only about her. She's spineless. If she wants to sit in her ivory tower than she must be ready because that only makes it easier to kill her."

"I must say," Jorge said with a smooth grin easing across his face as the SUV stopped again. "I do love it when you talk this way, *mi amor* but what about Diego? It is his sister that you want to kill."

"I think he's at the end of his rope with Jolene," Paige sighed and looked away. But she was *still* his sister and that was the fly in the ointment. "She has been disloyal to all us, including Diego. She used Chase to have someone on her side when we were against her, in the process, having an affair with the one man that she knew her brother loved. She had no qualms about you possibly being killed and hiding it from all of us."

Looking back at him, she saw his face soften into a peaceful expression that had disappeared in recent days, in the midst of so much tension. His hand reached out and touched her shoulder while he remained quiet; not a normal state for Jorge Hernandez who always had something to say, his silence often the strongest indication that his emotions were running high. She smiled and he continued to stare, as the weight of the moment was undeniable.

Traffic started to move again and they slowly made their way back to their dingy little apartment. Neither spoke for a few minutes as Paige watched the people on the sidewalks. The high of Christmas over, it was hard to stay upbeat when the cold weather overtook your body and dark clouds constantly lurked overhead during the longest month of the year. These factors were perhaps dampening her already dark disposition.

"How dare she think she can put your life in danger?" Paige said in a gentle whisper that caused an unmistakable passion to flow through the SUV as Jorge exchanged brief glances with her, as they moved closer to home. Even from the passenger side, she could tell his breath was growing labored as he shuffled uncomfortably in his seat and cleared his throat.

"And she always knew too," Paige continued to speak in a soft voice, which had a way of enveloping passion within her husband. "The day, when you first introduced me to your business associates, she looked so shocked. At the time, I thought it was because I had killed Luke Prince when she couldn't do the job herself and I thought she feared I would tell you the truth. But now I see it. She probably knew all along that I was *mistakenly* sent to your hotel room to kill you. Imagine her surprise when I walk in the door as your girlfriend?"

It was a bizarre way to meet. Paige had been given a last-minute assignment to kill another Hernandez on that particular night however, she wasn't aware someone had already ushered him away. Meanwhile, Jorge came along to the hotel and demanded his regular suite, something he had booked weeks earlier but the reservations were switched to the victim. Clearly, both Paige and Jorge were setup that night. Fortunately, she immediately sensed something was off upon entering the room.

"But *mi amor*," Jorge finally spoke, although his voice was weak, softer than usual. "Had she not done so, we may have never met. As much as we hate her, it was that night at the hotel room that we fell in love. It is, to me, worth the risk."

"I could've killed you that night," Paige replied, hearing the emotions creeping into her own voice. "That is something I will never forgive myself for."

"But you must," Jorge insisted as they drove down their street toward their apartment building. "I've told you, again and again, it was a mistake. It ended up being a beautiful night and that is all I think about now. That must be your only thoughts too."

Paige didn't reply at first. He was right but it was so hard to accept. Knowing the impact that Jorge Hernandez had in her life, it would've been a tragedy to have not known him. It made her briefly reconsider her work as an assassin. How many had she killed that were good people, people who changed someone else's life, influenced the world? Then again, she tended to only accept assignments that suggested otherwise; pedophiles, anyone who hurt children was at the top of her list but so were other despicable people who made the world a terrible place. Sure, there were other assassins out there who killed people who everyone loved; celebrities, public figures and everyday people who happened to get in the wrong person's crosshairs but she spent her life focusing on those who she felt brought the world down, rather than those who enhanced it. But had she ever been wrong?

"You're right," She agreed and saw relief fill his face. "It still makes me want to kill her though."

"Oh, *mi amor*, you may have to stand in line," Jorge spoke with his usual enthusiasm. "My distrust for Jolene only increases with the day, you know? But if there was one *policia* that wanted me dead, there could be another. That has to be our focus. Jolene, we cannot trust but it is unlikely she is a direct threat."

That was when Paige broke down. She had managed to stay strong when Jolene spoke casually of Jorge's potential murder and again when retelling the entire story to Diego; even when his eyes grew moist as he learned more hard truths about his own sister. But now, everything had somehow hit the tipping point as they drove into the underground parking, the dismal surroundings combined with the realizations of the day were now torturing her.

With her head down, Paige felt the abruptness of the SUV breaking as Jorge swiftly put the vehicle into park, his hand suddenly on her arm.

"Oh *mi amor*, please don't cry," Jorge said in a gentle tone, as Paige covered her eyes to hide her misery. She could hear his seatbelt clicking before he moved forward to pull her into an awkward hug. His breathing was loud in her ear as his soft lips could suddenly be felt on the side of her face as he kissed her, then tightening his grip. "Everything, it will be ok. We are fine."

"I'm sorry, I know," Paige began to speak as he let her go. Jorge's deep brown eyes stared into her own, a perfect combination of passion and love filled them as he listened intently to her every word. "It's been a long day."

"Ah, you Canadians, always apologizing," He said with a grin on his lips before leaning in and giving her another kiss, this time on the lips. "Is it not normal to have feelings? For this, we shouldn't apologize."

She responded with a half-hearted smile as Jorge moved away and they both got out of the SUV. He met her on the passenger side and slid a hand over her back, pulling her close as they walked toward the elevator in silence. It wasn't until they were back in the apartment that either spoke again.

"I'm setting up a meeting for tonight," Jorge commented as he tapped at his phone. "Jesús is on his way back and I want him, me and Diego to get together. I was thinking you could come too and I could ask Chase to babysit?"

"You know," Paige said after a moment. "That's fine. I think I know everything and maybe it would be better for you to invite Chase. I think he needs a reality check."

"I can arrange something at a better time, if you want," Jorge offered hesitantly. "If you wish to attend, I can work it around when Maria is in school?"

"That's fine," Paige replied. "I'm fine. You can tell me whatever I miss. I think I need a break from everything."

"*Mi amor*, are you ok?" Jorge suddenly asked her, his eyes on her face, he sat his phone aside.

"Yes, of course," Paige replied with a smile even though, lately she wasn't so sure herself. There were days when her life felt like a runaway train that wasn't about to stop. There was always so much going on with Jorge, with Maria, her life was vastly different from months earlier when she was single and although she loved every second of it, it still was an adjustment.

"Very well," He said and removed his jacket. She feared that his constant state of anxiety and unrest would make him sick. Although his health had vastly improved since the doctor's stern warnings the previous year, lately life had seemed more precious than ever and although that awareness was important, it was also distracting at times.

Jorge's eyes studied her face curiously as he approached. Leaning in, his lips met hers, his tongue boldly moving into her mouth as he pulled her tightly against his own body. Paige showed no reluctance to meet him halfway, as her fingers ran through the bottom of his hairline and her other hand traveled under his shirt, gently caressing the smooth skin on his back. It was just as he moved his hands down to her ass, greedily grabbing it and pulling her forward to squeeze tightly against his body that his phone rang.

"Oh for fuck sakes!" Jorge said after letting go of Paige, in a slight stupor, he seemed to forget where he placed his phone. Finally locating it, he grabbed it and hit a button. "Yeah?"

Jorge listened, his face relaxing slightly, he cleared his throat and looked away.

"We are having a meeting tonight," Jorge started and stalled. "Oh yes, ok, I do understand. Ok, I guess I can drop by now for a few minutes."

Ending the call, she could see the anger on his face. "I must go talk to Chase. As it turns out, he cannot attend tonight because he has a rock show at the club. So, we must meet now to discuss what is to happening."

"Will he need my help with the parties?" Paige asked as she watched her husband frown and shake his head.

"No," Jorge reached for his jacket. "Right now, I am seriously thinking of stopping the parties, selling the club and moving Chase back to the office. He can take over Jolene's space since I don't foresee her returning. I have plenty for him to do, that is for certain."

Paige nodded in understanding. "That actually sounds like a good idea."

"Others, they are already copying what we do anyway, so it is getting too competitive," Jorge said as he put on his jacket and shoved his phone in a pocket. "I am so sorry, Paige, I was hoping we could spend the afternoon together. But you know what? Once I have everyone organized, I believe we will have many afternoons ahead."

She smiled but was doubtful. It wasn't natural for Jorge to not be in disarray. He simply didn't know any other way to live.

It was after he was gone that she noticed a missed call from Alec. Paige knew he had shown some reluctance about having her husband as a backer for his potential campaign, so she was surprised by his message.

Chapter 26

The last thing he wanted to do was leave his wife but meeting with Chase was, unfortunately, quite necessary. It was on the drive there that Jorge continued to consider selling the club. He loved the idea but then again, the bar was the ideal place to launder money, so that fact made it a little more difficult to let it go. Fortunately, Chase had given it some thought too.

"We could end the sex club part of the business and make this a high-end nightclub," Chase suggested once they were in his office while on the other side of the door, the musicians scheduled to perform that night were setting up. Loud thumps, shouting and occasional shots of guitar could be heard while Jorge remained lost in a world of thought. "Or we could just have bands like tonight but in my experience, you want to get the rich people here because they spend a lot of cash so it wouldn't be unreasonable that we'd have a lot of money coming in if you know what I mean."

"I do," Jorge said with a nod as he continued to allow his thoughts to drift in various directions while listening to Chase at the same time. "So, tell me, are there any more parties scheduled."

"I hadn't added any new ones since Jolene started calling in sick," Chase commented as the loud thud of a bass drum could be heard on the other side of the wall. "We could have one, last party and make it a huge deal, charge extra and completely inflate the numbers due to the buildup?"

Jorge didn't respond at first, simply nodding as he quickly worked out the details in his mind. Perhaps it would be better to keep Chase at the bar since he was exceptional at keeping things on track and perhaps, once laws changed in the future, they could find a way to work it together with the pot shops. He decided to put aside the idea of selling for now. Who knew what the future would bring?

"Ok, Chase, I will trust you in this matter," Jorge said and slowly began to nod his head. "However, I am wondering if we should change the bar's name. JD Exclusive Club will always be associated with the sex club so if we created a new bar then we must also give it a new name. What do you think?"

"Sure," Chase said and began to nod. "I'm sure it's just a matter of some paperwork to change the name."

"We got lawyers for that," Jorge commented as he moved to the edge of the chair, already preparing to leave. "You can think of the name. Make it classy. I honestly don't care."

"Me? Are you sure?" Chase asked with some hesitation. "I…I mean, I don't know…"

"Neither do I," Jorge replied as he stood up and Chase did the same. "Name it after yourself if you wish. It does not matter to me."

"Oh, no," Chase said with a grin. "You might want to consider something a little classier than my name."

"Name it after Paige or Maria….or your kids, I don't care," Jorge suggested as he started for the door and suddenly stopped. Turning abruptly, he noted that Chase showed some reluctance at the last suggestion. "Anything you wish, Chase. You can name it after…"

He didn't even finish the sentence and Chase shook his head as a great sadness filled the room, causing Jorge to look away. It was perhaps insensitive to suggest that Chase name the bar after his dead son however in Jorge's mind, it would've been in honor of the little boy who had lost his life. Of course, Jorge wasn't exactly the most sensitive man on the planet so perhaps, it was still much too soon.

"I think….another name might be better," Chase said with some hesitation as he shrugged. "I appreciate it but you know, it's probably not the best idea. I think maybe Paige or Maria might be better."

"I know my wife and come to think of it," Jorge said as a grin curved his lips. "She would say no especially now that she might be working on a campaign with a politician." He turned to Chase who looked surprised and merely shook his head. "Don't ask, my friend, let's just say that this bar should get classy soon. We might be having some political functions here. Perhaps I will send Sylvana and you can discuss it from a marketing point of view. Her or Diego might have some ideas on how to change the interior to make it more….classy?"

"Whatever you think," Chase agreed as Jorge turned toward the door just as a loud shot of guitar vibrated through the building. Shaking his head, he glanced over his shoulder one last time as he reached for the doorknob.

"I'm thinking a nice, quiet lounge might be more suitable," He said with a raised eyebrows as Chase followed him to the door. "I see you are able to walk again, my friend, no more dates with the sadist?"

"I have one tonight," Chase replied.

"Well, so much for that," Jorge muttered before exiting the office.

Jorge glanced at his phone on the way out. A grin crossed his lips when he saw a text from Maria which included a picture of a recent assignment indicating top marks, followed by a message from Paige stating that she had heard from Alec and would tell him more when he arrived home.

Jorge wasn't crazy about working with Paige's ex-boyfriend, no matter how long it had been since they were together. The truth was that he was clearly the polar opposite of Jorge and even though that should've comforted him, there were times he feared Paige saw him as being a little 'too much' to contend with; his life was erratic, going off in several directions. Perhaps someone boring like Alec Athas might seem more appealing in comparison. Of course, it was his own insecurities that occasionally shone through, creating this idea in his mind, the dark enemy who would never let him fully experience joy. It was an evil bastard warning him that another shoe was about to drop.

Pushing the thought from his head, he realized that his low mood was probably because he hadn't eaten in hours. Jorge sent a quick text to Jesús asking him to bring food to the meeting. His stomach rumbled even thinking about it. Glancing at his watch, he wondered where the day had gone?

Fortunately, the aroma of pizza met him before even making it to the office. Pulling out his passcard, he quickly scanned it and walked into the dimly lit entrance. Making his way down the hallway, he found the others in the boardroom. Two large pizzas sat on the table and Jorge barely said hello to Diego before opening the cardboard container marked 'the works' grabbing a hearty slice and placing it on a paper plate.

"We got anything to drink?" He gestured toward Diego who had removed his blazer and started to roll up the sleeves of his white shirt. "You make us some of your coffee?"

"Of course," Diego said as he grabbed a piece of pizza and a plate with the other hand. "It should be ready shortly and Clara was just here so we're safe to talk."

"Fuck, I'm starving," Jorge sunk his teeth into a slice just as Jesús entered the room, covering the door handle with a paper towel before entering. "What are you doing, Jesús, some light cleaning before you eat?"

"I was washing my hands," Jesús spoke in his usual slow manner. "It is flu season, you do know that, right?"

"It's always fucking flu season," Diego spoke with his mouth full of pizza, waving his hand around as Jesús sat down. "We don't have time to get sick."

"This is exactly why you must wash your hands before eating," Jesús insisted as he tossed the paper towel in a nearby garbage can and reached for his slice. "Germs, they are everywhere."

"I'm sure Diego has had his tongue in places with a lot more germs than that piece of pizza," Jorge teased as he took another large bite of his pizza, while across the table Diego laughed, nearly choking on his food while Jesús started with a grin that quickly turned into a hearty laugh.

"Now, we gotta get to business," Jorge commented as he wiped his hands on a paper towel and sat down. "We got a lot of ground to cover."

"I'll start," Diego jumped in while he continued to stand. "Pot shops are *perfecto*, as long as we don't get raided, the ones opened are crazy busy and the others, are coming along on schedule. There have been some hiccups but nothing serious."

"And Jolene?"

Diego made a face. "Rehab."

"As of today?"

"As in immediately after we confronted her today," Diego insisted and gestured toward Jesús. "I already told him everything."

"Yes, it is unfortunate," Jesús said as he shook his head, barely nibbling on his pizza while Diego finished his first slice and was reaching for a second before sitting down. Jorge hesitated briefly before continuing to eat his pizza. "But now, at least we know where we stand and perhaps, we can work around it."

"I've been thinking about that but for now, what's going on in BC?" Jorge asked and took the last bite of his slice while reaching for the second one. Although it was hardly the best pizza ever, he was too hungry to care. He immediately sunk his teeth into the second piece, as the thick sauce swam over his taste buds. "Are we clear?"

"The body, it is gone," Jesús insisted. "Hector, he had a plan and it was taken care of quickly. No one has followed him and the lady he held a gun to, she will not talk. Marco spoke with her and she does not want trouble. She just wants a job. Of course, we gave her a week off with pay for her…troubles."

"I would say having a gun to her head would be trouble," Jorge said as he continued to eat, his mind-stretching in another direction altogether. "Are we sure that this man, he worked alone?"

"That is the only problem," Jesús said and hesitated to take another bite of his pizza. "We do not know who he is or where he came from so we will be more vigilant. I am having more cameras installed all over the property."

"And the news?" Jorge asked. "Is there any news of a missing person, anything like that?"

"No," Jesús replied as he shook his head. "There is nothing yet but it's early."

Although there was something unsettling about this report, he knew better than to overthink it. If the body was missing and no one saw a thing, they were pretty much home free. After all, the building was in a rural area, secluded from the few people who lived in the community.

Most people probably assumed that a local farmer owned the warehouse and thought nothing of the contents.

"Why was he there? What was he saying?" Diego spoke up. "Did he not ask for money? Drugs?"

"He grabbed one of our workers when she was trying to leave and put a gun to her head," Jesús replied. "He asked her what was inside the building but it was at that time, my men saw him and told him to put down the gun. He continued to ask what was inside the building and finally, one of my men got him on a perfect angle and shot him in the leg. When he collapsed on the ground, the woman, she got away and he was shot in the head."

Jorge merely nodded, he briefly sat his food aside but content with the reply, started to eat again, although more slowly this time.

"We must continue to monitor this situation."

"We are, day and night," Jesús assured him. "Do not worry, sir."

"I want to eventually get more grow ops started across the country," Jorge was insistent. "Maybe smaller ones, so that we can mix in a little better. Perhaps a large warehouse attracts too much attention."

"Perhaps so," Jesús nodded. "I will talk to the men in BC. I think I'm going back the day after tomorrow."

"Very good," Jorge said as he glanced at Diego. "I am thinking of something my friend and this affects you. How would you feel about getting Jolene's name off the business?"

"I was wondering the same," Diego spoke in a stern voice but his eyes carried some sadness.

"We cannot take any chances with her," Jorge continued as he leaned toward Diego. "And she's not in the position to say anything. What I would like is to also change the name of the bar. I met with Chase earlier and we want to get away from the sex parties, make the club into more of an upscale lounge. I originally thought of closing it and having Chase return to the office but, it is an asset when moving money through."

"Maybe *Paige* should come to the office," Diego suggested with emphasis on her name and then raised his eyebrows. "Or *you*."

"Perhaps," Jorge agreed.

"I'm hardly here anymore and we need someone to look after things," Diego insisted as he finished off his second piece of pizza and waved his hand around the otherwise, empty office. Jesús chewed on the last piece of his first slice and nodded. "Or the two of you could pop in, you know, from time to time, to make sure everything is ok."

"Yes, we could do that, this is true," Jorge considered and grinned. "Meanwhile, Diego, you must think of our new company name. I think we should keep it simple. Hernandez-Silva, something of that nature."

"Silva-Hernandez," Diego suggested.

"That there," Jorge pointed toward a grinning Diego. "That is *not* happening."

"It has a ring to it," Diego continued to tease. "I think."

"You would," Jorge shook his head. "Is there anything else we gotta discuss?"

"So the club," Jesús spoke up. "No more sex parties?"

"No, we're done," Jorge replied. "Chase, he got enough to do, there's too much planning and plus, I might be backing a politician so, you know, we might need somewhere classy to have events. This also provides a legit reason to change the business name since our business, it is no longer the same."

"Oh, can I make some suggestions on how to change the bar?" Diego's asked, his eyes expanding in size. "I got all these ideas."

"Go talk to Chase," Jorge said with a shrug. "You guys figure that out."

"Maybe it would be better to have Paige step into the office?" Jesús suggested. "You are not much of a detail person."

"I'm an end of the race kinda guy," Jorge said and took a deep breath, briefly considering if he wanted more pizza. "I know what I want to see at the end of the line but I don't give a fuck how we get there. I'll talk to Paige when I get home."

CHAPTER 27

"Sounds like I missed a few things," Paige commented when Jorge finally had the opportunity to tell her about both his meetings. They sat together on the couch with a bottle of wine after a long day. This was after he tended to Maria; helping her with homework, hearing about her day at school, all the things that he strived to do as often as possible. After she had learned the truth about his status in the world, it seemed even more important to spend time together and make sure that she was continuing to adjust to the many changes in her life over the last year.

Jorge let out a short laugh and wondered if he could persuade her to show up at the office the next morning. Not that he doubted she would but it sometimes seemed as if he was always asking her for a favor. Their marriage had never been about swallowing up Paige's entire life and yet, didn't her every day seem to center on his?

"Yes, well, I do think it is a good thing," Jorge said as he finished his wine and went ahead to pour them each an overly full glass before continuing, as she giggled at the gesture. "But change, it is good. Life, it is all about change."

"That it is," Paige said before easing the glass to her lips, attempting to carefully take a sip without spilling it. Jorge quietly watched her before gulping down some of the bitter drink; the sharp taste seemed to burn all the way down his throat, which was exactly what he needed at that point in the day.

"Do you remember, my love, when we first met?" Jorge decided to take the more sentimental approach as he put his free arm around her shoulders. "That night, we also sat on a couch and drank some wine together."

"Yes," Paige said as she rubbed her lips together and cleared her throat. "That was just after I almost killed you by accident."

"Oh, *mi amor*, you know what they say," Jorge squeezed her shoulder, moving closer to her as he did. "Almost is never enough."

"Who says this exactly?" Paige said with a sudden giggle and took another drink of wine.

"It does not matter," Jorge said and quickly switched gears. "The point is that we were together on a night very much like this one and both our lives changed drastically from that point on. We got married, I moved here from Mexico with Maria, we did some great work together…"

"Yes, that's true," Paige said with a nod, a grin spread across her lips.

"We work so well together, have you noticed?" Jorge said in a soft voice as he ran his finger over the back of her neck. "We make a great team."

"Of course," Paige replied and leaned toward him.

"How would you feel," Jorge started with some hesitation, "How would you feel if you and I were to pop by the office from time to time and help out? You know, just oversee what is going on, make sure the employees are doing their job, that kind of thing? Jolene is in rehab, Diego is hardly ever there lately because he has so much to do with the dispensaries. I am wondering if maybe we need to take over Jolene's office, perhaps share it?"

"You mean, *you're* going to spend time in an office?" Paige asked with some hesitation and took another drink of wine. "I somehow can't see that."

"And why is that?" Jorge teased her. "You do not think I have the smarts?"

"I don't think you have patience," Paige gently reminded him in almost a whisper that he thought was so sexy, so enticing. "I can barely get you to sit still long enough to have this conversation, how are you going to spend days in an office?"

"Who said anything about days?" Jorge replied and winked before taking another drink of wine. "You know me, I will be all over the place. I want to see what the employees are doing and make sure they know this and I will be going through Jolene's records and see what she has hidden. Of course, I would like to have you join me."

She thought about it for a minute and slowly began to nod. "I think that would work."

"*Excelente*!" Jorge replied with vigor and took another gulp of wine, noting that his glass was already half empty. "It will be fun! You'll get to work next door to Diego when he's there and we can work together. Maybe occasionally lock the door and have some afternoon delight, you know what I mean? And soon, the office will be Hernandez - Silva Inc. - *perfecto*!"

"You know, I do kind of like that idea," Paige said thoughtfully as she took another sip of wine. "That does have a ring to it."

"Ah! You and I, we will take over the world," Jorge said and leaned in to give her a quick kiss.

"There's a lot of changes happening awfully fast, are you sure?" Paige asked with some hesitation, her eyes suddenly appearing tired as she stared at the nearby bottle of wine. "This is a lot."

"I work fast, baby, if you have not noticed," Jorge teased before reaching for the rest of the bottle and offering it to Paige, who shook her head, he poured the rest in his own glass. "Everything I do is fast. I already sent a message to the lawyers to change the name. Jolene is out. I am not sure what to do when she gets out of rehab."

"Will she be leaving rehab?" Paige asked suspiciously, her long eyelashes flickering rapidly. "Or..not?"

"We will see," Jorge said and took another drink of wine. "However if she does, it won't be anytime soon. Her addiction, it is quite strong and we are paying for her to be well looked after for now. In the future, we will see."

"Fair enough," Paige nodded in agreement and took another drink of her wine. "I have to say, I've been thinking of making some changes myself."

"Oh?" Jorge moved closer to her, he could smell the delicious scent she wore; in her hair, her clothing, he wasn't sure but it was enticing. "And what would that be?"

"The life coach thing," She replied with a long, tired sigh. "I don't want to do it anymore."

"Well, *mi amor*, you do not have to," He gently reminded her as he kissed her neck. "You can do whatever pleases you now. You do not have to be an assassin either and if you wish to, we will find a way to work the money into our bank accounts with ease, through one of our businesses."

"The problem is that I'm sort of at the point," Paige continued as she snuggled up closer to him. "People are expecting me either to go on a speaking tour or write a book and I have no interest in either. This was only a front."

"I have an idea for you," Jorge suggested as he moved away from her briefly to finish his wine and set the glass on the table before returning to her side, his arm slipping over her back. "You can say you are taking a break to help your husband with his business. Does that make sense?"

"I was thinking kind of in the same line," Paige said, an apprehensive smile crept on her face. "Except that, I'm helping Alec with his campaign."

"Ugghh," Jorge said and moved back slightly. "I do not like this idea so much."

"It would make sense though," Paige insisted and turned more toward him. "Think about it. He's all for making the world a better place and I can say that I felt a calling to help him in his endeavor and of course, I will fade into the background during my hiatus. It works out perfectly."

"I like my idea better," Jorge spoke with some jealousy in his heart.

"You have nothing to worry about," Paige insisted and shook her head. "I thought you liked Alec."

"I do," Jorge insisted. "I like that I can contribute to his campaign if he does decide to run and that he will be in my pocket. I do not, however, like the idea of you working closely with him. This does not appeal to me. I want you to spend your days with me not…this Greek God."

"Ok, once again, he's an ex-boyfriend from a long time ago," Paige assured him as she gently touched his leg, a slight distraction from the topic. "There's nothing there and my contribution will probably be minor. It's more an excuse to get away from the site. I don't plan to run his campaign office or go door to door, nothing like that."

"I do not like you being front and centre in the media either," Jorge said while shaking his head. "You want to keep out of the spotlight."

"I'm kind of already in it with the site," Paige reminded him.

"I suppose," Jorge spoke with hesitation. "I guess, my dream is selfish. I want to spend every moment with you and I thought the office would be ideal."

"I can work at the office and help keep things organized," Paige assured him. "I mean, I don't know what Alec wants me to do yet but I'm thinking of helping him shoot videos to put online, social media, that kind of thing. Sort of behind the scenes."

"You mentioned speaking to him today," Jorge said with some reluctance and moved closer to his wife again, feeling his body relaxing with the wine. "Is this what you talked about?"

"Actually, that's what I meant to tell you," Paige said as she finished her own wine and sat the glass down. "I guess the people interested in him running for his party gathered for a meeting last night. Alec was actually feeling a bit apprehensive about everything. Like maybe he bit off more than he could chew and there was some reluctance about getting involved with you, given what that means."

"He felt apprehensive that he might be essentially working for me?" Jorge asked with a raised eyebrow. "Does this man not understand that politicians, they are put there by people like me? That they have a job because people like me invest in them and in return, we ask for a few favors from time to time?"

"Yes, honey, I believe he got the 'dance with the one who brought you' reference from the day you met," Paige eased in closer to him with a grin on her face. "I think that might've scared him a bit."

"Why? I am not a scary man, am I?" Jorge asked with a raised eyebrow as he moved his face close to his wife's as his breathing grew labored.

"Not to me but apparently, you are to him," Paige said with a grin as her hand ran up his thigh. "He essentially went to the meeting unsure of what to do. He thought the odds were against him because of some of the other people running in his district. They have money, more education, status in the community because he's merely a counselor in a poor neighborhood, he doesn't have a lot of disposable income and has no connections."

"He has me," Jorge smugly commented. "What more does he need?"

"Well, that's the thing," Paige continued. "He feared that someone who owned dispensaries and has sex parties mightn't be the best option as an investor, that maybe his party would turn their noses up at the idea. So he decided to go for broke and tell them who he had as a potential investor in his campaign."

"And?"

"And he wasn't able to read their reaction," Paige continued and paused briefly. "However, this morning, he received a call that every one of his opponents has opted to drop out for some reason. Do you know anything about that?"

"I can honestly say, no I do not," Jorge said with a self-satisfied smile on his face. "But, of course, the people, they love me! I also enjoy the fact that my name, it does carry some weight in this city."

"Not bad for someone who's relatively new to the country," Paige observed. "So apparently, each of the other people running will take turns officially dropping out of the race but in the end, Alec will be the last man standing. Everyone in the party will be backing him when the Federal election takes place."

"And that is?"

"This fall."

"And they are campaigning this soon?"

"Unofficially."

"I see, so it seems the Greek God will need my help after all," Jorge said and his eyes scanned the room as he thought.

"So promise me something," Paige gently asked as she squeezed his thigh. "You won't threaten him. You'll be fair."

Their eyes met again but before he could respond, Maria's bedroom door swung opened and she walked out in her nightdress. Glancing toward the couch, she wrinkled her nose.

"You guys aren't going to have sex on that couch are you?"

"Maria!" Jorge snapped at her without intending to and he noted that Paige moved away, if even slightly. "What have I told you about saying inappropriate things?"

"But *Papa*, the two of you, you looked as if you were about to do sexual things in the middle of the living room and…"

"We are having a glass of wine and discussing the day," Jorge said and took a breath, knowing that he was overreacting to the situation. "It is not unusual for a married couple to do such a thing."

"It looked very different from here," Maria insisted as she continued to walk toward the bathroom.

"Maybe you should tell her about the bar," Paige coaxed. "I think she would be excited."

"Oh, yes," Jorge said and began to calm slightly. "Maria, I was talking with Chase today and we think that the bar, we will be changing it in the near future. We want to make it more sophisticated, more classy and maybe change the name and Chase, he has suggested we name it after you."

His daughter's eyes lit up with excitement. "*Papa*, did *he* say that?"

"Yes, it was his idea," Jorge replied, knowing this was a bit of a stretch, as he watched his daughter's face fill with excitement. "This, I cannot take credit for."

Maria let out a squeal and rushed back into the bedroom, closing the door behind her.

"Chase, it seems, had a good idea," Jorge said with a smile.

"You do realize," Paige said as she gestured toward Maria's closed door. "That your daughter has a huge crush on Chase, right?"

"What?" Jorge said with the same sharp tone as he had used to speak to his daughter. "She's ten!"

"Ten-year-olds can have crushes."

"Oh, I do not like this," Jorge shook his head. "She is too young for this!"

"It's harmless and at least you know it's someone safe," Paige reminded him. "Let this one go."

"Me, I let everything go," Jorge was insistent and took another deep breath. "Eventually."

Chapter 28

"*Paige!*" Diego's voice could be heard as soon as they walked into the office the following morning. He excitedly rushed toward her with a bouquet of flowers in hand. Jorge watched with amusement as the Colombian immediately ushered Paige down the hallway leaving him standing at the door.

"I cleaned up Jolene's old office for you and I think you're going to love it," Diego continued to speak at a rapid pace while Paige nodded as she listened, the loud click of her heels could be heard as she walked away. Jorge stood at the door and reached for his buzzing phone while watching his wife's ass wiggle in the tight skirt.

What time is the meeting this morning?

Chase, we will meet with the staff for a short meeting and Jesús is now on his way. As soon as you can make it.

Sliding the phone back into his pocket, he looked up to see his cousin Sylvana walking toward him.

"So I see the king has arrived, does that mean we're starting our meeting shortly?" She asked with her usual attitude, showing little concern for what others thought; his cousin was as much a Latina as she was Italian.

"Well, I *have* arrived, however, our meeting, it will be in a few minutes," Jorge spoke candidly, showing little resistance to her sarcasm, he merely pointed toward the hallway and started to walk. "First, I must go remind Diego that I am also here. He seemed to have forgotten when Paige walked in."

"So you haven't been in the office yet?" Sylvana asked with humor in her voice before turning to walk with Jorge.

"Ah, no…"

To that, Sylvana merely grinned before slipping into the boardroom, where the other staff waited for the meeting. Jorge went into Jolene's former office and immediately stopped in disbelief. There were balloons, streamers, and a small cake placed before a rather stunned Paige behind the desk, while Diego continued to talk while putting the flowers in a vase.

"We can always paint the office too if you want."

"Diego! What the hell is this?" Jorge pointed around the room. "Is a five year old having a birthday party here later today or what? I feel like a unicorn is about to jump out from behind the door. Did you forget that we *both* will be working from this office?

"I didn't forget," Diego replied while standing up straight and fixing his tie. "Your desk is over there, in the corner."

Jorge glanced over his shoulder at the empty, pathetic desk and chair.

"Honey, we can share this desk," Paige commented as she slowly moved the cake aside. "This is for *you* too."

"Well…" Diego replied with a shrug, as he twisted his lips in an awkward pose. "I guess.."

"Yeah, where the fuck are my flowers, Diego?" Jorge asked as he continued to inspect the room. "We should probably go through Jolene's stuff. You know, to make sure there's nothing we should know about."

"I had Clara go through the office this morning," Diego referred to the 'cleaning lady'. "It's clean."

"The rest of the offices too?"

"*Perfecto!*"

"Well, then, we must get this meeting started," Jorge said while looking at Paige. "So do you need to put a tiara on my wife's head and escort her into the boardroom now or what is the procedure you have in mind, Diego?"

Paige grinned as she stood up while Diego shot Jorge a dirty look.

"I was trying to make her feel welcome," He spoke defensively while starting toward the door. "This is her first day at the office."

"As it is mine," Jorge reminded him. "And yet, nothing for me, I noticed."

"Honey, you can have some of my flowers," Paige spoke softly as she touched his arm on the way toward the door. Laughing, Jorge followed behind.

The boardroom consisted of the primary staff of the office minus a few recent recruits, as everyone chatted together. Abruptly stopping as the three of them walked in, Marco from IT flashed a bright smile at the couple, while Sylvana merely gave a mischievous grin before glancing at Benjamin, the company's creative accountant. Beverly rushed in at the last minute, the former assistant to Jolene and Diego who was now in charge of the dispensary managers.

"This is going to be a short meeting," Diego insisted as he made his way to the head of the table and sat down, while Paige and Jorge sat beside Marco and across from the other three other staff members. "We don't have time to sit around and chit-chat all day. Too much work to do."

Jorge nodded with an amused expression before glancing at Paige.

"Now, as you know, Jolene has been out for a week," Diego said and suddenly hesitated, as if he couldn't speak. His eyes shot toward Jorge who immediately realized that perhaps through all this, he had wrongly assumed that Diego had no emotional reaction to his sister's deceit and addiction.

"Yes, well," Jorge cleared his throat while dismissively nodding at his friend before returning his attention toward the others who watched him carefully. "What Diego is trying to explain, is that Jolene is quite ill and needs some time away from the office. However, as you know, we are now very busy. For this reason, Paige and I," He pointed toward his wife, who merely nodded in response. "We will be here on and off to help out. I would assume one of us will be here most days, if not both, depending on our schedules. Diego, as you know, is often out of the office with other responsibilities, so we must jump in to help where we can."

"So, if anything needs approval, we check with you?" Benjamin spoke up.

"Yes, that is right," Jorge replied and nodded. "Now, some of your responsibilities may change and we may also have to hire. But for now, we would like to keep the office staff to a minimum."

"And the name is changing?" Marco asked beside him and Jorge nodded.

"Yes, we will soon be Hernandez-Silva Inc, we are just waiting for our lawyer to take care of it."

"The club too?" Beverly asked this time, a laptop opened in front of her.

"Yes, we are not 100% on the name yet but it is looking like Maria will be in it."

"Hey," Diego suddenly found his voice again. "How about the *Princesa Maria Lounge?*"

Sylvana let out a laugh. "Does that mean we'll have to change the name of this place to 'King Hernandez'?"

"And *Silva*," Diego replied while leaning forward on the table.

"No," Jorge shot Sylvana a humored look. "We will stick with the Hernandez-Silva."

"Can you let me know the details for sure, as soon as you know them?" Sylvana asked, taping on her iPad. "I will ask my new assistant to create a press release."

"Of course," Jorge agreed. "Me or Paige, we will keep you posted on everything."

Sylvana nodded and casually leaned back in the chair.

"I believe that covers everything we need to discuss for this morning," Jorge continued, glancing toward Paige. "Do you have anything to add?"

"No," She spoke in her usual gentle demeanor. "But please, if anyone has any suggestions or thoughts on how to improve anything, do let us know."

Jorge nodded in agreement, glancing toward Diego who did so with vigor; he was like a cartoon character from the olden days, with his bulging eyes and rapid movements.

"Well then, unless anyone has anything else to add?"

"I may have to talk to your lawyer regarding the name change," Benjamin threw in and glanced toward Marco. "We'll need an official date when the change is to take place. Everyone at this table will need to be on the same page."

"Of course," Jorge replied and nodded as he glanced toward the door noting that Chase and Jesús were waiting with two large boxes of donuts. "Now, unless there is anything else, please have a little snack before you continue with your day."

The room quickly cleared; one box of donuts going to the staff room while the other made it's way to the centre of the table. Diego rushed out of the room to get the coffee, while Jorge reached for a chocolate donut before turning to wink at his wife.

"*Mi amor*, a donut?" He asked casually and watched her turn up her nose at the suggestion. "A little sugar, it won't hurt you."

"It's not me that I'm worried about," She spoke gently as Jesús made his way into the room, followed by Chase. Both sat across from Jorge and Paige and Jesús reached for a maple filled donut. Diego rushed back into the room with a coffee pot in one hand, a tray of mugs, cream and sugar in the other.

"Ah, Diego! No apron today?" Jorge teased as he wolfed down half the donut. "It was such a good look for you."

"I took it home to wash," Diego replied casually as if it were the most normal question. Jorge nodded and chewed his donut. Jesús grinned but remained silent as Diego placed the tray on the table and everyone reached for a coffee mug. He carefully poured coffee in each cup before disappearing down the hallway with the pot and quickly returned empty handed. Glancing back and forth, as if he were checking out the surroundings before returning to the boardroom, he seemed more at ease in this, the second meeting of the day.

"Ok," Jorge spoke up just as the door closed and Diego sat down. "Today, we are meeting to clear up a few things about Jolene and this fucking mess."

"I can't believe she's in rehab," Chase commented. "I mean, I thought she was drinking a bit but I didn't know that it was…that bad." He glanced at Diego who looked down at the table.

"It, apparently, was a problem," Jorge replied.

"It's not the first time," Diego surprised them when he spoke in a soft voice. "We dealt with this situation before she moved to Canada. Except that time, I forced her to stop, no rehab. She stayed with me in California."

No one replied.

"You know," Paige suddenly spoke up. "It happened and we're dealing with it the best we can. She's where she should be now."

"But boss, I thought she was trying to kill you," Jesús asked while beside him, Chase appeared stunned by this news. "That is not...that is more than an addiction issue. I mean, I do not understand."

"Essentially, it was the police officer wanted me dead," Jorge explained. "He knew the religious fanatics also had the same goal and Jolene was their go between."

"No offense," Jesús said and raised his hand in the air, while beside him Chase continued to look astonished. "But that does not quite sound right to me. I feel like we are missing the whole story, you know? Why did she hide this from us?"

"Scared," Diego spoke up this time. "Jolene, her biggest fear is ending up in jail or being sent back to Colombia. If someone threatens to do either, she puts herself first. She doesn't think of anyone else."

"Well, at any rate," Jorge continued. "She was to tell this man when I would be in town, where I would be located in order to enable the killers to find and get me. But this, fortunately, did not happen."

"She made a big thing out of nothing" Diego cut in again. "Had she come forward at any point and told us, we could've helped."

"Yes," Jorge continued. "She has killed the man who was behind this, I checked with Hector earlier today. It is true. However, I still cannot trust her."

"Is that why we're changing the name?" Chase pointed toward the door. "Cause of this."

"Yes, we would prefer to distance ourselves from Jolene and we do not know how long she will be in rehab," Jorge said and cleared his throat, making a point of avoiding his wife's eyes. "At any rate, Paige and I will be here to help out while Diego isn't here to continue his… reign of terror."

Glancing to his right, he noted that Diego had a sinister grin on his face as he nodded.

"Also, we want to be here to keep on top of what is going on and make sure we're all headed in the same direction, especially where things are changing so quickly," Jorge said and thought for a moment and glanced at his wife. "Also, Paige and I will be helping out a political candidate in the Toronto area who plans to run in the next election."

"Oh yeah, you mentioned that," Chase asked with interest. "What party?"

"The party that is going to fucking win," Jorge replied with a laugh. "Who cares? Is there really a difference?"

"To a degree, they go along with their parties beliefs and values but…" Paige hesitated.

"But we will own this man."

"What's his name?" Chase asked.

"Alec Athas."

"Greek?" Diego suddenly lit up.

"*Straight*, Greek, yes," Jorge replied and glanced at his wife. "Straight, still, right?"

She nodded with a grin, which in turn, Jorge did to Diego who shrugged.

"As if I even asked that," Diego spoke with a pout. "I was just *interested.*" He casually reached for his phone.

"Well, I do think that's it for today," Jorge directed his attention at Jesús and Chase. "Ah yes and name changes! We are changing both the business names, I forget if I told you both. This will be Hernandez-Silva and also, the bar…"

"*Princesa Maria Lounge,*" Diego belted out.

"That is the suggestion on the table," Jorge said with a chuckle.

"I like it," Chase nodded in agreement. "Maria will love that we used her name."

"I guess that is what we will choose then," Jorge commented as he pushed his chair out. "We will discuss it more later."

Everyone started to get up except Diego who appeared mesmerized by his phone.

"Diego, he's straight," Jorge reminded him.

"I was just looking at the pictures," Diego snapped, shoving his phone in his pocket. "Can't a man look?"

On the other side of him, Paige grinned.

CHAPTER 29

With Jolene tucked away in rehab, Jorge thought for certain that he would finally have some peace of mind but this wasn't the case. While his beautiful wife slept peacefully beside him, he would lie awake thinking. For so many years, his life had been a tornado of insanity and for most of that time, Jorge had enjoyed the ride. But things were so different now.

Maria knowing who he really was had changed everything. Now he would always feel that she was watching him a bit closer and in turn, it was up to him to appear as an exceptional role model. While he knew that no parent was perfect, most had flaws that were overflowing in humanity compared to his own. It was no coincidence that many called him the devil, a monster and other vile things over the years. He had given people many reasons to think of him in that way and yet, it had never mattered until now. His daughter was his world and it was important she grow up into a normal, law-abiding citizen. His wish was full of hypocrisy but yet, Jorge didn't want this life for her. He didn't want her awake at 3 AM thinking about the possibility that someone might be out to kill her.

Paige worried about him a lot. This filled his heart. Jorge never had anyone worry about him before; his parents and relatives seemed to ignore his existence after Miguel's death. The irony of those absorbed in religion and God to quickly turn their backs on him as a child hadn't been lost on him and in many ways, he had spent most of his adult life rebelling against those same people. Hadn't every person he ever killed, the lewd behavior he displayed, hadn't every cruel thing he had ever done in part because of their coldness? Deep down, he was a rebel that pushed boundaries further than most and had never second-guessed a decision; until now.

Life looked different when you're surrounded by love. It makes you question some of your decisions and perhaps, makes you wonder which direction your soul should follow. At one time, he would've laughed at such a notion. Paige and her meditation exercises had freaked him out at first but now, he admired her ability to stay balanced in the most frustrating and insane situations. He was a man full of passion but often, Jorge allowed it to take him too far. It had ruled him in a way that often made him lose control of his life. However, there were sometimes ways to harness this same passion and to do some good in the world.

Alec Athas would be the man who could change everything. Unlike the others, Jorge would be working with him from day one on his upcoming campaign, as opposed to stepping in later when he was already established. This meant that he would be able to shape him into the man he should be both publicly and behind the scenes. Ideally, he was grooming a future prime minister. Anything was possible. The beauty of a man like Alec Athas is that he had an honest look, large, puppy dog eyes that women loved and grandmothers trusted. This was the kind of man who appeared clean on paper and at the end of the day, didn't people want to believe that their politicians were pristine? That their motives were for the greater good?

It was over breakfast the next morning that Alec explained to both Jorge and Paige that he was, at the time, not allowed to campaign. Officially, an election hadn't been called so it was necessary to show caution in how he presented himself, making certain that people didn't feel he was out trying to win their vote but merely 'socializing' within his district.

"I do not understand," Jorge commented in between bites of toast. "So everyone knows that an election is coming up this fall and yet, we have to pretend that it's not going to happen? Is this what you mean?"

"Essentially, kind of," Alec replied, his attention switching to Paige and although it was an innocent look, Jorge couldn't help but feel as if they were communicating with one another through their eyes. The two had a history and even though it happened many years earlier, perhaps some connections never fully dissolve. Returning his gaze to Jorge, he shrugged. "We have to follow these rules, unfortunately."

"But like most rules," Jorge began as he took a drink of his coffee, hesitating a moment to look out the window. It was another bitterly cold day in Toronto, as people passed by in heavy coats, scarfs, mitts as they rushed toward their destination. The sun was pouring in and gently touching their faces as he finally shrugged and turned his attention back to Alec. "We can work around them."

Alec didn't reply but merely nodded, even if it was with some hesitation.

"Once the others have bowed out and you are officially the candidate for your party in this district, can we not have some kind of...introduction into the community? A little party?" Jorge asked as he picked at his eggs. "I would think that would be reasonable, no?"

"Yes," Alec answered eagerly, his eyes growing in size. "Of course, I need to connect with my community to learn about the issues that matter to them. That's an important part of the process. We could have a get together with free food and people will come because they're curious. I can speak to them about my values while asking what they feel is important. I just can't ask for their vote, hang up campaign posters or create any kind of literature. At this point, it's about mixing in the community and making myself recognizable."

"Yes, this, it sounds good," Jorge agreed and began to eat again despite the uneasiness he felt. Glancing at his wife, he noted that she hadn't said much since they arrived at the restaurant, instead, she was picking at her food and remained silent. "*Mi amor*, what do you think? Does this make sense to you?"

"Of course," She replied and glanced only briefly at Alec before looking back at her own food. "We need someone who knows more about running a campaign, someone who will make sure we follow the rules and be prepared for whatever is ahead."

"But that's why I was thinking of you," Alec insisted as his eyes grew in size, something that perturbed Jorge as he glared at him from the other side of the table. "You're smart, Paige, you can figure out anything and help me get things started."

"I can't," She spoke apologetically while shaking her head. "Look, you need someone who knows this kind of thing and how to deal with the media, the proper procedure and that's not me. I think my role should stay behind the scenes, maybe social media or something."

Her gaze met Jorge's and he smiled, silently relieved that his wife wouldn't be getting too engrossed in this campaign. Before Alec could respond, Jorge quickly jumped in.

"And also, we are taking on extra responsibilities with the business for which I invest," Jorge commented as he boldly leaned forward with his dark eyes focused on Athas who, in turn, seemed to sit back in his seat. "We had to…remove someone from her position and Paige and I, unfortunately, had to step in to oversee the office. We have many changes coming up including the nightclub, our hope is to create a more sophisticated lounge to host future political events and, we are continuing to open more Our House of Pot locations throughout the city and eventually, the province and country."

"Wow, you're really tapped into what the public wants," Alec quickly commented as he pushed the rest of his food aside. He hardly touched his meal as if not hungry but only ordered it to appease them. "I walked by one of your shops the other day and it was quite busy."

"Give the people what they want," Jorge insisted with a smile. "That's my job as a businessman and that is also your job, as a politician."

"That's the problem, you can't always give people what they want," Alec replied with a shrug.

"But that is the thing, my friend," Jorge casually commented and finished the last of his eggs. "It is not for you to worry about giving them exactly what they want, you're merely the salesman, you convince them you are capable of solving all their problems. What you do after the election, is a whole other thing."

"But I do want to help," Alec insisted with undeniable sincerity, the kind that people would believe and vote for, Jorge was sure of it. "I want to do more for those who are living in poverty, so they can get ahead."

"I do appreciate your noble goals but people, they don't work that way," Jorge commented, noting a look of defeat in Alec's hopeful eyes. "Again, I do appreciate your hopes and dreams but my friend, I must tell you that many people are not self-motivated like you and I. You assume they are because you're that kind of person and so it is natural that you also feel that others would be the same if they could. Unfortunately, this is not always so."

His words came from experience. There were people like Diego and Jesús who had proven themselves ambitious and hard-working while many others had failed. Jolene would be a prime example of this; she had all the chances in the world and yet, she wasn't a strong woman but someone who turned to addictions during a time of weakness. Although the jury was still out on her, there were many others who had attempted to get his help along the way and most, Jorge noticed, grew to expect him to pick them up and carry them and not walk on their own two feet.

"I like to believe that if most people had a chance," Alec gently countered, "That they will prosper and thrive. I think most people need some hope, for someone to believe in them and to give them a boost. That's what our world needs."

"We do," Jorge agreed and nodded. "But even with that, there are only a few that will do what they must to thrive. These people are a small percentage of the world. They are the people who get up at dawn, the people who work beyond the hours that most think are suitable for their lifestyle. Do you think I sleep in most mornings? Do you think I do not deal with sudden, unexpected emergencies in the middle of the night? That is why I'm successful. Many, they would not do the things that I have done and that is why their lives never meet their expectations. Many want the pot of gold at the end of the rainbow but not many are willing to take the journey necessary to get there, unless it's convenient, unless it's easy, and unless it doesn't interfere with the football game that they want to watch or require them to sometimes lose a little sleep. That is, unfortunately, the reality of people."

Alec listened to his words, his face suddenly full of despair. "But if I'm not here to help, then what am I doing this for?"

"You *can* help," Jorge insisted, leaning ahead in his seat, making intense eye contact with the man across the table. "But do not believe you can help everyone. Do not extend your expectations when it comes to people because people, they often will disappoint you."

It was a harsh lesson and although Alec Athas was the same age as him and Paige, it was clear his idealistic ways had led him off into a fantasy world. Some people accepted a helping hand and made it matter while others just looked for more help. Some people are wolves but many, as Diego would say, were merely sheep. It was necessary that Alec be aware of this truth now from a man who had been a leader in his own world.

This was only one of many lessons he planned to teach Alec Athas.

CHAPTER 30

"I don't think he has the stomach for politics," Paige repeated a comment she had made a few times since Alec first approached them for help with his campaign. This time, it was in the SUV on their way home after they met with Alec for breakfast. "I think his intentions are good but when he gets out there and sees everything involved, I feel like it's going to crush him."

"Perhaps though," Jorge intercepted, his right hand in the air as he gestured toward the streets ahead of them. "Perhaps you are not giving him enough credit. This man, he's not the 19 or 20-year-old man who you knew long ago. We will do what we can to help him."

"While helping ourselves out?" Paige asked in her usual smooth voice; a question that would seem more like an accusation had anyone else asked it. She turned slightly and they made brief eye contact at the lights. "Even if he gets in his district, that doesn't mean that he will be able to help us as much as you think. His powers will still be limited."

"Ah, yes, limited today but he will still have connections," Jorge commented with a huge grin on his face as he reached out and gently touched his wife's hand, if only briefly. "However, it is the future I think of. My wish for him is to move up further and further until he has power over this country, until he has power in the world."

"You want him to become prime minister?" Paige's voice took an unexpected high pitch when she spoke and she began to laugh. "Wow! That seems….I don't know, that seems really far off if you ask me."

"But that is ok," Jorge spoke with determination as they drove into the underground parking. "I am a patient man."

"You're not a patient man," Paige replied with a giggle in her voice. "You're anything but patient."

"In *some* circumstances, yes, I am a patient man," Jorge corrected her as he parked the vehicle in the assigned spot, attempting to ignore her laughter. "However, I agree, I am not, for the most part, a patient man. In a situation such as this one, you must think long-term, not the here and now. This is a man I can work with and once he eventually gets to the top spot, he can do so much for me. His word, it will have a lot of power."

"I don't think you should get your hopes up," Paige replied after Jorge turned the SUV off and they sat in the dark parking garage. "I'm not sure if he is fierce enough to be a leader."

"That is the beauty of it Paige," Jorge replied as he turned toward his wife. "I am fierce enough for the both of us."

Alec would show a different side of himself later that week. Paige was at the office when he sent a brief message to Jorge indicating that a slight problem had developed. If she had been home that day, Paige would've witnessed a very different man arriving at their door.

"I need your help," Alec spoke abruptly as he rushed into the apartment and swung around just as Jorge closed the door behind him. With fury in his eyes, he jumped right into the issue. "Everyone has dropped out of the race except this one asshole who claims he had a change of heart."

"Really?" Jorge calmly asked as his brain quickly shot through the list of candidates that Alec had been up against. Gesturing toward the couch, Alec rushed across the room and sat down while Jorge chose a seat across from him. "So this man, who is he?"

"His name is Nicolas Costa Lambropoulos," Alec said while shaking his head, his face growing red. "And he's an asshole, always has been."

"Another Greek man? You know this man well?" Jorge asked as he relaxed in his chair. It was interesting to see this man, who normally displayed a calm, relaxed exterior, suddenly blow up over a rival. Now this, *this* was the kind of fire he wanted to see in a political candidate, if even just behind the scenes. "Tell me, is he any competition for you?"

"I don't know him well," Alec replied as he sat ahead on the couch.

"But he is full of himself. Plus, he attends the Greek Orthodox church every fucking week, so he's got all those people on his side and, some rich people in the community want to back him. *And* he's a lawyer so his job is more prestigious than a youth counselor."

The look of defeat on his face was undeniable. Alec was already expecting to lose to this guy, therefore, making Jorge have some, if only temporary, second thoughts about his choice of candidates.

"But you, my friend, you have me backing you," Jorge spoke with determination as he made brief eye contact with Alec who quickly looked down while shaking his head. "And you are also Greek, can you also not go to the church every week? Talk to the people, get to know their concerns?"

"I don't normally go to church," He commented sheepishly. "Religion, it's not my thing."

"Well, it is *now,*" Jorge corrected him and watched Alec slowly nod. "I'm not saying you have to do this for the rest of your life but for now, I would definitely make some efforts to get to know the people in that area in any way possible. People in the Greek community will want to see one of their own represent them, it only makes sense. Maybe you're more down to earth, more familiar with the real problems whereas the lawyer, he only knows the rich life. What does he know of the everyday people who are struggling to pay their bills or find affordable housing? Is this not a right? You must downplay his education as being mere window dressing but point out that he does not know the real struggles of people. You must point this out to your party. They will see."

"Actually, he worked while going to law school and paid his own way," Alec commented with a sigh while leaning against his hand. "Also, his parents were immigrants to this country, just like mine. Their son turned out to be a lawyer, it speaks of his drive and his ability to overcome. I'm just a counselor working with street kids and the poor."

"Do these poor people, do they not vote? Jorge was quick to point out. "Do you think they would vote for you?"

"But they don't have money and at this stage, my goal is to have a lot of people sign up as party members," Alec replied. "These people, they can't afford to pay for a membership."

"So in other words, the person with the money, they choose the candidate?" Jorge replied and shrugged. "And you, my friend, you have me and I have a lot of fucking money. Paige, she is the same, so you do not have to worry about this other man. We will pay for these memberships…on the sly, of course."

Alec seemed to brighten up slightly although his eyes were full of anxiety.

"At the end of the day," Jorge spoke thoughtfully. "This man, Lambropoulos, he will not give you trouble. He's holding out, trying to save the last of his dignity but I predict he won't stay in the race."

"I'm not so sure," Alec commented with a hopeful look in his eyes as he shook his head.

"My friend, you must lose this defeatist attitude," Jorge replied as he stood up to indicate their meeting was over. "You cannot allow such things to discourage you and you certainly can't focus on the opponent's good points and compare them to your own. This will only set yourself up for disaster."

His eyes were full of uncertainty when he left the apartment. Little did he know that he had chosen the perfect man to discuss his concerns. In fact, it briefly crossed Jorge's mind that perhaps that had been the plan all along. Perhaps Alec Athas was much more clever and conniving than he originally appeared. Had Jorge not seen a fire in his eyes? Had he not recognized a silent agreement between the two of them as Alec left the apartment?

Jorge made a few phone calls and the following morning, he contacted Diego.

"Do you have a few minutes to join me this morning?" Jorge asked as sat alone in the kitchen while his wife and daughter could be heard shuffling around their bedrooms. "I had a meeting with the Greek yesterday and there's a little situation we need to take care of first thing."

"Oh! I was hoping to meet Alec Athas," Diego spoke eagerly on the phone.

"Now, let's cool our heels for a second, Diego," Jorge spoke sternly into the phone. "First, unfortunately, we must take care of something but then, possibly we will drop by his office if he's free."

"Whatever he needs," Diego continued to speak excitedly into the phone. "You just tell me."

"I'll give you an address," Jorge commented while glancing at his laptop. "Meet me there as soon as you can."

Thirty minutes later, the two men stood outside a dingy apartment building in a less prosperous area of the city. In fact, it was the area where Alec worked with troubled youth and the poorer demographic of the city. If Diego was wondering why they were there, he didn't ask. He simply slipped on a pair of black leather gloves and followed Jorge up the staircase, since the elevator was apparently broken.

"You know, Diego, I hate my apartment," Jorge commented when they reached the third flight of stairs. "But at least, it is not this bad, you know?"

"I know, I know," Diego commented. "You should've seen the building I was in when I first moved to California as a kid."

"That, I have no doubt," Jorge commented and glanced at his phone briefly before gesturing down a dark hallway, the smell of fried food and garlic surrounded them causing his stomach to turn as they approached an apartment. A quick glance at Diego, he knocked at the door. The sound of rustling could be heard but no one answered. He knocked again and once again, no one answered.

"Moments like this, *amigo*, you gotta ask yourself," Jorge calmly posed the question and glanced toward the ceiling. "What would God do in this situation?"

"Pick the lock? Break down the door?" Diego offered.

"Let's try something else first," Jorge reached forward with a gloved hand, turned the knob and with a grin on his face, he noted the surprise in Diego's eyes. "Just a feeling I had."

Carefully opening the door, the two reached for their guns as they quietly eased into the small apartment. Automatically met by a pungent smell, Jorge ignored the cramped and unclean living room and kitchen combo and pointed toward a closed door. The two men eased closer and after making brief eye contact, Jorge abruptly pushed the door opened. On the other side was a man and woman in bed, naked; the man holding a crack pipe. Diego quickly reached for his phone and started to take pictures.

"Finally, I get the opportunity to meet the prestigious Nicolas Costa Lambropoulos in the flesh," Jorge jubilantly commented while pointing at the Greek man scrambling to hide a crack pipe while beside him, his whore merely pulled the covers up over her breasts, a look of disorientation on her face. "Although, I must say, *amigo*, much more flesh than I had hoped to see."

"Who the hell are you?" Nicolas shot back as he rushed to grab his clothes. "You can't just break in here."

"Well, you might say I'm an associate of Alec Athas and he thought that you and I, we should meet," Jorge continued to calmly explain while at his side, Diego continued to take pictures with his phone. "I guess this is perhaps not how he thought we would meet."

Beside him, Diego let out an evil laugh.

"Unfortunately," Jorge continued to watch Nicolas as he hastily dressed, his expensive suit sitting on a nearby chair. "Your beautiful wife, she did not know where I could find you. But of course, I have unlimited resources at my disposal."

With his shirt and underwear on, the Greek man suddenly stopped and turned in his direction, giving him an angry glare, while in the bed, the woman collapsed back as if this entire conversation was exhausting to her.

"You're Jorge Hernandez, aren't you?"

"Ah! My reputation, it proceeds me," Jorge smugly commented as the man continued to quietly dress. "Yes, I am the one and only Jorge Hernandez and I'm here to tell you that this day, it will be the day you step down from your campaign."

"Or you'll release the pictures?" He glared toward Diego.

"If you're lucky," Jorge commented casually. "But I'm thinking the police, they may be curious how you are associated with a dead crack whore." His eyes glanced toward the semi-conscious woman in the bed. "And this, my friend, could easily be arranged."

CHAPTER 31

….In an unexpected move, Nicolas Costa Lambropoulos has dropped out of the race leaving Alec Athas as the lone candidate. Lambropoulos said that he intends to fully support the campaign for Athas….

"Oh, he's so handsome!" Maria piped up from the kitchen as she watched the news, while slowly eating her bowl of cereal. Paige stopped what she was doing to turn around. Her eyes immediately swiped past her stepdaughter to Jorge, who sat beside Maria with a coffee in hand. Giving his wife a quick wink and grin, he shook his head.

"Not you too, Maria!" He teased and sat down his coffee cup. "Everyone's in love with the Greek God!"

Turning toward his wife, he noted that she was raising her eyebrows.

"Who else is in love with him?" Maria immediately asked.

"Ah, no one," Jorge replied and shook his head. "I heard a lot of people find him attractive. But tell me, Maria, if you were old enough, would you vote for him?"

"Oh yes!" Maria insisted as the story switched away to a stabbing in the Jane/Finch area of the city. "He's so handsome and he looks nice. He has pretty eyes."

"Pretty eyes, well that always works for me," Jorge teased and stood up from his seat, coffee cup in hand, he approached Paige who stood near the sink. Rinsing out his cup, he muttered. "Diego and I will meet with Alec shortly to discuss this turn of events."

"I'm not in love with Alec," Paige whispered as he got closer to her.

"I know," Jorge whispered back before leaning in to kiss his wife before winking at her again. "I was thinking Diego."

"Oh no," She sighed and shook her head.

"I got a feeling since he's got this thing for straight men," Jorge shook his head. "I'm going to talk to him."

"Please do."

After swinging by the table to give his daughter a quick kiss, Jorge headed for the door, phone in hand. Glancing at his messages, he noted that Diego was already on his way to the diner where the three of them were about to meet. Unfortunately, he would probably get there first and hopefully managed to keep calm and not show Alec his hyper, slightly fanatic side that was a little too much for most people to deal with, especially when first meeting him.

As he suspected, the two men were already seated in the diner when he got there. Even from across the room, Jorge immediately recognized Diego's usual bug-eyed, overly zealous demeanor but if it was making Alec nervous, he wasn't showing it. Instead, he appeared to take the conversation in stride as Jorge approached but he still appeared relieved to see a familiar face.

"Oh, Jorge," He stood up respectfully.

"There's no need to stand, my friend," He insisted while glancing around for a waitress. Catching the eye of an older woman rushing table to table, he shot her his usual charming smile. "Coffee, when you get a chance?"

"Yes, of course," She replied before rushing off and Jorge joined the others at the table. He immediately noted that Diego suddenly got quiet.

"I see you've met," Jorge asked as he looked at the two men. "Did I miss anything?"

"We were just talking about his campaign," Diego replied, his eyes growing larger with each word. "We gotta find an office for him."

"That shouldn't be too difficult," Jorge replied just as the waitress brought his coffee to the table. After thanking her, he returned his attention to the two men. "So, tell me, Alec, did you see the news this morning?"

"I...I don't know what happened," Alec started to speak with a look of doubt in his eyes while a grin crept on his lips. "I didn't think Lambropoulos was going to drop out. He seemed quite determined earlier this week and late last night, I learned the news. I was surprised."

"That's what I thought," Jorge said while giving an expressionless Diego a quick look before returning his attention to Alec. "You know, to save face, he would wait a few days before dropping out. He probably never wanted it in the first place. Now he has brought some extra attention to his law practice…perhaps that is why he got involved in the first place, no?"

"He *did* mention his law practice when he dropped out," Alec commented, his eyes jumping from one man to the other. "Come on guys, be straight with me here. If we're going to work together, I want to know, did you guys speak with him?"

"As a matter of fact, we did," Jorge confirmed, impressed by Alec's directness. Once again, he felt there was more to this man than met the eye. "Diego and I had a brief word with him yesterday."

"What did you say?" Alec asked and then put his hand up. "Wait, do I want to know this?"

"Well, it's not so much what we said," Diego said as he twisted his mouth into a pout. "It's more, you know, when we chose to speak with him."

"Ah, yes, your nemesis, he has some interesting ways of spending his free time," Jorge said as his lips fell into a sadistic smile. "Diego, maybe you should show him the pictures."

"With pleasure," He replied with too much enthusiasm but then again, that was Diego, always extreme in his moods and desires. Reaching for his phone, he pulled it out, tapped at the screen briefly and moved closer to Alec, his fingers swiping across the screen while the Greek politician didn't appear as surprised as Jorge expected.

"I had heard about this," Alec said as his hand pointed toward Diego's phone and he seemed to freeze, a smile spread across his lips. "But, I mean, it was a rumor. How the hell did you ever get these?"

"Sometimes, *amigo*, you got to sniff out the bread crumbs and follow the trail," Jorge replied as his eyes squinted with his smile while Diego put his phone away. "Fortunately, I happen to know some people in the right places and well, Diego and I paid him an early morning visit. Apparently sticking his mouth on a dirty whore followed by a crack pipe is his idea of a breakfast of champions. I guess his soccer mom wife and her bowl of Cheerios weren't quite doing the trick."

Alec laughed, almost in shame, as he looked away and calmed only briefly, to only look back again and laugh even harder. "Holy fuck!"

"So you see, this is not a good man to represent your district," Jorge quietly commented, as he enjoyed Alec's reaction to this news. "The last thing Toronto needs is another politician being outed as a crackhead. Your city, it barely recovered after the last fiasco."

"Toronto is a city that bounces back," Alec said after finally composing himself. He reached for his coffee and took another drink. "Besides, there's been some more scandalous politicians since, that have taken the attention off our city."

"Yes, well, to some it is all about power," Jorge replied and cleared his throat. "And do not misunderstand, power is good but there must be a nice balance between power and humility, between strength and understanding in order to be a successful politician. I've been a political observer for years and the ones who get the furthest are the ones who stay calm, balanced and in control and yet, listen to the people. Unfortunately, those who are weak, those who have something to prove, they tend to choose the more tyrant approach because deep down, they know they have nothing of substance to offer."

"You, my friend," Jorge continued. "You have much to offer and with our help, I assure you, there is no problem we cannot resolve." He glanced at Diego. "Me, I enjoy solving problems."

"Thank you," Alec said with sincerity in his eyes and voice. "I do appreciate it."

"As I've said before, we will work together on this and you *will* get in."

Jorge noted how quiet Diego was throughout the short meeting but this was about to change after Alec left.

"I *like* him," Diego said as he leaned forward as if sharing a big secret with Jorge.

"Not this again, ok?" His reply was abrupt but it was clear that Diego needed a quick reality check. "I am not having you crying on my couch again because you fell for a straight man. I am telling you, Diego, you must stop doing this, you are only hurting yourself."

With a slightly defeated expression, he slumped over in his chair and Jorge immediately felt bad.

"Look, Diego, look outside," Jorge gestured toward the nearby window as the sun shone in. "There are tons, *tons* of gay men out there and that, *that* must be your focus. As a straight man, I tell you that we don't wake up one day and suddenly feel like we want to put a cock in our mouth or anywhere else. It's not happening."

"You would be surprised," Diego countered. "How many so called straight men actually would."

"Yes, well, let's think about what you just said," Jorge insisted. "Do you think they are *really* straight? Clearly no and also, if they are hiding this part of themselves, what does that say to you? Do you want to be someone's secret boyfriend?"

Diego fell silent, his eyes full of sadness. "I know, I don't know why..."

"Because Diego, you do not value yourself enough," Jorge was insistent. "And perhaps it is because you once had to hide this part of yourself while growing up in Colombia. When you finally did tell your father, how did that go? Not well, correct? Perhaps that left you with a negative message. This is perhaps something Paige would be more helpful with than me."

"I think it's, you know, the challenge," Diego said thoughtfully. "Like, gay guys are easy to get but straight guys...."

"Why do you need a challenge?" Jorge countered. "Relationships, they are challenging enough without finding new ones."

"I don't know."

"Exactly, talk to Paige."

"I'm planning your wedding," Diego piped up, his eyes bulging out again. "That's a challenge."

"Yes, *amigo*, this is not news."

"No, I mean, I'm setting a date for your wedding," Diego spoke with insistence. "Because you people are fucking impossible. I can't properly plan anything without a date so I'm picking one for you. That's *my* challenge."

"When I say challenge," Jorge spoke calmly. "I meant, take up a sport, go boxing with Chase, I don't know."

"I think he's moving soon," Diego suddenly grew quiet again, his emotions all over the place, it was hard to keep up. "He's been looking at some places this week."

"Well, Diego," Jorge spoke with affection in his voice. "I hate to say it but I think this is the best for you both. I don't feel this is healthy."

"It's hard, you know? I'm so used to having him around."

"I know, Diego, I do," Jorge spoke gently. "But you, you must focus on other things. Before me and Paige get married, we need a house. This real estate agent is a fucking *idiota,* we are no better off than before when we were looking for ourselves."

"Let me find your house," Diego perked up slightly. "I will talk to Paige and see what she wants and we will do it together."

"*Perfecto!*" Jorge grinned and nodded. "You find us a place, then we'll pick a wedding date."

"I know Paige, she don't like looking," Diego spoke with his usual vigor, showing that his disposition improved upon giving him a more feasible challenge. "She's getting frustrated."

"As am I, my friend," Jorge replied. "As am I."

"Look, I don't normally do this," Diego leaned forward with some apprehension in his face. "I don't normally break a confidence but between you and me, Paige is worried."

"About?"

"You."

"Me? I'm fine, I'm eating better, exercising more, I'm healthy," Jorge insisted even though, it concerned him that his wife continued to worry.

"Nah, not about that," Diego replied and looked apprehensive to continue. "She's worried about the police, the man who tried to kill you, she worries there are others. Please don't tell her I said anything but she's checking with her sources to see if there is anything going on behind the scenes."

Jorge slowly shook his head. "I wish, I wish she would not worry so much, you know? I think a missing police officer might actually send a strong message."

"She's afraid they will retaliate."

Jorge fell silent.

CHAPTER 32

He should've taken it more seriously and yet, he didn't. It wasn't impossible that one of the *policia* was trying to kill him but yet, the concern didn't weigh him down. For some reason, having Jolene out of the picture brought him some relief and the truth was most of the time, someone probably wanted him dead. He was a man who incited anger in many so it seemed a bit redundant to worry about it. Being vigilant was necessary.

Of course, Paige wouldn't see things that way. She loved him so much and in likelihood, valued his life much more than he did himself. This was often hard to comprehend, having grown up a neglected child followed by spending his youth as a lone wolf, a man who boasted of having no emotional connection to anyone. Those were the days when alcohol and drugs were his temporary relief on the occasions when loneliness filled his heart but it never lasted. A part of him felt he deserved this misery therefore, he simply allowed it to flow through him, taking out his torment on others. It was only after the birth of his beautiful daughter that this changed. Both her and Paige were his whole world and without them, he would disappear into a world of darkness.

He spent the rest of the day touring all the pot shops with Diego, followed by a brief conversation with Jesús about progress at the BC distribution centre and finally dropping by the office to go over numbers with Benjamin. Around 6 o'clock, Jorge finally went home. Although the day had been hectic, his thoughts were never far away from the confession Diego shared with him that morning. He needed to figure a way to relieve his wife's fears.

It wasn't until they were climbing into bed later that night that he decided to slowly work his way to the topic.

"So earlier today, I mentioned to Diego that we were having a lot of difficulties finding a house and he volunteered to help out," Jorge commented while watching his wife take a drink of water, her blue eyes glanced at him as he spoke. "I thought, you know, why not? He seems to enjoy these kinds of things and perhaps he will have more luck than us."

She didn't reply at first, setting the glass back on the nightstand and pulling the covers up over her nightgown. Although the apartment was warm enough for him, he noted that his wife was often cold. Perhaps it was a woman thing? Her eyes were pensive as she shook her head.

"That's sweet of him but he doesn't have time," Paige replied as she moved closer to Jorge, a faint hint of vanilla swept over him as she leaned in. "Every time I talk to Diego, he's so crazy busy."

"That is just Diego, he's wired all the time," Jorge reminded her as he slid his arm around her shoulder. "The thing is he needs to have something productive to do so he won't do something destructive in his own life."

Paige didn't reply but quietly listened.

"Chase is moving out," Jorge announced but could tell by the expression on his wife's face that this was not new information to her. "And I do think it is for the best but at the same time, I know it is hurting Diego a lot. I thought perhaps it would be a good time to find him something to preoccupy his mind, something he might enjoy. It is a different experience for him since he does not feel the pressure as we do."

Paige grinned and looked down, her long eyelashes fluttered as she took a deep breath and shrugged. "If you think this will help him?"

"Trust me, the alternative, it would not be good," Jorge shook his head as he thought about Diego's intrigue with Alec Athas earlier that day. "For some reason, that I do not understand, Diego has this obsession with men who are not gay. I don't know if this is because his *daddy* years ago actually started off as a married, supposedly straight man, that he believes that every man is secretly gay or because he had to pretend to be straight as a teenager but it is not healthy for him. He is becoming slightly interested in Alec and so I say, Diego, you must let this go. This man is not attracted to other men. Why do you do this when there's a whole world of gay men out there? I do not understand."

"Yes, I hear what you're saying," Paige nodded in understanding as she briefly glanced at her wedding ring before sharing a smile with Jorge. "I think he's lonely and having Chase leave is kind of like taking another hit. You know Diego, he's not someone who relates to people well. He's erratic and sometimes a little crazy but under all that, he has a big heart. Plus with his lifestyle, it's not like he can share everything with just anyone. Chase knows who he really is."

"And accepted him," Jorge agreed as he squeezed her shoulder. "As you do with me."

"Of course I accept you," Paige confirmed as she moved closer and he momentarily had to fight his desires in order to remind himself where he was going with this conversation. "Am I really that different from you?"

Her eyes were studying his, as she crouched down slightly, like an animal about to devour her prey, it was almost impossible to fight off his natural inclination to give into his lust but it was necessary to first relieve Paige of her worries.

"You know, then again, maybe Alec is gay," Jorge's sudden comment seemed to send a bolt of lightning through Paige as she sat upright again. "I mean, you know, maybe Diego senses something from him, you know? I noticed he doesn't seem to have a girlfriend either."

"Alec?" Paige made a face and shook her head, a halted grin seemed to touch her lips. "I don't think so."

"But you did say that your relationship ended many years ago," Jorge pointed out and briefly looked away from her before continuing. "Maybe there are some things you do not know about him."

"I'm pretty sure that's not one of them," Paige was insistent but he noted that she had no emotions in her eyes and that gave him some relief. "Alec is a complicated guy. He has strong ideas about marriage and commitment and unfortunately, they've been a bit too confining for most women."

"Oh really?" Jorge let out a laugh. "Not one of these 'women need to be in the kitchen' kind of men, is he?"

"No, not like that," Paige appeared reluctant to continue. "Like, if he goes on a date, he's overly analytical of the woman and not just enjoying their time together. No one can ever survive that for long because eventually, he'll spot something that makes him reluctant and he pulls back. He sees that as a 'sign' rather than possibly a potential lesson, it's hard to explain."

"So why did you two break up?" Jorge asked bluntly and immediately noted the strange look on her face. It wasn't that he wanted to bring up painful memories, but it was something that had weighed on his mind since meeting the moralistic politician. "I mean, I'm curious what happened."

"It was…." Paige appeared hesitant. "It was a long time ago, we were young, not very mature."

"I understand that," Jorge commented. "But I am surprised you have remained friends. Many former lovers don't stay in each other's lives after a breakup."

"I don't know, I guess because he was my first, serious boyfriend," Paige continued to appear uncomfortable with the topic which caused fear to creep into his heart. What if she still had some leftover emotions for him? "He was a genuine, nice person who accepted me and then after I killed that man for him, I guess it connected us on a different level."

"A secret that connected you?" Jorge attempted to understand while his heart raced.

"Yes, I guess you could say that," Paige nodded and their eyes met. There was more. He could see it. "To be honest, I regret doing it. I knew that he'd eventually have a hard time accepting his role in the murder. I feel that is why he goes to such lengths to help people now…because he feels the need to give back what he took away."

"Very noble," Jorge replied and took a deep breath. "I guess, it depends on one's view. Me, I don't feel regret for my role in anyone's death especially if I feel they have or want to hurt me or my family."

Their eyes met in silence.

"You know, if anyone ever *thought* of hurting you or Maria," Jorge whispered. "I would kill them in the most barbaric way possible. I would make them suffer for every last second of their lives and wish they had not been born."

"I would do the same for both of you," She whispered back.

"*Mi amor*, you know of course, that we are safe," Jorge spoke gently as moved closer to her and Paige leaned in to hug him. "Jolene is away, our enemies know that we are a powerful force, everything, it will be fine."

As she let go of him, he saw tears in her eyes.

"I don't know that," She finally spoke in a whisper. "I keep thinking about that woman who was with the cop that threatened Jolene. The one who saw the cocaine in her purse. Who was she? What if there are others after you?"

"This is not happening with me," Jorge was insistent. "We will not allow them to control us with intimidation or fear. Plus this other policeman, I was assured that he was working on his own."

Paige didn't respond.

"Look, *mi amor*, what will make you feel better about all of this?" He finally asked, unsure of what else to do. "You tell me what I can do to make you feel better and I will do it."

Her silence continued as her eyes stared at her wedding ring for a long time while beside her, he patiently waited.

"We can never be sure," Jorge finally continued, nervous when she didn't speak. "But I have control in this situation. I've spoken to the people who I…deal with in both local police and RCMP and I think you're worrying about nothing."

She started to cry and he automatically pulled her close.

"You must not worry," Jorge felt his heart lurch in fear. "I am fine. *We* will be ok."

"I lied to you earlier," Paige sobbed and pulled away from him. "When I said Alec and I broke up just because we were young and stupid."

"It does not matter," Jorge automatically assured her, his voice gentle as he rubbed her back. "Please forget I asked. That has nothing to do with us."

"I can't have children," She blurted out through her tears.

"Paige," He spoke affectionately as he pulled her closer. "This is not a concern to me. You know I'm content with just Maria. This was never an issue."

And then he realized something. This wasn't about him.

CHAPTER 33

"It's a beautiful day for some beautiful tequila," Jorge had the full attention of both Chase and Diego as he walked in the door of the closed nightclub, holding a bottle in the air. While Chase had no reaction other than a look of curiosity, Diego's eyes bugged out in their usual way and a rare smile lit up his face.

"Oh, that stuff is the *best!*" He remarked as Jorge joined them at the bar. Sitting the bottle on the counter, he didn't even have to ask for shot glasses because Diego had already rushed past Chase to grab some from the corner. Slapping them on the counter and rubbing his hands together in delight, he resembled a kid on Christmas morning as Jorge opened the bottle and poured them each a hearty shot. "This *must* be good news!"

"It is my friend," Jorge replied and pushed one toward a reluctant Chase, who appeared nervous. "Drink up my friend!"

"It's barely noon," Chase said with a nervous laugh. "We're drinking this early in the day?"

"Come on! What's going on?" Diego interrupted Chase, who reluctantly joined the other two picking up a shot glass, his nose wrinkling slightly. "Did you guys find a house? Set a wedding date *finally?* Did you kill someone today?"

Although Jorge was well aware that the last question was to tease more than a sincere inquiry, he merely let it go with a laugh.

"Diego, not everything is about our personal lives," Jorge reminded him. "Some things, they are still about business and this, my friend, is good news! We are now standing in *Princesa Maria Lounge* and when you return to the office later today, you will be stepping into Hernandez-Silva Inc. That, I do believe is worth a shot."

"Ohhh!" Diego commented before letting out an evil laugh as the three men tapped their shot glasses together before knocking them back at the same time.

"Ahh! That's the good stuff!" Diego exclaimed while beside him, Chase made a face.

"Only the best for us, Diego, only the best," Jorge was insistent. "We must celebrate the fact that Jolene is no longer connected to this business, the sex party business is *terminado* and we are officially all about pot and this here, our classy lounge bar."

"So now what? What do I do?" Chase appeared confused and Jorge immediately began to shake his head. "I mean, I'm a little lost."

"Benjamin is sorting things out at the office today and he will be here tomorrow to go over the details for accounting," Jorge replied as he poured himself and Diego another shot, while Chase shook his head no. "But essentially, we clean up this place and make it more upscale. Apparently, our new friend Alec Athas knows some contractors that can help us immediately."

"Ahhh…the Greek!" Diego said with a smile before knocking back his shot. Jorge made a face and did the same.

"Yes, indeed, the Greek is already becoming a valuable asset to me," Jorge replied as he pushed his glass aside. "It is unfortunate that he is from my wife's past."

"So, he was an ex-boyfriend of Paige?" Chase asked with a raised eyebrow. "I'm actually kind of surprised that you're working with him."

"Because you're super fucking jealous," Diego added in his usual blunt way. "You don't even like *me* hanging around Paige and I'm *gay*."

"Ok, first," Jorge said while putting his hand up defensively, "Diego, I have *never* said that it's just that in the beginning, I felt it was necessary to keep business and personal separate."

"But we aren't separate," Diego spoke with passion as he waved his hands around. "We're family here, not just business associates. Our connection runs deeper than that."

"Yes, Diego and now I see that," Jorge admitted. "But you are right, I can be a *tad* jealous, ok? I know."

"More than a tad," Diego said with widened eyes. "Remember that time some guy was hitting on Paige in the grocery store lineup."

"I leave for a second to get an avocado," Jorge attempted to defend himself to Chase while Diego stood nearby with a sadistic grin on his face. "I come back and this man is flirting with my wife! How disrespectful! It is not as if he didn't see us together or the ring on her finger."

"Paige said you made a scene."

"I did not make a scene," Jorge insisted to them both. "I raise my voice a bit, that is all."

"But Paige said…."

"No no, we are not talking about this anymore," Jorge immediately cut him off and noted the humored look on Diego's face while Chase was expressionless. "The point is yes, I can be a *little* jealous but that is a normal human emotion."

"So, this Athas guy is helpful?" Chase asked as if to steer the conversation away from the jealousy issue, while Diego started to make a pot of coffee.

"I tell you, this man, he knows everyone," Jorge commented as he tapped his finger on the bar as if to make a point. "People that actually want to work, they are more than happy to have this job. So, we will hire them, make this place beautiful and have a grand reopening."

"Oh! Can I plan the party?" Diego piped up while Chase joined in with an enthusiastic nod.

"Yes, can *he* plan the party cause this here," Chase now started to shake his head. "Isn't for me? This grand reopening, I have no idea what to do."

"Leave it to me and The Italian," Diego referred to Sylvana. "We will work out the details. You hire the staff and order in what we tell you and that's it."

"I was thinking," Chase began as he glanced at the coffee as it started to drip into the pot. "I'm not exactly used to working or being in a classy, upscale bar. What do I know?"

"Chase, it's really the same," Jorge replied with a grin. "People are people, you know? Rich people, poor people, they are all the same. Except that the rich people, they will pay to be made feel as if they are special. They want to believe they are more important than they actually are and you cater to that illusion. It is not different from the sex parties, either way, you're catering to a fantasy because most of these people, they are no better than anyone else but they need to feel as if they are and that, my friend, is what you make them believe."

"Smile, be polite, compliment the women," Diego piped up as he leaned more toward Jorge as he spoke. "Act as if they are VIP…"

"Charge them about three times what the watered down liquor is actually worth," Jorge added while waving his hand in the air. "Have some expensive beverages available so they can be seen drinking liquor that secures their status in the community. Give them nice chairs to sit on, beautiful paintings on the wall and we will put some windows facing the street so people can see them inside because, in the end, that is what they want; am I correct Diego?"

"That is what they want," Diego agreed with a nod. "*And* attractive, well-dressed servers."

Chase seemed satisfied with the answer and Jorge quickly moved on.

"We must make this place *perfecto* for Alec's political events because we will definitely have some here. That will also help get the bar some extra attention."

"You gotta meet this guy," Diego said to Chase then back at Jorge. "He's a smart man, good ideas, he seems to care about people."

"Yes, a regular saint," Jorge sniffed and gestured toward the pot of coffee. "Diego, I could really use a cup. I didn't get much sleep last night."

"Ah, a night of romance keep you up?" Diego asked with a menacing grin on his face as he reached for three coffee cups.

"What?" Jorge made a face. "Oh, Diego, you make it sound like we are an old married couple who schedules sex. No, I do not mean that I mean….it wasn't a good night."

Diego stopped in the middle of the floor, cups in hand. "Is everything ok?"

Jorge took a deep breath and shrugged, "Well, it depends on how you define ok, I guess."

"Is Paige still worried about what we talked about?" Diego glanced toward Chase, as if unsure to continue and Jorge shook his head.

"It is ok," Jorge commented. "Chase is family, as you would say, he can know."

"What?" Chase asked as he turned toward Diego, who sat down the cups on the bar and was now reaching for the coffee pot.

"Diego was talking to Paige and she confessed she fears someone else is trying to kill me," Jorge said as a frown formed on his face. "She worries, which I love but I also hate it, at the same time."

"She's afraid another cop is going to try to kill Jorge," Diego added and started to slowly pour their coffee. "Which is a legit concern."

"But the last cop, I thought he was working alone," Chase asked as he accepted the cup of coffee that Diego pushed toward him.

"Yes, I mean, we believe so," Jorge replied as Diego sat a cup of coffee in front of him. "But really, we cannot be sure. It's not something that my people or hers would be able to check. If someone wants me dead, they will be working alone because this, this was never an order from the top. Originally, I had felt it was but the police are paid too generously to not be loyal to me. Why would they want to destroy that relationship?"

"Why don't you try to turn them against one another?" Chase replied as if it were the most natural thing. "Let the right people know that you won't stand for it and they may try to intimidate one another."

Jorge was impressed that he was moving away from his innocent nature to finally start to view the world as he and Diego already did.

"Yes, you are right, Chase and that is what I am doing," Jorge replied. "Unfortunately, some may not care about these things. But no, this is not why I had a late night, I'm afraid."

Both men fell silent and Jorge debated whether to bring up such a personal issue. It wasn't in his nature.

"Paige confided something to me that I do not care for," Jorge said as his forehead wrinkled in anxiety. "She told me that when she and Alec broke up it was…it was because she is not able to have children."

To his surprise, both men looked genuinely sympathetic.

"So, I have many mixed feelings about this," Jorge replied. "He gives the impression of a man who has morals and is authentic and yet, he broke Paige's heart because she was not able to have children. This is after I learned that he once had my wife kill a man for him."

Chase looked shocked while Diego's jaw almost hit the ground.

"He had her kill someone?" Chase quietly asked.

"Yes, but this was long ago and it does not matter now," Jorge replied. "But how he hurt Paige, that I have an issue with."

"Oh my God! Paige, she must be heartbroken," Diego spoke with compassion, his hand reaching for his own chest. "I mean, I didn't know she wanted to have kids…we never discussed it."

"Neither did we," Jorge spoke honestly. "I do not care. I have Maria so to me, it is good. I do not need more children but if she wanted one, well, yes, of course, I would be happy to have a baby with her but it is not a deal breaker to me."

"But it bothers her?" Chase finally spoke.

"See, that is the confusing part to me," Jorge confessed as he watched Diego slowly get the cream from the fridge under the bar and set it on the counter. "She does not seem to want a baby so I say, you know, are you upset because you couldn't have a baby with Alec many years ago but she said no, that it was for the best but I did not understand…"

"You know just because she doesn't want kids," Chase spoke slowly, carefully as if unsure to dive in. "Doesn't mean that wouldn't bother her. I mean, I don't want more kids but I also wouldn't get a vasectomy or want to find out I wasn't able to have more either. I think it's more about not having the option if that makes sense."

"Yes, it does," Jorge spoke appreciatively. "Paige, she spoke about this last night but at first, there was some miscommunication. I thought that she was suggesting that she regrets not having a child with Alec and to be honest, it killed me to hear."

"No, Paige wouldn't mean that," Diego spoke defensively.

"But sometimes, when I'm upset, I think I hear my English wrong so she switched to Spanish," Jorge admitted as he thought back to the emotional conversation of the previous night. "I am glad we sorted it

out but it was quite difficult in the beginning. I must admit, I was a little nervous but now, I'm annoyed at Alec Athas."

"But that was a long time ago too," Diego reminded him. "Plus, now you're with Paige, so it worked out better."

"Yes, I know," Jorge agreed and reached for the cream. "It didn't leave me with a pleasant impression."

"Let it go," Diego advised.

"And regarding Paige," Chase jumped in. "Did she think you would be upset she couldn't have kids?"

"I think yes," Jorge replied and made a face. "I think because of this old experience, she feared I would feel the same."

"You know, doctors are wrong," Diego reminded him. "All the fucking time."

"That is what I say too," Jorge realized he was still holding the cream in his hand and poured some into his coffee. Grabbing a straw from behind the counter, he stirred the drink and took a deep breath. "I said, Paige, come on, if you wanted to get pregnant, I would have you pregnant like that," He snapped his fingers and watched Diego roll his eyes, a grin on his face. "I'm Latino, we are passionate people."

"I can't picture Paige pregnant," Chase spoke thoughtfully as he reached for the cream

"I can't picture me changing diapers in the middle of the night," Jorge made a face. "But on the other side, I was often not there when Maria was a baby so, you know, maybe it is an experiencing I missed out on."

Chase made a face. "Well, yes and no. Cleaning explosive diarrhea and vomit in the middle of the night is hardly a delight."

Diego started to laugh while Jorge made a face.

"Paige will be fine," Diego insisted. "Now that the truth is out and she sees you don't care, she'll feel better and if not, you look at other options."

"Meanwhile," Diego continued, "I will find you a house, we open the pot shops, clean up this place, you guys get married and we all live happily ever after."

Jorge laughed in spite of himself. Feeling his phone vibrating, he pulled it out of his pocket and answered.

"*Hola* Jesús, you are missing a celebration, my friend," Jorge spoke with enthusiasm and immediately hesitated. Something was wrong. He knew it right away.

Chapter 34

"Boss, the news I have, it is not good," Jesús spoke in a calm tone despite the fact that his face was full of anxiety. The two men sat alone in Chase's office only moments after Jesús arrived at the club, immediately following his return from British Columbia. Running a hand over his face, he continued after a slight hesitation. "We had another man come around the warehouse. It was very suspicious and the middle of the night. He was trying to break in when we caught him and pulled him inside."

"I got there as soon as possible but he would not talk," Jesús continued with a worried expression on his face. "He was reluctant to tell me what was going on or why he was there so I, unfortunately, had to put on a little pressure, you know."

Jorge nodded. Jesús was quite brutal when it came to getting answers. There simply was no way this man would get away without talking.

"I cut off his toe," Jesús replied to the unanswered question; not that this surprised Jorge because this was a method he had also used in the past. There was no scream as primal as that from a man being brutalized in such a violent way. It was a way of reminding him underneath a tough exterior that we are all human; it was humbling in a way and yet, there was a power he felt when bringing out the most vulnerable side of an enemy.

"Did this make our friend more inclined to speak?" Jorge asked while attempting to ignore the tension climbing up his back, gripping on to his shoulders, his neck, forcing him to stay in control and listen carefully to everything. "Do we know what he wanted?"

"Unfortunately, he did not want to speak much even at this point so, I cut off another toe," Jesús continued to speak calmly as if they were merely talking about an average business meeting where associates sat around listening to a PowerPoint presentation. "This seemed to prove that I was serious and he talked."

Jorge opened his lips as if he wanted to speak but no words came out.

"This man, he tells me that he is connected to the last man who was snooping around and he was looking for him, assuming he was held captive," Jesús continued and seemed to sit up a bit straighter in his chair, "He told me they both were sent by a man named Urban Thomas, a *gringo* from British Columbia that is not happy that you're trying to take over the pot business in Canada. He has heard all you've done so far and is angry that a Mexican has moved in on what he believes is Canadian territory."

Jorge laughed in spite of himself. "Yes, just another immigrant here to take away the Canadian jobs, am I right?"

Seeing the look of seriousness on Jesús' face, his laughter halted and his stomach was in knots. "What is it? You are not telling me everything."

Jesús looked away briefly before continuing. "There is more, yes."

"Please…" Jorge recognized the vulnerability in his own voice. "What is it?"

"He tells me that the man who stopped Jolene, also worked for Urban Thomas and they thought we may have him captive as well since he's been..missing. This man was a former cop so he knew exactly what to say to Jolene to make it seem official. He was fired for shooting an unarmed black man and then worked for Urban Thomas."

"I'm surprised he was fired."

"It was recorded," Jesús continued and Jorge nodded and waited for the other shoe to drop. He could sense it, feel it in his bones. Terror filled his body and he knew these simple questions and comments were merely a distraction for himself, a denial of what was to come. It was necessary to get right to the point.

"Paige or Maria?" Jorge felt emotional even saying the words but he immediately recognized a look in his longtime associate's eyes that confirmed he was right. "The man said that this Urban piece of shit is threatening one of them, am I right?"

Jesús slowly nodded and with a hushed voice answered, "Paige."

Jorge broke out in a cold sweat and felt his stomach churn when his longtime friend and associate gave details of what this man planned to do to Paige. Anger quickly followed.

"Then," Jorge spoke with determination in his voice. "I'm going to find him and I'm going to kill him myself. You don't threaten me or my family and live to talk about it."

"I know, sir, I know," Jesús replied with compassion in his voice. "I told him that the only way I would allow him to live was if he told me where this Urban Thomas lives, his address, otherwise, I would torture him until I got bored, then I kill him."

Jorge nodded.

"He was not willing to talk until I took out a razor blade and said I was going to slice his eyeball, piece by piece. I now have his address and it has been confirmed. I have sent someone to get him."

"Are you sure it's the right person?"

"I have checked it out," Jesús confirmed and nodded. "Boss, this is the right man, he is the one who has been behind these threats since you came to Canada. He is powerful but sir, not as powerful as you. If we take care of him, we send a strong message to the others but I will do it for you, you do not need to concern yourself with this kind of details."

"Jesús, I have every intention of doing this myself," Jorge spoke sternly, his eyes glaring across the room at the empty wall, his mind racing in several different directions. "I need to know that there will be no retaliation though. I don't want to always look over my shoulder or worry about my wife and daughter."

"Sir, this man is big," Jesús confirmed. "You kill him, the others, they will fall away. Even if someone else rises to the top, they will be aware of what you are capable of and they will *keep* out of our way, as they did in Mexico. Remember the fire?"

Jorge thought back to his early days with the cartel when some questioned his abilities; he quickly proved his tenacity with a massive fire that trapped rivals inside a small house. Their screams could be heard from a distance as he watched them attempt to break out but the flames and smoke quickly engulfed the entire building. His heart pounded in fear, his body felt weak with anxiety but it had been necessary; there was simply no other way to prove that he was a dangerous and powerful man, willing to do whatever was necessary. Now Urban Thomas was about to learn this the hard way as he died in the most excruciating way possible; his death would be slow and performed by a man pushed to the edge. You do not threaten someone Jorge Hernandez loves and think you will simply walk away.

"Ok, so, this man, where and when can I take care of him?" Jorge asked as his mind ran in several different directions.

"I can bring him here but it may be a struggle and the chances of getting caught are too great," Jesús replied with some hesitation.

"Too risky, I will go there," Jorge replied. "However, I will need a cover story for this visit to BC. Perhaps I will bring Alec Athas with me to tour the warehouse for an alibi. We can discuss opening one in his district, which will create jobs and bring attention to his party. Meanwhile, I will have someone else, maybe yourself show him around, keep him busy and I will take care of this man."

"Sir, I would rather be with you," Jesús spoke in a low voice. "I do not want you left alone with this man….maybe you would like to have Paige help? This is her line of work."

"No, Paige is staying here and I want someone with her at all times until this is finished," Jorge insisted. "I will ask Chase to watch over her and I will bring Diego with me."

"Yes, sir, this makes sense," Jesús replied and fell silent for a moment. "I am sorry sir to bring this to you and my wish was to take care of it myself, however, I felt you should know everything. I do not like to hide things from you but I also do not want to trouble you with such upsetting news."

"It is fine, Jesús, this is something I had to know," Jorge confirmed with a faint smile. "I want to take care of this myself. I want to make this man suffer."

"I understand."

"I will need a few things," Jorge continued as he started to stand and Jesús did the same. "I will need a chainsaw and an ax. I suspect some plastic too since blood, it does not clean up well, does it Jesús?"

"No sir," He replied with a note of understanding in his eyes. "It does not. I will make sure you have the appropriate….attire for this as well."

"Good idea Jesús," Jorge replied as they started toward the door. "The last thing I want is for this *hijo de puta* to get his filthy blood all over me."

Opening the door, he headed toward the bar where an anxious Diego waited and Chase stood beside him, a concerned expression on his face.

"So, there's a problem," Jorge announced with his usual confidence even as his heart raced in both panic and rage. "I will need both of your help with something very important."

"Of course," Chase replied while Diego continued to look worried.

"We have a situation and we must act quickly," He turned toward Jesús. "Could you contact Alec Athas about what we discussed. See if he can clear his schedule for the rest of the day and tomorrow to come with us? Book the flights?"

"Absolutely boss," Jesús replied and turned, heading back into Chase's office.

"I do not want to get into a lot of details now," Jorge commented and took a deep breath. "It has come to my attention that the death threats to me, the man who was recently around the warehouse in BC and the cop Jolene spoke with are connected to a man named Urban Thomas. He is heavily involved in the Canadian pot industry and felt that he was going to find a way to bring me down and when that didn't work, he started to come up with a plan to instead…to target Paige."

Both men looked alarmed but Diego had unmistakable fear cross his face.

"I know my wife, she is capable of taking care of this man," Jorge continued and took a deep breath and pushed down his emotions. "But I, I want to take care of it myself. No one threatens my family. *No one.*

I am traveling to BC as soon as possible and Chase, I need you to stay with Paige until we come back. I do not suspect there will be any trouble but I need you to keep a close eye on her and Maria. If these people find out we have their leader, they may try to retaliate but I suspect once his remains are discovered, they may not be so inclined."

"Sure," Chase replied. "Whatever you need."

"Diego, you will come with me," He said to his old friend, a man he saw as a brother. "We will take care of this man. I need you there to make sure I don't lose control and to watch my back."

Diego nodded with fire in his eyes. "If he threatens Paige, you know I will do anything to stop him."

"I know, Diego, I know, that is why I want you there," Jorge replied and the two men shared a look that went beyond words. "Jesús will bring the politician and give him a tour of our warehouse, with hopes of opening the second one in his district. This will be our alibi because he will say we were with him during this tour and discussion. Not that anyone will ever look at us but in case. So we will all be traveling together."

No one replied.

"Boss," Jesús started to speak as he walked out of the office. "Athas is on board and is cancelling everything on his schedule for the next couple of days. I have arranged our tickets for the plane tonight, four first class seats."

"*Perfecto*, thank you, Jesús." Jorge replied and turned his attention to the other two men in the room. "Chase, I need you to pack a bag and go to the apartment immediately and Diego, Jesús, you need to get ready for a business trip."

CHAPTER 35

"I don't understand," Paige's gentle words touched his soul, causing him to fight the urge to break down as soon as he looked into her eyes. Someone wanted to kill the most important woman in his life because of *him;* of all the words he had no problem saying, this time, he couldn't speak. His mouth grew dry as he rushed to throw some clothes in a suitcase, he sucked in a deep breath and hoped to keep it together as an intense wave of emotions overwhelmed his soul. This couldn't be real. This couldn't be happening.

"I..I just have to go," Jorge attempted to explain but the words caught in his throat with a tight grip that made him suddenly stop as her hand gently touched his arm. It was the moment that he turned around and looked into her worried eyes that he fell apart.

Crumbling to the floor, his breathing turned shallow as the world around him began to spin and he closed his eyes. He immediately felt Paige by his side, grasping his arm.

"Jorge!" Her voice was full of fear as he opened his eyes again. "Are you okay? Should we go to the hospital?"

"No no no! I gotta go, Paige," He took a deep breath and felt his body relax as he attempted to stand but she put a hand out to stop him.

"No, wait a second," She spoke calmly, her hand resting on his leg. "What's going on here?"

"I have to go to BC," Jorge started to answer but his mouth was dry so he hesitated for a moment to clear his throat. "I…there's a situation I have to take care of right away."

"Ok," Paige said with a nod as she continued to run her hand over his leg. "I understand but what happened? What's the emergency?"

"I….I have to take care of someone," His answer was short as he tried to avoid looking her in the eyes.

"Do you need me to come too?" She asked and leaned in. "I can get someone to look after Maria, maybe Chase?"

"No, please, you have to stay here," Jorge replied, as he suddenly started to feel normal again. "Look, *mi amor*, I'm sending Chase over here to keep an eye on you and Maria, to be cautious. It would make me feel better while I'm away."

"What?" Paige asked with slight alarm in her voice. "Jorge, what is going on here? This isn't like you? Did someone threaten Maria? I can look after her."

Their eyes met for only an instant and she began to nod in understanding. Immediately reaching for his hand, she squeezed it and smiled.

"Jorge, I'm gonna be ok," She said with a self-assurance that he wished to have in his own heart. "I'm a trained assassin. I dare anyone come in here and tries to hurt or kill either me or Maria."

"I know..I just, you have to do this for me," Jorge stumbled over his words, suddenly lost for what to say. "*Moriría si algo te sucediera alguna vez.*"

"I'll be fine," Paige whispered and leaned in to hug him. He felt his body grow heavy as if he would never be able to get up from the floor again. "I know the precautions to take."

"Chase, I want him with you and Maria," Jorge hurriedly explained as she released him, his brain suddenly in overdrive. "I need to know…"

"It's ok," Paige insisted as she looked into his eyes. "I know you're scared but it will be ok. I'll be fine. I can keep Maria home from school tomorrow and if Chase is here too, don't worry about us. We'll be ok."

"Chase, he's dropping by the school to pick up Maria before he comes here," Jorge said as he took a deep breath and found himself beginning to calm. "I am going to BC and I will take care of the man who made the threat."

"I don't want you going alone," Paige insisted.

"I'm not," Jorge replied. "I will take Diego and Jesús and Alec is coming to tour a warehouse and I guess, to be our alibi."

"Does he know that?" Paige asked.

"He will," Jorge insisted. "It will be fine but I'm not going to lie, *mi amor,* this man who threatened you, he's doing so to get to me. There is nothing in this world that pushes me over the edge like trying to hurt my family. This man, he will die a very painful, miserable death."

Jorge's final words shot a fire into his soul as he started to rise from the floor, while beside him, Paige did the same. Her face was expressionless as if attempting to absorb his words, she finally reached forward and pulled him into another gentle hug, a warm kiss landed on his cheek.

"Please be careful," She whispered in his ear before letting him go, her eyes full of concern. "Call me, as soon as you can."

"I will," He assured her.

Chase and Maria arrived at the apartment shortly after, giving Jorge some sense of relief, as his daughter skipped through the room. Excited to learn that Chase would be spending the night, she immediately launched into a whole slew of questions that Jorge simply didn't want to answer.

"Are we in danger?" She boldly asked. "Is that why Chase is here, to *protect* us?"

"Actually, I'm here so you two can protect me," Chase spoke up causing everyone to grin, even Maria, who began to giggle. "I'm too scared to stay home alone when Diego is away."

"No, you're not!" Maria laughed. "You're not scared of anything."

"Oh, yes I am, I'm scared of everything," Chase spoke with sincerity causing Jorge to join in on the fun, just as his phone beeped.

"Maria, he's a very nervous man, please look after him for me while I'm gone."

"*Papa*, when will you return?" Maria asked as she rushed forward for a quick hug and kiss.

"Maria, I will be home tomorrow night," He replied and glanced around at everyone in the room. "Now, I must go, Diego and Jesús are waiting for me downstairs."

As it turns out, Alec Athas was also with the men. Looking slightly uncomfortable, he sat silently in the back seat, while Jorge merely gave him a nod when he got in the car.

"So," He pulled Jorge's attention away from his many dark thoughts. "We are doing a tour of this warehouse and you're thinking of opening another one in my district?"

"Yes," Jorge replied, secretly welcoming a distraction. "I have given this a lot of thought and I wish to open another warehouse here in Ontario and yes, I think your voting district would be ideal for both of us."

"We could use the jobs," Alec spoke appreciatively. "Good paying jobs."

"They will be," Jorge spoke with assurance. "I want the jobs done correctly and to do so, you must pay your staff."

From the front seat, Jesús drove in silence while Diego quickly found his voice.

"I did a quick search for places in that area and I found a building that would be *perfecto*!" He spoke expressively as they drove through the busy Toronto streets, the airport still a distance away, while Jorge tried to stay calm. His thoughts were bouncing between Paige's face and the moment when he would slaughter the bastard who thought he could threaten Jorge Hernandez's wife.

"Oh, really?" Alec asked and the two immediately got into a discussion about the precise building. Diego pulled out his phone and showed Alec the location, pointing out all the reasons why it would be an asset.

"Yes, that building has been for sale for a couple of years," Alec said as he studied the picture and handed the phone back to Diego. "Warehouse shut down, a lot of jobs lost in the area, it was devastating to the community."

"Well, we," Jorge spoke up with assurance in his voice. "We will change that."

"That would be incredible for my district," Alec spoke appreciatively. "We need some hope in our community."

"You got your hope in the way of a grow-op," Diego spoke bluntly from the front seat, causing Jorge to grin. "Those places, they won't be shutting down and moving jobs to some country like *Mexico.*"

"Hey, *amigo*, come on," Jorge retorted with a touch of humor in his voice, recognizing that Diego was attempting to tease him. "We got people who want to work down there too."

"Actually," Alec tactfully jumped into the conversation. "The last owners for that building went bankrupt, that's why they closed."

"It's the nature of business my friend," Jorge replied and glanced at Alec Athas. "You gotta make changes when necessary, change with the times, that is why I'm now in the pot industry."

"What were you in before, again?" Alec asked with his huge eyes looking at Jorge.

"Coffee," Jorge replied with a grin.

Alec merely nodded with a smirk on his face. "And *coffee*, it's not as popular now?"

"Not as popular as pot," Jorge insisted and avoided his eyes. "Sometimes, my friend, we must see the bigger picture. Sometimes we must recognize how society is changing and this, this was one of those times. You will see, pot is about to become more popular than alcohol and porn, two of our *other* favorite things."

"I don't know, alcohol is often abused and porn's become quite degrading over the years," Alec commented while on the other side of the car, Jorge lifted an eyebrow while looking out the window. "I mean some of it is kind of shocking."

"Some people, they like that kind of thing," Jorge replied and took a deep breath. "Everyone, their tastes are different."

"I know but it's a bit disturbing what some people find as… pleasurable," Alec commented in a schoolboy-like way that caused Jorge to roll his eyes.

"I agree," Diego piped up from the front seat and turned slightly and Jorge grinned when he considered where this conversation was going. "There are some things I see online that's completely disturbing to me."

Jorge had to bite his lip to keep from laughing.

"Well, that's what I mean," Alec continued to speak. "When it involves minors or like, four guys and one woman, sometimes things get a little…scary…"

"And yet, my friend, you clearly watch it," Jorge commented as he avoided eye contact, still managing to barely hold back his laughter. "Otherwise, how would you know?"

"Just stumbled on it while looking for something more…digestible."

Jorge nodded and continued to look out the window.

"Yeah, I know what you mean," Diego seemed to get more in the conversation as he turned around in his seat. "There are some videos I accidentally stumble upon that I *really* wished I hadn't seen."

"It's true," Alec agreed and made eye contact with Jorge, whom finally turned his head.

"Except, my friend," Jorge spoke directly to him. "I guarantee you and Diego are not watching the same kind of porn."

"I'm gay," Diego spoke up while twisting his lips and shrugging. "He's right, we're probably not watching the same thing."

Alec merely nodded in acceptance while Jorge continued to grin. From the driver's seat, Jesús spoke for the first time.

"It's about the direction of the production," He commented in his slow, calm voice as if attempting to pull the words from his brain. "You must find an actress or in your case, Diego, the *actor* that gives the kind of performance that appeals to you."

To this, the three men agreed while Jorge continued to grow antsy.

"How are we for time? I don't want to miss the plane," Jorge spoke anxiously.

"We're fine," Diego assured him. "You worry too much."

"I just want to get there and get things sorted out," Jorge commented and turned his attention to Alec. "Jesús will be showing you around the warehouse and giving you the presentation involved but if anyone asks, me and Diego were there too."

"But…"

"Me and Diego," Jorge repeated. "Were there *too.*"

Alec didn't reply but nodded in a quiet understanding.

"This business," Jorge continued as Alec attentively listened. "It will prosper your district and I will have someone at the office let the press know that you and I had long conversations about how to bring hope back to your community and me, as a businessman felt that we would open and operate our business where it was most needed in the city."

"You and I, we will make a good team," Jorge continued as he glanced toward the window again, seeing signs indicating that they were getting closer to the airport. "I will make sure to have this all over social media as well. The warehouse should be opening for business hopefully before the next election is called."

Alec understood.

Chapter *36*

"Some people like their television with a lot of sex and violence," Jorge commented as they entered the dingy, dark warehouse, miles away from civilization. The smell was immediate and although his brain searched to distinguish the piercing odor, he quickly decided that perhaps it was best that he did not. Beside him, Diego wrinkled his nose and made a face but Jorge acted as if he hadn't noticed the terrible pungent smell that surrounded them as they began to walk. "Me, I like my *life* with lots of sex and violence. People deny their true passions, Diego, it is not natural."

"No one can ever say that you deny your passions," Diego commented gruffly as he glanced at his feet as if he was unsure of what he would find under them. "What the fuck was in here….or *is* in here."

"Oh, my friend, does it really matter?" Jorge asked as they found their way to the back of the building, where Jesús stood beside a white man lying motionless on the ground. The *gringo* wasn't tied or handcuffed but was so lifeless on the thick, clear plastic covering the floor that Jorge briefly wondered if he was already dead. However, the man's eyes were alive, indicating that he was aware of where he was and perhaps, what was about to happen to him. Nearby sat a chainsaw, an ax, towels, safety boots and two Hazmat suits.

"I see you have found us with ease," Jesús spoke in his usual slow manner, almost as if it were the most normal thing in the world to stand in the middle of a dingy, abandoned warehouse with a stranger lying on the ground beside him. "This man, here," He hesitated for a moment and kicked the *gringo* in the ribs before he turning his attention back to Jorge and Diego. "This is Urban Thomas."

"Ah! So we finally meet," Jorge spoke bitterly while glaring at the large man who vulnerably lay before them; he was tall, husky and had he not been injected with a drug that made him unable to move, there was little doubt that he could've put up a good fight against the three of them. He struggled to speak but yet, nothing more than a moan came out of his mouth. "I see my associate gave you a little something to relax. Very considerate of him because you're about to undergo a *delicate* procedure, Mr. Thomas."

The noise coming from deep inside the man was a struggle but could be heard while his semi-conscious, icy blue eyes begged Jorge, who ignored this and turned his attention toward Jesús. "I believe, my friend, you have to do a tour now? We're fine here."

"But you," Jorge returned his attention toward the man on the floor as he continued to make long, incoherent noises from deep in his chest. "You, *amigo*, you will not be fine today. In fact, I think I'm being quite generous by allowing you to be under the influence of some powerful drugs now because you're about to experience your worst fucking nightmare."

The man continued to make noise while Jorge returned his attention to Jesús who was glaring at Urban Thomas and nodded. "Sir, he will not be able to move anytime soon, that I promise you. We have some extra help when you need it."

"Very good," Jorge replied while beside him, Diego's face grew angrier by the second.

"Why don't we just shoot this fucker and leave him for the rats to eat?" Diego shoved both hands into his pockets while Jesús raised an eyebrow before turning to walk away. "This is the man who wanted to kill Paige?"

"And me," Jorge reminded him before turning his dark glare back at the man who now had tears in his eyes while further away, the door could be heard opening and closing again. "Don't forget me."

The warehouse seemed to grow darker, an early morning chill was in the air, something that was not noticeable to Jorge before that moment.

His anger had warmed him and although it certainly wasn't as cold as it had been in Toronto the day before, it wasn't exactly comfortable either. Both wore suits, ties, dressed for success and not a gruesome act of violence. It was only the leather gloves on their hands that gave away the weather outside as much as their true motives.

"How could I forget?" Diego countered and glanced around at the few items that Jesús had left them. "So how you want to do this?"

"Well, first, my friend, we must put on the Hazmat suits," Jorge made his way toward the large, white garments sitting nearby, which included a clear shield that would protect their faces. Turing his attention back to Urban Thomas on the floor, tears running from his vulnerable, eyes, he directed his comment toward the pathetic man on the floor. "Since Diego and I, we like nice things like expensive suits, we must wear something to protect our clothing."

"These suits, they're designer," Diego piped up, his eyes bugging out as he spoke to the man on the ground. He showed no compassion, completely expressionless, he turned his attention back to Jorge. "It would hardly be *practical* to do it any other way."

"This is true my friend," Jorge spoke very matter of fact like and nodded. "Cause this, my friend, it's about to get really messy."

Urban Thomas was unsuccessfully fighting with his own body to move, the noises from the back of his throat only grew louder but still was merely a grunt, mixed with a deep sense of fear. Jorge and Diego ignored him and began to dress in the Hazmat suits. They were large, protectively fitting over their clothes. It wasn't Jorge's first time wearing one.

Finally dressed in the awkward outfit, Jorge glanced back to see some towels and grinned when he realized why they were there; to wipe the blood from the shield over their faces when it splattered back. Jesús, he thought of everything! His eyes returned to Diego's, who was still adjusting the suit, which caused him to grin and lift an eyebrow. Exchanging his own shoes for the large boots, he sat them far away from the place where this murder was about to take place.

"It does not have to be perfect, Diego," His comment was low, while he shot him an amused smile. "As long as it protects your clothing, you know?"

"So, Mr. Thomas," He returned his attention to the defeated man on the ground. "I hear that it is ironic that we give you a drug to make you defenseless, unable to fight back. Since my understanding was that your intention was to do the same to my wife."

Diego suddenly stopped fidgeting and turned his attention toward Jorge. His black eyes, a mixture of shock and pain, quickly replaced by a fire so strong there was no doubt that the Colombian would've thought nothing of committing this brutal murder on his own.

"Yes, Diego, he was going to drug my wife, *rape* her then slit her throat," Jorge suddenly halted the conversation and turned toward Urban Thomas and saw nothing; just an animal on the ground, a wild, filthy pig that would be slaughtered, put out of its misery. He was garbage. "But obviously, that will not happen. If anyone comes near my wife, this *animal's* wife will die in the most excruciating way possible. I will burn her alive, fully conscious with no luxury like drugs, such as this man is now experiencing. She will scream for every last second of her life until she passes out from the pain and eventually burns to death."

Fear overtook the man's eyes as he watched Jorge calmly reached for the clear shield on the ground. "But of course, I will show a little compassion, this is something I've learned from Paige of course because I don't got any feelings. But I will wait and I will see. But at this time, Diego, I think I will allow his wife to live. But I'm a man who changes my mind a lot, so who knows how I feel tomorrow."

"If anyone touches Paige," Diego began to fidget, his face scrunching up in a frown. "I will kill this man's wife myself and every fucking associate he has."

"Ah, Diego, now that's why you're such a great team player," Jorge spoke calmly while putting his shield on and pointing toward the other one on the floor. "You will need that my friend. Sorry, it might mess your hair a bit but it's better than having blood splattered on your face or even worse.... You don't want that."

"It wouldn't be a good look," Diego responded in a serious tone and the two of them started to laugh as Jorge reached for his chainsaw.

"You actually know how to use that?" Diego asked as he reached for his shield and put it on.

"This ain't my first fucking rodeo," Jorge replied dramatically before reaching to roughly pull the cord, starting the chainsaw. A loud roar filled the warehouse and suddenly, the man on the floor was doing everything in his ability, although limited, to move away. To this, Jorge merely shook his head before bringing the blade down, savagely cutting through the man's hand, he observed the blood pouring out, some splattering back on the shield, as he detached Urban Thomas' five fingers, followed by the rest of his hand and a portion of his arm.

Turning off the saw, Jorge ignored the man's reaction; he could care less about the life draining from his eyes, whether he had any sensation in his now, missing body parts or whether the man was willing to negotiate in any way. This did not matter to him. Urban Thomas threatened Paige. There was no coming back from that, no amount of money, nothing that could ever be exchanged for his life. He was dead the minute he even suggested it, the second he even thought of hurting the one person Jorge loved the most in the world.

Grabbing a towel, he wiped the shield while nearby, Diego looked frozen, his face full of fury.

"Diego, we have just begun," Jorge replied and stopped to look into Urban Thomas' fading eyes. "You see, I once told my wife, that if anyone ever hurt her, even suggested hurting her, I would cut them up. Piece by piece. I would make the last minutes of their life terrifying and horrid. I would kill them in the most agonizing way imaginable and you know me, Diego, I like to keep my promises to my wife."

Blood poured out of the man, collecting around Jorge's feet, the smell of death lingered in the air.

"Speaking of which, Diego, we must get to work," Jorge continued. "I also promised Paige that I would be home for dinner."

"The ax?" Diego gestured toward the shiny new tool sitting on the floor.

"My friend, I know how you like hitting things with a baseball bat,"

Jorge spoke as he threw the towel aside. "I figure this is the next best thing, am I right?"

A smug grin appeared on Diego's lips as he picked up the ax and without hesitation, swung it up over his head and with great force brought it back down to lodge into the man's chest, possibly near his heart, giving Jorge a satisfied smile.

It was less than an hour later after both gave up on the original plan to cut the man into pieces, that they had an associate of Hector's help clean up then get rid of the body. His eyes would be delivered to the next man in the food chain with a very stern warning that only a fool would ignore. Jorge Hernandez was not fucking around and anyone who thought otherwise would face the consequences.

After removing and disposing of the hazmat suits, helmets, boots, towels, ax and chainsaw, the two men left the warehouse in the middle of nowhere and decided to go for breakfast. On some level, Jorge recognized why this was perhaps incredibly twisted however, he couldn't deny that the morning had given him a hearty appetite.

"Diego," Jorge announced as the two sat in a sunny, bright diner after getting back to the town where their warehouse was located. "I know I tell my wife that I will eat better but today, my friend, I feel I deserve a treat."

"Did you text her," Diego lunged forward across the table, his dark eyes loomed over Jorge. "She's gonna be worried."

"Yes, I texted her," Jorge replied with a grin and gestured toward the window. "When we turned our phones back on in the parking lot. I texted her immediately and she received it."

"Is she ok?"

"Of course," Jorge replied calmly as the waitress approached. "She said Maria and Chase are watching a movie. Ahhh, but life, for some, it goes on."

After ordering their food, Diego insisted they call Paige. Humored, Jorge agreed reached for his iPhone, but his friend was way ahead of him and on his own phone.

"*Paige!*" He spoke with great emphasis on her name. "Is everything ok?"

He nodded toward Jorge.

"Hey, *amigo*, let me talk to my wife," Jorge said as he reached for Diego's phone. Reluctantly, he passed it to him.

"Learn to wait your turn," Diego spoke gruffly.

"Me, I'm not a patient man," Jorge replied as he put the phone against his ear.

"I've noticed that about you," Her voice was soft, immediately bringing him back to life after a morning of brutality. "So, how's the warehouse tour?"

"It went exceptionally well, *mi amor*, we're just waiting for Jesús and Alec to go over a few things and then, I believe they will be meeting us here for breakfast. Diego and me, we were too hungry to wait."

"And you're coming home?"

"Later today, my love, just as soon as we finish up with Alec."

"I can't wait."

"Me neither."

His heart full after the conversation with his wife, Jorge felt the need to confess a secret he had held back for months.

CHAPTER 37

The confession stunned Diego. Although up until that point, he had eaten with great gusto, Jorge's words seemed to suddenly repeal him, causing him to push his food aside while his face turned ashen. It hadn't occurred to him that sharing medical information would have such a strong impact; this only made him more certain he shouldn't tell Paige.

"When did you find this out?" Diego quietly asked. His eyes widened and he pressed his hands together anxiously, as an awkwardness took over the table. "Why haven't you told me? Have you told Paige?"

Jorge shook his head.

"What? Come on! You gotta tell Paige," Diego leaned forward on the table while he studied Jorge's face. "She's your wife, she needs to know."

"I cannot tell her," Jorge insisted and broke their eye contact. "I found out right after we got married and I...I couldn't. Besides, we are monitoring it and I feel great. The doctor told me he sees a vast improvement since I quit smoking and except for today, I almost always eat healthily. I'm working out more, you know? The body, it wants to heal itself."

"Jorge, this isn't like you just have a little blood pressure problem," Diego reminded him. "You could die."

"Ok, Diego, stop being dramatic," Jorge spoke more aggressively this time, feeling the need to get a grasp on things. "I didn't tell you this information for a lecture but because I felt the need to share it with someone. I'm fine. I had a doctor's appointment recently and he was happy with my overall state of health. So do not worry, my friend."

"I still think you should tell Paige," Diego said and took a deep breath, reaching for his coffee. "I think I need a drink."

"You're blowing this way out of proportion," Jorge said and began to laugh. "The doctor simply said it was something we would have to watch. So, please, please do not say anything to Paige. I will talk to her but it will be at the right time."

"Don't leave it," Diego said and shook his head.

"Diego, how much time do any of us have?" Jorge posed the question and leaned back comfortably in the booth "Even me, with this, I could live till I'm 100 or I could walk out and get shot by some of Urban Thomas' people. We do not know. That is unfortunately how life works. None of us know how much time we have."

"How did you…not tell anyone this long?" Diego quietly asked. "How did you keep that to yourself and not go crazy?"

"It's actually, you know, it is better in a way," Jorge replied and glanced out the window, watching a woman and child walking into the diner as the sun continued to brighten in the sky; was it just him or had it suddenly grown in size after he revealed this hard news to Diego? "You see the world differently when there's a chance that you could die. In a way, I've been living this way for years simply because of my line of work. I see something I want, I grab it. That is why I married Paige so fast. I knew she was perfect for me, that I loved her, so why wait? That is how we must live, for the moment and from the heart."

Diego remained solemn and looked away.

"*Amigo*, I tell you, I am fine," Jorge said with a shrug. "As I said, the doctor was happy with my latest reports. Perhaps because I didn't overthink the entire situation or worry about it, perhaps that was the best thing I could've done."

"You gotta promise me you will tell Paige," Diego jumped in abruptly, almost as if he hadn't heard anything Jorge just said. "Please, she has to know."

"Ok," Jorge spoke reluctantly. "But you know, it's almost better she doesn't know. I don't want to scare her."

'I can't believe you didn't tell her before," Diego said and shook his head. "I couldn't have kept a secret like that."

"I found out and it was at a sensitive time," Jorge replied while reaching for his coffee, having already inhaled most of his food. "It was when everything happened with Jolene and I wanted to tell her a few days later but when I went to, I couldn't. You know?"

His heart was heavy when he thought back to that day. It was late at night as he watched Paige get ready for bed. Changing into shorts and a tank top, pulling her hair back in a ponytail, her fingers gently patting cream on her face, all the nightly routines he had watched so many times before but suddenly they were relevant. What if this was one of the last times he would see her do such things? As trivial as they may have seemed before, they suddenly were fascinating, beautiful in their simplicity and it was while he watched her that night, Jorge decided to not say a word. He wanted to enjoy these moments.

"I did not want her to worry," Jorge said, sure he was simply repeating himself at this point but it was an important factor. Why would you want to scare someone you love if it wasn't necessary? "Because I knew she would. Even when she found out that my blood pressure was high, she worried, you know? I do not want to see her worrying about me."

"I get it," Diego finally seemed to come around. "I do, I understand why you didn't tell her but I think, you should now. Especially if things are looking better."

"They are, my friend, they are."

"Then tell her," Diego said while reaching for his coffee. "It's important she knows if you suddenly get sick. She would be very hurt if you got sick and she found out you hid this from her."

"This is true," Jorge replied and looked away in shame. He hadn't thought of it that way. His logic made sense at the time but perhaps it was for selfish reasons.

"But also, she wouldn't want you to go through this alone."

"There's nothing to go through," Jorge countered with a shrug. "I just look after myself, something I never used to do. I mean, the idea of worrying about my health when I was in such a dangerous lifestyle, it seemed kind of redundant, you know? Like why worry about getting sick when you could have your head blown off by some crackhead or cop?"

"I suppose."

"And married life was still pretty new to me," Jorge said and glanced down at his wedding ring. "It's still new, telling someone everything and anything, this is nothing I have experienced before, you know?"

"I believe this about you," Diego said and glanced out the window. "There's Alec and Jesús. Again, you're going to talk to Paige?"

"Tonight, when I get home," Jorge promised.

Relieved to see the two men join them. Diego's intensity had unnerved Jorge more than he expected. At the time, his decision felt like the right one but now, he regretted hiding the truth from Paige. He hadn't done so with malice intent but because he simply thought it was the right thing to do; now he feared she would be angry.

Alec was studying him as he reached the table and behind him, Jesús gave a brief nod that said more than any words could've; the two men had worked together so long that often, words weren't necessary. Although Jorge remained silent and showed no reaction, he briefly wondered if he died, would Alec attempt to get back together with Paige? He turned as the Greek man sat beside him, his eyes watching Jorge before he briefly looked away.

"The meeting, the tour, it went well?" Jorge asked, ignoring his thoughts. "You like what you saw, Alec? What do you think?"

"I like what I saw," Alec insisted as he sat forward, leaning on the table and turning toward Jorge while Jesús sat beside Diego on the other side. "My only concern is that my potential constituents may not like the idea that its pot that will be creating jobs. Especially when I saw the security around your building. That might make people uneasy."

"*Amigo*, we're growing pot, of course, we need security," Diego butted in but yet, his voice was calmer than usual. Jorge suspected that he was still slightly haunted by their conversation only moments earlier. "We gotta, it's worth a lot of money."

"I know," Alec said in a defeated voice while Jorge bit his bottom lip, his mind lost in thought. "I'm wondering if I want armed guards to be so…visible when we're in the middle of the city. It's not the same as where your warehouse is now."

"We will have them mostly inside in the Toronto location," Jorge spoke up, unsure if this was a fact or because it was the easiest way to deal with this situation. "And people will get over the product once they find out that the jobs, they pay well."

"But my opponents will clearly use it against me," Alec said with a shrug.

"Then, my friend, you must find the reasons why people shouldn't feel so negatively," Jorge replied. "You're a man who has no obligation to them since the election isn't called and yet, here you are, looking to bring well-paying jobs to their community. Educate them on the benefits of pot, whatever you need to do. Figure out the demographic and take it from whatever angle works."

"There's always an angle," Diego spoke up as he glanced at the waitress returning to their table. Jesús and Alec received menus, while Jorge and Diego said no when she offered them more coffee. After the waitress left, Diego quickly returned to his train of thought. "When the time comes, we will make the people see that you are the only candidate to win in your district. Even if it means destroying your opponents."

"Oh, I don't know if we need to go that far," Alec said with an awkward laugh as he closed his menu. "I mean, I think I can win on my merit."

"Politics, they are dirty, my friend," Jorge spoke smugly. "You say that *now* but when the gloves come off, you might not feel the same because you can be assured, they will do it to you."

"I have nothing bad in my past," Alec spoke honestly.

"Oh really?" Jorge challenged him and he automatically looked away.

"What?" Diego asked innocently as if he had no idea. "What happened in your past?"

"Nothing I want to talk about," Alec looked toward the approaching waitress. Passing the menu to her, he ordered a breakfast.

"Me too," Jesús finally spoke up. "Same."

After the waitress was out of earshot, Jorge turned back toward a reluctant Alec. "My point is that we *all* have skeletons in our closet if someone chooses to dig. Now yours, yours won't get out and if someone discovers them and tries to do so, there will be hell to pay. You must remember, you are protected when you work with us."

Alec gave a reluctant smile and Jorge felt his confidence rise.

"So, this morning, it went well?" Jesús asked as he shared a look with Jorge, who nodded in response.

"Very good."

"Am I allowed to know where you were this morning?" Alec asked reluctantly.

"I was with *you*, *amigo*, touring the warehouse," Jorge glared at him and Alec merely nodded in response. "Then Diego and I came here to eat and discuss some things while you and Jesús went through the finer points at his office. That is all."

"That is all," Jesús repeated.

"I know," Alec said with a nod. "I'm seeing how this works."

"That is good," Jorge replied, his eyes continued to watch him. "Because we will be working closely together and if we don't have trust for one another, we have nothing."

"You trust that we're going to get you voted in and we trust that you're gonna keep your mouth shut," Diego spoke firmly while his eyes studied Alec with a sense of admiration. "I think that's reasonable."

"I understand," Alec assured him, turning his attention to Jorge. "I do appreciate everything you are doing for me."

Nodding, he didn't say anything as he looked away. It was only a little later, when he was alone with Alec at the airport while Diego and Jesús went for a drink at the bar, that their conversation returned to something said at the diner. It was while they sat away from others waiting for their flight later that morning, that Alec brought it up again.

"You know everything," His words were simple, to the point while his eyes stared at a space on the floor. "Paige told you."

"Yes," Jorge replied, also not looking toward Alec but the floor. "She told me everything."

"I guess, you're married, it's natural that you share everything," Alec spoke gently and Jorge felt his heart drop with guilt, suddenly overwhelmed with emotion. He managed to push everything down and merely nodded.

"I want you to know," Alec said and slowly started to turn in his direction. "I was young and maybe acted rashly.."

"*Amigo*, do you know who you are speaking with?" Jorge was slightly humored by this reaction, his face lifting in a grin as he turned toward Alec. "You do not have to explain your actions to me. If it were my sister, I would've done the same thing as you and perhaps, much worse than what you did."

Alec didn't respond but merely nodded. He turned away from Jorge and was silent for a moment.

"I regret it, actually," Alec confessed. "I've been carrying this with me for every day since. Secrets can be heavy."

"Oh, I know, *amigo* but unfortunately, there are few that we can share them with," Jorge replied. "As I said, in your shoes, I wouldn't have hesitated to do the same."

"But did I have a right?" Alec asked.

"Did he?" Jorge countered and turned his head. For a moment, the two men made eye contact and Alec slowly nodded.

"I see what you mean," He quietly replied.

"My friend, Diego," Jorge pointed toward the two men at the nearby bar. "He always says that we have two choices. We either can be a sheep or a wolf. The sheep will let life happen to them while the wolf, he takes what he wants, fights for what he believes in. Now, tell me something, Alec, which one are you?"

"I'm not sure," Alec replied with some hesitation.

"You, my friend, are a wolf but yet, it's almost as if you doubt this," Jorge spoke honestly. "As if someone told you that to be likable, you must be a sheep. You must confine to what the world tells you but this, this is a lie. People crave powerful people. They think that sheep, they are weak. You cannot be weak in politics."

"So you're a wolf?" Alec asked with interest. "Is that what you're telling me?"

"No, my friend, I'm not," Jorge replied and looked away. "I'm much more dangerous. I'm the lion."

Chapter 38

It was one of the hardest conversations he ever had. The anxiety Jorge felt when his daughter learned the truth about *who* he was had been easier than having this conversation with Paige. The look on her face was a mixture of hurt and shock, quickly replaced by intense sorrow. He wasn't used to seeing his wife like this; always a pillar of strength, it was rare that she cried and when she did, it was usually a soft, gentle cry like a summer rain but this time it was very different. Her tears were forceful and angry, depleting, if only temporarily as she collapsed on the bed in shock and disbelief.

Unsure of what to do, he reached out and touched her arm, running his hand up and down her smooth skin, Jorge immediately regretted telling her the truth. It wasn't worth it. He felt helpless, weak as if nothing he could do or say would ever make it better. As if her heart were permanently broken and he wasn't able to fix it when he was usually able to fix everything.

"Mi amor, por favor, por favor no llores," Jorge whispered, the words catching in his throat and he felt uncertain of what else to say as she sat up and looked in his eyes. Her face pale, her eyes red, she silently studied his face and he had to look away.

"Paige, this is why I didn't tell you," Jorge confessed as he hesitantly looked back into her eyes with some reluctance. "I didn't want to upset you."

"But…how could you keep this from me?" Her voice was hoarse as if she could barely get the words out. "This is your health."

"I thought…you know, I thought I would work on getting better and I didn't want you to worry about me," He replied, feeling as though his explanation fell flat when he actually said it out loud. "There's nothing we could do about what already happened."

"You had a heart attack!" Paige said with panic in her voice. "You could've died!"

"I had a small, *tiny* heart attack," He attempted to correct her but it was as if he hadn't spoken at all, as she stared at him in disbelief.

"Is there such a thing?" Paige countered while shaking her head. "There's permanent damage. You can try to trivialize it but it's still a big deal, Jorge. When did it happen? Was it when you were passing out?"

"They are not sure," He replied with a sense of shame as his heart raced. "Paige, I am sorry, I didn't hide this to hurt you. I sincerely felt that it was better you not know. I wanted you to not worry about me. As soon as I found out, I changed my entire lifestyle and I'm working closely with a doctor."

"You told me that you had the body of an 18-year-old? Remember?" Paige reminded him. "You made it sound like you were doing better."

"That is because I *am* doing much better," Jorge insisted and moved closer to her. "I started smoking when I was around 12 and I quit. I barely touch liquor now, I eat healthy most of the time, I exercise, I try to cut back on stress….I'm doing everything I can do, *mi amor*, I cannot do much more and really, my doctor, he is quite impressed, so this is true. I wasn't lying. He said he sees a difference."

"But the damage is already done," Paige repeated her earlier words. "That's scary."

"It doesn't have to be," Jorge insisted. "It was…what you say, a warning, a reminder that life is precious and it was a hard lesson but at least you are in my life. If you weren't and Maria wasn't, I probably would have kept doing things how I used to but you know, I do feel better. I had no idea how bad I felt over the years until I changed everything. I *feel* like I'm 18 again or at least, how I probably would've felt back then if I hadn't abused my body so much with drugs and everything else."

Much to his relief, she began to calm down, slowly nodding her head. "I suppose…"

"Paige, I promise you, I didn't keep this from you to be deceitful, I did it because I wanted you to not worry," Jorge insisted. "I did not tell anyone until today when I told Diego and he insisted I tell you right away."

She appeared satisfied with this comment and he cautiously moved closer to her, attempting to read her reaction.

"From now on, I want to go to your doctor appointments with you," She spoke defiantly her eyes watching him carefully. "I don't want you to hide anything from me anymore. You have to promise."

"There is nothing else," Jorge assured her. "Just this, *mi amor*, you know all my dirty secrets."

"And today," Paige asked cautiously. "Is there anything else I need to know about today?"

"The people we were up against now know why they should never fuck with Jorge Hernandez," He commented and watched as a smirk formed on her lips. "They will not be bothering us again, not unless they want an all-out war. I think they will get a strong message about what will happen if they do."

"But you didn't hide anything about that situation from me," Paige quietly asked as she reached for his hand. "To protect me?"

"No, unfortunately, I had to tell you everything *to* protect you," Jorge admitted and squeezed her hand. "I would have preferred not to tell you but I want you to be safe and warned, just in case."

"What did you do to this man?" She quietly asked, as if cautiously trekking into unknown territory. "I want to know."

"Well," Jorge moved closer to her, sensing an intimacy growing between them. "Diego and I, we both took care of him. I learned that he had intended on kidnapping you and putting a drug in your system that would more or less paralyze you."

He stopped and cleared his throat, feeling uncomfortable when remembering what Urban Thomas had intended to do to his wife. "He….he wanted to torture you, I believe," Jorge wasn't about to tell her that Urban Thomas planned to rape her, it made him too angry to even think about and simply moved past that part of the story. "So, Jesús, he gave the man something so that he couldn't move but yet, he was fully conscious of everything that happened. Remember how I always said that if anyone ever hurt you, I would cut them up into pieces, that I would torture them?"

"Is that what you did?" Paige barely whispered. "You….cut him up?"

"We started but it ah….it gets messy, you know?" He quietly replied. "But we did butcher him, there was a lot of blood and ah, I would say that he died right about the time Diego took his ax to him…" Jorge stopped for a moment, a smooth grin crossed his lips. "And you worry about *my* heart, *mi amor*, I assure you my heart looks better than his right about now."

Her eyes lit up with this last comment as she leaned in closer to him, her breath was hot on his face. "You did this for me?"

"Of course, Paige, you know I would do anything for you," Jorge spoke honestly as she moved closer. "Have I not told you that many times? Anything to protect you, anything to make you happy. Anything, you just tell me and I will do it."

"Was it difficult?" Her question seemed seductive in nature as her hand ran over the stubble on his face.

"It was actually way easier than it should've been," Jorge replied honestly as his lips formed into a smile. "I, quite literally, tortured him to death."

"I bet you did," She moved closer and he felt his heart begin to race as she moved in to kiss him, her tongue quickly slid into his mouth, as a soft moan erupted from the back of her throat. Jorge reached out and grasped her hips, as their kiss grew more intense, he pulled her body on top of him as his breath grew labored. Moving away from him for a moment, she quietly asked. "Can you still do *this?* With your heart?"

"Fucking shoot me if I can't," Jorge replied and heard Paige giggle as he pulled her toward him, his tongue quickly moving back into her mouth as his hands slid back down her body to grip her hips while he simultaneously squeezed her torso against him, as he grew hard in response. Her lips moved away from his to slowly trailed down his body as he gasped in reaction to her tongue as it teased him, sending a rhythm of pleasure through his entire body as he felt himself let go of everything that didn't matter at that moment. He drifted off into a state of intense euphoria as she worked her magic with both her mouth and fingers, sending him into a state of intense gratification. For a few minutes he was free, he was healthy and life, it would never end.

It was after he drifted off that Jorge slipped away from his world of beauty to one of terror. Although he felt no remorse for his barbaric actions, it was during his sleep that he would be haunted by the evil that sought him out. His dream started with him walking into a room so beautiful, so comforting and bright that he briefly wondered if he was dead, crossing to the other side. Did he suffer from a heart attack and die during the night? It was when he saw Paige in the distance, lying on a bed that a smile formed on his lips and he realized it didn't matter if she was there too.

As he approached her, something changed. The room suddenly grew cold, dark and he barely could breathe. A sense of panic filled his heart when Jorge finally stood beside his beautiful wife, with a knife drove in her chest. Screaming, his heart pounded erratically as he pulled the knife out and blood started to gush all over him as he tried to save her, his hands moving quickly to cover the wound as her white dress turned red. He cried, screamed, begged for help but no one appeared. That's when he woke in a cold sweat.

Sitting up in bed, he glanced toward Paige to see her quietly sleeping, her body moved the covers with each breath and he began to calm after reaching out to touch her. Nausea suddenly overtook him as he jumped out of bed, rushing toward the adjoining bathroom, he barely reached the toilet in time to vomit. He coughed and retched until his stomach was empty. Behind him, he could hear Paige rising from the bed and rushing up behind him, her hand on his shoulder.

"I'll get you some water," He heard her say before leaving the room. Taking a deep breath, he flushed the toilet and waited for a moment until he heard Paige returning. The chill of the night air met with his naked body upon her return, as she passed him the water before rushing off and returning with his robe. After rinsing his mouth out a couple of times, he finally rose and put on his robe, flushing the toilet again.

"Are you ok?" Paige appeared alarmed, yet half asleep, her hair disheveled, a blur of black makeup below her right eye as she struggled to understand.

"I'm fine," Jorge insisted as he walked across the room and searched for some mouthwash in the cabinet. "I don't know what happened. I was having a nightmare and suddenly, I woke up and was sick. I'm fine."

Paige didn't look convinced. "Are you having any other symptoms?"

"Ah, *mi amor*, I am fine," Jorge assured her. "Everything is not a heart attack, so please, do not worry."

"You would tell me if you had any other symptoms?" She asked.

Jorge hesitated for a moment, as their eyes met through the bathroom mirror. "*Mi amor*, I promise you, this is all. I probably ate something that didn't agree with me or maybe it's just been a long day but I assure you, I am fine. I feel much better."

Paige gave a hesitant smile.

"Go back to bed, Paige, I will be there shortly."

She quietly followed his suggestion while he stared in the mirror briefly before looking away. There was one other thing he had to tell Paige.

Upon turning out the lights and returning to bed, he felt comfort when she snuggled up close to him.

"Paige, there is one other thing, I forgot to mention earlier," He reached out and pulled her closer. "I am going to change my Will this week. Not because anything is wrong but all these issues lately, they worry me. What would happen to Maria if anything were to happen to us?"

Paige leaned in, her eyes huge in the dark.

"Right now, you are listed as being her parent if anything happens to me but if something were to happen to both of us, we need to have someone named as a guardian otherwise, I'm afraid my mother or other relatives will try to take her back to Mexico and I want her to stay in Canada."

"Of course," Paige seemed calm. "I know it's not a pleasant conversation to have but it's realistic that something could happen and we should be prepared."

"I am thinking Diego," Jorge continued slowly. "I did bring this up to him earlier today but he seemed unable to consider the possibility of anything happening to us, however, he did agree that if anything did, he would take care of Maria."

"I think that's a wise choice," Paige agreed as she leaned her head against his shoulder. "Diego would take good care of her. She has a stronger bond with Chase but that…concerns me a bit."

"I know, I am seeing the infatuation that you mentioned," Jorge confirmed. "I did not want to see it but you are right, it is there. He also has his own children, so regardless, it is better to consider Diego as a potential guardian, if we ever need one. He is like a brother to me and he loves you and Maria, so this is a good decision."

"Don't ever die," She whispered.

"Paige, I am like the Phoenix," Jorge insisted as he pulled her close. "I will always rise from the ashes."

CHAPTER 39

"Why are you acting as if I'm already dead?" Jorge asked, immediately bringing an awkward silence to the table. Paige and Diego exchanged looks as the waitress returned with their coffee. Jorge thanked her and turned to his wife and friend.

"*This* here, *this* has to stop. I am fine. I am alive and actually, probably in the best health of my adult life. I don't do drugs and drink excessively like I did in my 20s, I don't smoke, I eat better. Come on!"

"It's like Paige said," Diego spoke abruptly as he leaned forward on the table, facing Jorge head on. "You had a heart attack! That's serious! You can't fix that damage, Jorge, *amigo*, it is there forever."

"I had a *minor* heart attack," Jorge decided to put an end to the insanity, reminding them how ridiculous it was to fixate on this issue. "A *tiny*, small heart attack. Not a massive heart attack, just a small one. The doctor was happy with everything on my last visit. That is all."

"But you won't take your medication," Paige spoke quietly and he felt his heart melt. She had such sadness in her eyes and once again, Jorge regretted sharing the truth with her about his health. "I'm not someone who is crazy about pills either but what if you do need them."

"No, you know what, Big Pharma wants me to think I need them," Jorge corrected her and put his hand up in the air as the server returned again. "Now, this topic, it is over. I am fine."

After placing their order with the waitress and she walked away, Jorge noted a slight look of defiance on his wife's face while across from him, Diego merely avoided his eyes. Feeling somewhat guilty for his harsh remark, Jorge began to calm down.

"Look, I wouldn't have told either of you about this if I knew that you would take it this way," Jorge spoke slowly, carefully picking out his words. "I appreciate your concern, I do but this, this here is not living. We cannot focus on what could go wrong. Please, can we let this go."

"Well, it's a little hard to let go of when we just watched you sign your Will at the lawyer's office, you know?" Diego complained as he reached for his coffee and made a face before taking a drink.

"Lots of people, they have Wills, Diego," Jorge calmly reminded him. "Do you not have a Will?"

"Yes," Diego slowly answered. "But that's different because I'm fine."

"And so am *I,*" Jorge insisted as he turned his attention away, glancing at some men at the next table, who seemed overly interested in their conversation. "Look, this here conversation, it is done. The point is that I have a Will, I'm healthy and whatever happened in the past, it does not matter now. Can we move on?"

"Well, I'm not just depressed about this," Diego confessed as he spoke more in Paige's direction. "Chase is moving out soon."

Paige frowned and reached out to gently touch Diego's hand while Jorge felt his own face drop. He did not like to see his brother in pain.

"When does he plan to do so?" Jorge asked in a quiet voice as he reached for his coffee. "Is this certain?"

"He found a place and yeah, I mean, he told me the other day that he wants to move in at the end of the month," Diego said and immediately looked away. "It's, you know, it wasn't like I didn't know but it still bothers me. I know he's not gay or didn't see me that way but I guess I kinda thought that would change, you know?"

"These things, Diego, they don't change," Jorge commented as he glanced toward the waitress once again approaching, this time with their food. "Anymore than if a woman lived with you and wished you were straight, it's not going to happen."

Diego reluctantly nodded just as the waitress arrived at their table with three plates of food. Jorge automatically felt his stomach rumble as the aroma of eggs filled the air; even if it was a boring omelet, he was starving. Beside him, Paige had a poached egg while across from him, Diego quickly dug into a grease filled breakfast of bacon, fried eggs, hash browns, and toast. After they thanked the waitress and she walked away, Jorge turned his attention to the Colombian, as he shoveled a forkful of hash browns into his mouth.

"Seriously? And yet, *you* worry about my health?" He gestured toward Diego's plate and turned his attention toward Paige. "This man is eating the same as I used to, remember?"

"Yeah but I haven't had a heart attack," Diego countered while he chewed on his food. "Plus, I'm having a bad day."

"And this, this will make it better?" Jorge asked defiantly. "Food isn't the solution."

"It's *comfort* food," Diego corrected him. "I know it's not going to make anything better but I don't care. Between Chase leaving and dealing with my sister, everything is a fucking mess."

"What's up with Jolene?" Paige asked as she put pepper on her eggs. "Have you spoken to her?"

"No, she's not allowed to talk to anyone yet but when I called and spoke to the counselor or whatever it was," Diego said as he swung his hand around dramatically in the air. "She's going through a lot of emotional stuff. I know I'm going to get pulled into all of this and to tell you the truth, I don't want to go down that road. What if she tells them something about *us* and what we do."

He spoke these last words in a quiet voice but still managed to send a note of alarm to Jorge. It was something that he had considered when Jolene went to rehab, however, at the time, the short-term plan seemed much more relevant. Now, he wasn't so sure. What if Jolene spoke of their work? Could they trust her? Jorge didn't comment as he quickly ate his flavorless eggs.

"Do you think she would say anything?" Paige calmly asked as she picked at her food. "I mean, she's in it as much as us."

"Exactly and I want to remind her of that but I'm not sure when I will be able to actually talk to her," Diego complained before stuffing a slice of bacon in his mouth. "The patients aren't allowed to communicate with anyone outside the centre for the first couple of weeks."

"Try her now," Jorge instructed abruptly. "We gotta make sure she's not going to say anything about us or we're hauling her the fuck out of there. Say it's a family emergency."

"Right now?" Diego glanced at his phone. "Here?"

"Yes, call…."

"But I'm eating," Diego continued to shove food in his mouth.

"Give your body a break for a second and call," Jorge said more abruptly this time.

With some reluctance, Diego reached for his phone and hit a few buttons. Holding it to his ear, he spoke pleasantly on the phone, insisting their father was quite ill. He made a face and glanced toward Jorge.

"What? When did this happen?" He snapped into the phone. "And why did no one let me know? I'm paying for all this…"

Jorge exchanged looks with Paige who stopped eating her food and watched Diego.

"You fucking imbeciles!" He snapped before abruptly ending the call and dropped the phone on their table. "She left!"

"What?" Jorge shot back. "You've gotta be kidding me?"

"I'm not and I can't believe they didn't let me know," Diego said as he ran a hand over his forehead and took a deep breath. "Aren't they supposed to call me so I can find out what is going on or in case she was in danger?"

Jorge didn't reply, his mind already jumping ahead.

"Ok, let's calm down," Paige spoke with insistence in her voice. "Let's finish our breakfast and think."

Jorge followed her instructions and Diego hesitantly did the same.

"Why would she do this?"

"Cause she probably planned to all along," Jorge replied and shared a look with Diego who made a face and nodded. "She knew no one could talk to her the first week or two so she used it as her time to come up with what to do next. We would think she was off the radar so she could escape."

"Escape?" Diego spoke with a mouthful of eggs. "They said she just had to sign herself out."

"I mean us," Jorge corrected him. "She got out and skipped town."

"Skipped town? But…."

"I assure you, *amigo*, we will go to her apartment and she will not be there," Jorge continued to eat and enjoy his food, despite the situation. "She's long fucking gone. She is scared of us and you know, that might be a good thing."

"But where would she go?" Diego appeared confused. "She doesn't have friends anywhere. What if she's with the cops? What if they have her in some program and she's telling them everything?"

"I got people if she talks, she…" Jorge hesitated to finish his sentence but merely shared a look with Diego. "Look, my friend, we go far back but there comes a point where…"

"I know," Diego cut in and shook his head. "I know, we can't risk it. Can you find out for sure?"

"I will make a call but the last time someone tried to turn on me, they called me."

Diego nodded.

"I own too many people for that to be a concern," Jorge contemplated everything for a moment. "No, if I had to put my money on it, I would say she's left town. She's scared for her life, but where? We must go to her apartment and see. Do you still have the camera in her place? Can we look back to see if she's been there?"

"I'm not sure how far back it goes," Diego admitted and thought for a moment. "But I will do that after breakfast."

"Once we figure that out, we can find out where she is," Jorge considered for a moment. "And if she's in hiding, the main thing is she doesn't talk. As long as she stays away from the police or our enemies, I don't really care what she does."

"Maybe we should let both Jesús and Chase know," Diego spoke in a hushed tone especially when saying the latter of the two names. "They should be aware."

"I will text them," Paige said as she reached for her phone. "Maybe they can find out something for us?"

"We should still go to her apartment," Diego commented. "I have a key so if she's not there, we can at least go in and take a look around."

Paige nodded and Jorge finished his food, pushing the plate aside. "I wonder if anyone was there to pick her up when she left the facility?"

"Maybe we can go to the clinic," Paige suggested to Diego. "See where it takes us."

"And me," Jorge spoke up. "Me and Chase will go to her apartment and look around. I will ask Jesús to check with airports and some of his connections to see what he can learn. We will do this and meet later today?"

Everyone was in agreement. It was after they were outside in the parking lot that Jorge began to second-guess his original decision. "You know, I think I will instead have Jesús help me."

"You don't trust Chase?" Paige asked with surprise in her voice while Diego's eyes expanded as he waited for the answer. "Do you think he might help Jolene?"

"I...I hope not but she has wrapped him around her finger before," Jorge reminded them as he shoved his hands in both pockets as the cool, January air swirled around them. "I would like to think his loyalty is with us but of course, we cannot be certain."

No one replied but merely stood in silence.

CHAPTER 40

"In a way, it don't bother me," Jorge commented to Jesús as they drove to Jolene's apartment while Paige and Diego headed to the rehab facility. Reaching ahead, he turned up the heat in the SUV. "To be honest, I just want her to get the fuck out of the way. As long as I know she's not out there feeding information to the fucking *policia or* our competition, I don't give a fuck where she is or what she's doing."

"That's the problem, sir," Jesús spoke in his usual slow drawl as he looked out the passenger window, almost as if he expected to find Jolene walking down the Toronto streets. "We don't know where she is *or* what she's doing. Chances are good, she is trying to avoid us because she fears for her life but on the other hand, maybe she has turned on us."

"I think she knows better than to turn on me," Jorge gruffly commented as they arrived at her apartment building. "Now, we can do this the old-fashioned way and ring her buzzer and see if she answers or we can just walk into her apartment."

"I assumed the last option," Jesús returned his attention to Jorge as they parked in the visitor section. "But, whatever you think, boss."

"I think that there is something about the element of surprise, Jesús," Jorge commented as he turned off the SUV and glanced around. "I'm not seeing her car, are you?"

"No sir, I do not see," Jesús commented as he unfastened his seatbelt while Jorge didn't move. "And you said that Diego did not see anything when he checked the camera."

"Unfortunately, no," Jorge said as he bit his bottom lip and thought for a moment. "If her car isn't here then that suggests she got back from the facility and left town. I don't think she would stay here because she knows we would eventually find out she left the rehab and would come looking for her."

"Let's go look, ok?" Jesús commented as if he recognized Jorge's apprehension. "We must check her apartment."

Neither said a word as they slowly made their way into the elevator then to Jolene's floor. The doors opened and they walked into an empty hallway that was modern, yet not very appealing as far as apartment buildings go; the carpeting was old, the decor was quite plain, even the light fixtures were dim, almost as if they hadn't been cleaned in a decade.

Finding Jolene's door, Jesús reached into his pocket and pulled out a key, carefully sliding it into the lock and opening it.

Jorge let out a long sigh as they entered the apartment, his hand slipping into his jacket to find his gun; just in case. One never knew what they were walking into especially when it concerned someone like Jolene. However, the apartment was empty. The place looked like it had when they dragged her off to rehab; dirty dishes, empty bottles and a disarray of clothing scattered throughout the apartment. It was a fucking mess and the last thing Jorge wanted to do was to go through all her shit to look for anything but unfortunately, he didn't have much of a choice.

"Do you think, boss, that she even came back here after she left the facility? Maybe she jumped in her car and left."

"I'm not sure," Jorge replied. "But we are talking Jolene. It's not as if she would be happy without her makeup and expensive clothes, so I cannot see her out there winging it. Plus, did she even have her car keys with her? My guess is that she was here but she didn't stay long."

"Laptop," Jesús pointed toward the kitchen counter. "Marco, he can get into it."

"I already have him trying to hack her emails but she probably would be careful," Jorge commented as he approached the counter and grabbed the laptop. His eyes dancing around the apartment as if to find something that would tell him exactly where they could find Jolene but nothing was jumping out. Meanwhile, Jesús started to comb the room, going through every section, every corner as if he would discover a clue. Jorge instinctively went into her bedroom and glanced around. More clothing was tossed around but when he looked in her small closet, he noted that there was no suitcase; where had she normally kept it? Plus the room was such a mess, it was difficult to tell if she had packed a bag to leave.

A vanity table sat in the corner. He noted that there was no makeup on it. A grin formed on his lips. Leaving her bedroom, he went into the bathroom and after opening a few cabinets, he discovered the shelves were empty; no face creams, hair products, nothing that a woman like Jolene enjoyed having in her possession. Then again, what had she been allowed in the facility? He set the laptop down and grabbed his phone to send a message to Diego.

What is something that Jolene wasn't allowed in rehab that she would definitely want to have?

His attempts to get Verónic into rehab had taught him that there were certain stipulations. He couldn't recall; at the time, he simply wanted to get her ass off cocaine, personal comfort was of little interest to him. Not that it mattered since she refused to go and if she did, the stay was probably as short as Jolene's had been.

A razor. They weren't allowed anything sharp in rehab and her gun. It would be in her nightstand.

Of course! Her gun! Approaching her nightstand, he secretly wondered what else he would find; but when he pulled the drawer open there was only a Bible. This was an interesting choice for her. Grinning to himself, he moved to the other nightstand and opened that drawer to find various samples of hand lotions, lavender essential oil and empty notebooks and junk like bookmarks, vitamins, and other random crap; but no gun.

Diego, would she have a gun anywhere else in her apartment?

He glanced around the room and walked toward her vanity. Opening a small drawer he found nothing more than makeup brushes, more samples of various creams and more vitamins.

Are you kidding? Do you know how paranoid Jolene is? She would have it by her bed.

Unless someone else had taken the gun, which was unlikely, so apparently Jolene had returned to the apartment to collect a few things. Returning to the bathroom, he noted that there was no sign of a razor. Where did women usually keep one? He checked the drawers again and glanced in the shower; nothing.

"She was here," Jorge called out as he walked out to find Jesús, standing in the kitchen eating a large, red apple. "Taking a break?"

"I was hungry, sir," Jesús replied with a shrug and took another bite. "I was thinking."

"Well, her gun is gone and we know she didn't have that in rehab," Jorge commented and Jesús smiled, slowly nodding. "So, she was back here."

"Perfect, sir," Jesús managed between bites. "Do you have the laptop?"

"Ah yes," Jorge commented as he turned and went back into her bathroom. Before getting in the room, his phone buzzed. Pulling it out of his pocket, he saw another message from Diego.

She was only here a couple of days before signing herself out.

Meaning, Jolene had only agreed to go to rehab long enough to get them off her track. She never intended on staying.

Let's all meet back at the office.

Jorge had enough time to swing by the club first, deciding to casually mention Jolene's disappearance to Chase. He wanted to see his reaction.

"Are you kidding?" Chase almost appeared pissed off with this news. "Why wouldn't she stay and get the help she needed?"

"Maybe she didn't need as much help as she led us to believe," Jorge replied with a shrug, while Jesús made himself a drink. Contractors were in the building making plans for some work that would be done in the near future. The club was officially closed for renovations. "Maybe it was her way of getting away from us."

"No, I think she had a problem," Chase confirmed with no hesitation. "I mean, I didn't want to see it at first but when she went to rehab, it did make sense. I know I'm kind of naïve sometimes but it was clear that she was drinking more than normal."

"I guess it don't matter," Jorge confirmed with a shrug. "She's gone now. We don't know where….*yet*. Do you have any ideas?"

Chase thought for a moment and slowly shook his head. "I don't know. Maybe she went back to Calgary? Did she move or is her stuff there?"

"No, her apartment is still full."

"If she left things that were meaningful to her, then she's planning to come back," Chase reminded him and Jorge found himself slowly nodding. "Check with Diego, he might have some ideas."

This was exactly what he would do later when the four of them met at the office. Having passed off her laptop to Marco to check, he told him to interrupt their meeting if he found something.

"Going to rehab was fucking useless," Diego complained as soon as they all sat down, each with a coffee in hand. "They barely told me a thing. I'm her *brother* and paying the bills and yet, they won't tell me anything! Suddenly, the world is concerned with privacy!"

"It's probably some legal thing," Paige reminded him with a calm voice that seemed to instantly relax Diego. 'She probably didn't reveal anything then."

"Yes, Diego, we do not need to know what she talked about in group therapy," Jorge commented with some abruptness in his voice. "Unless she happened to share something about us or where she's going next."

"I can't believe that these people can just *sign* themselves out, I mean, really," Diego swung his hand in the air dramatically while rolling his eyes. "What's the fucking sense of going to rehab if they can't make you stay?"

"Well, it's not jail, Diego," Jorge commented and leaned back in his chair. "And my main concern is that we'll all end up *there* if she's off talking to the police."

"I thought we were protected?" Diego countered as his eyes bulged out. "You always say you got people."

"I do but sometimes, there is a limit for even me," Jorge insisted as he reached for his coffee. "How come we never buy donuts anymore?"

"Why do you think?" Paige replied with a smooth grin then reminded him. "We had some last meeting."

"We are trying to keep you from dying," Diego shot from the end of the table. "Or having another heart attack."

"You had a heart attack, sir?" Jesús appeared alarmed. It was the first time he spoke since the meeting began.

"A *minor* heart attack," Jorge shot Diego a dirty look. "It was nothing. I'm fine. Can we get back to the topic at hand?"

"But sir, there are *no* minor heart attacks," Jesús continued, unable to let the topic go. "I had a conversation with my doctor last year and he tells me that I had to start looking after my health better and lose weight because of potential issues with the heart, it is bad, sir."

"I'm fine, it's ok," Jorge rushed to change the topic. "Plus, one donut now and then, probably isn't going to kill me."

"I wouldn't be so sure, sir, they have a lot of fat and sugar," Jesús said as he made a face. "The heart, it can't take such things."

"*Especially* Jorge's heart," Diego piped up while Paige grinned and looked away. "Its like ready to explode."

"Diego, if my heart explodes, it is because you and your sister are irritating me so much," Jorge countered and put his hand up in the air. "Now back to the original topic, we must find out where Jolene is and fast. I doubt she would've brought a gun if she was going to talk to the police, so it does look as if she probably is just on the run from us."

That was when the door opened after a short knock. Marco stuck his head in and looked directly at Jorge. "Mr. Hernandez, I think I have something."

CHAPTER *41*

"The room is clean so give it to me, what you got?" Jorge asked after Marco eased into the room with an apprehensive smile on his face. His eyes glancing around the table. "Have a seat, my friend and tell me what you discovered."

"Mr. Hernandez, I, unfortunately, could not find anything on the computer, however, I was able to find something on the app," He said the last word softly, his eyes downcast as he sat beside Jesús.

"What app?" Diego automatically responded before anyone else could get a word in. "What's he's talking about? You put an app on Jolene's phone?"

"We all put an app on our phones," Jorge corrected him, understanding why Marco appeared somewhat reluctant to reveal this information. "The one for the club? That is what he means."

"What's that got to do with anything?" Diego pushed while his lips scrunched up and suspicion crept on his face. "Got a tracking device on us now, is that it?"

"No, Diego, I got a tracking device on everyone who downloads the app," Jorge corrected him as if it were common sense, merely shrugging it off while Jesús appeared intrigued and beside him, Paige was expressionless. "It's part of what people agree to when they accept the free app."

"Wait! What?" Diego shot back as he leaned forward at the end of the table. "What the hell are you talking about?"

"Apps, in general," Paige cut in at this point and Jorge was somewhat relieved because Diego had a tendency to take her words with more ease.

"There's a lot of them that can track what you're doing on your phone, your location and even watch you with the camera."

"What the fucking hell?" Diego's eyes doubled in size, his mouth fell open. "Are you serious?"

"Yes, it was on the news not long ago," Paige reminded him but Diego continued to look confused. "When you agree to the terms, it's usually a long document that no one actually reads and it essentially can allow them to track where you are, see your text messages, have access to your camera, that kind of thing. It's not *just* our app, it's many apps."

Diego continued to look stunned while Jesús appeared at ease with this information, nodding his head. "Oh yes, I also was watching that program online, it was very informative. It's a good thing we turn our phones off when we're on special missions."

"Yes, that's why I had always insisted on it," Jorge replied calmly while noting that Marco still appeared uncomfortable. "It is, you know, a good idea to be careful. But also, when we received new iPhones after the holidays, Marco created an app to put on them that deactivated the camera or mic for most apps so that you cannot be heard or watched without knowing."

"I don't understand," Diego said while shaking his head, turning his attention toward Marco. "How does that work?"

"Sir, it is complicated but essentially, I created an app that is only for us," Marco slowly explained. "It blocks other apps that might be potentially spying on us. It's something that might be used in government or other corporations with their phones because of the nature of secrecy and sensitivity of the information. We are merely doing the same here. However, it is still a good idea to turn off your phone when going to a place that you may not want to be tracked."

"I agree," Jorge insisted, as his eyes scanned everyone at the table. Jesús nodded while Paige continued to show no expression and Diego appeared anxious. "At any rate, what did you find?"

"No, wait," Diego cut in, putting his hands in the air. "Hold on! So you're telling me that companies are spying on people through their apps and that we are also doing this with the club app?"

"In general, yes, companies are doing this," Marco attempted to explain while his face grew red. "However, they cannot because of the app I created for us when we received our new phones, that blocks them. But our club app, it does do these things but I am not watching our actions and I would be the only one with access."

Diego slowly nodded as if he was beginning to understand.

"Makes you rethink sexting, doesn't it Diego?" Jorge teased and was automatically shot a dirty look, which he ignored and turned his attention toward Jesús.

"So this here, we could specifically target and watch Jolene through her phone, is this correct?" He directed his question toward Jorge, then turned to Marco, who was already nodding.

"Yes, sir, that is true," Marco replied but before he could go on, Diego cut in again.

"Why weren't we told this about the app?" He asked suspiciously, his question directed toward Jorge. "Are you secretly watching us?"

"No, as Marco said, he is the only one who can and he does not do so unless it is a case such as this one," Jorge hesitated to figure out how to explain it better. "Then, he can get access and see what is going on."

"Why didn't we just do this in the first place?" Paige asked in a calm voice. "If we knew the app would track any of our phones?"

"Tell the truth," Jorge said with an awkward shrug. "I never thought of it. I guess I was assuming that we couldn't get that much from the app, maybe just see her through the camera but it was my assumption she would turn her phone off if she suspected we were looking for her since she is certainly not answering it."

"No sir, she hasn't turned it off or if she did, it's not turned off now," Marco replied and appeared to grow more comfortable with the conversation. "Because I was able to see her but the audio, it was difficult to hear so she must have it turned down and also, I'm having some issue tracking her. It almost seems like she is somewhere where her signal is not being picked up very easily. Maybe a rural area or somewhere that has poor reception?"

"I had poor reception when I went to Chase's hometown," Diego commented with some apprehension. "Do you think she's there?"

"Unlikely," Jorge shook his head. "And besides, poor reception is common in many places, not just in Chase's hometown. Why would she go there? To hang out with his ex-wife? That doesn't even make sense."

Diego made a face and thought for a moment. "Are we able to see anything in the video?"

"That is the thing, she seems to be driving," Marco replied. "I can hear music playing and see her at the wheel but I'm unable to track her location. So, you see, it is not a lot of information to go on so far but it gives a place to start."

Jorge nodded. "Can you continue to watch, see what you notice and keep me updated?"

"Of course, Mr. Hernandez, this is no problem," Marco replied and stood up. "I will go back now and see what I can learn."

After he left, Jorge noted that Diego still appeared uncomfortable with everything he had just learned while Paige and Jesús were taking everything in stride.

"I still can't believe that companies are *tracking* people," Diego said with a naïvety that surprised Jorge. "I can't believe it's legal."

"As you know, my friend, many things happen that are not ethical or shouldn't be legal but the law, it picks favorites, this is not news," Jorge commented and paused for a moment before continuing. "For example, these music streaming services, do you not think that they are tracking people's habits too? Do you not think they were invented merely to see what people listen to, how much, how often so that they can manufacture the next pop sensation? Everything, it is about money."

"That doesn't make sense," Diego commented even though, he didn't appear too convinced. "They don't need music streaming services for that, they just have to see what sells on iTunes or whatever site people buy music from."

"No, but my friend, those sites only tell sales, they do not tell how often people necessarily listen to the songs," Jorge corrected him. "For example, I can download two songs today. One of which, I may listen to once or twice and grow bored but the other, I can listen to repeatedly, perhaps all day. A streaming service can track that and give more exact numbers."

Diego appeared stunned while Paige nodded her head and Jesús raised an eyebrow.

"They can get a more accurate sense of what is popular and with what age group, demographic, that kind of thing," Jorge continued as he shuffled uncomfortably in his seat. "That way, they can see what audiences want to hear whether it be to manufacture a new pop star or perhaps in say, a commercial for chewing gum or laundry detergent. It's fancy market research, my friend, nothing more."

"Wow!" Diego shook his head. "Unbelievable, this world we live in."

"True, but the trick is to make this work for us," Jorge spoke with persuasion in his voice. "It is about, taking any given situation and creating an advantage for us and in this case, it's gathering data to sell to marketers. That is why we have an app that does things like track people, things that morally is wrong but then again when was the last time I had morals?"

Beside him, Paige let out a laugh.

"Sir, I think it was forward thinking of you," Jesús spoke up. "I would not have thought of such things but you, I know you're always on top of new ways to improve our work."

"There is a lot of information out there,' Jorge insisted as he leaned back in his chair again. "If you choose to look into it. There are many ways to see our world but you must always ask yourself, how can I make this work for me? You cannot get stuck on how the world works against you but how you can make it work for you. This is important."

"How did you know about the music streaming services?" Diego asked bluntly. "I mean, it does make sense but still, how did you know?"

"I get approached a lot about investing in various things and you know," Jorge said before clearing his throat. "People tell me the bottom line in these situations. They do not waste their time on PowerPoint presentations, they just tell me what I need to know and this is one such thing. I do not care about much else except how much money will it make me and what is the real motives behind the business. As with us, all businesses have real motives, even if they claim to care about the customers or other such bullshit, at the end of the day, it's all about money and power. That is our world."

Everyone fell silent.

"So, if that is all…."

"Actually, boss, did you see the news today?" Jesús asked before Jorge was able to stand up. "The police already found Urban Thomas' remains."

"They should've, we practically placed him on their fucking steps!" Jorge boasted with a grin as he recalled the limited details on the news. The reporter merely suggested 'human remains' were found without saying how the man had been brutally murdered. "It is sometimes good to leave these things where people can find them. It sends a strong message. Although the second in command for Urban Thomas' business received a beautiful set of eyes this morning."

"Well sir, it did have an effect because these men, they have suggested they would like to work *with* us," Jesús spoke with humor in his voice. "Perhaps they now see what they are dealing with?"

"Perhaps they see differently with that extra set of eyes," Jorge mocked the situation and laughed at his own dark humor. "It is nice when people understand me. I find I'm so often misunderstood. Perhaps it's my English, it is not good yet."

"Your English is fine," Paige commented beside him. "But there's something to be said about actions speaking louder than words."

"Yes, *mi amor*, this is true," Jorge replied as he reached out, briefly touching her hand. "Often actions, they speak so much louder than words."

There was a hushed silence in the room. Everyone knew who the murder was really for and everyone knew why.

CHAPTER 42

"What do you want me to do, Diego? Ask Siri?" Jorge replied with a certain amount of sarcasm, something that didn't seem to go unnoticed at the table. Beside him sat Paige, looking out the window of the small restaurant while Diego merely gave him the usual response; a look of disgust carefully mixed with his lips twisting into an awkward pose. "As advanced as Apple technology is, I somehow doubt that it can find your runaway sister. All we can do now is wait and see what Marco can find out."

"It's been a couple of days," Diego was quick to point out as the waitress reappeared to fill up everyone's coffee. After they thanked her in their own way, she disappeared and he picked up where he left off. "I thought this app could track her. There must've been a location identified by now or something…a clue, a hint? Is she ok?"

"From what Marco is telling me, she is in a car driving," Jorge answered honestly, surprised that he wasn't anxious about this situation but something told him that Jolene was too smart to turn on him at that point. "That says to me that she is trying to get away from here and perhaps, that is the best thing for all of us."

"So, what? She's going to leave her apartment and never come back again?" Diego asked suspiciously. "Are you sure you don't know anything more and you're not telling me? This is stressing me out plus I'm having nightmares about…"

"Diego, I do not know anything more about this," Jorge abruptly replied and took another drink of his coffee. "Why you so paranoid? Have I ever lied to you about anything? No, I have not. This time is no different. We have to wait and see. My guess is that she will eventually reach out to you but who knows? We are talking Jolene."

"If she were to talk to anyone here, it would probably be Chase," Diego spoke thoughtfully. "I'm going to stop by the club after I leave here. I want to see the progress with the renovations anyway."

"Chase, he said they are going quickly," Jorge replied as he glanced around the restaurant, suddenly feeling tired. "I would say, we can soon plan our grand re-opening party, or whatever you wish to call it."

"Well, it's gotta be perfect cause that's where I'm having the wedding," Diego spoke casually, directing his comment at Paige, who appeared somewhat surprised. "By the way."

"Just tell us when and where to show up," Jorge replied, automatically rolling with the punches, while beside him, Paige looked slightly alarmed.

"We're getting married at the club," She spoke skeptically. "I don't know, is that a good place, all things considered?"

Jorge turned and noted that his wife's question seemed directed toward him. "I mean, that Telips girl was…"

"Yes, well, that is a good point too," Jorge nodded in understanding. He had killed a woman at the club a year earlier, after learning that she was causing trouble for Chase and his family; and maybe getting a little too close to some truth about him too. "However, I sometimes wonder if we need to have another wedding at all. In the beginning, this was more for my daughter and as of late, Maria now seems disinterested in the idea."

"Oh no!" Diego spoke abruptly with his hand in the air. "*You* told *me* that I could plan this wedding and now, you're trying to say that it's off? After all the time and research that I've put into this? Are you fucking mad?"

"Diego, what difference does this make, really?" Jorge replied with a shrug. "Don't you have enough to do without this extra task? Plus, Paige and I, we are already married. Why does it matter?"

"Because it just does," Diego replied with a shrug and leaned back in his seat. "This was something I was looking forward to and it would give us a reason to celebrate for a change. Everything is something negative, meetings about problems, this was something that I actually wanted to see happen. You can't take this from me."

"Ok, I thought," Paige gently cut in, her hand reaching out and touching Jorge's arm as she spoke. "We agreed to wait till we find a house and sort out this mess with Jolene. Right now, there's too much stuff."

"There always will be too much stuff," Diego reminded her as he gestured toward Jorge. "If you haven't noticed, this man is a freight train flying down the track and nothing slows down. Today, it is Jolene or whatever else but in the future, it will be the election and a million other things. There's always something going on with Jorge Hernandez."

"I'm a busy man, *amigo*," Jorge responded with a fake modesty, his hand gently reaching toward his heart. "The world of a busy man, it never stops."

Diego rolled his eyes while Paige merely grinned, causing Jorge to lean forward and give her a quick kiss. Of course, this show of affection wasn't just because he suddenly wanted to shower his wife with love but also because he noticed that Alec Athas had just walked in the door; the others hadn't seen him yet. There was always a need to make people see what belongs to you.

However, his attempt was for nothing. Alec was immediately swept into a conversation, meanwhile, Diego looked crestfallen. This had not been his intention.

"Do not worry, Diego," Jorge addressed his response with sincerity. "It is a delay. Who knows? Maybe we should renew our vows in the fall on the same day we were married, what do you think, Paige?"

To his surprise, she made a face and shook her head. "Everyone does that. It's so…*not* us."

"This is true, *mi amor*, this is true," Jorge admitted while Diego let out a loud sigh. "How about we see what the next few weeks bring. I would like to find a new house first. I'm about to lose my mind in that cramped little apartment."

"You and me both," Paige quietly added.

"Well, you can move into *my* place," Diego abruptly commented. "It will soon be all but empty, now that Chase is moving out."

Paige frowned while Jorge wasn't sure how to react, which was rare. Not that he had to, his wife was ready to show comfort.

"I think it is better," She spoke with the gentleness of a mother to her child, as she reached out and gently touched Diego's hand. "I don't think it was healthy living together considering how you feel about him. Deep down, you know it too."

Diego merely nodded, just as Alec arrived at the table.

"Sorry, I'm late," He spoke apologetically. "I have a lot of people asking me about the warehouse and…"

"Hey, I gotta go," Diego rose from his seat before Alec could sit down. "You sit here, I'm heading out."

Sliding across the booth, he stood up as Alec stood aside to let him out.

"I will call you," Paige said to Diego as he buttoned his jacket and reached for his gloves. "Maybe we can meet back at the office later?"

"Sure," Diego spoke glumly before walking away.

"Is he ok?" Alec asked as he slid into the booth across from them. "Did I interrupt something?"

"Nah, that's just Diego," Jorge replied and took a deep breath. "So, you have a lot of interest in jobs at the warehouse?"

"Jobs, concerns," Alec replied, the second word coming out in a lower tone than the first. "As you can imagine, some people worry about criminals being around if there is a grow op in the neighborhood while others are looking for details about jobs, but I keep telling them it's too early yet."

"We barely have acquired the building," Jorge replied with a nod. "The rest will be sorted out soon. Jesús is on the job."

"Keep me posted," Alec said as he removed his gloves and began to unbutton his coat. "I know these things don't happen overnight, obviously, but as long as I know what to tell the people in my district."

"You tell them that lots of well-paying jobs are on the way," Jorge replied curtly. "That's what you tell them."

Alec suddenly looked awkward and hesitant, as if unsure of whether or not to speak. He glanced at Paige and then returned his attention to Jorge.

"Look, I'm going to be honest with you," He slowly began as he carefully moved his gloves aside, his attention suddenly averted by an approaching waitress. After ordering a coffee and she rushed away, Alec returned his focus to Jorge. "When I first contacted Paige about helping me, that's all I wanted. Just someone to help me win the nomination for my party, maybe with my campaign this fall."

He stopped speaking as the waitress returned with his coffee. After a superficial conversation with her about the weather, she left and Alec continued.

"Now," He continued as he stirred some sugar into his coffee, slowly as if he were apprehensive. "Now, suddenly, I feel like you're such a huge part of my political future."

"This is because I am," Jorge replied and took a deep breath. "You and I, we will work together."

"I did some research," Alec seemed to ignore his last comment. "I did some research on you online."

The table fell silent and an unease swept over them.

"I found some disturbing things about you when I did," Alec spoke in a hushed tone. "And although I certainly want to work with you, I'm a little concerned because if I managed to find this information, then that means others can too."

"And you think this will hurt you during the campaign this fall?" Jorge asked, showing no reaction to this news. He knew of the articles in question. In Mexico, many called him *intocable* or untouchable, something that spoke to how much influence he had in his old country, despite any wrongdoings.

"It has crossed my mind," Alec replied, his eyes jumping between Jorge and Paige.

"But you did notice that you got the position for your party in your district despite the competition you originally had," Jorge pointed out and paused briefly before continuing. "So this theory, it is not strong."

"That was different though," Alec calmly answered. "Winning the voters over may not be as easy. We can create jobs but on the other hand, some may learn of my involvement with you and your reputation…I have some concerns that it will be held against me when the pressure is on. The media will be all over this."

"Please tell me, what did you find?" Jorge was curious. It was rare that he searched his own name online but occasionally he did for fun. In Mexico, there was a whispering of his crimes but yet, nothing could ever be proven. What if he underestimated Canada? Perhaps there was something to Alec's concerns.

Reaching into his pocket, Alec pulled out a phone and after tapping on the screen, he passed the phone to Jorge. He noted the translation under the Spanish title.

El narco más famoso de México se muda a Canadá.

He only glanced at a few lines but wasn't surprised. The article talked about how he was notorious for slinking away from trouble despite the general belief that there was blood on his hands. It suggested collusion within the police department and government. It made him laugh, while beside him, Paige was reading over his shoulder.

"He could be right," She quietly commented. "This isn't good."

"*Mi amor*, this is hardly a reputable news source," Jorge said, handing the phone back to Alec. "This, it has been my whole life in the independent media. It is not new. This is like one of those gossip rags that print lies."

"But people may not know that," Alec calmly pointed out while shaking his head. "Journalists have managed to put a lot of pressure on the government and organizations in the past. If you're in the media, this could weight down on me and in turn, also my campaign."

"Alec, you misunderstand," Jorge spoke casually. "This article is mere speculation from a questionable source. If someone were to research me here and now, I own various dispensaries as well as one, soon two, warehouses in the marijuana market as do many other businessmen. Before that, I invested in various, *legal* Canadian businesses and before that, I was working for my father's coffee company."

Alec slowly nodded.

"Anything else is merely speculation," Jorge spoke arrogantly, perhaps on purpose to get his point across. "I have never been arrested. Not here in Canada or Mexico so you see, everything you see online is exaggerated. Most public people and businessmen have bad things about them on the internet too. It is the nature of the beast, is it not?"

Alec appeared apprehensive while beside him, Paige merely nodded her head.

"He is right," She commented. "It's easy to turn this around to say that the media is merely grasping at anything to create a story and that right-wing extremists are in protest of the liberal lifestyle since Jorge sells marijuana. There's always a way to spin things. We just have to get our own journalist."

Alec didn't say anything and neither did Jorge.

CHAPTER 43

"He's concerned that what you got away with in Mexico won't fly here," Paige explained later that day as they got ready to meet with Chase and Diego for drinks. It had already been a long week and Jorge suggested that perhaps they needed to get together and unwind; at least, that was what he told Chase. In actuality, he was hoping that after a few drinks, the normally quiet club manager would admit if he had any communication with Jolene in recent days. Although Marco had attempted to learn what he could, there was some connection issues making it difficult.

"Oh, please!" Jorge laughed as he slid his arms into a fresh shirt on the other side of the room from Paige, who was fixing her makeup. "The only difference between the people I pay off here and the people I pay off in Mexico is that you Canadians are a little more polite. But for some reason, you like to believe that you're an honest country with no corruption or wrongdoing and I'm here to tell you, that's a fantasy you've been brought up to believe. It's kind of like believing in the legal system or trusting the police. When the day comes you see the reality, it's always a bit of a shock, no?"

"Maybe people believe what they have to believe," Paige gently pointed out as their eyes met in the mirror. "They *need* to believe that there is order and that the good guys always win."

"I guess that depends on how you define 'good guys'," Jorge commented flippantly as he approached his wife, giving her a quick kiss on the top of her head. "Now, *mi amor*, we must get going or we will be late."

The upscale bar where Diego chose for them to meet was actually one of the places he had looked at when deciding on a new image for the club. It smelled of money as soon as you walked in the door. Small groups of people gathered together, many dressed in expensive clothing, women with designer handbags while the men were passing their gold cards to the staff as if everyone had the same luxury. To Jorge, that was merely a blatant way of making the world know that they were important. He probably had more money than anyone in the room and yet, he didn't feel the need to show it off. The only reason why he wore a suit and not just a shirt and tie with his usual leather jacket was that it was more suitable for this establishment; plus, he wanted to look good for his wife.

Paige was wearing a very fitted red dress that captured attention as soon as they walked into the establishment, having checked their coats at the door, they wandered past the small crowd to the back of the room where Chase and Diego were waiting. The two were already enjoying a drink and fully involved in a lively conversation. Jorge felt his heart twinge a bit when he considered that Diego might be making one, last attempt to seduce Chase before he moved out in a few days.

"It looks like you two already started without us," Jorge observed as he pulled a chair out for Paige before sitting beside her. Two empty shot glasses sat on the table while both Diego and Chase were drinking some girly drink. "So, tell me, what's good?"

"The tequila, it's good," Diego automatically replied with a joyous grin on his face. It reminded Jorge of twenty years earlier when it was more commonplace for his friend to share a smile. These days, it was his dark brooding appearance that stood out, now that life had pulled him into a much more cynical place. "But when is tequila ever not good?"

Jorge started to laugh. "I recall at least one tequila experience that wasn't so pleasant but that was many years ago."

"What happened?" Chase asked with his usual wide-eyed innocence. Perhaps, Jorge considered, this was one of the things that Diego found attractive about him. Maybe we look for in partners, a part of ourselves that we have lost.

"Cheap brand?" Diego guessed and puckered his lips up, arrogantly lifting his head and nodded.

"No, actually, Diego, it was an expensive brand and probably the best I ever had in my life," Jorge paused and shared a look with his wife and grinned. "Until the next morning, when I vomited what I believe may have been part of my liver. I do not know but there was definitely a vital organ of some kind that came up in that mess."

Paige snickered while across the table, Diego let out a boisterous laugh, just as a young waiter came to take their drink order. After he left, Jorge immediately continued.

"Nine months later, I learn that I'm a father and that's my tequila story."

"No way!" Diego encouraged him on. "You're telling me that you were drunk on tequila that night."

"Had to be, *amigo*, cause there was no way I would ever have sex without a condom otherwise," Jorge said while shaking his head. "I barely remember a thing. I was high on cocaine, drunk on tequila and *there*….and barely at that. It was hardly ideal but I got Maria out of it, so I guess everything does work out in the end."

The waiter returned with his Corona and Paige's glass of wine. Diego immediately jumped in and requested another Zombie for both him and Chase. Jorge said nothing. A quick glance at Paige and he knew they were thinking the same thing.

After the waiter left, the usually subdued Chase spoke up with his own story.

"You know what?" He spoke with a slight slur in his speech, making Jorge wonder how many drinks he already had; although Chase was one to rarely indulge so chances are it wouldn't take that many to make him talk. "I…I totally relate to your story. That's how I ended up with my ex-wife. I went to a party right after my high school girlfriend dumped me and somehow hooked up with Audrey. I had a drink or two but she gave me a pill and the next thing I know, we're in bed together and a few weeks later she shows up at my house and tells my mom that she's pregnant."

"What? Your mom?" Jorge began to laugh as the waiter returned with their drinks. "How fucking old were you?"

"Barely 18."

Diego laughed just as the waiter placed the drinks on the table.

"That's insane," Jorge agreed while Diego quickly thanked the young, handsome waiter for the drinks. "I have to say, at least I was a little older, but 18, that's young. I could not handle such news at that age."

"How old were you when Maria was born?" Diego asked with interest as he began to sip on his Zombie. "In your 30s, right?"

Jorge didn't answer just nodded and glanced at Paige.

"I was a kid," Chase continued to confess and Jorge watched him carefully. "I had just graduated high school, I didn't know what I wanted to do with my life but I knew I wanted to leave Hennessey. The next thing I know, I'm forced to marry this girl that I didn't love, all over one mistake."

"Ah, this is the thing," Jorge commented while shaking his head. "Men, we get so much anger from women because we supposedly make a baby then leave and yet, no one talks about the women who try to get pregnant to keep you around. The only difference between you and me, my friend, is that I was older and more headstrong than you. There was no way anyone was going to tell me what to do."

"Of course," He continued as the lounge suddenly grew louder. "I looked after my daughter but I wasn't about to get married to her mother."

"It was a terrible mistake," Chase confessed and his face grew sad. Of course, he was referring to the same son that died at the age of four, after wandering into a nearby wooded area and shot by a local hunter. That same man was later hunted down and shot by Paige.

"Well, at any rate, we all do crazy things in our youth," Jorge attempted to change the mood before it dipped too low. "I could tell you all a few stories from when I was younger, situations that I got into that were hilarious in retrospect, if not at that time."

"I think that most people could," Paige weighed in with laughter in her voice. "We all have those days when we feel as though the joke is on us."

"God, he has a sense of humor, this is for sure," Jorge replied and took a drink of his beer while watching Chase carefully. He was definitely enjoying his Zombie, maybe a little too much, especially after the topic of children arose. Although it hadn't been on purpose, it definitely would help them out with their plan for that evening.

Diego lifted his drink in the air. "To life, and its many strange events."

With a grin, Jorge raised his Corona while Paige and Chase picked up their glasses; a beautiful moment shared, the four of them tapped their drinks together.

"Where is Jesús tonight?" Diego asked and glanced at his phone before putting it away. "Looking after Maria?"

"No, Maria, she is at another school event," Jorge replied and glanced toward Paige. "Was it that play she is working on?"

"Yes," Paige nodded. "That's why we have to leave by 7:30."

"Of course," Jorge glanced at his phone, noting it was only 6:25. This gave him enough time to find out what he needed to know. "Jesús is actually in BC again, taking care of some business."

"How did your meeting with Alec go?" Diego switched gears as he leaned forward on the table.

"Good, he does have some concerns though," Jorge replied with a shrug. "Just some news stories he has found about me on the Internet."

Diego's lips changed from a smug expression to laugher very quickly and he nodded. "When I recently met with him about buying the warehouse, he said that every time he talks to you, he feels as if he is approaching The Godfather."

Jorge laughed at this remark and looked down at the table.

"I said, 'you know, you kinda are *amigo*' and you should've seen the expression on his face," Diego continued to laugh as he glanced toward Chase, who quickly joined in. It was almost as if the two were having a party on their own, while he and Paige were merely observing.

"Well, I cannot disagree with that statement," Jorge grinned and reached for his Corona, briefly glancing at his wife. "I like to think I make an offer people can't refuse."

"You usually do," Paige quickly agreed, her hand gently gliding down his arm. "Look at everything you've managed in only a few short months."

"All of that and yet, I cannot find Jolene," Jorge spoke with regret, he looked down at his drink before glancing up at Chase. Concern filled his eyes but it was unclear if the concern was for Jolene or for the fact that they were unable to locate her. "Let us hope that wherever she is, that she is ok."

He couldn't look at his wife. They both knew that Jolene's safety wasn't a concern to him.

"I don't understand why she didn't stay," Chase appeared irritated. "She had the opportunity to get help and she walked away? If she had a problem, why wouldn't she want to get better?"

"It's addiction," Diego spoke up and shook his head. "It runs in my family and Jolene, it is not the first time that she's run into this kind of problem. Unfortunately, she does not listen to anyone."

"We are unable to locate her," Jorge continued with a sigh. "She avoids our messages, our calls, she does not want to talk to anyone."

"I don't understand," Chase asked, his eyes sincerely full of concern. "She really should come back and get the helps she needs.

"You know, maybe *you* should call her," Jorge suggested in the most sincere voice he could find. "Maybe you can get through to her. You've always had a close relationship with Jolene, she might speak to you."

Noting Diego's downcast eyes, Jorge felt a tinge of compassion but it was necessary to continue.

"Perhaps you will be the voice of reason."

"I tried before and she wouldn't answer," Chase admitted. "I was so angry when I learned that she wasn't finishing her treatment."

"But today, it is a new day, am I right?" Jorge coaxed. "Maybe try again?"

While a disoriented Chase attempted to remember which pocket held his phone, Jorge sent Marco a quick text message to watch Jolene's app. This didn't go unnoticed by Diego who remained silent and continued to sip his drink, while beside him, Paige squeezed her husband's arm. Although he wasn't sure what they would discover, he had a feeling that something would come out of this attempt. What he didn't expect, however, was for Jolene to answer.

CHAPTER 44

As soon as he saw Diego's eyes bulge out, Jorge quickly gave him a warning look. Shaking his head, he put his hand up in the air, indicating for him to stay calm while Chase talked to Jolene. She wasn't about to speak to anyone else at that table, so it was important they remain patient and see what they could learn.

"Where are you? Why did you leave rehab? I don't understand," Chase slurred his words, something Jorge hoped Jolene would notice. If she knew he was drinking, perhaps she would assume he had drunk-dialed and lower her defenses. Jorge sensed his motivations were sincere as opposed to helping them out, which would translate perfectly to Jolene. It might actually work.

It was when Chase stood up that Jorge grew nervous.

"Sorry, Jolene, it's hard to hear, just a second," He was saying as he headed towards the door, leaving an uncertain group behind. His eyes on Diego, Jorge recognized a mixture of sadness and anxiety as he slumped back in the seat while Paige remained calm.

"I have to pick up Maria soon," She glanced at her watch. "The school gets pissed off if we're late. I'm gonna follow him outside and see if I can catch anything on my way out. You two, stay here. Give him some space. If Jolene suspects either of you are with Chase, she won't say a thing."

"What if she doesn't anyway?" Diego spoke in his usual abrupt way but his eyes were full of sadness. "Or what if she does and he doesn't tell us?"

"I have Marco on the app," Jorge replied with a heavy sigh. "This here is getting to be too much, Diego. Your sister, we need to find her and make sure she keeps her mouth shut. I do not need trouble from her. If she wants to go her own way, that is fine but I need to know she isn't working against us in any way."

"I know," Diego nodded with traces of defeat on his face. "I understand."

"Paige," Jorge continued as his wife got up to leave. "Do not bother trying to find out anything. I think Marco can take care of it and if Chase sees you, he might let it slip that we are all together here tonight."

"Good point," Paige agreed, turning her attention toward Diego. "I'm sure he won't hold anything back from us."

"Unless she tells him about the day we put her in rehab," Diego reminded them both. "Maybe she will try to get him on her side."

"I do not think," Jorge shook his head and leaned forward on the table. "If Jolene works against all of us, she also will be working against him. He will not walk away unscathed."

"It will be fine," Paige reached for her purse. "I think she understands the severity of this situation."

Leaning in, she gave Jorge a quick kiss, which he graciously accepted. After she left, he returned his attention to Diego.

"We gotta sort this out," Jorge insisted as he reached for his beer.

Diego didn't reply. His eyes slightly downcast.

"So when is he moving?" Jorge finally asked. "Is it the end of this week, no?"

"Yes, in a few days," Diego glumly replied.

"That is why you are not sleeping?" Jorge asked. "Your eyes, they are dark like you haven't slept in weeks."

"Partially," Diego replied and leaned in. "Look, you know me, I'm not opposed to violence, right?"

"I know this, yes," Jorge replied with a casual shrug.

"What happened, in BC," Diego quietly replied. "I'm having nightmares about it."

"Really?" Jorge asked with surprise in his voice. Although he knew their attack on Urban Thomas was quite brutal, it never occurred to him that it would upset Diego. He was hardly a sensitive man when it came to violence.

Diego nodded, the concern in his eyes quickly turned to fire as he leaned ahead. "That day, I wanted nothing more than to make him suffer. What he wanted to do to Paige; we had to send a message back that we weren't fucking around. So, I don't regret it and *amigo*, I would do it again. I would not give it a second thought."

"Ok, so you do not have second thoughts?" Jorge attempted to understand. "But since that time, you've had nightmares?"

"Yes," Diego appeared regretful as his eyes drifted across the room and back again. "Every night I see that ax coming down. I hear him, that sound that came out of his throat and I see it, the blood, everywhere, all around me. I'm drowning in it and I can't breathe. I wake up and I feel as if the walls are closing in on me."

His voice was shaky as he continued, while Jorge remained fascinated by his words. "Every night, the same nightmare except sometimes, it is worse than others. Sometimes, when the ax comes down, it is as if I'm sinking down like I'm being pulled into the ground with Urban Thomas. As if I have no strength like I'm powerless."

"And this, this has been happening since that day?" Jorge asked with surprise in his voice. "Diego, this is not like you."

"I know, I never," He started to speak and shook his head no, just at the young waiter returned to see if they wanted anything to drink.

"No, my friend, you can give me the bill for everyone," Jorge commented and gestured toward the empty seat across from him. "Both my wife and associate had to rush away, so I will take care of everything."

"I can pay," Diego said as he reached into his pocket.

"No, this is fine," Jorge insisted as he nodded toward the waiter. "Please, bring me the bill unless, Diego, you wish for another drink?"

"You know, I will see what Chase wants to do," He appeared unsure.

"Ok, well, I will pay up until this point," Jorge replied and watched the waiter walk away. Returning his attention to Diego, he wasn't sure what he would say until the words were out. "Well, my friend, I am sorry to hear this although, I'm somewhat surprised to learn this news.

I had no idea that this would disturb you so much and you know me, I would've easily taken care of it on my own."

"I didn't expect this either," Diego said with a heavy sigh. "Maybe I'm getting soft with old age."

"You're younger than me, so that there, it is not going to fly," Jorge commented just as the waiter returned with their bill. After he was given cash that also allowed for a generous tip, the waiter walked away.

"I don't know," Diego spoke solemnly. "This is not *me.*"

"Perhaps it is a combination of things, no?" Jorge considered with a shrug. "You know, Jolene taking off, that whole situation was stressful. Then you have Chase leaving…it is, perhaps, a bad time overall for you?"

"Everything is a disaster."

"Ah!" Jorge shook his head as a grin appeared on his face. "And yet, everything is beautiful. You know, we are about to find Jolene and sort everything out, soon the new club will be opening, that will be fun too. We have this situation with our enemies under control. Good things are ahead, my friend, many good things."

"It's just," Diego frowned as his face darkened. "I always thought that once I found success, money, that everything else would fall into place but it's not. Here I am trying to help with your life, looking for your house and planning the wedding because I got no life of my own."

"See, this is something you must work on," Jorge spoke with intensity in his voice, he leaned forward on the table and looked into Diego's eyes. "I've known you for what? Twenty years now? If there is something I've always known about you it is that even when it seems you are in a weakened position, you are strong. Even in those early days, with your *daddy* back in California. He had the power but yet, there was something that told me you were always in control."

Diego's eyes widened as he listened as if this information was something new that he had never considered. He remained silent.

"Perhaps, it is me," Jorge considered. "I have been known to steal other people's fire without meaning to simply because mine is so strong. It always has been and always had to be. I did not have a choice. At a young age, I learned that it was up to me to make my life as I wished and no one was going to help me. I set out and made things happen. I never asked anyone's permission to have what I wanted, I just took it."

"But Paige?" Diego asked and glanced at Chase's empty seat. "You can't make people be a part of your life if they don't choose to be. You can't make them care."

"No, this is true," Jorge replied and thought for a moment. "But do you think Paige would've stayed that first night, had I not been persistent? I remind you, she came to my suite thinking that I was the man she was paid to…take care of. Once she learned I was the wrong person, she wanted to leave. I had to think fast. So, I asked her to share a drink with me. Just a simple drink, nothing more. That is the key. You keep it simple, my friend and each time, you push a little further. Sometimes it is about reading the situation and sensing what that other person needs at that moment and giving it to them. But we, we get tied up in our own insecurities and fears. You cannot allow this to own you."

Diego seemed to relax as he took in his words.

"Look, I don't think that this situation with Chase is necessarily the same," Jorge admitted and searched for the right words. "I do feel, however, that sometimes we must listen and not talk. Maybe you should ask him why he's leaving. What does he need?"

"I'm guessing to be away from me," Diego spoke glumly.

"See, you are personalizing this situation when perhaps, it has nothing to do with you," Jorge spoke thoughtfully. "This is the time, my friend, he has a few drinks in him and his conversation with Jolene, perhaps will bring out emotions too and I feel that maybe tonight is the night you say what you need to say to him. It is sitting in your heart now."

"And this thing," He continued. "With Urban Thomas, we are sometimes locked in anger and the reality, it does not hit until later. I regret I did not work alone."

"Do you," Diego started in a hushed voice as he moved forward. "Do you regret it? Do you have nightmares?"

It took Jorge a moment to process the question and although his first instinct was to say no, he suddenly recalled his recent nightmare about Paige.

"I have no regrets because what I did, it was out of love for my wife. You do not threaten someone I love and think you will walk away. I did have one nightmare where Paige was killed. If anything, it made me more certain about what I have done. She and Maria, they are my heart and if that day ever comes that I lose one of them, it will be half of my heart ripped out. And I assure you, my friend, no one wants me with even less heart than I have now. The world, it would be a very dark place."

Diego seemed to take everything he said in stride and quiet contemplation.

Jorge finished his beer just as Chase returned. Looking drained, he sat back in his seat.

"So, where's my sister?" Diego immediately jumped in. "What did she tell you?"

Chase didn't reply to Diego's questions but looked to be in shock.

Diego opened his mouth to say something but Jorge shot him a warning look and spoke instead.

"So, Chase, I take it that this conversation, it did not go well?" Jorge calmly replied. "I will order you another drink." He turned to catch the waiter's attention.

"I'll have a water, I'm driving," Diego said as soon as the server arrived at the table. Jorge nodded before turning his attention toward Chase. "And you?"

"Another one," He pointed toward the empty glass in front of him.

Jorge ordered another beer. Across the table, Diego appeared nervous while Chase was unusually quiet. Jorge remained silent and sent a quick message to Marco. Relieved to learn that they now had established Jolene's location, he forwarded the information to Paige and then looked up to see Diego's eyes studying him while Chase remained aloof. The waiter returned with their drinks.

"I guess Jolene, she has a way of rattling us all from time to time," Jorge spoke gently. "However, you know, we cannot allow her to upset our night. Here, we are having a beautiful time, making plans for the future. It is going to be good."

Chase grunted miserably and put his attention on the drink,

knocking back most of it in one gulp, causing Jorge to make a brief glance at Diego, who appeared somewhat alarmed by this reaction.

"I guess that's one way to look at it," Chase muttered as he set the glass back down.

"My friend, why so sad, we, here, we can solve any problem," Jorge spoke boastfully, knowing his arrogance shone through and didn't care. Perhaps this would be a lesson to Diego on this night when he was full of insecurities. "So, what is wrong, we can resolve this for you."

"What did she say?" Diego asked in an unusually calm voice as if he had taken some of Jorge's earlier advice to heart. "You seem upset."

Chase glanced at Diego then back at Jorge. At first, it didn't appear he was going to answer any of their questions but both men remained calm, open and yet, neither prepared for his answer.

"Jolene thinks she's pregnant."

CHAPTER 45

"Me, I think she's making it up," Jorge said while removing his shirt and tie. Across the room, Paige was sitting in bed, already changed into the beautiful silk nightdress he gave her for Christmas. The vibrant colors and richness of the fabric made her skin glow when combined with the dim light from the nearby lamp. She watched him with interest, her head tilted to the side. "If we think she's pregnant, we're not going to hurt her."

"And Chase is soft-hearted too," Paige agreed with a nod, her eyes quickly looking away while sadness crossed her face. "But then again, maybe it is true."

"No, not likely," Jorge insisted as he removed his pants and tossed them on the same chair with his shirt and tie. He took off his socks before crossing the room and getting into bed beside her. His thoughts were quickly moving away from their conversation as he inhaled the soft, vanilla scent his wife wore. "She's like, what? In her early 40s?"

"Wait, what?" Paige spoke abruptly, despite the fact that her voice was soft, soothing by nature. Jorge noted that she was backing away from him slightly, a cold vibe took over their bed. "Are you suggesting that a woman can't get pregnant in her forties? Do you really believe that?"

"I did not say that they could not," Jorge rushed to defend himself as his hand gently touched her arm. "What I mean is that it does not necessarily happen as easily with age, isn't this correct? I did not say she was too old."

He quickly realized that this was perhaps not the best choice of words as her eyes filled with hurt.

"Ok, let me go back," Jorge attempted to ease the situation before it got any worse. "Obviously, I am saying this wrong. I mean that my understanding is that women in their forties aren't as quick to get pregnant as let's say, a woman in her 20s? I mean nothing offensive by this comment."

"I know," Paige quietly replied as she tilted her head forward. "I'm sorry, I wasn't trying to pick a fight."

Jorge grinned at her comment since any 'fight' with Paige was nothing compared to some he had with women over the years, especially with Verónic. Maria's mother was constantly angry with him and the two had some brutal confrontations that on occasion became violent. Moving closer to his wife, he merely kissed her on the cheek and shook his head.

"*Mi amor*, this is ok, it was a misunderstanding," He said and snuggled up closer to her. "Let's not worry about it. The point is that she *says* she *thinks* she is pregnant and Chase, of course, he believes anything Jolene says and me, I don't believe *anything* Jolene says. So while Chase is sitting across from me, upset that he might be a father again, worried since Jolene was a cokehead and drinking while possibly pregnant, Diego looks heartbroken over the matter and is oddly quiet. So, I'm feeling quite uncertain of what to say to either. It was not a fun evening."

"Were they still drinking when you left?"

"Diego was not but Chase, he was drinking a lot," Jorge replied and he shared a look with his wife. "I feel that this situation is about to get quite messy and it's been complicated by Jolene. She's the constant problem. She's a problem for me, she causes problems for Chase, for Diego, it is always something with her. The woman is angering me more and more every day."

"So what are we going to do?" Paige leaned against him and he slid his hand over the smooth material around her waist, her head brushing up against his shoulder. "Now that we know where she is?"

"Yes, we do," Jorge confirmed as he closed his eyes, breathing in her perfume. "She was North of Toronto but it does not seem she got very far. To answer your question, I do not know what to do. I am tired of dealing with her, one way or another. She is nothing more than a headache."

"She must plan to speak with Chase in person," Paige pointed out as Jorge continued to run his hand over the material, his thoughts disappearing from the worries of the day and into another, more pleasurable place. "Does that mean she's coming back or he is going to see her?"

"I do not know," Jorge whispered as his lips briefly touched her shoulder as his fingers continued to explore. "Chase is our key here. He will lead us to her."

"What a mess," Paige replied as he slid her nightdress strap from her shoulder and began to kiss her smooth skin while his other hand slid under the silky material and up her leg, his breath quickly becoming labored as he pulled her on top of him.

Having a perceptive child in the next room, they were often rushed, unsure of when she would show up at the door. It was necessary to keep as quiet as possible but they somehow made it work. They had each position down to a science.

Jorge laid back as she straddled him. He suppressed his natural impulses as she quietly rocked her body on his as waves of pleasure filled him, his fingers working roughly to intensify her experience. Although he felt quite limited in such a small apartment with thin walls, he was up for the challenge. He thought his body was going to explode when she tightened the grip around him, as he fought his natural impulse to gasp loudly when he finally was able to release into a euphoric moment of pleasure and perfection.

Attempting to catch his breath, she fell against his chest as her own heart pounded wildly against his chest. Jorge wrapped his arms around his wife. "We must find a house, *mi amor*, one with thick walls and a separate floor for my daughter."

She let out a giggle and kissed his neck.

"Your phone rang while we were doing it," She whispered. "I'm not sure if you noticed."

"I noticed nothing but you at that time," He insisted and for a long, beautiful moment, he pushed it aside until the phone rang again. Feeling as if he had been ripped from a perfect dream and back to the bitter reality, he reached for the phone. It was Jesús calling from BC.

"Sir, it is the alarm, someone tried to break into a shop," He gave the address for the first location they had opened. "I tried to call both Diego and Chase but there is no answer, sir, I'm sorry but I need you to check it. I do not think they were successful but the police are there now, so you must go unless you can find the others."

"No, that's fine," Jorge started to sit up and looked for his robe. "I will go. Could you do me a favor and call....maybe Marco to meet me? He knows about the security system."

"Yes, sir, I was thinking the same thing," Jesús replied. "I will contact him immediately."

"Thanks," He ended the call and tossed the phone on the nightstand.

"What's going on?" Paige asked. "Is something wrong?"

"Someone tried to break into one of the shops," Jorge replied as he reached into the nightstand for a gun while glancing at his clothes across the room. "I must go see the police there. As if those fuckers will do anything useful."

"Is Diego meeting you?"

"No, apparently both him and Chase aren't answering their phones," He turned and gave his wife a look that made her silently nod in response. "So, I must meet with Marco and you, you stay here with Maria. It will be fine."

"Be careful," Paige commented as he slowly crossed the room, gun in one hand and phone in the other.

"Do not worry for me, *mi amor*," He said with laughter in his voice. "Worry for the person who thought they were going to break into my store."

He glanced back for a second to see the grin on her face as she pulled the blankets over her.

Leaving the apartment, the night air was shocking to the system when he arrived in the parking garage. Checking the back of the SUV, he quickly jumped in and pulled out of the apartment complex.

Exhausted, he drove through the Toronto streets to what had been their first of many dispensaries. He just hoped the police didn't stick around for long. He certainly didn't want their help.

Marco was already there when he arrived. Of course, he lived much closer and despite his wrinkled clothes and exhausted appearance, Jorge noted that his IT specialist was taking care of this situation with ease. The young, black officer beside him seemed content with the answers.

"Mr. Hernandez, I was just discussing our security system with the officer," He appeared relieved to see him. "Fortunately, they were not able to get in and the alarm probably scared them off."

Jorge nodded and glanced toward the building, which looked undamaged. They had added bars on the windows and doors, making it almost impossible to get in, regardless of how clever the criminal. The irony was that being someone who committed crimes gave you insight into all the ways someone might do the same to you. Of course, whoever tried to break in his shop would've been better off if the cops caught them.

"We checked out the area and were unable to find anything," The officer reassured him and Jorge didn't reply. "I notice you have a video camera outside."

"Yes," Jorge calmly replied. "Unfortunately, it is not working well, so it may not have been useful. I wanted to update the system for the shops but was waiting until they were all opened."

"Sir, is there anything you wish for me to do?" Marco interrupted as if unsure of his role in this situation. He pointed toward the shop, where the alarm continued to roar.

"Yes, if you would go inside," Jorge reached in his pocket for the massive key chain, he searched for the correct one and handed it to Marco. "Take a quick look around, then reset the alarm, if you do not mind."

"No sir, I do not mind," He agreed and rushed off while Jorge returned his attention to the officer.

"Check the camera, Mr. Hernandez," He seemed to change his tone immediately after Marco walked away. "You know the drill if you need our help, let us know otherwise, I will leave it in your capable hands."

Jorge merely grinned and nodded. The officer knew him.

Watching the young man get back into the car and drive away, the few people who were hanging around began to leave. It was only a few minutes before Marco walked out of the building, locking it up behind him. He approached Jorge and handed him the keys.

"Sir, I was checking the camera on my phone but wasn't sure if you wanted me to tell the police of what I found?" He spoke skeptically as he slid his fingers over the screen. "I can send the video to you and I will zoom in on the faces of the men involved."

"*Perfecto*! And no," Jorge shook his head. "The police, we do not need. We are our own police, so what you got?"

"I will send it to you sir but it looks like…."

Jorge immediately checked his phone when it beeped and watched the video and looked at the still images. He simply nodded and returned his attention to Marco. "Thank you, I do appreciate your help Marco. We will discuss this more tomorrow."

This could be a problem.

CHAPTER *46*

"I don't got all day so everyone better get here soon," Jorge impatiently muttered to Paige the following afternoon as the two sat alone in the company boardroom. Although they arrived early, he was eager to get the meeting started. The previous night's attempted break-in was cause for concern and it was important that everyone be aware of the circumstances.

Paige met this comment with silence, her hand touched his arm as Jorge stared at his laptop. She glanced over at the still image that Marco had forwarded the previous night but neither said a word. It wasn't necessary. They had already discussed it at great lengths.

A sound alerted them and both turned to see Jesús outside the glass doors, a smooth grin on his face while his eyes had dark circles underneath. He had taken an early flight to arrive back in time for the meeting. There were many new concerns that had presented themselves in a short time and Jorge wasn't one to waste time.

"Good afternoon," Paige greeted him with a smile as he entered the room and sat across the table. "Sorry, there's no coffee yet. I actually thought Diego would've been here by now. He usually makes it better than I do."

"Yes, where the hell is he?" Jorge complained, glancing at his phone. "And Chase, how much did they have to drink last night?"

"They were drinking, sir?" Jesús asked with a raised eyebrow. "I thought Chase, he did not drink."

"He *was* last night," Jorge said as he exchanged looks with Paige, his eyes quickly shifted across the table. "*Amigo*, you will not believe what happened."

"You found Jolene," Jesús replied as he slowly nodded. "I remember you mentioned this last night."

"But you do not know the entire story," Jorge grunted. "There is more."

"Is she back into the *cocaína*, sir?" Jesús asked appearing only mildly interested as he reached for his phone, his eyes briefly glanced at the screen. "This would not surprise me."

"She says she is pregnant," Jorge spoke abruptly, his eyes blazing across the table. "And it is for Chase."

Regaining Jesús' full attention, his eyes expanded in size as he exchanged looks with both Jorge and Paige. "This here, is this true? Do we know if she is telling us the truth?"

"Well, that, we intend on finding out," Jorge commented gruffly. "We are not playing any more of these games. I do not have time for this nonsense."

A sound caught his attention and he turned to see Chase abruptly walk into the boardroom. Lagging behind was Diego, who looked pale and tired, as if he hadn't slept a wink. It momentarily threw Jorge off guard because it was as if they traded bodies since the previous night but then again, did he want to know what had taken place after he left the bar?

"Good afternoon," Paige said in her usual gentle tone while Jorge observed them both suspiciously and gestured toward the seats. He noted that Diego took his usual spot at the head of the table after returning Paige's greeting, but Chase sat down without acknowledging anyone. There was an awkward silence as Jesús quickly glanced down at his phone while Paige silently took everything in.

"Very good," Jorge spoke up in his usual abrupt way and glanced at his laptop. They had arrived just in time. "We have a lot to discuss today, so let's get started."

"Was Clara in?" Diego asked in a hoarse voice that took Jorge a bit off guard, if only for a moment.

"Yes, everything is clear," Jorge insisted and glanced around the table, noting that Chase looked angry while Jesús appeared somewhat nervous. "So we must start. As you all know, we had an attempted break-in last night."

"Sorry, I didn't see your call until this morning…" Diego's voice drifted off self-consciously. Jorge nodded, attempting to wade through the tension in the room.

"That is fine," He replied with a shrug. "Actually, it worked out ok because Marco knows more about the security system anyway so he was able to assist me at the shop."

"The police, they are not going to give us trouble?" Jesús asked, his confidence seemed to reappear despite the elephant in the room. "We do not need them investigating."

"Officially, the only thing they would have to work with was our camera outside, which I told them," Jorge couldn't resist but grin. "Is not working well. You know how those cameras can be sometimes, no?"

Jesús smirked as he glanced down at his phone. "And this here, this is the picture you were talking about? This is the man trying to break in?"

"Yes, it is," Jorge replied and glanced around the table. "I trust everyone has seen it?"

"What picture?" Chase finally spoke and much to Jorge's surprise, his face suddenly seemed troubled, as if his original mask had fallen to the ground and broken into pieces. "I don't think…"

"I sent it to your phone," Jorge confirmed and glanced at Diego.

"I saw it," His longtime friend quickly replied. "Fuck!"

"We," Jorge pointed toward the same image that was on his laptop in front of him. "We do not need this."

"I will look into it more, sir," Jesús commented while beside him, Chase expanded the image size.

"Is that a swastika on his neck?" He finally asked in stunned disbelief. "Are you fucking kidding me?"

"No, we are not fucking kidding you," Jorge replied with a certain amount of sarcasm in his voice, slightly irritated with Chase's naivety. "So we have to wonder, is this racially motivated or is it just some fucking redneck out to break into our shop. We must find out."

"Remember in California," Diego spoke up, his eyes bulging out as they normally did when attempting to make a point. "The skinheads back in the 90s? Remember the time…."

"Yes, Diego, let's not talk about that," Jorge quickly cut him off, knowing that a trip down memory lane would potentially get the entire conversation off track. "That was another time and place, so let's focus on the now. This could mean nothing or it could lead to something more serious. However, it is well known that Latinos own these shops and are taking over. Plus, our staff, many are from various ethnicities so, perhaps this is why or maybe it means nothing but we must keep on top of it."

"I've dealt with these people in the past," Paige spoke up, her voice was oddly comforting to Jorge, despite the topic of the meeting. "It's probably a powerful suit and tie guy at the top giving orders to some kids on the street. They feed them these insane ideas that there's a white genocide and they are somehow soldiers in an army to save *their* people."

"At least you don't have to worry," Chase commented with some attitude in his voice. "You're white."

Although Paige appeared slightly alarmed by his remark, she didn't reply. Not that she had to because Jorge was quick to jump in.

"Yes, but she's a white woman married to a Mexican man, working with a group of Latinos and clearly, she isn't a racist," Jorge snapped, suddenly perturbed by Chase's ignorance. "To them, she is a traitor, she is worse than us."

"Oh sorry," Chase replied and seemed to sink in his seat. "I didn't know."

To this, Paige merely shrugged while Jorge shot him a dirty look.

"Well, now you know," He snapped and turned his attention to Diego. "And do not worry, this is nothing like California. We will not allow these people to get out of hand."

Diego didn't reply but nodded, his eyes suddenly full of vulnerability.

Jorge quickly looked away and back toward Paige.

"We must learn who these people are," He sternly commented. "This is not something we can allow to get out of control. I do not have a good feeling. And my instincts, they are always right."

"I'm looking into it," Paige commented just as Jesús was about to speak up, he hesitated while she finished. "I have some connections that might be able to give us some information. I know it has been in the news that a couple of synagogues as well as a mosque, were recently vandalized. I wonder if there is any connection."

"If there is a connection," Jorge spoke up before Jesús could speak. "We can reach out to others that they are attacking. We may be the minority, however, if you put enough like-minded minorities together, then we have an army."

"Sir, I have my people looking into it as well," Jesús spoke eagerly while beside him, Chase appeared depressed and defeated. "I spoke to some people in BC last night and they said it perhaps is a smaller gang, due to the current climate regarding refugees and immigration, it is possible that people are gathering and creating their own groups."

"Let's hope this is a random thing and nothing more," Jorge spoke hopefully even though he didn't believe it. He had dealt with this before and couldn't believe that in Canada, he was dealing with it again. "We will figure it out."

The meeting concluded on a bit of a tense note. Jesús had to rush away for another appointment, while in the corner, Chase approached Paige, apologizing for his rudeness. Jorge gestured for Diego to meet him outside the boardroom. The two went into Diego's office.

"So," Jorge closed the door behind the two of them. "What the fuck is going on?"

"I don't know, Jolene, she still won't take my calls," Diego replied with sadness in his voice. "I text her again this morning…"

"Not that," Jorge replied as Diego sat behind his desk while he stood nearby. "What the fuck was going on with you and Chase this morning? I don't know what it is, my friend, but you need to get over it because we must work together. Especially right now."

"It..it will be fine," Diego assured him with a hand in the air. "It was…a rough night."

"*Amigo*, do I want to know how rough it was?" Jorge asked with some humor in his voice. "Ah! But if that were the case, you would be a happy man today, not walking around like the world is sitting on your shoulders."

Diego didn't reply but merely looked down at his desk.

"Right?" Jorge asked but quickly realized that he wasn't about to get an answer. "Look, it is none of my business what takes place between you and Chase. I do not want to see you miserable. You're my brother, remember, I don't need to worry about you too."

"It's fine," Diego assured him but with much sadness in his eyes. "Last night was perfect and terrible at the same time. That's all I can say about it."

Jorge nodded and didn't reply.

"It won't interfere with anything here," Diego insisted and shook his head.

"Ok," Jorge replied. "Maybe, we should talk about this later?"

Diego nodded while Jorge stood awkwardly, his mind analyzing Diego's words; *perfect and terrible.*

"Well, I must go," Jorge finally commented and headed toward the door. "This conversation, we can have it again. If you wish."

Diego didn't reply as Jorge walked out to find Paige waiting in the hallway.

"Should I talk to him?" Paige asked as her eyes glanced at Diego's office. She reached for his hand and Jorge turned his head to see Chase walk out of the boardroom and toward the main door. Taking a deep breath, Jorge nodded.

"Yes, you do that and me," Jorge glanced around the office. "I gotta get out of here. See you back home later? I can come pick you up?"

"Diego will drop me off," Paige gently commented as she leaned forward and gave him a quick kiss.

He was barely back in his SUV when he got the call.

CHAPTER 47

Few things shook up Jorge Hernandez. He had spent his life on high alert and was ready for anything but for some reason, this call was different. Perhaps it was because he knew it was merely a symptom of a bigger problem, something that was about to escalate to a dangerous level. Maybe it was because deep down, he knew that he had somehow contributed to his own fate.

On the surface, it was merely a fire. The damage enough to receive his insurance but yet, this time it wasn't the money that concerned him. This had been the last property he purchased for a dispensary, scheduled to open in upcoming weeks; fortunately, there was no product inside but as he stared at the building from afar, he recalled the scrawny, white kid that had attempted to pull out of the original deal. Perhaps it was merely a coincidence but Jorge wasn't one to believe in such things; to him, two separate attacks on his shops in less than 24 hours, indicating that someone was targeting him.

He slowly got out of the SUV and stood in stunned silence. Jesús was on the way but he wasn't sure whether or not to text Paige and Diego. He usually was in control and knew exactly what to do but this time, Jorge felt slightly defeated. In the few months he had lived in Canada, he had already taken on religious fanatics and competitors in the pot industry, neither of which had worried him. However, something felt different this time.

It was only a few minutes before Jesús swiftly pulled up beside the SUV, jumping out of the car, he rushed to Jorge's side. For a moment, the two stood in silence and watched the smoke rise from the small building as fireman continued to inspect the property.

"Sir," Jesús finally spoke in his usual, slow manner. "We must get security at every location immediately. I know we have security during the day but we must have someone for nighttime to watch, to guard the buildings."

Jorge merely nodded and felt some comfort with his longtime associate's words. He was right, of course, and he silently chastised himself for not doing this sooner, for not thinking ahead to potential issues.

"Sometimes, I wonder," Jorge turned toward Jesús and paused for a moment before continuing his thoughts. "If I should have stayed in Mexico. Canada, it is giving me so many problems, things I never dealt with before. In Mexico, I had to deal with rivals, potential issues with the media, things that I could handle. Here, I feel faced with people who are against me personally, not just me as a businessman. It is very strange."

"But sir, you cannot leave," Jesús quickly protested. "That is what they want, don't you see? People like the religious people who were protesting the business, your competitors and if your theory on white supremacist is correct, these are people who want you to go. You must not let them win. We can take on anyone. We have taken on worse and we always win."

Taking a deep breath, Jorge agreed. His true fear was that they would go after either Paige or Maria; he didn't care about himself. He had already outlived most with the same lifestyle but his family, that was another matter. Love created vulnerability and hadn't that been why, as a young man, he had decided that he would never marry or have children? A naïve man in his 20s, Jorge assumed he was unable to fall in love and children could easily be prevented, that he would live his life as a lone wolf with no attachments; no one else to worry about other than himself. Yet here he was, a man in his 40s with both a daughter and a wife. Not that he would have it any other way but there was no denying that they created a weakness in him.

"I can deal with this," Jesús continued, gesturing toward the building that was now nothing more than rubble. "You should leave and I will take care of this situation."

Jorge nodded again and although a part of him felt that it was necessary he be there, another part wanted to go home to think. It was time to make some big decisions. Also, he had to get in touch with his own boss, the man who had helped to finance this business. He would not be pleased.

It was on the drive home that Jorge briefly thought about stopping at a convenience store and buying a pack of cigarettes, his body suddenly craving an old habit. It frustrated him because it indicated another weakness that owned him, crawling back into his mind after weeks of being avoided. He could not let it win.

He welcomed the quietness of his apartment. The only sound was the heat kicking in, as he mindlessly looked in the fridge but then decided that he couldn't eat. Instead, he made a phone call to his boss, leaving a detailed message before laying on the couch, placing his iPhone on the nearby table, he ignored it when it beeped. Several text messages came in, the phone rang and yet, he couldn't answer it. He couldn't move.

Closing his eyes, Jorge was unable to sleep. Instead, he attempted to push everything from his mind. He felt weightless as he slipped into a restful state and although it didn't last long, something happened in those few minutes. His eyes suddenly opened, his heart began to race and he took a deep breath before sitting up. He knew what he had to do.

Reaching for his phone, he found a series of messages. One was from his daughter, telling him something about an acting school she wanted to go see and how her teacher said she had a 'flare for the dramatic'. His response was blunt.

We will discuss it when you get home.

The second was from Paige informing him that she and Diego had found a house online, one that looked perfect. She sent a link but he didn't bother looking at it. If it made her happy, it made him happy.

Book an appointment and we will go see it, mi amor.

The next was from Diego, essentially repeating the same message, only with his usual passion and exaggeration. It made Jorge laugh.

Thank you hermano, your help is appreciated.

The next was from Chase.

After our meeting this morning, I decided I want to step up. Whatever you need me to do.

This surprised Jorge. Chase had once been the man who stayed on the sidelines but apparently, something had sparked his fire. It was the loyalty that Jorge appreciated especially since his faith in this young Canadian had lacked in recent weeks.

Perfecto.

The next was a message from Jesús stating that everything was taken care of regarding the fire. The building was no longer salvageable, however, the insurance would go toward rebuilding, if that was his wish. Jorge wasn't sure.

Let's just wait.

The last message was from the man who he called his boss, although the term was probably not the best for their relationship. He was the person who had given a fiery young man named Jorge Hernandez a chance many years before, back when most had written him off as a *perdedor* because of his erratic and unstable nature. However, the older, Latino respected his boldness and arrogant insistence that the two of them could make a lot of money together. In retrospect, there had been many reasons to write off the young Mexican but he instead took a chance. The decision turned out to be a good one.

Si necesitas un ejército, te enviaré un ejército.

Although Jorge hoped he wouldn't need an army to fight this battle, it was better to be prepared. He had worked too hard to back down. This was his home now. No one had ever taken anything from Jorge Hernandez and walked away unscathed. Whoever burned down one of his shops and attempted to break into another would pay. He would take them on and win.

The afternoon had slipped away. Making some calls back to Mexico followed by a productive discussion with Jesús, he hadn't paid attention to the time until he received a frantic call from Paige.

"Maria isn't at the school," Paige's voice was full of emotion that sent a jolt of fear through his heart. In the background, he could hear

Diego attempting to calm her. "I can't find her, she's not answering her phone for me or Diego. I asked the principal and they have no idea. She was in her last class and then she disappeared."

Paige was crying while Jorge felt his heart race.

"Should we call the police?" She asked in a weak voice as she quietly sobbed. "I don't know what to do. I was a few minutes late! Oh my God, do you think she started to walk home?"

"Ok, let's remain calm, Paige," Jorge replied, suddenly overwhelmed with emotion, he felt his body break out in a cold sweat. "Call Chase, have him check the school again and bus stops in between here and there and you, *you* come home in case she arrives here. I will go look."

"Have you heard from her today? Did she call home looking for a drive, anything?" Paige asked and she cleared her throat. "I don't understand."

"Ok, yes, she contacted me about an acting school…" His voice drifted off and he closed his eyes. "Fuck! She probably decided to go visit the school herself. I told her we would discuss it when she got home but you know Maria, she does not listen."

"What school?"

Jorge shook his head. Had she told him the name of the school? He had no idea.

"I don't think she said," Jorge spoke absently in the phone. "I will do a quick search online and we all need to keep calling Maria. I will try her in a moment and…..hey, maybe she will answer if Chase calls her?"

"Text Chase to call her," Paige's muffled voice could be heard moving away from the phone. Diego was in the background agreeing, "Ah yes!"

"Ok, I will come home soon and if she doesn't answer Chase, we will look up all the acting schools and try to figure out where she is."

"Yes," Jorge agreed and ended the call and immediately phoned his daughter. There was no answer. He left a message demanding her to call him immediately.

Panic encompassed his heart as Jorge sat the phone down. What if it was somehow connected to the events with the two dispensaries? What if someone kidnapped his daughter? He thought about the recent threats to Paige. Fear filled him and he did something that was rare for him; he prayed. He had long turned his back on the church but at that moment, he would've done anything to make sure his daughter was ok. It was not like Maria to ignore his calls. Something was wrong.

Taking a deep breath and wiping a tear from his eye, he grabbed his phone and looked up acting schools, specifically the ones directed toward children and jotted down a few names and numbers when his phone rang. It was Chase.

"I found her,"

These simple words caused Jorge to break down; his entire body weak, he couldn't even speak as his eyes filled with tears of gratitude. Barely able to hold the phone in his shaking hand, Jorge took a deep breath.

"I'm on my way to pick her up," Chase continued. "She decided to check out an acting school and thought you wouldn't take her, so she decided to look up the bus schedule and go herself. I told her not to move. I'm going to get her."

"Thank you," Jorge spoke in a weak voice, slowly feeling his body coming back to life. "I feared…"

He couldn't finish the sentence and the beauty was that if anyone would understand, it was Chase. He was a man who had lost his own child after hours of him being missing, so there was no need to express the fear in his heart. He knew.

"Don't," Chase immediately responded. "She's fine. I promise you, Maria is just being…Maria."

"That child will be the death of me," Jorge finally managed as he relaxed and continued in a heartfelt voice. "I thank you."

"It's not necessary," Chase gently insisted. "I know."

He ended the call and was about to send a message to Paige when she walked in the door, followed by Diego.

"She's ok," He immediately put his hand in the air, seeing the automatic relief in Diego's face while Paige was still upset. "Chase, he got in touch. Just as I suspected, she decided to go check out an acting school on her own."

"Oh Jorge, she can't do that," Paige quietly commented as she crossed the floor and hugged him.

"That little girl, she has a mind of her own," Jorge spoke with emotion in his voice as he kissed his wife on the cheek. "I cannot seem to make her understand."

"She knows who you are," Paige reminded him. "You have to let her know that there are dangers involved without scaring her."

"Good luck with that," Diego commented with the usual amount of attitude in his voice. "She's too much like her father."

Jorge slowly agreed and with some hesitation, told them about the fire. Diego and Paige exchanged looks but neither said a word. They knew what this meant. It wasn't a coincidence that two dispensaries were attacked within a day of the other. Everything was about to get a bit more dangerous.

Time slowly crept by, each minute dragging until finally, the door flew open and Maria pranced in, excitedly talking to Chase as if nothing out of the ordinary had happened; as if she hadn't scared them all or disobeyed Jorge's rule to never leave the school unless it was with one of them. He felt anger fill his heart as he slowly rose from his seat and watched as she casually approached him, chattering on about the school that he *had* to let her join, how great it was and how 'next time' he would have to join her for a tour.

Jorge stood in silence as he looked into the eyes of the girl who suddenly reminded him of Verónic, a woman who was reckless and stupid, someone who pushed his buttons on purpose with no care or consideration for anyone else. Without stepping back to calm down, he felt rage fill his body as Jorge raised his hand and slapped his daughter across the face.

CHAPTER *48*

There was a stunned silence in the room. Maria's face immediately crumbled and Jorge's heart filled with regret. He opened his mouth to say something but was unable to speak. Maria burst into tears and dramatically swung around, flying into her bedroom. Slamming the door behind her, he didn't have to turn around to see everyone's reaction. He couldn't look any of them in the eye. Filled with remorse, he suddenly remembered his own father's rage on the day Miguel died and his heart dropped.

Jorge hesitantly walked toward his daughter's bedroom door and gently knocked before slowly turning the knob and going inside. Closing the door behind him, he found his daughter sitting on the edge of her bed, her tiny body trembling as she loudly sobbed. Heartbroken, Jorge didn't say a word as he slowly walked over and awkwardly sat beside her on the bed.

"*Papa, lo siento*," Maria said in barely a whimper as she reached for a tissue and abruptly wiped her face. "I know I wasn't supposed to leave the school and I wasn't answering your calls and that's why you're mad at me. I disobeyed you."

"Maria," He reached out and put his arm around her shoulder and kissed the top of her head. "You're right, you shouldn't have disobeyed me but I, I should *not* have slapped you either."

"Why did you?" She countered, her brown eyes suddenly met his and it was as if someone kicked him in the stomach. He could see the hurt and vulnerability of a child who had already lost so much "You've never slapped me before."

"*Niñita*, you're only ten years old," Jorge gently reminded her. "You're too young to wander the city alone. It is very dangerous."

"Lots of other kids my age do it," Maria protested with a shrug. "I didn't think it was a big deal."

"Maria, you are not those other kids," Jorge replied as he pulled her closer. "Must I remind you that when we lived in Mexico, you also weren't allowed to do something like this there either? Do you remember why?"

"You said I could get kidnapped," Maria replied with some hesitation. "Because you were a prominent businessman. But *Papa*, that was Mexico, Canada is much safer."

"See, this is the thing," Jorge said and took a deep breath, wondering how to approach this situation. "Maria, I am not always sure that it is safer. Do you remember when you recently told me that you know what I do for a living?"

"You're part of the Mexican cartel," Maria spoke bluntly, no longer crying, her eyes met his with determination. "That's why we were in more danger in Mexico but here, you're involved in legal things, right? So we are ok? We are safe here."

"No, *bonita*, we are not necessarily safe here," Jorge's mind wandered back to the fire earlier that day. "Always be careful, Maria, no matter where you are because the truth is that we never know. This is why I was so worried when you weren't answering my calls today. This is not just about my work, it is also about respect. You disobeyed me and left the school property alone. It is not like you to take off or not answer your calls so naturally, I was terrified."

His daughter's face filled with regret and she quickly looked away. "I was excited when I learned about this acting school and I was dying to see it! I knew you wouldn't take me so I went on my own."

"Did I say that I would not take you?" Jorge countered and she shook her head.

"You're always busy and I don't feel you take my dreams seriously," She stubbornly insisted.

"Maria, you're only 10," Jorge replied with a grin. "It's not that I don't take your dreams seriously but I think you need to relax. You have many years ahead of you. Why not enjoy being a little girl?"

"I don't feel like a little girl," Maria insisted as she turned more in his direction. "I feel like I'm older."

"I understand," Jorge nodded. "You've always been mature for your age but do you know how many adults would do anything to be your age again? To not have worries or responsibilities? There are days I wish I had none."

"*Papa*, I really want to take acting classes," Maria spoke with determination in her voice. "Can you at least come see the school? They have a class during spring break. I would like to go."

"I will take a look," Jorge replied and leaned in and gave her another quick kiss before rising from the bed. "Email me the information and Maria, I am *very* sorry…I should *not* have slapped you but you cannot do things like you did today. There are some very bad people out there and I was *terrified* when you weren't answering my calls."

"I'm sorry, *Papa*," Maria spoke with regret. "I promise I won't do it again."

Leaving her bedroom, Jorge closed the door behind him and was immediately met with three sets of eyes. Filled with shame once again, he felt humbled as he returned to the living room. It was Diego who spoke first, while Chase and Paige looked uncertain.

"Is everything *ok*?"

"Yes, it is fine," Jorge replied quickly and noted the relief on Paige's face while Chase offered him a knowing look. "I was upset…."

"You don't have to explain it to me," Chase spoke up and shrugged. "I'm a parent."

Jorge felt some shame. Chase's own son was only 4 when he went missing and unlike Maria, the ending was not a happy one.

"You were scared," Diego commented with bulging eyes. "Considering everything going on now, it's understandable."

He looked towards Paige but she didn't comment.

"Speaking of being a parent," Chase spoke hesitantly while glancing at his phone. "While all this was going on, Jolene sent me a message. She's back in town."

Noting that Diego was now the one looking upset, Jorge thought quickly.

"We must make sure she's pregnant," He turned toward Paige. "We must make her take a test in front of us to prove it."

Paige quickly nodded in agreement. "Should we go now?"

"I see no reason to wait," Jorge commented and glanced at Diego and Chase. "I'm not sure who is interested in coming with us? Could one of you stay with Maria?"

Noting the awkwardness between them, Jorge hadn't expected Chase to volunteer to stay with Maria while the others went to see Jolene. Insisting he wasn't ready to deal with her, Jorge nodded in understanding and thought that perhaps it would also be better to have him there for Maria since they were so close.

Glancing at his phone on the way out of the apartment, he noted that Jesús had a handle on everything regarding the fire. He was already in contact with their insurance company while at the same time, upping security at the other locations. Fortunately, he knew people who would be happy to watch the shop and unlike official security, they would protect the properties with a fierceness that was apparently required.

The last person Jorge felt like dealing with was Jolene. This woman was long past the point of being a liability but what could he do? She was Diego's sister and although his loyalty apparently was with Jorge, this news of a pregnancy complicated things. He regretted not getting rid of her before; he had left it too long and now, perhaps it would be impossible.

"So how we gonna do this?" Diego spoke up from the backseat as they drove to Jolene's, after a brief stop at the nearest drugstore. "She might try to fake this."

"Not if one of us is in the bathroom while she's peeing on the stick," Jorge commented and glanced toward Paige. "I'm thinking, that should be you."

"It's not gonna be me," Diego insisted with frustration in his voice.

"I will do it," Paige replied as she read the instructions on the box. "She won't try to get anything over on me. It looks pretty simple. Two lines mean she's pregnant."

"I still think we should go to the doctor," Diego repeated his original thought when they first headed out. "To make sure it's 100% accurate."

"I think these tests are accurate," Jorge commented. "Plus, do we want to sit at the hospital or a doctor's office all fucking day?"

Diego shook his head.

"Paige, what do you think?" Jorge asked, noting that she had been quiet since they left the apartment. "Are these tests accurate?"

"I've never taken one, so I don't know," She commented evenly while looking out the window and again, he felt as though he had hit a nerve without realizing it. "I guess, it should be fine."

"I know when Verónic was pregnant, we went to the doctor," Jorge commented as he watched the traffic ahead. "To make sure she was pregnant and that the baby was mine. I did not trust her."

"If she is pregnant, do you think it is Chase's?" Diego asked glumly and Jorge glanced back to see the concern in his eyes. "Maybe it's not?"

"We will see," Jorge replied while his mind quickly jumped back to Paige. She was oddly quiet.

"Paige, is something wrong?" Jorge bluntly asked her as they got closer to Jolene's apartment building.

She shook her head no.

"You know that when I hit Maria back there, this is not something I normally do," Jorge took a jab at what might've been bothering her. Although uncertain, she hadn't said much since witnessing him slap his daughter. "I was frantic. I thought, what if something had happened to her..."

"Jorge, I'm not upset with you over that," Paige calmly replied and when their eyes met, he felt certain she was telling the truth. "In fact, I understand your frustration and I think she needs more boundaries, not less. You had a right to be angry. She was out of line today. She scared all of us."

"Oh, ok, you did not say anything at the time," Jorge commented with some surprise in his voice.

"You do know she was listening at the door, right?"

"Oh, no, I did not," Jorge admitted. It hadn't occurred to him.

"Trust me, she was," Paige replied with a smooth grin. "Your daughter, she's smart and she's cunning. You have to remember that."

Jorge didn't reply. He knew she was right.

They arrived at Jolene's apartment and she quickly buzzed them in, something that surprised Jorge. Her cooperation made him suspicious. This was unusual. Perhaps his daughter wasn't the only cunning female in his life.

The three made their way upstairs and although he didn't say anything to the others, Jorge made sure to bring his gun. He didn't think Jolene was setting them up but then again, who knew? He suspected his wife was thinking the same but Diego was perhaps naïve about his sister.

However, when she met them at the door, Jolene looked tired, defeated, wearing a pair of yoga pants and an oversized sweater. Once the door closed, all hell broke loose.

"So what the fuck were you doing?" Diego immediately shot out. "I put you in a fucking good rehab to help you and you run? Why should we trust anything you say at this point?"

"I run because I found out I was pregnant and I was scared," Her eyes automatically shot toward Jorge then back at Diego. "I didn't know what to do. I didn't want anyone to know about this baby. I feared that I had hurt it with the cocaine. I was so confused. I could not think."

"Not thinking seems to be what you do best lately," Jorge snapped and glanced toward Paige. "Anyway, you're doing a test for us. First, we need to know that you are pregnant."

"What? Do you think I would lie?" Jolene asked with tears in her eyes. "About this?"

"It wouldn't be the first time you lied," Diego pointed out. "Paige is going to go with you to do the test."

"What? You think I know how to create fake results?" Jolene shot back at her brother.

"Who fucking knows?" Diego snapped back.

"Ok, let's keep the sibling rivalry to a minimum for now," Jorge cut in, feeling exhausted by the day. "Paige, can you go with her to the bathroom. Make sure she does the test correctly."

Paige merely nodded but was still oddly quiet, which concerned him. He would talk to her more when they got home.

Neither Paige nor Jolene looked thrilled with the idea but followed Jorge's instructions, heading toward the bathroom. After they were in the room and the door closed, Diego turned toward him and raised an eyebrow.

"What a fucking mess!" He exclaimed and shook his head.

"This is not you," Jorge reassured him.

Diego continued to look apologetic as he glanced at his phone.

"So what is going on with you and Chase?" Jorge muttered. "Are you going to tell me now?"

"I don't wanna talk about it," Diego spoke sadly and Jorge nodded.

The toilet flushed, the water could be heard running and the two women walked out of the bathroom. Paige was holding the plastic device in her hand and nodding.

"She *is* pregnant."

Jorge noted that no one in the room looked happy.

CHAPTER *49*

In the midst of all the craziness, they found a house. It was smaller than Jorge had hoped but with such outrageous prices in Toronto, perhaps it was better he dropped some of his original expectations. The place he owned in Mexico was much more beautiful, with creative architecture but in Canada, people had very different ideas for their overpriced homes; practicality seemed to outweigh all else and in the end, did it matter? As long as he had a reasonable place to live with his family.

Although the house was little more than a shack by his standards, Paige argued that three bedrooms and a full basement apartment would be too much.

"But *mi amor,* you never know when we will need the extra room," Jorge replied with a shrug. "Unfortunately, I think I must now sell the house in Mexico."

Paige crossed the living room floor to sit beside him on the couch. "Do you ever miss it?"

"Sometimes but it is not the best place for my daughter," Jorge replied and reached for her hand, giving it a squeeze. "I want her to get an education here, to live and work, whatever she wishes to do."

"Become an actress?" Paige softly added with a smirk on her face.

"Ah!" Jorge shook his head. "Such a smart little girl and yet, she wants to get involved in a superficial and ridiculous profession!"

"It's not all bad," Paige countered. "I know what you're saying but we can't assume that she will become caught up in the craziness of Hollywood."

"Believe me, I know my daughter," Jorge insisted as he moved closer to his wife. "She will get involved in the silliness, the pettiness, the Twitter arguments, all of that stupidity. I have the money to educate her at the best schools to become a professional but yet, she wants the glamour and what she thinks is exciting. It's really not. I knew some of these big shot actresses when I was working in California. Many were fucking train wrecks and classless *putas* and that, that will not be my daughter."

"Keep in mind the world you were in back then might've had something to do with the kind of actresses you met and your daughter is *only* 10," Paige reminded him as he snuggled up close to her. "What she wants now can change a million times by high school. Acting classes would be good to gain confidence, to learn how to present herself well…"

"You think my daughter, she does not have confidence," He grinned. "Are we talking about the same little girl?"

"Don't confuse confidence with boldness," Paige commented as Jorge began to run his fingers up her thigh, easing over the soft material as his mind began to drift.

"She gets that from me," Jorge replied. "It's a curse and a blessing."

"I keep thinking about how you slapped her the other day," Paige quietly commented. "I never saw that side of you before."

"It is not a side that I'm proud of," Jorge said as he moved away slightly. "But for a minute, I saw her mother. I saw that woman who pushed all my buttons and I was furious. I cannot have her turn out like Verónic but at the same time, I cannot be like my father."

"You're not your father," Paige assured him while shaking her head. "And Maria was just excited about this school and wasn't thinking. She's young and so impulsive…"

Her words drifted off and Jorge squeezed her thigh and moved in to kiss her. Their lips fused together with an intensity that it took him off guard. Following his natural instinct, he slid his hand between her legs, feeling the intense heat through the thin material of her pants. A soft moan came from the back of Paige's throat as she pulled him closer and their kiss grew more aggressive, fiercer, as their natural inclinations came out as opposed to the quiet encounters necessary when Maria was in the next room. Alone in the apartment, they could both unleash the animal that wanted to claw it's way out.

Jorge's lips released hers and drifted down her neck as his breath became labored. With his hands working to unbutton her blouse, a task that suddenly seemed almost impossible, his primal instincts caused him to grab the delicate material and unapologetically rip it open. Pushing the material aside, his tongue slid down her chest, while he quickly unfastened her bra and she simultaneously removed the blouse, followed by the bra. Jorge's mouth greedily took in her breast while his hand slid under the waistband of her pants and sunk into the soft place between her legs.

Although Paige was attempting to remove his tie, she seemed to stall, overcome with pleasure as she sank back on the couch and let out a loud gasp as his fingers worked roughly while his tongue continued to travel, he pulled his hand out of her pants and in one swoop, he tore off both her pants and the thong underneath. Within seconds, she was completely naked and he was removing both his tie and unbuttoning his shirt, only to leave it open and swoop in between her legs.

She continued to moan and wiggle beneath him with the combination of his fingers and tongue working together, until he felt the familiar indications of her pleasure with that sound that came from deep inside of her, a soft pulsating beneath his tongue, he sat up and removed his shirt and tossed it on the floor then stood up to unbutton his pants as Paige lay back with her eyes closed. He observed her hard, pink nipples, her flat, smooth stomach that led down to the softness of her thighs as he threw the rest of his clothes aside and wasted no time getting on top of her.

Paige spread her legs as he teased her for a few minutes, squeezing his body against hers, he knew this drove her wild with anticipation. The truth was that regardless of how much pleasure she got out of various sexual acts, at the end of the day, nothing quite quenched her physical thirst like having him inside of her; nothing sent her to such a state of uncontrollable pleasure as his powerful thrusts, roughly pushing her over the edge.

After a satisfactory amount of time was dedicated to heightening her desires, he finally slid in between her legs, causing her to gasp. Quickly wrapped her legs around him, she tightened her grip on him causing Jorge to loudly gasp, his movements rapid and forceful, as Paige threw back her head. An animal-like sound escaped her lips as his hands slid down to grasp her full, round hips, unable to hold back any longer as his last thrusts were stronger than usual, her nails driving into his back as he finally collapsed on top of her.

Feeling his heart racing erratically, his breathing loud, a rhythm of pleasure rang through him as he closed his eyes, his hands slid over his wife's back. Her body seemed to relax under his, her hand ran over his arm and through his hair as the smell of sweat and sex filled the room. He laid there for a long time before finally rising in silence. She awkwardly sat up as if feeling off-balance, her appearance disheveled, he went into the bathroom and grabbed a towel and quickly wrapped it around his hips. Finding her robe, he made his way back to the living room, where Paige was attempting to gather her clothes.

"I brought you..." He started to say but his voice somehow got caught in his throat. Passing it toward her, she smiled and accepted it.

"I'll be right back," She quietly said as she put the robe on before gathering the last of her clothes and went into the bathroom. Jorge sat on the couch. Looking at his own clothes, he briefly considered picking them up but decided to wait and enjoy the peacefulness that filled his body.

Paige returned, still wearing the robe but looking slightly refreshed. She sat beside him and he put an arm around her. Kissing her on the side of the face, Paige snuggled up close to him and for a moment, neither said a word.

"So now what?" She finally asked in her usual, soft voice. "We almost have a house, Jolene's back, she's pregnant....the dispensary burned to the ground..."

"Arson," Jorge replied even before she could ask. "The police are 'investigating'. I may as well be investigating my own asshole, they are so fucking useless."

"We will find out who did it."

"Jesús is looking at some neighboring cameras before the police get to them," Jorge replied and gave her another kiss. "We suspect who is behind it. This is not a good place to be. I do *not* make a good enemy."

"No, you do not," Paige confirmed as a shy grin crossed her lips.

"And tomorrow, Alec will be touring our first dispensary," Jorge spoke as if he were in a daze. "If it has not been burnt to the ground by then, that is, and we will talk more business. I know he has reservations but his district, it will be getting a lot of jobs from me and in turn, he will get voted in. Mark my word, people are very basic in what they want."

"Hopefully things work out with the house this week," Paige said as she also stared into space. "Finally get out of this apartment and into our own place."

"Yes, *mi amor*, yes we will."

"Maria still wants a cat."

"Oh, fuck me!" Jorge complained and Paige laughed at his response. "Yes, let's get a cat to scratch our furniture and barf on the hardwood floors. This is what I work so hard for, to have an animal destroy my home."

"Not necessarily," Paige laughed.

"I'm half thinking of moving Clara in the apartment in the basement," Jorge referred to the 'housecleaner' that Paige always insisted was much more valuable than the older, Latina was given credit. "I want her to monitor both the house and the businesses by the cameras along with checking for devices. She is a huge asset to us and plus, have you seen where she lives? It's a dump."

"Oh! I love Clara!" Paige spoke excitedly. The two had actually met years earlier in South America and were reacquainted the previous fall. "That's terrific! Did you ask her? Did she agree?"

"I just mentioned it," Jorge replied. "I was going to talk to you about it but it was an impulsive thing and I thought, you know, it was just a suggestion, nothing confirmed. If you said no, I would accept your decision."

"I can't wait," Paige said and gave him a quick kiss on the cheek. He turned and stared into her eyes for a long moment.

"It's going to be ok, Paige," He reassured her. "Whatever the problem is now with these people trying to destroy me, it will be fine. No one has taken me down so far and they never will."

"I know," Paige reassured him. "I just worry."

"As I worry about you too and that one fact, it makes me more fierce," Jorge spoke gently and pulled her close. "When I am worried, I become a person they do not want to deal with because I will *not* back down."

"I wish we could have a normal life without worrying about someone trying to kill one of us," Paige said while looking into his eyes. "I thought once you got into pot that would be possible."

"Unfortunately, *mi amor*, it is not that simple," He replied with a compassionate smile. "We will always be a target to some especially if we take over the Canadian pot industry as I dream we will but that is fine, we can take them all on."

"Can we?"

"You're one of the best assassins in the world, you can take on anyone," Jorge confirmed as he swooped in to give her another kiss. "And me, I'm just fucking ruthless."

Chapter 50

One never knows when life will give them a moment that they will forever hold in their heart. Each day starts the same; we open our eyes, look around, sluggishly get out of bed and start our morning ritual with no expectations but often, a sense of dread. Life has taught us to fear what's around the corner and not anticipate it; fear plaques us from the moment we look at our phones in the morning until we collapse in bed at the end of the night. The key is to find some moments of pleasure that make it all worthwhile. It's simply a matter of seeing every day as if it could be the last.

Jorge Hernandez wasn't immune to waking up with a sense of apathy. His life rarely slowed down, his problems never ended but yet, wasn't that the life he had chosen for himself? As a young man, he had the opportunity to join his father's coffee company as a sales rep until the day he would take over the family business. However, this was not for him. He sought a bigger life. He wanted more than a regular, boring job. He yearned for adventure and excitement. He wanted to be rich. He wanted to be a legend.

Over twenty years later, he had managed to do all these things. There were days when he briefly flirted with the idea of what things would've looked like had he taken a different path. A quiet life, living in a modest home, probably with a boring, religious wife and a couple of kids, while he went to a secure, yet miserable job every day, silently wishing for his death. There simply was no comparison. One must always follow their heart, even when they weren't sure that they had one to follow.

That particular day started off like any other. He woke to a silent apartment and slowly turned toward his wife. She was sound asleep. Jorge stared at her for a moment before sitting up on the bed and hesitantly grabbing his phone; what a terrible way to start a day but unfortunately, it was necessary. He never knew what would take place while he was in the vulnerable state of sleep. Fortunately, that morning looked clear. No messages from Jesús or Diego, indicating any problems had arisen overnight.

Slowly moving his legs to the side of the bed, his body felt stiff like a man who slept on his problems and not an expensive mattress. He ignored this, refusing to believe that his body would ever age. There was a momentary sense of dread but he pushed past it as he located his slippers and slid them on his feet. Stretching, yawning, he slowly got up and made his way toward the bathroom. The day had just begun.

Two hours later, he still didn't feel awake. Sitting across from Alec Athas in a coffee shop, Jorge silently considered that *this* would be the man he would've been, had he decided to toe the line and not take the road less traveled. Charming, handsome, smart and yet, had Alec ever truly lived a day in his life? Sure, he spoke passionately about politics and how he wanted to make the world a better place - helping with lower-income housing, community outreach centers and programs for youth - but would that someday be enough? Glancing at his wife beside him, Paige was taking everything in stride but remained silent.

"Look, my friend," Jorge finally interrupted Alec, who politely clasped his mouth shut, as Canadian society had trained him to do. "This here, this is window dressing and politician talk. You need to tell people what they want to hear and that is jobs. People, they like the sounds of many things but realistically, most live in fear of not having a roof over their head. You give them jobs, you give them security and the rest, it will fall into place. Don't be another bullshit politician."

"But you don't understand," Alec began to speak again. "We need all of this to propel society into.."

"Nah Nah," Jorge cut him off again and put his hand in the air. "You must be bold. This here, this is you repeating the same shit every other politician says, no matter what province in this country, no matter what country in the world. These ideas, they are nice, don't get me wrong but I'm telling you, at the end of the day, people don't give a shit about community outreach centers unless they have a need for them. They don't care about youth programs unless there is a kid in their home. They don't care about lower-income housing unless they have a job that isn't paying them enough for their rent. Now, tell me something, Athas, would you live in a low-income home?"

Alec's eyes grew in size and he appeared stunned by the question. He didn't respond. Beside him, Paige raised her eyebrows.

"Exactly," Jorge acted as if he had answered the question. "When people think 'low-income home' they think of welfare street. They think of trailer trash. They think of dirty people. Not to say that this here is always the case but the entire image of lower-income housing is not a pretty one in most people's eyes. It says poor. It says poverty. People want to at least have the belief, maybe even the illusion, that they can work up in this world. That they can have a nice place, nice car, nice things. This, my friend, is the dream you have to sell to them."

Alec relaxed in his seat and glanced out the window for a moment before replying. "You're right."

"Of course I'm right," Jorge spoke bluntly with some frustration in his voice. "Stop talking like a fucking politician and start talking to people like a regular human being, that's what they want."

Alec opened his mouth as if to say something but Jorge had once again taken over, this time, turning toward his wife.

"You know, when I lived in Mexico, I often thought that one day, I should run for *presidente* and now, I wonder if I should run in politics here, in Canada."

Paige raised her eyebrows and grinned. "Ok, let's take one thing at a time. You have a lot of stuff on your plate now and remember, we promised to help Alec…"

"I know but what if I did," Jorge considered for a moment. "Maybe even I could run against Alec here, in his own district."

He noted that Alec's face fell at the suggestion.

"You can't, there's no…."

"I can do anything, my friend," His comment was smooth, yet forceful. "I'm Jorge Hernandez and I do what I want."

"What?" Alec leaned forward with fire in his eyes, he spoke in a quiet yet stressed tone. "What are you going to do, threaten someone in the opposing party to run against me? Are you serious?"

A smooth grin flirted with Jorge's lips until he suddenly started to laugh and turned to wink at his wife.

"See this," He pointed toward Alec while speaking in Paige's direction. "This is the kind of passion he needs. Not this compliant politician with the nice haircut bullshit, he needs balls."

Alec appeared stunned, his body pulling back. "I don't understand."

"He's messing with you," Paige spoke evenly.

"Yes, my friend, she is right," Jorge said with a sly grin and leaned in to kiss Paige on the cheek. "I'm fucking with you. I don't got time or the stomach for politics, however, you're going to need a lot more fire to stand out. You Greeks, you do have passion, do you not? That's what people want. Now give them what they want."

Whether or not his speech made a difference to Athas, he wasn't sure but it certainly wouldn't be the last time that Jorge intended on pushing this man a little harder to get results. The problem with the world is that people looked toward those they admire and attempted to mimic them and not be themselves or to take it a step further, and be better.

After their conversation, the three went to one of the local dispensaries in order for Alec to learn more about their business. Jorge was thinking about opening one in Athas' district, creating some of those better-paying jobs that they were discussing in the coffee shop. The beauty of paying more, as Jorge had learned over the years, is that it allowed you to expect more too. This was something businessmen that were a little less savvy didn't understand.

It was when they stopped by the dispensary that Jorge immediately sensed something was off. Glancing around, he shot Paige a look and gestured Alec to stay back. Standing by the door, the politician didn't move an inch as Jorge and Paige crept toward the cash, where an obnoxious customer was giving a young, Indian woman associate a hard time. Jorge's eyes scanned for security. Employees weren't allowed to work alone. It wasn't until they got closer that he saw it. He noted that Paige quietly moved aside and behind a shelf.

The young *gringo* swung around, his pale blue eyes shot through Jorge while he pointed a gun at the employee. Jorge felt his heart race as a chill ran through his spine when he finally noticed the security man was lying on the floor behind the counter. It was the first time that Jorge truly thought he was going to die. The swastika tattoo on the man's neck only managed to confirm the hatred in his heart; this time, he stood before a man who didn't hate him for what he was but for the color of his skin.

"Not a*nother* fucking spic," The ignorant young man spat out, his pale blue eyes narrowed on Jorge as he slowly turned the gun away from the woman. Jorge's mouth was suddenly dry, his heart pounding in fear. The one time he had left his gun at home and he was suddenly in a vulnerable position. It was as the kid was about to turn the weapon on Jorge that Paige suddenly lurched forward and raising her leg, she drove a sharp heel into the man's back, causing him to drop the gun and fall to the floor.

Behind the counter, the young Indian woman whimpered and started to cry while Jorge jumped forward, quickly grabbing the gun before the maniac could get close to it. Feeling his heart race, he glanced toward Alec who was frozen by the entrance, his face white as a ghost.

"Lock the fucking door!" Jorge commanded while glancing around the shop quickly to make sure no one else was inside. He pointed the gun at the white kid laying defenseless on the floor. He attempted to move, causing Paige once again to stab him in the back with her heel. It was as he screamed out in pain that she eased down, her knee sitting on the place where the wound would be, she pressed down while shoving a gun against the back of his head.

"Who the fuck are you and what are you doing in my shop?" Jorge felt his confidence return, his heart raced now for a very different reason, as both him and Paige pointed guns at the asshole on the floor. "And for the fucking record, *she's* Indian and *I'm* Mexican you racist prick! If you must be a white supremacist, at least know who the fuck you're hating."

"I hate all you," The kids muttered in obvious agony. "You immigrants ruin our country. You're ruining Canada."

"Fuck you!" Jorge glanced at the Indian girl behind the counter. "Security, is he dead?"

In between sobs, the Indian girl shook her head.

"Athas, come over here and check this guy on the floor," Jorge gestured behind the counter, noting that Alec wasted no time rushing across the room and toward the man on the floor, who was now starting to move. Glancing back at his wife, Jorge silently shared a look with her and then returned his attention toward the man who lay motionless on the floor.

"He's fine," Athas commented as he helped the security guard sit up.

"Now you, fucker, who sent you here?" Jorge demanded. "I want a fucking name or you are going to die."

"Fuck you!" The kid snapped back as he tried to move again and that's when Paige drove her knee further into the guy's side, causing him to let out a loud gasp.

"Tell us a name!" She forcefully demanded, causing Jorge to feel an excitement shoot through his body. "Or your brains will be like fireworks shooting through the sky." She jabbed the gun harder against his head causing the man to flinch.

"There is someone at the top," Jorge insisted in a somewhat soothing voice. "You, your friends are just this person's bitches, out doing his work while this man, he is hiding behind a desk, wearing a nice suit. Probably has a nice wife, some kids. But you, you think your part of an army. You're the one out there, maybe doing his dirty work? Am I right?"

"I do what I want to do," The man suddenly spoke with defiance. "I'm a white nationalist and I am for the betterment of our country. We want our country back! No one has to tell me to do anything."

"Oh, is this right?" Jorge asked with interest while gesturing for Paige to get off the man. She did so slowly, carefully, watching him as she moved away, continuing to point a gun at his head. She had barely stepped away when Jorge shot the man in the hand. Ignoring the kid's cries of pain, his pathetic begging, Jorge continued to speak as if nothing out of the ordinary was going on. "Or should I say, 'far right' isn't that what you fuckers call yourselves?"

Grinning at his own bad joke, he stepped back and watched the blood pour from the man's hand. He had been defeated.

"Tell me the name or I will keep shooting you and the places that I choose to do so, may be less pleasant next time," Jorge continued. "This hand, it can be fixed and you can have a life again but I cannot guarantee that the next time, I will be as thoughtful."

"I will die for what I believe in," The man whimpered but it was clear from the look on his face that he was bluffing.

"Oh, and you think," Jorge paused for a moment and glanced toward Paige who watched with interest. "You think that they will die for you. That the man who is at the top, that he will do the same for you? Not a fucking chance. You're a puppet on a string. Some dumb, white kid who's angry at the world. That is you."

"If I tell you," The kid finally whimpered, his face now red, his eyes bulging as he gasped and made a failed attempt to move. "You won't kill me?"

"All I ask for is the truth, *amigo*," Jorge replied in a gentle tone. "Why would I kill you if I have what I want? What kind of man would I be?"

Taking a deep breath, obviously in a lot of pain, as blood continued to drain from his body, the kid seemed to bite his bottom lip before answering the question.

"His name is Fulton Harley," The kid finally whimpered in defeat.

"What?" Alec suddenly spoke up after spending the last few minutes sitting on the floor, attempting to help the security guard. "He's a politician! He's running in one of the rich districts."

"Do tell," Jorge replied calmly and glanced at his wife who merely nodded.

"Thanks for your help, *amigo*," His tone was condescending as he pointed the gun at his head. "But unfortunately for you, I need to send Fulton Harley a surprise in the mail. A little warning that he picked the wrong immigrant to fuck with this time because I never back down from a fight."

He shot him quickly, perhaps so quickly that the man didn't even know what happened. He was dead instantly.

Turning toward his wife, they shared a long, intense look while everything fell apart around them. The Indian girl was crying hysterically while Alec Athas stared in stunned disbelief, covering his mouth while beside him, the security guard began to slowly stand up, rubbing his head in confusion. A dead man lie nearby, soaked in the same blood that now covered the floor, quickly moving toward Jorge's feet and yet, he was oblivious to everything except his wife's smile.

"Baby, we got ourselves a war," Jorge commented in a calm voice as he reached out to gently grasp Paige's hand, his dark eyes blazing with passion as she squeezed his fingers. "But the good news is that we're going to win."

"We always do," Paige spoke softly, her voice smooth like the most gentle music. The love in her eyes shone through with such intensity that even as they stood in the midst of chaos, of pure insanity, in the centre of hell, he could feel the strength of her commitment to him, as he had the same for her. It was a beautiful moment and one that he would never forget. He was a devil named Hernandez and she was his angel.

Can't get enough of the Hernandez series? Check out We're All Animals, Always be a Wolf and The Devil is Smooth Like Honey. Go to <u>mimaonfire.com</u> **and sign up for the newsletter and to learn more about this series.**

Printed in the United States
By Bookmasters